ONLY
THE
INNOCENT

Rachel Abbott

Only the Innocent

ISBN 978-0-9576522-1-7

Find out more about the author and any future books on

http://www.rachel-abbott.com

Prologue

Bright sunshine flooded through the tall windows, touching each surface with its dazzling light. Every corner of the room was bathed in a soft yellow glow, and its elegant proportions were displayed to their best advantage. It was a disaster. The one thing she hadn't allowed for was a sunny day.

Maximum impact—that's what she was striving for. The clothes, the hair, the jewellery; her attention to detail had been impeccable, and any false note would influence his perception of her credibility. But instead of completing the illusion by creating subtle lighting and atmospheric shadows, the room was more akin to a floodlit stage. It was the end of October in London. It was supposed to be raining.

She didn't know what to do. Should she close the curtains? No. That would never work. Too obvious by far, and he wouldn't like it. But time was running out, and she had to think fast. She adjusted everything quickly until she was sure it was as perfect as it could be, angling a wingback leather armchair so that it almost faced the door, sufficient that she could see his face without turning her head. But not straight on. That would give her nowhere to hide. And the light from the window had to be behind her, of course, throwing her face into enough shadow to disguise anything that her eyes might inadvertently reveal.

Her preparations were complete. All she could do now was wait, and think of the inevitability of what was about to happen. Every muscle in her body was taut, and her shoulders were rigid. She forced herself to relax. She heard the sound of a taxi drawing to a halt and a car door slamming. She quickly glanced in the mirror to check that everything was perfect, and was alarmed to see the inner turmoil betrayed in her eyes. She breathed deeply and suppressed the thoughts and images that were crowding her mind, fighting to compose herself.

She heard nothing more for several minutes, but she knew he was in the house. There were no footsteps; the deep pile carpet in the hall and up the staircase to the third floor smothered any sound. But he was moving straight towards the bedroom. Every nerve ending in her body told her so.

The door opened slowly but he remained in the doorway, his expression inscrutable. He didn't speak for several moments, and she steadily returned his gaze. Nobody could deny that he was a handsome man. His tailored black suit hung perfectly on his tall, lean frame, and his grey-flecked hair was as immaculate as always. He looked every inch the successful man that he was. It was no wonder the media loved him so much.

Finally he smiled, the curve of his lips suggesting only the slightest trace of the victory he was no doubt feeling. Her heart jerked unsteadily, but her eyes didn't falter.

"I knew you'd come." He paused, and his glance raked her body. "You really had no choice, did you?" He nodded, as if with a sense of self-satisfaction. "You look perfect."

Knowing she could afford no mistakes, she had chosen carefully—selecting a black leather knee-length skirt with sheer black stockings coupled with a white silk-knit V-necked top, designed to cling lightly to her breasts and offer a just a hint of what was beneath. Her legs were artfully crossed showing a glimpse of thigh, and her simple but elegant gold jewellery completed the picture. It seemed that he was pleased. She had passed the first test, and prayed that she could keep her emotions in check for just a little longer.

"Why the gloves?" he asked, noticing for the first time the elbow-length black silk gloves she was wearing.

"I thought you'd like them."

He smiled again, and she knew he was mocking her. "And you were right."

He pointed to the ice bucket that she had placed on the marble-topped console table, together with two flutes.

"Champagne! I see we're celebrating." He chuckled without mirth.

She reached across and, willing her hands not to shake, she poured a thin trickle of the pale golden bubbles into both glasses. He walked towards the table, picked up a glass, and took one careful sip.

"Delicious, but a bad idea. I don't think we should be dulling the senses, do you?" He carefully put the glass back on the table, and looked straight into her eyes. "You've taken the initiative. That's good. Does this mean you're going to take charge today?"

She stood and walked purposefully towards him, her high stiletto heels sinking into the pile of the carpet. She knew exactly what he wanted, and she touched his cheek with a single gloved finger.

"It does. I hope you're ready for this."

She didn't need to wait for a reply. All she had to do was sound authoritative, and she knew he would comply. "Take your clothes off. All of them. Then lie down on the bed, and wait until I'm ready."

His eyes narrowed, but she knew he was pleased.

"And what are you going to do to me?" he asked, feigning a coolness that he was clearly no longer feeling.

"For now, I'm just going to watch." She forced herself to look into his eyes. They were glittering with excitement, although his face continued to betray little or no emotion. She had seen that look before, and she knew just how dangerous it could be. She pushed the fear to the back of her mind.

He walked across the room, and slowly began removing his clothes, facing her and watching her all the time. Each item that he removed was carefully folded and laid on a chair, until he was completely naked. As always, the sense of the unknown was arousing him and she desperately wanted to look away.

"And now?" he asked.

"Lie on the bed, just as I told you," she answered, her voice becoming stronger as she gained confidence.

He moved towards the four-poster bed in the centre of the room, his proud stance betraying how conscious he was of his near-perfect body. His lightly tanned back, muscular buttocks, and long firm thighs could have belonged to a man half his age. He turned and lay down on the bed, smiling with a sense of triumph.

"I'm ready." His voice was deepening with barely suppressed desire, and she smothered a shudder.

"See what I've got for you," she said with what she hoped was a convincing smile.

From her bag she drew out five matching silk scarves, in a deep rich crimson. "Your favourite colour."

He started to lick his lips as his excitement mounted. His features had transformed into an expression that was almost animal, his lips swollen with lust and his eyes blazing with expectation.

She moved over to the bed, and carefully and expertly tied first each arm, and then each leg to one of the four wooden bedposts. She took the fifth scarf, and hesitated just for a second.

With a quick intake of breath and a visible straightening of her spine, she advanced towards the head of the bed.

"Today's going to be special—I don't want you to see anything until the very last minute."

His answering smile held more than a trace of self-satisfaction, clearly believing that her only aspiration was to give him pleasure.

Without a word, she firmly tied the scarf over his eyes, and moved towards the door. His naked body displayed his excitement, and in a voice barely recognisable he asked, "What happens next?" She glanced across at him and forced herself to respond.

"Now you must wait. I promise you, it will be more than you are expecting."

Quickly she moved into the luxurious bathroom adjoining the master bedroom. She was out of her clothes in seconds, and carefully slid into her costume, never removing the long black gloves. In less than three minutes, she was ready.

As she moved back into the bedroom, she could see that his arousal had not diminished for a second; the anticipation had simply heightened his passion. But a note of uncertainty crept into his voice when he heard a slight rustle as she moved, and then the almost imperceptible sound of two objects—one by one—being carefully placed on the bedside table.

"What are you wearing? I thought it would be silk."

She moved her gloved hands down to the scarf that was blindfolding him, and quickly and firmly slid it down from his eyes to his mouth, where she pulled it tightly into place.

He blinked a little, and looked at her in her costume. His arousal had reached such a peak that it took several seconds for him to register what he was seeing, and he stared at her with a look of horror as he tried in vain to cry out.

The mask over her face revealed only her eyes, and they were filled with a mixture of feelings too complex to interpret. Only the few who knew her well would have recognised the most significant of those feelings—that of sheer determination.

She reached across to the bedside table where moments before she had placed a syringe. With a quick indrawn breath she parted the dark hairs in his groin with a gloved hand, and plunged the syringe in as deeply as possible. A low moan was all that could be heard as he fought a futile battle to break free. She knew that the syringe hadn't hurt too much, but she also knew that he understood what it meant.

And then he was still.

1

Detective Chief Inspector Tom Douglas glanced out of the window of his apartment as he quickly moved around the room collecting the few things he needed. The view across the wide, murky river to Greenwich was one that normally gave him real pleasure, but right now he needed to focus and not waste time looking at the scenery.

Bloody stupid having a couple of glasses of wine with his lunch, but then again how could he have known that his first big case with the Met was going to fall on his day off? Sod's law, no doubt. His performance in the coming days had to be impeccable, and he needed to win the respect and trust of his new team. Asking for a car to be sent as a result of midday drinking was certainly not the start he'd been hoping for.

He hurriedly looked around to make sure he hadn't forgotten anything, but his mantra of "phone, keys, wallet, notebook, warrant card" was so ingrained that he didn't think it likely. Nevertheless, he checked and double-checked that he had everything. Slamming the apartment door behind him, he raced down the six flights of stairs and arrived at the double front doors of his apartment block just as a dark blue car screeched around the corner and drew to a halt. Recognising the driver as his new sergeant, Becky Robinson, Tom opened the passenger door and jumped in. The car was moving again before he had so much as fastened his seat belt.

"Sorry about this, Becky. I didn't mean to drag you all the way out here," Tom said.

"That's okay, sir. A pretty posh place you've got, if you don't mind me saying so."

Tom turned slightly in his seat to look at Becky. He couldn't quite decide if this was just an observation or if she was fishing for information, but her dark, shiny hair was swinging forward and obscuring her face, so he wasn't able to judge. He really didn't have any wish to explain how a policeman, and a divorced policeman at that, could afford to live in a smart apartment in the heart of Docklands. Now was neither the time nor the place.

Fortunately Becky was concentrating on her driving, which seemed to involve a lot of rapid acceleration interspersed with fierce braking. He was in for a bumpy ride, and was slightly hesitant about distracting her.

"Think you can drive and talk at the same time, Becky?"

"No problem. The traffic's a bit heavy, but I can weave around it."

Tom had little doubt about that, and was relieved that she didn't apparently feel the need to look at him as she spoke.

"Okay, what do we know? All I was told on the phone was 'suspicious death'—and that it was one for me. I gather the incident took place in central London, so I guess that's where we're heading?"

"Yep. To the heart of Knightsbridge. The victim is none other than Hugo Fletcher. He's dead. Obviously. The first officers called to the scene said it looks like it could be murder, but it's not a sure thing. That's all I know at the moment."

Becky swerved violently to the left to avoid a black cab and pressed her hand hard on the horn. The cabbie stuck his middle finger up at her, and Tom couldn't help feeling some sympathy for him, despite Becky's mutterings about taxi drivers.

In the interests of arriving in one piece, he kept his thoughts to himself for a few moments. Hugo Fletcher, of all people. What a way to start his career in the Met. He knew something of the victim's public life—everybody did. The media couldn't get enough of him, and the man in the street thought he was some sort of demigod. But Tom actually knew very little about his private life. He remembered that there was a wife whom he had proudly, and rather nauseatingly in Tom's opinion, presented as his "soul mate" a few years ago. But then there was a bit of gossip about her that he couldn't quite remember and now she seemed to have dropped out of the public eye completely.

Bugger. This case was going to have a hell of a high profile, and they were going to have to suffer a relentless stream of inane questions from the press. People often asked how he coped with having to convey the worst possible news to families, but at least he could show how sorry he was. He didn't stick a microphone under a grieving relative's nose and ask how they were feeling.

The heavy traffic had slowed Becky to a crawl, so it seemed safe to ask her a couple more questions.

"Who found him?"

"The cleaner. She's waiting to talk to us at the house, although I gather she's pretty incoherent. DCS Sinclair's off at some fancy wedding in Bath and a car's gone to pick him up and take him directly to the scene. He's asked me to be family liaison officer on this one because of its high profile. I did the job for yonks before my promotion, so it's no problem."

"Have we managed to get hold of the next of kin?" Tom asked.

"Afraid not. He was found at his house in Knightsbridge where he usually stays during the week, but his family home is in Oxfordshire. The local police have been despatched but there's nobody home. There's a daughter from his previous marriage, but as far as we know at the moment that's it. We'll send one of the locals to the ex-wife's house as soon as we know what's going on with the current wife. It would never do for the ex to know first, would it?"

Becky spotted a gap in the traffic, and put her foot down—dodging between cars and changing lanes before slamming her brakes on again. Although it was only about eight miles from Tom's apartment to Hugo Fletcher's house in Egerton Crescent, the early-afternoon London traffic was a nightmare.

"I'm going to put the siren on, sir, if that's okay. We need to get a shift on." Becky tucked her hair behind her ears and flicked the switch on the dashboard. Immediately what looked like an ordinary saloon car had flashing headlights and a siren to clear a way through the dawdling Saturday shoppers.

For the sake of his safety and sanity, Tom decided that silence would be the best option, but he was actually quite impressed. Although Becky's driving appeared erratic, she didn't miss a single opportunity to nip into the smallest gap between two cars, or swerve into the next lane when the narrowest of openings presented itself. Her face was a picture of concentration and determination.

Despite her best efforts, it still took a good fifteen minutes to get to the scene, which had already been sealed off. Tom looked at the elegant crescent of white painted houses, adorned on the outside with clipped box and bay shrubs. Clearly money was no object in this family—but even that hadn't prevented the untimely death of such a famous and well-respected man.

He was less impressed with the crowd gathered in the street outside, cameras at the ready.

"Shit. Becky—if the wife's not been told yet we have to keep a lid on this. Have a word, would you? I'm not at my best when dealing with that lot."

He made a beeline for the front door before anybody could shout any questions at him.

"Top floor, sir," the young PC on the door helpfully informed him as Tom struggled into his coveralls. He made his way up the stairs, taking in the sumptuous surroundings. Over recent months, luxury had become no stranger to him—but somehow this house spoke of centuries of wealth in a way that was not so familiar.

He stopped at the bedroom door. The crime scene team had just about finished and were packing up to go. The pathologist was by the bed, performing his usual tricks. Tom looked around. It was a light and airy room, but strangely only the carpet seemed to have any relationship with the twenty-first century. For Tom's taste, the large four-poster was better suited to a country house, and the heavy pieces of dark wooden furniture made the room feel more oppressive than it should have done. Mind you, Tom acknowledged to himself, the dead body on the bed didn't do much to lighten the atmosphere.

He took in the two glasses of champagne, now gone flat, and could see that prints had been taken from them. And there was still condensation on the outside of the bucket, suggesting that the ice hadn't long been melted.

There was something tragic about this setting. An occasion that had clearly begun as a celebration or romantic tryst had ended with a dead body and an endless stream of men in white coveralls. Tom could picture the scene: glasses raised in a toast; a private smile full of promise; a kiss, perhaps. So what went wrong?

A young crime scene technician with pale skin and a spotty face looked up from where he was packing up his equipment and pushed his glasses back up his nose.

"Not much to go on, sir. We've got some prints, but nothing to compare them with other than the victim, so they could be legit. The only thing we have found of any consequence is one very long hair. Discovered it in the bathroom. It's a red hair—I don't know if that's significant. We'll have it checked out and get back to you. If we're lucky it might have some root attached to it. And then there's the knife."

Tom turned and glanced back at the bed, with a puzzled frown. "Based on a conspicuous absence of blood, I can only presume he wasn't stabbed?"

"No—he wasn't. Which is what makes the knife a bit odd. It was on the bedside table, right next to him. No sign of blood, no fingerprints. It's one of a set from the kitchen, and I think it's what you'd call a boning knife so it's very sharp—it appears to have been very recently sharpened, actually."

"Any idea what it could have been used for?"

"None at all, I'm afraid. But we'll take it back and do some more tests to see if anything shows up."

Tom nodded to the other technician, who was leaning casually against the wall, having clearly finished his work.

"Thanks, guys. I presume you've taken the cleaner's prints?" Tom asked.

"Yep—all done. She's in a bit of a state, though. We'll leave it up to you to find out from her who might come into this room in the normal course of events, so we can rule out their prints." He closed his bag of tricks with a decisive *clunk*.

"Right. That's us done. We just need to bag the scarves, when you're ready, then we'll be off."

Tom turned towards the bed where a large man with an equally large girth was leaning over the body, peering over a pair of half-moon spectacles. The deceased's arms and legs were tied to the four corners of the bed with dark red scarves, and the mouth was gagged. The body was naked and in good shape for a man of Hugo Fletcher's age. Tom stood and stared at the body. First champagne, then some form of bondage. But it didn't look like a typical BDSM scene. There were no physical signs of discipline or sadism.

He hadn't had the pleasure of meeting the pathologist before, and walked over to introduce himself. He always liked pathologists; he'd never met one that wasn't a bit quirky.

"Good afternoon. I'm DCI Tom Douglas. Thanks for keeping the scene intact for me, but I think we can release his hands and feet now."

"Rufus Dexter. Won't shake your hand just now," he said, waving a gloved hand that had been God knows where in Tom's general direction. He leaned over to start the untying process while the crime technician started on the other side of the bed.

"Strange one, Tom. He's tied up, so foul play? Probably. Sexually motivated? Scarves would certainly suggest that. Died on the job? Don't think so. Possible, though. No evidence that he actually was on the job. Penis is clean—I'd say it hasn't been inside a woman since his last shower. Have to check that, though. Could have been oral, I suppose? Don't know."

Tom interrupted this flow of information. "A bit of an assumption that it was a female, don't you think?"

"Hmph. Suppose so. Always appeared pretty straight to me when I saw him on the box. Ever hear a whisper about him having the remotest interest in men? Thought not, though anything's possible, I suppose. No signs of anybody being on or around him—female or male. The bed is undisturbed.

I've been over his body and haven't found any hairs—pubic or otherwise—that don't belong to him. He's clean as a whistle."

Strange, thought Tom. All the evidence suggests that sex was on the cards, but nothing appears to have happened.

"Any idea on the cause of death?"

"Can't see any immediate signs of anything being done to him. Possibly he was tied up and left, and the resulting panic caused a heart attack, or he's been poisoned in some way? We'll test the champagne, of course. Won't have any answers until I open him up and get some tox results. Sorry."

Tom asked if they could turn the body over—just to check for any marks that could suggest some form of erotic sexual preference that might be linked to the bondage. The back was clear, but bruising left by the scarves on both the wrists and ankles did suggest a struggle.

"Can't take that to mean anything," announced the young spotty technician. "They're supposed to writhe around in ecstasy when they play these games. It's how they show they're enjoying it. Doesn't mean he was struggling. And they don't always have sex—you know, in the usual way. She could have just jacked him off."

Tom looked at the crime tech with interest, but resisted the temptation to ask him how he knew so much about bondage. And fascinating though this speculation was, it was time to get some facts.

He turned to Rufus Dexter. "Any idea of the time of death?"

"Cleaner's a silly bat," he responded. "Didn't call it in for over an hour. In too much of a panic, she says. She'd been here quarter of an hour before she found the body. How long had he been dead when we arrived? Max three hours, more like two and a half."

The minute the pathologist paused for breath, Tom jumped in. "I understand we were called to the scene and arrived just before two, and you got here at about two thirty. So time of death was between eleven thirty and noon. Yes?"

Rufus nodded.

"Okay, Rufus, feel free to get the body moved when you're ready. When are you going to do the PM?"

"Tomorrow morning okay? Prefer to do it early. Press will want some answers. Bloody Prime Minister too, no doubt, considering who it is! Eight a.m. okay for you?"

Tom winced as he thought about the phone call he was inevitably going to have to make. "Put it like this—I'm going to be in enough trouble as it is for buggering up Saturday, so I don't think Sunday's going to make things any worse. We get an extra hour anyway—the clocks go back tonight. I'll speak to DCS Sinclair to see if he wants to attend. Sounds like he's here now, actually."

Through the open door, the quiet but authoritative voice of Detective Chief Superintendent James Sinclair drifted up the stairs. Tom knew that he would be giving orders in such a way that they seemed more like suggestions, but ones which nobody would even question. His strange lopsided face had left him burdened with the nickname Isaiah, which Tom was ashamed to admit he had failed to comprehend until it was explained to him, but it was always spoken with affection. He had infinite respect for this man, and although Tom hadn't known him long, he was genuinely delighted when he was appointed to work as his deputy in the murder investigation team. Although he had other reasons for moving to London, working for James Sinclair was an absolute bonus.

The undertakers had been summoned to move the body, and Tom took the opportunity to have another look around. He now realised what seemed wrong with the room. There were no feminine touches at all. He'd never seen a woman's bedroom that didn't have at least a couple of bottles of perfume and some evidence of makeup or face creams. But here there wasn't a trace. He opened the wardrobe door and looked inside. Nothing but smart suits. He walked over to the chest of drawers and found the same story. Laundered shirts all perfectly folded, and underwear and socks in another drawer.

Leaving the men to do their work, he wandered down the corridor and into a second bedroom. This one was just as featureless as the first, with similar furnishings. The chest of drawers was completely empty, and only the wardrobe held any evidence of a female member of the family, with a few dress bags containing evening gowns but no day clothes at all. It was abundantly clear that the apartment was only used by Hugo Fletcher as a rule, and then only during the working week. Even somebody as apparently important as this man would be unlikely to wear a smart suit or dinner jacket to relax in at the weekend. And from what he could see, the wife only came for special occasions.

Deep in thought, he made his way downstairs to where the DCS was talking to Becky Robinson.

"Becky, one of the PCs has been trying to get some joy out of the cleaner, but apparently she isn't making much sense and just keeps going on about the embarrassment of seeing the victim 'in the buff' as she puts it. Could you have a go, please? You know better than most how important this is—and time is everything."

"Okay sir, I'll see what I can do." Becky made for the stairs to the basement, having already got the lay of the land, it seemed.

Tom looked quickly around him. He hadn't noticed much on his way in, but now realised that the ground floor was mainly laid out as very smart offices, each of which looked more like an elegant study than a place of work, whilst the two floors above seemed to be living space.

Now that they were on their own, he turned to his boss and filled him in on his conversation with the pathologist. He could see that James Sinclair was quietly assimilating the facts.

"What do you think about the knife, Tom? Do you think he died of a heart attack, and the knife was originally there to cut him free if he'd stayed the course, so to speak?"

"It's possible, but we won't really know until after the PM. The knots were tight, but not so difficult that you'd need a knife. I'll get someone on the make of the scarves and see if we can find anybody who was daft enough to buy all five in the one shop with a credit card, but somehow I don't think so. He clearly knew whoever was with him; there's no sign of forced entry, and the champagne certainly suggests it was planned. We need to check if anything was taken, but there are no obvious signs of ransacking the house, and there's some valuable stuff around."

"I don't need to tell you that the eyes of the world will be on us for this one. But there's nothing like a high-profile case to test your credentials, eh, Tom?"

Tom glanced around the hallway at a series of pictures he hadn't noticed before. They were mainly framed photographs of the victim taken with various high-ranking politicians and several with other famous philanthropists. It was strange, somehow, to relate the smiling man in an impeccable dinner jacket with the bound and gagged naked body on the bed.

James Sinclair followed Tom's gaze. "Old Hugo may have been loved by the general public and the media," the DCS said, "but he ruffled a lot of feathers in his time, you know, and quite frankly I'm surprised that somebody didn't seriously beat the shit out of him before now. I understand that he had bodyguards. Where the hell were they today?"

Tom looked towards the front door. "This place is very well protected. I expect he thought he was safe in here, and perhaps didn't want the bodyguards to know what he was up to. I'll have them tracked down and see what they can tell us. I think I'll go and check on Becky's progress, though. With those vultures outside I'm not sure how long we can keep this to ourselves."

Tom headed down into the basement where Becky was seated on a low sofa in what appeared to be a very pleasant staff sitting room, gently holding the hand of a person who he could only assume was the cleaning lady. Although not in any way doubting her genuine distress, Tom could see that she was making the most of the attention. A PC was making her a cup of tea in the adjoining kitchen, and what looked like a small brandy sat in front of her on a low coffee table.

Still wearing her coat and a rather oddly shaped brown knitted hat the like of which Tom had never seen before, he would have put her age at about sixty. Becky was talking to her in a soothing voice. Tom decided to stay in the background and leave her to it.

"Beryl, you've been incredibly helpful. I know it must have been a terrible shock for you. But we desperately need to find Lady Fletcher. Do you have any ideas?"

Tom was momentarily surprised to hear the title. He'd forgotten that Hugo Fletcher had been knighted for his charity work. He never kept up much with the Honours List though.

"That poor Alexa. She loved her dad so much, you know."

"Beryl, I don't want to nag—but we can't tell Alexa until we've told Lady Fletcher."

Becky's pretty face was starting to go quite pink, which Tom assessed as frustration.

"You should ask Rosie—she'll know where she is."

"Who's Rosie, and how I can get hold of her?" Becky asked, with a hint of desperation.

"Rosie Dixon—she's one of Sir Hugo's secretaries and looks after all the diaries and stuff. Her number's in the red book in the office. Try her mobile first, because if I know Rosie she'll be in Harvey Nick's. She spends the best part of every day there, as far as I can see. Why he puts up with her behaviour I'll never know." Instantly realising her inappropriate use of the present tense, Beryl's face fell.

There was no time to comfort her now, though, and Tom turned towards the stairs and made his way hastily back to the main office. Becky followed, leaving the PC to look after Beryl.

"Rosie Dixon's number—found it," he said a couple of minutes later. "Can you phone her, Becky, and get her here fast. And ask if she knows where we can get in touch with Laura Fletcher urgently."

Tom made his way to the front of the house where the DCS was talking to the policeman who had been first on the scene. Within a few minutes, a shout came from the office.

"Result, sir!" Becky raced out of the door waving a piece of paper. "Rosie's on her way here, so we need to get somebody to talk to her. But I've found out where Lady Fletcher is. Rosie says she's due back from their place in Italy this afternoon, arriving at Stansted any time soon. We need to intercept her."

Tom stopped briefly to give the DCS a quick update, then followed Becky out of the door. "Okay, we can do the organising from the car—let's get to her before the news breaks."

2

Becky was doing her best to get them to the M11 as quickly as possible. She tried to concentrate on the road ahead in order to shut out the difficult conversation that her boss seemed to be having, but it was impossible. Especially as she could hear the strident voice of a very angry female on the other end of the line.

The conversation ended abruptly, and she heard DCI Douglas exhale slowly as he leaned back against the headrest. She risked a quick glance and saw that his eyes were closed. For the first time she realised that he carried an air of sadness about him, and the skin around his eyes had a bluish tinge as if he didn't sleep well. She felt a strange urge to grab his hand and give it a reassuring squeeze. Ridiculous notion. Telling herself to get a grip, she was wondering how to break the silence when he saved her the trouble.

"Sorry, Becky. I would have preferred you not to hear that."

"That's okay, sir. Sorry for you, really."

"Under the circumstances, I think we can dispense with the formalities. When we're on our own, call me Tom. After all, you've just heard my ex-wife berating me and generally making me feel even more of a bastard than I did already."

"Ex-wife's prerogative, sir—sorry, Tom. My mum used to scream at my dad all the time."

Tom gave a half smile. "I don't blame her for being mad, if I'm honest. I was supposed to be picking my daughter up today. She was going to stay with me overnight for the first time since I arrived in London. We were both looking forward to it."

"Your daughter will understand, I'm sure," Becky said.

"Lucy's only five. All she knows is that her dad can't have her for the weekend like he promised. And do you really think that her mother will present the reason in a positive way?"

Tom gazed out of the window, obviously not expecting an answer. After a brief pause, he turned back towards Becky with a self-deprecating smile.

"Okay, back to business," he said. "Before I got a bollocking from my ex-wife, I passed on the details of Lady Fletcher's flight to Ajay in the office. I told him to contact the airline and ask a flight attendant to have a quiet word, and take Laura Fletcher into a private room when they land."

Becky glanced at Tom. "You do realise she's on a budget airline, don't you?

She could see that Tom didn't appreciate the relevance.

"There are no assigned seats," she explained. "It's like a bus. You get on and find a seat wherever you can. And with a plane full of Italians, not known for their queuing skills, I can't imagine it's a bundle of laughs for somebody of Laura Fletcher's wealth and status."

"Christ—how the hell are they going to find her then? I suppose they'll make an announcement. What on earth is Laura Fletcher doing using a cheap airline?"

"You'll have to ask her that. Given her husband's apparent gazillions I would have thought they'd have had their own Lear jet, or something."

"Well, it's intriguing, but not exactly relevant to the enquiry. Did you get anything interesting out of the cleaner, by the way?"

"Not really, except that apparently she shouldn't actually have been at Egerton Crescent that day. She doesn't work Saturdays, but she'd left her purse on Friday. I had a massive long tale about an argument with her husband who wouldn't lend her any money to take the grandchildren to McDonald's. So she had to come all the way on the bus to pick up her purse. Luckily for her, the argument made her miss the first bus, otherwise she'd have got there at about the time Sir Hugo died. She said she wouldn't have gone upstairs normally, but she realised the alarm was off, so she assumed Sir Hugo was in the apartment. She went up to explain what she was doing there. That's when she found the body, and she was so terrified she locked herself in the staff room for about an hour in case there was a killer still in the house. There was no phone, so she couldn't call us."

"I heard her mention Alexa," Tom said. "Sir Hugo's daughter, I presume?"

"Yep. Lives with the ex-wife."

Becky was about to make some tactless remark about ex-wives when fortunately her mobile rang. Fiddling briefly with the earpiece behind her left ear, she answered, "DS Robinson." Nothing. "DS Robinson," she repeated.

With an irritated tut, she pulled the offending object off her ear and flung it over her shoulder onto the backseat.

"Sodding Bluetooth headset. It never works when I want it to. When whoever it was calls back, I'll have to put it on speaker if that's okay."

Almost immediately the mobile rang again and Becky pressed the speaker button.

"DS Robinson."

"Yeah, Bex. Finally! It's Ajay. You with Throb?"

Tom turned his head and looked at Becky with raised eyebrows.

Becky winced. "Yes, Ajay. I am."

"Better put this on speaker then so he can hear too."

"Splendid idea, Ajay—if a tad too late."

"Oh, bollocks. Sorry, sir."

Clearly deciding it was better to get on with the message in the hope that his gaffe would be overlooked, Ajay continued. "I thought you might like to know that Laura Fletcher's definitely on the flight, and has checked in a bag. No bags were unloaded for no-shows, and the flight manifest shows she's on board. They'll make an announcement just before they land, and they'll call you on this number to make arrangements for you to meet up with her."

The conversation over, Becky disconnected and glanced nervously at Tom. She knew she was blushing, but bloody Ajay should have had more sense. They had nicknames for all the senior officers, but they usually had the wits to keep them private.

"Care to explain, Becky?"

Becky groaned. "I get all the dirty work. I'll kill Ajay. Oh well…You know when you came for your interview? Florence in the office saw you, and she said you were a bit of a heartthrob. When you got the job you became "The Throb,' and it's kind of got shortened to Throb. That's it—simple as that."

Tom didn't say a word, but Becky was fundamentally incapable of being silent.

"Mind you, Florence is about ninety and blind as a bat!"

"Ah, that would explain it then," Tom responded sardonically.

The thing is, Becky thought, he really is a bit of a dish. Not her type—she preferred them a bit less contained. A bit rougher round the edges, if she was honest. But she wouldn't chuck him out of bed, and he had quite a body on him.

Quickly changing the subject, Becky pointed to a folder on the backseat. "You might want to look in there. I got some photos e-mailed to me while you were upstairs with the body, and printed them out in the secretary's office. The techies said it would be okay to use that computer. They make interesting viewing."

❖ ❖ ❖

Tom was grateful to get away from the subject of himself, good looks or otherwise. He didn't know Becky well, but he suspected that the last hour or so had proved quite illuminating for both of them. He didn't think she was a gossip, though. She was tough and ambitious, and he was pretty sure she would respect his privacy. What little he had left.

He opened the folder.

The first image he came to was of a young and vibrant woman. Long, wavy red hair tumbled to her shoulders. She was wearing a pewter-grey silk evening dress, cut low at the front with wide shoulder straps, and she had a gorgeous figure. Not pencil thin, but slim with lovely curves. The thing that struck Tom the most was her amazing smile. It lit up her whole face, and she looked on top of the world. Becky glanced across.

"Laura Fletcher. That was taken about ten years ago. She'd just met her husband, and this was their first public date together. Did you notice the red hair? I'd have thought we were on to something, other than the fact that we know Laura Fletcher was in Italy."

Tom started looking through the rest of the photos. The odds were always on the wife in these cases, so that made her the number-one suspect. But there were too many things that didn't fit. Apart from the fact that she was apparently out of the country, the whole bedroom setup, the champagne, the silk scarves—it didn't feel like a rendezvous with a wife, particularly as the evidence suggested she rarely stayed at the apartment. Far more like an assignation with mistress. Wife out of the country; living apart during the week—a perfect opportunity for a visit from the other woman, Tom thought.

He had now reached the last photo in the pile, and couldn't help but utter an expletive.

"Shit—what on earth happened?"

"I thought that might be your reaction when you saw that one," Becky said. "The others are interesting too, though. They were taken over a period of time, but she looks different, somehow. What do you think?"

Tom studied the other photos. In none of them did Laura Fletcher shine as brightly as she did in the first one. Her clothes were undoubtedly expensive, but somehow she managed to look less sexy in each one. Still beautiful, but thinner. And in the third of the formal photos her hair was no longer red. She looked like a brunette and it suited her. But she also looked stiff and uncomfortable in a dress that came unflatteringly halfway up her chest with small cap sleeves. He dragged his attention back to the last photo and turned to Becky.

"Do you know when this was taken?"

"About six months ago, I believe. Apparently there have been very few photos in the last four or five years. She's stopped accompanying her husband to functions, and she's spent a lot of time in and out of private care homes, of the psychiatric variety. At least a couple of reasonably long stays that we know of. That last photo was taken by some very opportunistic paparazzo who was actually at the hospital to visit his mother. He didn't recognise Lady Fletcher, but he did recognise the car that was picking her up. Hugo Fletcher's car has a very distinctive number plate."

Tom looked again at the picture. The woman in the photo could easily pass for fifty, although he knew that Laura Fletcher was only in her mid thirties. She was wearing a pair of trousers that looked as if they were at least two sizes too big, with a baggy jumper and flat shoes. Her hair was scraped back from her face and was a dull mousy colour—not red. She looked pale and lifeless. He could only think that she must have been quite ill to have changed so dramatically. It was a sad picture, and he wondered how Hugo's very public life had been affected by his wife's illness. He hated to admit it, but the mistress theory was definitely looking like a very plausible scenario.

"Do we know what was the matter with her?"

Becky had done her research. "We've contacted the hospital, but of course patient confidentiality prevents them from saying anything. Anyway, you'll be meeting her in a couple of minutes—because we're about to turn off for the airport. We've made good time, so she probably hasn't even picked up her bag yet."

"Let's just hope the airline staff have done their stuff."

3

Laura indicated left and swung her car abruptly from the main road onto the unlit lane that approached Ashbury Park. Slamming her foot hard on the brake, the car slowed to a crawl as she stared nervously at a strange white glow, lighting up the sky above the trees ahead. She cautiously turned the final bend towards the gates of her home, and was met with a shattering sight.

"Oh, dear God," she whispered.

There was no escape. The hordes of press, hearing the deep hum of her Mercedes coupé, rapidly whipped their cameras round towards her. The television teams swiftly adjusted their arc lights to point at her approaching car, the bright beams penetrating the interior with their harsh glare, momentarily blinding her. It wasn't unusual to see photographers at these gates, and she could practically taste their excitement. After all, Hugo's fame and near celebrity status had virtually been built by these very same individuals, as he skilfully fed them just enough information about his work to maintain their interest.

But this was different. This was a feeding frenzy.

And there was only one way that she could gain access to her home. Hugo had insisted that the electric gates had a keypad opening system rather than a remote control. That way, he could change the code regularly. Remotes could be lost, or even sold to the highest bidder.

As she drew to a stop, she could do nothing to prevent the ruthless flashing of cameras from exposing her anguish, and as her window wound smoothly down so she could type in the entry code she heard frantic shouts from the press, each one trying to secure the best picture.

"Look this way, Lady Fletcher."

"Have you been told the news yet, Lady Fletcher?"

"Do you have anything to say, Laura?" As if use of her first name would elicit a more favourable response. Yet nobody actually said what the news was. This in itself spoke volumes.

A multitude of cameras caught her look of utter despair as she wound up her window. She felt certain that this image would feature on the front page of several newspapers the next morning.

Manoeuvring the car as quickly as possible between the overgrown shrubs towards the front of her home, she was almost overcome with nausea. She knew the police would be waiting. They had the code to the gate for security reasons, and she was certain they would be at the house. What would they expect of her? It had been a long time since Laura felt that she could simply react instinctively to life.

So it was with a sense of surprise that she saw a solitary policeman standing as if on guard on the steps to the front door of Ashbury Park. He seemed small against the huge black doors. Glimpsing his face in the headlights, she could see he looked wary and uncomfortable, and was speaking urgently to somebody on his radio. It was evident that he was not expecting to have to do this job himself.

She pulled up in front of the steps. The policeman pocketed his radio and rushed down to open the door for her, but he was too late.

"Lady Fletcher? I'm so sorry, ma'am, but we weren't expecting you yet. At least, I was here just in case, but the senior officers are on their way. They went to meet you at Stansted, but…"

Taking a deep breath, Laura interrupted in a voice quivering slightly from tension. "It's okay, Officer. Just tell me what's happened."

"We tried to keep the animals at the gate at bay, your ladyship. There's a press embargo until you've been told, and they know not to say anything. They didn't say anything, did they?"

"Enough. Enough for me to know that this is very serious. Tell me."

"Do you think we should go inside, ma'am, and perhaps wait for the senior policemen to arrive?"

Laura just wanted to get this over, and then to be alone as quickly as possible. She tried to control her mounting panic. "It's my husband, isn't it? If it were anything else, he would have called me. And he hasn't. The reality can't be any worse than I'm imagining, so for God's sake just tell me. Please."

The young policeman took a deep breath. "All I know, ma'am, and I'm really sorry to have to tell you this, is that your husband was found dead at your London home sometime earlier today. I realise that this must be deeply distressing for you. Would you like to go inside? Surely that would be for the best?"

Laura couldn't trust herself to speak. She stared mutely at the policeman for just a few seconds, and then turned her back on him and walked towards the house without a word. It wasn't his fault, but she couldn't bear the thought of anybody being with her now. Forcing herself to place one foot in front of the other, she climbed the steps to the front door as if her legs knew what had to be done, even though her mind seemed to be a total blank. She felt as if she were somehow outside of her body, looking down and watching a performance—and a bad one at that. The policeman clearly hadn't known what to say, and she hadn't known what she should do, or how she should behave. A scream was hovering just below the surface, but she somehow prevented it from breaking through. She couldn't fall apart yet.

As she reached the top step she heard an unwelcome sound. The press at the gates were out of sight, but a steady throbbing noise growing in volume indicated that a helicopter was fast approaching, and as she inserted the key into the front door lock, to her horror a huge overhead spotlight flooded the area, illuminating both her and the hapless policeman. The spell was broken.

She hurriedly turned the key and pushed the door open, relieved to escape the probing lenses of the television crew overhead. Slamming the door with force, she leaned back heavily against it, and only then did she let the tears come. They flowed in relentless channels down her cheeks, but her weeping was soundless. Slowly, her legs gave out and she sank to the cold stone floor, her back still pressed hard against the door. She bent forward and rested her forehead on her knees, her arms tight around her head, trying desperately to stop herself from falling apart completely.

Her mind was filled with images of Hugo and how he'd looked the very first time she had seen him. How handsome and self-assured. And she had been as bright as a butterfly, flitting through life without a care in the world, loving her job, her family, and her friends. How had it ended like this?

The silent tears turned to deep, wrenching sobs of regret, and she was still huddled by the door fifteen minutes later when she heard the unmistakable sound of a car racing up the drive, its door opening practically before the car had stopped. She heard muffled voices consulting with the policeman, but she couldn't make out the words. Hastily she pulled a sodden tissue from up her sleeve—a habit that she had never been able to break even though Hugo always thought it was the height of unsophisticated behaviour—and wiped the tears from her face. She pushed herself shakily to her feet, and before the new arrivals had a chance to ring the bell, she opened the door.

Standing before her was a man who she guessed was around forty, dressed in a leather jacket, black T-shirt, and jeans. She vaguely registered that he was tall with dark blond hair that was slightly messy. She didn't know how she expected a senior policeman to look, but it certainly wasn't like this.

Having parked the car on the far side of the drive, a young dark-haired girl in a conservative black trouser suit was quickly making her way across the gravel to the front steps.

As she stood in the open doorway, Laura felt herself swaying. The policeman leapt up the last two steps and grabbed her forearms gently but firmly.

"Come on, Lady Fletcher. Let's get you sat down."

She saw the policeman signal with a flick of his head to the girl, who gently eased past them and disappeared down the hallway.

"I'm so sorry," Laura said. "I'm not usually so pathetic. I'll be okay in a moment."

"You're not being pathetic. You've had a shock. Which way to your sitting room?"

Laura felt oddly relieved to hear a northern accent. It felt like a million years since everybody in her life had spoken like this. It was a reminder of an untroubled life.

With the policeman holding her right elbow, obviously fearing that she was about to keel over, she led the way across the stone-flagged hallway to the drawing room. This had never been her favourite room, with its gloomy dark panelling and drab furniture, but it seemed the most appropriate to the occasion. The young woman had clearly found the kitchen, and was hovering with a glass of water in her hand.

The policeman guided Laura to a sofa and waited until she was seated, and the glass was placed on the table at her side. She was so cold, but although the fire was made up and ready to light, she felt no inclination to make the effort.

"Lady Fletcher, I'm Detective Chief Inspector Tom Douglas, and this is Detective Sergeant Becky Robinson from the Metropolitan Police. We're expecting Detective Chief Superintendent Sinclair to join us, but he got stuck on his way to the M40. He'll be with us in about ten minutes."

The two police officers sat down on the facing sofa, and Tom Douglas took a deep breath. It was clear that he wasn't enjoying this moment.

"I'm so very sorry that we weren't here when you arrived home, and that you had to run the gauntlet of the press out there. It must have been a very stressful experience, and I'm not at all surprised that you're feeling a bit shaky. I know you've heard that your husband was found dead this afternoon in your London home, and you have our deepest sympathy for your loss."

Laura closed her eyes and clamped her top lip between her teeth to stop it from trembling. She dropped her chin to her chest in a vain attempt to hide her lack of control. The tissue that had remained clutched in her hand was somehow torn to shreds in her lap. She had no recollection of doing that, and now her nose was starting to run. Bundling the bits into a ball, she attempted to wipe her eyes and nose. She felt a clean tissue being pressed into her hand, and knew she was being rude to not thank the thoughtful young sergeant. But she couldn't bring herself to look at them or to speak. She just held the tissue to her streaming eyes and nose.

The chief inspector began to talk again, and she tried to concentrate on what he was saying.

"Police officers were called to the apartment in Egerton Crescent at around two p.m. following a call from a Mrs. Beryl Stubbs, who had discovered your husband's body about an hour earlier."

She looked up sharply, her hands dropping to her lap. "Beryl? What on earth was *she* doing there on a Saturday afternoon?"

The sergeant answered, "She came to pick up her purse, but it was helpful having her there to be honest. She told us how we might find out where you were. We did try to catch you at the airport—there was supposed to be an announcement on your flight, but I gather you didn't come forward. I'm sorry we missed you. We could perhaps have saved you some distress."

Laura managed a barely audible response. "I'm afraid I slept all the way home. I didn't hear any announcement."

At that moment, the shrill peal of the doorbell shattered the quiet of the house.

"I'll go," Becky said.

Laura could feel the chief inspector's eyes on her. But she said nothing. Not even when the sergeant and the DCS entered the drawing room did she feel able to speak. She simply gave a fleeting look at the new arrival and then returned her gaze to her hands, which were tightly clasped around the now soggy ball of tissue.

"Lady Fletcher, I'm James Sinclair. I do apologise for my delay in getting here. May I offer my sincere condolences on your loss. Your husband was a great man, and was much loved in this country and elsewhere in the world."

Laura felt her body jolt at the policeman's words.

"I'm also sorry to say that the minute you drove through the gates it provided a signal to the media to go public. Given your husband's profile, I'm afraid it's bound to be given priority coverage. We're informing Sir Hugo's former wife, but is there anybody else that you would like us to notify on your behalf?"

Laura knew she should respond, but somehow the words just wouldn't come. All she could do was shake her head.

"I know that my two colleagues here have hardly had a chance to talk to you, but we will need to ask you some questions, I'm afraid."

The DCS paused and glanced at his colleagues. "We still don't know exactly how your husband died, but we do have to treat his death as suspicious. We'll have to wait for the results of the postmortem, but some new evidence has just come to light that strongly suggests foul play. You're probably aware that the faster we act in such a case, the more chance there is of finding the perpetrator of this monstrous crime."

Fighting hard to keep her feelings in check, Laura glanced up briefly. She was conscious that both the other police officers were looking at the DCS with interest.

At that moment, a woman officer pushed the door open and brought in a tray of tea. The conversation paused briefly whilst the tea was poured, and Laura was grateful for the respite. She needed to retain some vestige of self-control until they left, but at least the shaking had stopped.

James Sinclair was the first to break the silence. "I'm sorry, Lady Fletcher, but we also need to ask you to identify the body. This is just a formality, but it has to be done. The postmortem is scheduled for tomorrow morning. I would prefer you to see him beforehand, but that would mean you coming in first thing."

"I don't sleep much, Chief Superintendent. Just tell me where and when." Laura felt herself fading. The stress was wearing her out. She was keeping her emotions under control, but just barely. She just needed them to leave.

"We could send a car for you at about six thirty if that's not too early. And then we would like some time with you so that we can learn everything possible about your husband. We do think that if he was murdered, it was by somebody he knew. I'm sure that you can assist us with that."

Laura answered quietly, "I'll do my best."

"Do you know of anybody who was threatening your husband, or anybody who could be harbouring a significant grudge?"

"Nobody. Well, nobody obvious. Because of his work there was always a perceived threat—but he didn't tell me of anything specific. I'm sorry."

"We know all about his work, Lady Fletcher. Who doesn't? So we'll be looking into that in great detail, of course. Think about it overnight and then perhaps we can talk to you some more tomorrow."

The policeman paused. When he started to speak again, his voice had softened. "I'm really sorry to have to ask you this, but I'm afraid I must. Do you believe that your husband had any relationships with women outside your marriage?"

Laura couldn't stop a shudder from running through her body. She paused for just a beat, and then looked up. "I don't know. I'm sorry," she replied, almost in a whisper.

"Is there anybody that we could call to be with you, Lady Fletcher?" the young sergeant asked.

"I don't want anybody, thank you. I would really prefer to be alone." Laura paused for a second. Glancing up, she cast a worried glance out of the window through the still open curtains. "But if it's not too much trouble, do you think you could ask somebody to bring my case in from the boot of the car, please? I don't really want to go outside if that helicopter's still hovering."

The ever-helpful sergeant jumped up. "I'll get it."

Laura was vaguely conscious that the chief inspector was asking if she wanted them to call her doctor, but she had tuned out of the conversation and was in another place and time. The sound of their voices was echoing hollowly in her head, but the words were no longer registering.

She was relieved when the sergeant reappeared, carrying a small suitcase.

"Excuse me, Lady Fletcher, there's a lady here to see you. The policeman let her as far as the front door, because she said she's a relation of yours. Should I let her in?"

Before Laura could gather her wits about her and answer, the door was pushed open farther. A slender young woman stood in the doorway, her long strawberry-blonde hair shining in the light of the chandelier behind her.

"Laura, I just heard the news. I'm so sorry. I had to come. I couldn't possibly let you face this on your own."

The slight but unmistakable North American accent was the last thing Laura was expecting to hear.

She felt her heart begin to pound, and she leapt out of her chair. She couldn't stop herself, and all her pent-up emotion exploded from her lips.

"What the *fuck* are *you* doing here?"

4

Within a matter of minutes of the arrival of the evidently unwanted guest, all three detectives left in Becky's car, edging their way past the growing number of press blocking the gates. None of them had uttered a word since leaving the house, other than for the chief superintendent to dismiss his driver in favour of travelling with Becky and Tom. No comment was passed until they were out of sight of the cameras. A close-up of three visibly agitated police officers on the evening news would only result in unnecessary speculation, so they had kept their faces impassive until they were well out of range. Becky was the first to break the silence.

"Does anybody apart from me think that was truly weird? Hardly a word uttered—and then such an outburst. And she was certainly keen to see the back of us, once that sister-in-law of hers turned up."

Tom knew she was right. Laura's distress had seemed very genuine, but once her visitor had arrived she had practically pushed them out of the door. And Becky's offer to stay overnight with Laura had been abruptly turned down, much to her obvious disappointment. No doubt she would love to be a fly on that particular wall right now.

"Tom, you're the motivational analysis expert. What were your first impressions of Lady Fletcher?" James Sinclair's sharp eyes turned towards Tom, who was deep in thought in the back of the car. All he could think about was how fragile she felt when he had tried to stop her from crumpling to the floor. He forced himself to revisit the scene in the drawing room in his mind.

"She's a difficult one to read. Distressed, without a doubt. She seemed to be focused on holding herself together; so much so that she seemed almost detached, as if none of it was real. Except, of course, in her reaction to her visitor. That was certainly real."

"Well, her visitor—what was her name again, Becky?"

"Imogen Kennedy, sir."

"Thank you. Well, as Imogen used to be married to Lady Fletcher's brother, there could be all sorts of reasons for her response—some family feud, perhaps. But definitely worth pursuing. With that level of antagonism, there could be more to it. What did you think, Becky?" James asked.

"I thought that Lady Fletcher looked as if she'd given up on life. Unlike her very attractive sister-in-law."

Tom thought Becky's forthright observations were sadly completely accurate. Laura Fletcher had been wearing a sort of paisley skirt in shades of purple, gathered unattractively at the waist, and a short-sleeved and round-necked jumper that was a washed-out beige colour. Her hair was tied back with a plain elastic band, and of course the understandably pale skin, blotchy through crying, did nothing to enhance her appearance. Imogen Kennedy, on the other hand, had arrived to her less-than-warm welcome looking immaculate. It was certainly a contrast.

"I would have liked to have seen her reaction when she found out the news. That young PC was too flustered to have picked up on anything."

"Do you know how you missed her, Tom?"

"Not really. They assured us they had made an announcement on the flight, but nobody came forward. She said she must have slept through it."

Becky gave a derisive snort. "Yeah—and just two minutes later she said she doesn't sleep much."

Tom nodded. "I suppose travel does that to some people. Anyway, we asked the airport to check the status of her baggage, and they got back to us about ten minutes later to say that she appeared to have collected her suitcase as the carousel was empty, so we expected to see her come through any time soon."

"They put out several announcements in the airport, and we waited another half hour before we gave up and accepted that we'd missed her. We got here at about ten past eight. I'm surprised we were so close behind her, given the head start she must have had."

The DCS interjected. "Are we absolutely certain that she was on that flight? Can there be any doubt at all?"

Becky was quick to respond to this. "Absolutely none. And when I got her case out of the car, the airline's luggage label was for the Ancona flight, with today's date."

"From what you saw of her this evening, Becky, would you have recognised her at the airport, do you think?" James asked.

"The latest photo we had wasn't that great so on that basis we could easily have missed her. But I do have an almost photographic memory, and I can't believe that skirt could have walked past without me registering it. She could have been wearing a coat, though. There was one on the back seat of the car."

Tom had no idea how they'd missed her, but they obviously had. As Becky said, there was no doubt that Laura Fletcher was in Italy at the time of the murder. But something was nagging at the back of his mind. He had felt her body shaking so there was no question that her suffering was real, but there were a couple of odd reactions. It was strange that she didn't seem interested in any of the details. In fact, she hadn't asked a single question about how her husband had died. But the fact that the cleaner was there on a Saturday seemed to have come as a surprise. Why did that matter? Even they hadn't known at that point that it was definitely murder. Becky's thought patterns seemed to be mirroring his own as he heard her speak to James.

"You said it looks like murder. What have they found, sir?"

"Apparently when they got the body to the mortuary, Rufus Dexter had another go over the body with a magnifying glass. He may be short on complete sentences, but he's a detail fanatic and couldn't resist a bit of further investigation prior to the PM. He noticed a tiny spot of blood in the victim's pubic hair. There is definitely a puncture wound there, and given that no sane person would inject themselves anywhere near their own scrotum, he felt he should alert me, although as yet he doesn't know what was injected. He doesn't really think there was any intention to hide the puncture wound—there are better spots for that as we all know—so the site was probably chosen for speed of absorption into the blood stream."

"We've still got to tell her that he was naked and tied up. It's going to be difficult for her to block out that bit of information," Becky said.

Tom gazed out at the dark night as they sped down the M40, and thought about Hugo Fletcher. It seemed increasingly improbable that this would turn out to be a simple murder by an angry wife, so they needed to consider other possibilities. He couldn't help thinking that Sir Hugo's charitable work might be related in some way. His fortune was inherited, but his fame came from his high-profile charity and the help it gave to help Eastern European prostitutes. Given the sexual overtones of the murder scene, there was an obvious link to the prostitutes. But why would one of them want to kill him?

James Sinclair was sceptical. "If we're to believe the media, they all thought he was God Almighty. I could believe that a disgruntled pimp might have done it, but he would hardly drink champagne with a pimp and then let himself be tied to the bed. I'm sure there's a logical link here, but it's eluding me."

They had reached the end of the motorway, and Becky's driving had reverted to its usual ducking and diving style along the dual carriageway, which was heavy with traffic even this late on a Saturday night. Tom could just make out a slightly nervous expression on his boss's face each time they passed under a yellow streetlight, and he couldn't resist a smile, which he managed to erase as James turned to face him in the back of the car.

"Let's get back to the facts. We all know the statistics on murder by spouses, so let's rule out the obvious first. We have established beyond reasonable doubt that Lady Fletcher was on the flight from Italy. Are we absolutely certain that there is no way she could have murdered him, and then got herself to Italy for that flight from Ancona?"

"No way at all. We've checked."

"What about private planes, given their wealth?"

"We're checking that out too, but it would be a bit obvious. She may be many things, but I don't think she's stupid, and she might as well wear a hat that says 'guilty' on it as take a private plane from London to Ancona and fly back on a scheduled flight an hour later."

"Fair point. We'll check of course, but it certainly wouldn't win any awards for subtlety."

There was one point that Tom thought they'd failed to mention, and that was Laura Fletcher's lack of response when they asked about other women. He thought that most wives would have looked shocked, horrified, or mortified at the thought. But she didn't react at all.

Tom could feel they were all flagging a bit, and James Sinclair obviously had the same view.

"Okay," the DCS said. "Let's just try to sum up what we've got. Lady Fletcher's looking unlikely—although that doesn't mean that she couldn't have paid somebody else to do it. What about the rather extreme reaction to her visitor?"

They had hardly had time to absorb Lady Fletcher's passionate outburst before they had effectively been shown the door.

"She demonstrated a much more intense response to the arrival of her sister-in-law than she did to the news that her husband had been murdered. I would say it was an absolute gut reaction. She seemed to be genuinely angry—as if this were the last person on earth that she wanted to see."

"My bet," Becky said, "would be that Laura suspected Hugo of having an affair with Imogen. That would certainly explain the reaction."

"Which also suggests that we need to look in detail at Mrs. Kennedy's movements over the last twenty-four hours," James Sinclair said.

On that note, they settled down to their own thoughts, only to be rudely interrupted by Tom's mobile. He quickly answered, listened carefully, and hung up.

"Good news. The house to house has resulted in a sighting of somebody leaving the house in Egerton Crescent at around eleven forty-five today. A slim woman of average height, carrying a large black shoulder bag. The two things he noticed most about her were that she had incredible long red hair, and she was wearing a rather tight black knee-length leather skirt."

"Good lord, somebody's very observant," the DCS commented.

"Apparently he stood and watched her for a few minutes, because he thought she was 'sexy as hell,' in his own words."

They continued the journey in silence, Tom pondering quietly on the difference between a sexy black leather skirt and the hideous one that Laura was wearing. Some of this would unavoidably be made public, and he wondered how she would cope with the inevitable comparison and the obvious implications.

Less than a hundred miles southwest of Oxfordshire, a young girl stood at a window, looking out into the night beyond. Even though the room behind her was in total darkness, the unlit country lanes and the lack of a moon left nothing more than vague shapes discernible to the human eye. She could just make out the shadowy forms of the treetops against the black night sky, swaying in the strong winds coming off the nearby sea. But there was not a sign of human life anywhere. Nevertheless, she scoured the landscape, her eyes straining to penetrate the dense, high hedgerows, praying and fearing in equal measure that she would see the twin headlights of a car in the distance, weaving their way towards her.

It was several days since he'd been, and he'd never stayed away for this long before. She knew he was angry with her, but perhaps — just perhaps — she could make things right when he came. Maybe she had been too hasty, or maybe she had expected too much.

Seeing nothing, she pushed aside the vague sense of relief. She knew the feeling would soon be replaced by a creeping dread. The room was cold and she realised she was shivering in her flimsy clothes. She took a tiny sip of water and pushed herself under the thin bedcovers, dragging them around her to cut out the icy draughts, then burying her head beneath them to let the warm air of her breath bring a little comfort to her trembling body.

5

The fire crackled in the hearth, where Imogen had finally put a match to the firelighters. The logs had caught and were burning well. It made a very dreary room only slightly more cheerful.

Laura glanced across at Imogen, who was busying herself searching through Hugo's bewildering collection of brandy bottles. The minute the police had gone, the argument had begun. Brief but ferocious, it had left Laura exhausted. She had run the full gamut of emotions, and finally had abruptly ended the row by racing to the downstairs bathroom to be sick. Intense stress often had this effect on her. Now she lay on her side on the sofa, her head on a pile of cushions, her arms around her stomach—more to provide a sense of comfort than to ease the cramping. When she spoke her words were difficult, but not impossible, to decipher. No longer capable of shouting, she was still furious with Imogen.

"You shouldn't have come. It was a stupid, stupid decision. You just didn't think, did you?"

"You've already made your feelings quite clear, thank you. I believe I've got the message."

"You should be on your way to Canada by now. And why on earth did you have to tell them that you're my sister-in-law?"

Imogen seemed completely unmoved by Laura's anguish, and answered in a brisk, no-nonsense voice, "Because I *was*, until it all went pear shaped. I guess Will isn't going to like me being here either, but that's his problem. Look, Laura, what was I supposed to do? As soon as I heard the announcement that Hugo was dead, I *had* to come. And after everything that you've asked me to do for you, I actually thought that you might need some support. Silly me."

Gone was the gentle, sweet conciliatory tone that had been used to impress the police. Laura sighed. "Yes, I know what I asked, and it was a *big* ask, but..."

"A big ask? Is that what you call it? I would say that a 'big ask' is asking to borrow a brand-new Armani jacket, or asking for my last two thousand pounds. Not, of course, that you would ever need either of those things. But your 'big ask' was way off the Richter scale, lady, and you know it."

"I explained all that to you. You said you understood."

"But now it's different, isn't it." Imogen let out a huge breath, as if releasing a mountain of pent-up tension. "The next few days—possibly weeks—are going to be horrendous. You are going to need a lot of support. Who *knows* what is going to crawl out of the woodwork, and the police are inevitably going to want to understand what happened to you, and why you ended up in that madhouse."

Laura swung herself round into a sitting position. Not even Imogen was allowed to get away with a comment like that.

"You have a charming way with words, as always, Imo. Both you and I know quite well why I was there, but whatever the reason it doesn't make me feel any better about it."

The fight seemed to drain out of Imogen, and Laura could read regret in her eyes. That was the trouble with Imogen. She often spoke first, thought later. She'd always been that way.

Imogen placed an extremely large cognac that Laura didn't want on the table next to the sofa, and sat down beside her.

"I'm sorry," Imogen said. "That was tactless of me. But what are you going to tell the police? I'm here to give you the strength to go on. There are going to be moments when you really won't know what to do. You're going to have to deal with Alexa, then there's the will, the funeral, no end of things to do. You'll need somebody to talk to, and I'm the only person who understands."

Laura wasn't quite ready to let Imogen off the hook yet. "Ah, but there's the rub. You *think* you understand, but you actually don't have the faintest clue."

They were hurting each other, and it was a pointless exercise. The damage was done, and sticking the knife in Imogen wasn't going to help or change a thing. Perhaps the cognac wasn't such a bad idea. She took a mouthful and shuddered. She hated its cloying sweetness.

"Look, I don't want us to keep fighting," Laura said at last. "God knows my emotions are on enough of a roller coaster as it is. I do understand why you came, even though it was a crap idea. It was irresponsible and impulsive. And the police are definitely going to want to know why I was so horrified when you walked through the door."

"Then tell them the truth! Hugo hated me, your brother loathes me, I have been banned from this God-awful house for years—and your husband forbade you to speak to me ever again. And you were my best friend in the world. The truth is hideous enough without you trying to fabricate some unrealistic story."

Laura couldn't help but agree. From the age of five right up until the first year of her marriage, she and Imo had been as close as any two friends could be. Imogen's parents had moved from Canada into the house next door to Laura, and she could clearly remember the day they'd met. It had been one of the bad days in the Kennedy household, and Laura had crawled into her private den in the midst of an area of dense shrubbery at the bottom of their long garden, far enough away from the house so that she couldn't hear the argument. She'd never heard a real live North American accent until she heard Imogen's first words: "I saw you from my bedroom window, and thought you looked like you could use some chocolate. Can I come in?" Laura must have said yes, because this smiley kid in denim dungarees came scuttling into the den on hands and knees and gave Laura a quick hug and a rather dirty packet of chocolate buttons. "You'd better tell me why you're crying. 'Cos I'm staying till you do."

And that set the pattern of their relationship. Imogen had discovered a gap in the hedge between their houses and said it could be their secret. Any time she wanted, Laura could wriggle through to come and play with her and she would do the same. From that day forward they were inseparable. Laura believed that she knew everything about Imogen and vice versa. But she was wrong.

Imogen had never told Laura that from her early teens she was absolutely besotted with Will Kennedy, Laura's older brother. And when her feelings were reciprocated, Laura had felt side-lined. It took her a while to forgive Imogen for harbouring such a secret, but their happiness was infectious. Her best friend and her brother were married when Imogen was just twenty years old, and they had remained just as smitten with each other until one dreadful night here in this very house.

Now somebody was going to have to tell Will and her mother about Hugo. She hated the fact that Will had chosen to work in Kenya, but thankfully her mother was on her way there for a visit. She should have arrived by now. God knows, she was never Hugo's greatest fan, but Laura could really do without hearing her mother's views on her choice of husband at this precise moment.

"I need to tell Will. And Mum. Otherwise they're going to just see it on the news, and that wouldn't be great. I'm not sure if I have the energy to deal with my mother, so I'll tell Will and let him pass it on."

Laura knew what Imogen's response would be. She would never miss such a golden opportunity to speak to her ex-husband.

"I'll phone Will. Leave it with me. I'll do it in a minute," Imogen said, a thoughtful expression on her face.

"Oh, and can you check that the message light is on? And if it is…"

Imogen interrupted her. "Yes, I know what to do, don't worry."

"And then there's Alexa. I really need to do what I can to help her, poor kid. She's only twelve—and a very young twelve at that. It's going to hit her so hard. I can guarantee her mother will be totally useless. Alexa needs to be able to grieve for her father without getting Annabel's version of what a shit he was. I know she's his ex-wife and almost duty bound to loathe him, but surely she will just this once put her daughter's feelings before her own?"

Aware that she was babbling, Laura glanced across at Imogen, who was looking at her in a strange but determined way. Her next words confirmed that she had just been waiting for an appropriate pause in Laura's ramblings to jump in.

"Before you digressed somewhat, you said—and I quote—'You think you understand, but you actually don't have the faintest clue.' I think you'd better explain that statement."

Laura stood up from the sofa. Imogen was watching her too closely, and it made her uncomfortable. She walked over to the fireplace and crouched down to poke the embers. She didn't have the energy to justify her statement to Imogen right now. But Imogen hadn't finished.

"I'm not a hypocrite, Laura, and I detested your husband with a vengeance. There's more to this 'not having the faintest clue' than meets the eye, and I need to know what it is. I promise you, I won't give up until you've told me. I'm not here as your enemy. I'm here as your friend."

Having poked the fire to death, Laura played for time whilst she added more logs, arranging each one with unnecessary care. She knew that Imogen deserved an explanation. She had lied to her, or at least she had never told her the whole truth. But they had gone years without seeing or speaking to each other and too much had happened. Too much to explain in a single evening.

"I'm honestly not in any fit state to tell you. I know nowadays we're all encouraged to bare our souls at the drop of a hat, but I don't entirely subscribe to that theory. When I was in the home I saw enough instances of people regurgitating the same problems over and over again, when it would have served them better to push them to the back of their minds and just get on with life. However, you do have a right to know. I will concede that."

There was a long, drawn-out silence. Laura was fighting an internal battle, and it was clear that Imogen wasn't going to help. Finally, Laura made a decision, and not one she had been intending to make.

"I wrote you some letters."

"What letters? I haven't had a letter from you in years. What on earth are you talking about?"

"I didn't send them."

Laura paused. She didn't know if she could do this.

"The first time I wrote to you was when you and Will started seeing each other, and I was sulking. I wrote to tell you how I felt—and then I read it. I was appalled at my selfishness and I tore the letter up. Since then, there have been times in my life when I've desperately wanted to know what you think, and times when I just wanted to clarify my own feelings and resolve any dilemmas, so I wrote you letters. Several of them. It all started when I first met Hugo. I wasn't allowed to tell anybody about our relationship, so I wanted to capture every moment so that I could relive it with you when the time was right. I hated the fact that I couldn't share it with you. But after that, the time never was right. Things moved on and when I reread the first letter everything I'd written seemed so immature and childish. So as things changed, I wrote to you again. I fully intended to let you read everything— but gradually there were too many things that prevented that. And so it became something almost therapeutic. I felt as if I was talking to you, but I didn't have to suffer the humiliation of seeing your reaction. It won't make sense now, but it will when you read them."

Laura took a deep breath.

"Go, Imogen. Go and call Will. I'll go and find the letters—they're well hidden. I suppose you might as well start at the beginning—from the night I met Hugo. But we need to do this at my pace, Imo. I don't know if I can let you read them all."

6

Dear Imo,

There's something I'm dying to tell you—but I can't! It's so frustrating. I understand why I can't, but it's difficult for me. You're my best friend, and I want to share this with you. So I'm going to write it all down, and that way I won't forget anything. Not one precious moment. You see, I've had an amazing couple of weeks. I truly believe that in the last fourteen days, my life has changed forever.

I've met a man.

It all started with the awards night. The one I told you about. I've never been to an event in the Great Room of the Grosvenor House Hotel before, but it's famous for all the best awards nights. And this time one of my programmes had been shortlisted (and I was a complete bag of nerves).

Simon—my boss—was waiting for me when I arrived, and we pushed our way through the throngs of people crammed into the small lobby, all laughing and smiling and looking wonderfully elegant. We made our way down to the mezzanine overlooking the Great Room where the champagne reception was being held.

I have to say (somewhat immodestly) that I was really pleased with how I looked, which was a huge confidence boost, particularly as I was trembling with nerves. I'd splashed out on a gorgeous dress in aquamarine silk. It's got tiny shoestring straps, and a plunged neckline, and it's cut on the bias so that I look shapely rather than chubby—at least, that's what I'd convinced myself! And of course, my hair helps. I love being a redhead! So all in all, it was one of those nights when I felt good about myself.

Looking into the Great Room from the reception area, the sight was breathtaking. Enormous chandeliers created a warm and welcoming light, and there was an endless sea of beautifully decorated circular tables each with its own candelabra, the soft yellow flames gently illuminating the white cloths, which shimmered like pools of gold below us. The stage had been set up with a stunning backdrop of silver and gold stars, but best of all was the long table that held all the crystal pyramid awards for the winners. Just looking at them made me shiver with excitement. It would be such an honour to win, and such a boost to my career.

But I don't just feel ambitious for myself anymore. It's all about the company. Since Simon gave me some shares I feel I need to prove myself, and a win would surely make him feel his faith in me had been justified?

As we sat down at our table I realised that I wasn't going to be able to talk to everybody. I couldn't even see some of the VIP guests that Simon had invited because of the tall candles and a mass of wine bottles in a huge silver ice bucket, but as the night wore on and the wine was greedily devoured, I caught the eye of the man sitting opposite me. He seemed vaguely familiar, and very interesting! I guessed he was about forty, and he had thick, dark hair that like the rest of him was impeccably styled. Every man in the room was wearing a dinner jacket, but somehow his looked better—blacker, better fitting, more elegant. I couldn't see the colour of his eyes, but I made a bet with myself that they're dark blue. And he was watching me! He lifted his champagne flute and raised his glass just a fraction higher, offering me the most subtle of silent toasts as it reached his lips. It was so charming...I can't think of another word for it (except sexy, perhaps!). But I didn't have time to respond to his little flirtation, because there was a loud drum roll, and over the speakers came the voice of the master of ceremonies.

"Ladies and gentlemen, please be seated. The awards ceremony is about to commence."

You could practically feel the thrill of anticipation in the room. Now I know how people feel at the Oscars. I sat back, trying to look nonchalant whilst all the time my heart was pounding so hard I thought it was going to burst from my chest!

And just like the Oscars, they showed a clip of each of the finalists. My film was all about domestic abuse. Not necessarily the physically violent kind, but more the controlling and demeaning type. Honestly, the things that go on behind closed doors! The clip they showed was from one of the dramatic scenes that we built in. The acting was great. The guy who played the bullying husband managed to just create the right feeling of threat without ever laying a finger on his wife. But did you know that quite a lot of men are bullied too?

You wonder how they allow it to happen to them, but when we were planning the show I spoke to quite a few people who were not at all what you would expect of a typical victim. Many of them were intelligent with good jobs. As one of them said to me: "The slow, relentless destruction of self-confidence is something that is impossible to explain." I bet you thank God that you're married to Will!

We had to sit through the clips from the other nominations in my category, but finally it was the moment of truth.

The host stepped back up to the microphone.

"And the winner is... 'It's All in the Family.' Please welcome to the stage the producer of the programme, Laura Kennedy!"

The next half hour passed in a complete blur for me. Congratulations abounded, and champagne flowed. Everybody was great—lots of smiles and best wishes even from those we'd beaten (although no doubt through gritted teeth). But I could feel that I was still being watched...and I loved it.

I tore myself away from our crowd for a moment, because I thought I should have a quick word with the judges—just to say thanks, really. But there was one woman who looked completely stone faced.

"Don't thank me, Laura. I didn't vote for you," she said.

With that, she stood up from the table and walked away. I recognised her. It was the journalist Sophie Miller. She's pretty well known herself for reporting on sensitive subjects, so I was a bit shocked, but I tried to keep my cool. I smiled at the others to cover my embarrassment, and made my way back to our table.

I was feeling slightly deflated, but I think I hid it well. Then I heard a quiet voice behind me.

"Miss Kennedy?" he said (how very formal!). I turned round, and it was him. "Hugo Fletcher. Congratulations on a well-deserved award. I was impressed with your film tonight—at least, the part I saw. I'd appreciate an opportunity to talk to you about it in more detail, and tell you something of the work that I do in my charity. But clearly tonight is not the occasion. Would you care to have lunch with me one day? There's a rather good restaurant off the King's Road that I would very much like to take you to. Here's my card. Have a think about it, and give me a call."

He gave me a little bow—yes, really—and made his way out. I have to say I was sorry to see him go. Just knowing he was there and watching me had added an extra frisson of excitement, and everything felt a little less sharply defined once he'd gone, if you can understand that.

Anyway, I pulled myself together and was about to jump up to dance when I saw that awful Sophie woman heading for the stairs, so I dodged around the tables and made my way after her. I caught up with her whilst she was queuing for her coat.

"Hello," I said in a pleasant voice. "We didn't get a chance to chat properly earlier, but I got the impression that you didn't like my programme. I'd be really interested to understand what it was that you had a problem with."

She didn't blink or look even slightly embarrassed. Her eyes were dark and unsmiling, and her response was short and to the point.

"Your film was well made. It was well paced, and the drama sections were decently acted. Unfortunately it had one major flaw. It was abundantly clear to me that you know absolutely nothing whatsoever about the subject. Now, if you'll excuse me?"

With that, she walked past me without a backward glance and out through the double doors.

I just stood and watched her leave. There was no suitable response to this, and there was really no time to ponder as Simon came chasing after me to drag me to the dance floor.

The rest of the night passed in a blur—but I remember thinking that my life was about to change forever.

I know that by the time you read this, you will know all about the award—so sorry to be boring. But it all somehow fits together, so it was important to capture the whole atmosphere of the evening and my swirling emotions!

Predictably the next day was *not* a good day for working in the TV production office. Nobody had made it to bed much before four a.m., and our heads were throbbing. I, however, was still smiling. I actually didn't mind the headache and the mild feeling of nausea.

I'm not sure if it was the hangover or not, but I kept seeing images of the previous night flash before my eyes in Technicolor. *Flash:* a sea of faces as I look down from the stage, clutching my precious crystal pyramid. *Flash:* a single face; the face of a man, offering me just a suggestion of a private smile.

Strangely, the second of these two occurred with rather more frequency than the first.

My past performance with men hasn't really been that great, has it? It's been so different for you, with Will. But I've never had a really serious relationship. Everybody seems to want casual sex these days. Some men think they just need to buy you a quick beer in the pub, and then it's back to your place. I know I sound cynical, but I need to make some connection with a man I'm going to have sex with. And I've never met anybody who makes me feel the way you do about Will. Certainly no man has constantly intruded on my thoughts. Until Hugo Fletcher.

I was dying to ask Simon about him, but he didn't make it into the office until three o'clock! One of the privileges of being the boss, I suppose. Of course, everybody wanted a verbal rerun of the previous night's events—but strangely enough, I just wanted to get Simon on his own, so I could pick his brains. Finally, I managed to corner him.

"Laura, I don't miss much, you know. You want to talk to me about Hugo Fletcher, don't you? He couldn't take his eyes off you all night, darling." (TV speak—please don't let me slip into that—I love Simon, but I even heard him call the electrician "darling" the other day.)

Anyway, this was music to my ears, and I sat there entranced as Simon told me everything he knew about the man, his charity, his business, his investments…and his wife!

Why had it never occurred to me that he's married? And I *don't do* married men. Never—at least knowingly—would I become a party to the inevitable misery. Somebody always suffers, and I've seen enough of it in my life to recognise this. I know you'll understand that.

I was getting a bit ahead of myself, though. We'd only exchanged a few words! But there was such a spark, or at least, that's how it felt to me.

Having just about decided that I wouldn't follow up on his offer of lunch, Simon surprised me.

"I think you should meet him. You should flirt with him a little. I know that's as far as you'll let it go, because you are who you are. But he's important to us. He's very wealthy, but also he's never allowed anybody to make a documentary about his charity, and it would be a major coup. You have to learn to use your assets, darling. You underestimate how gorgeous you are, and if it's okay to win business by brains, why not by beauty?"

What do you think of *that*, Imo? I wasn't quite sure if he was suggesting that I didn't have a brain, but I don't think so.

❖ ❖ ❖

It might have been a dangerous decision to make, but I finally arranged a lunch date with Hugo. I'd put off making the call, but I'd thought of little else. So it had to be done.

I wanted to look perfect—business-like, but attractive—so I'd splashed out on a Donna Karan suit, and a gorgeous pair of long grey suede boots. I decided to leave my hair in its natural waves, and I felt good.

The taxi driver was droning on about Arsenal and Manchester United fighting for the top of some league or other. I feigned interest, as you do, but I really just wanted to tune out and focus on the hours ahead. We turned into Egerton Crescent, and what a charming place it is, with the beautiful white painted houses all looking pristine even in the grey February weather.

I did feel a few butterflies as I ran up the path to get out of the rain, and the young woman who opened the door somehow managed to make me feel like a country hick, even in my smart new suit. She had that look of class that comes with years of shopping in the right places. Wearing what was unmistakably Chanel, I felt that I had altogether missed the mark. But I wasn't going to turn tail and run, so I gave her my brightest smile.

"Hello, I'm Laura Kennedy. I have an appointment with Sir Hugo Fletcher," I said, putting out my hand to shake hers.

A rather limp hand was extended. I never know what to do with people who just let their hands drop into yours, do you? Are you supposed to squeeze them reassuringly, pump them frenetically, or match like with like and let both hands hang lifelessly together for a few seconds? I opted for a gentle squeeze and a mild shake, and hoped that would do. Obviously I was being judged, and I suspect found wanting, by this rather po-faced girl. She didn't quite look me up and down with a sneer on her face, but it was a close thing!

"Good morning, Ms. Kennedy. I'm Jessica Armstrong, Sir Hugo's personal assistant. He's expecting you. Please come in."

I was shown into Hugo's private office where he rose to meet me from behind his desk. It was like no office I'd ever been in, with dark green walls covered in classical art, and walnut furniture that was clearly antique. The desk itself was enormous, and was devoid of a scrap of paper. There was a large blotter, unmarked by ink or doodles (which shows enormous restraint) and a Mont Blanc silver fountain pen was lying perfectly straight against the upper edge. The only other thing on the desk was a huge leather-bound diary, with the current year stamped in gold on the front. Thank God I didn't invite him to my office, which is the exact opposite to this in every way possible.

Hugo moved around the desk. "Welcome, Laura. You don't mind if I call you Laura, I hope?"

Rather bemused at what else he might want to call me, I wasn't sure how to respond.

"It's good to be here finally, and I'd be delighted if you would call me Laura. I have to admit, though, that I haven't a clue what I should call you!" God, how crass! Why does this man make me feel so *edgy*?

He smiled at me benignly.

"I hope we're going to be good friends, Laura, so please call me Hugo. Do have a seat. Jessica will be bringing some coffee through, and we have an hour to talk business before I have the pleasure of taking you to lunch."

He told me all about his charity, and he's so passionate about it! It was wonderful to just sit and listen. Apparently he inherited a "rather considerable sum" from his father, mainly in property, which is managed by his company in Canary Wharf. But Hugo prefers to focus as much of his time as possible on a charitable foundation that he set up, which helps young prostitutes who end up on the streets through no fault of their own. Isn't that an amazingly good cause? I asked him why he had chosen this type of charity, and it's the most incredible story, so I asked permission to tape him as research for a programme. He said I could record it, but he wasn't sure if he would let me use it. Anyway, this is what he told me.

"A bit of rather embarrassing family history came to light some years ago. The wealth of the family is inherited, of course—but it turns out that the family fortune was built on slavery back in the nineteenth century. My great-great-grandfather failed to adhere to the Abolition of the Slave Trade Act in the early part of the century, and continued trading in various areas of the British Empire until well into the middle of the century. He invested his ill-gotten gains in property. There was some talk of my great-grandfather—his son—also doing rather well out of prostitution, although we haven't been able to prove that. But most of the working girls in that era were considered of a lower class, and he's reputed to have founded a few clubs with 'clean' girls for his rich friends. I can't find any evidence to that effect, but apparently there was one prostitute to every twelve adult males in London in his time, so I wouldn't be surprised. Now *that* would make rather a good subject for a documentary!"

"So that's why you chose to help prostitutes?" I asked.

"Well, I could hardly help slaves, and as this all came to light when my father was alive, he thought of the idea and I've developed it from there. I called it the Allium Foundation."

I love alliums. Then Hugo told me that they are part of the onion family. Did you know that?

"I like the analogy," he said. "What starts off as a rather pungent, multi-layered bulb forces its way out through the ground with a strong and straight stem, culminating in a glorious and complex flower. I like the parallel with the girls' families—what's beneath the surface is not very sweet, but given some appropriate cultivation it has the potential for a beautiful result."

I can only conclude from everything that he said that he is not only charming, but he is sensitive and compassionate. At this point, I was beginning to feel that I really shouldn't have come. It was dangerous.

We set off for the restaurant, and it was all that I thought it would be: discreet, sophisticated, and subtly decorated in relaxing stone colours. We were shown to our table, and Hugo quietly moved the waiter aside so that he could personally pull my chair out, making sure I was comfortably settled before he sat down himself. The waiter came back to the table with menus, but Hugo waved them away.

"Tell me what you like, Laura. What sort of food gives you pleasure, and what wine do you enjoy the most?"

Nobody's ever asked me this before, and I didn't know where to start.

"All right, why don't you tell me any types of food that you don't like?"

That's a pretty short list, as you know, but as I talked I felt that Hugo was really interested in me. So I told him about the meals I'd eaten that I'd enjoyed the most. He prompted me from time to time with ideas, and after about ten minutes he called the waiter over and placed an order—without further reference to the menu. *Really* impressive stuff. I was bowled over.

"I'm glad you let me order for you, Laura. I consider it an honour to look after a lady, particularly one as beautiful as you are. I find these days that there are fewer and fewer women who are prepared to relinquish control."

I have to admit that the idea of him controlling me flashed through my mind in rather lurid detail. Then I brought myself up short when he mentioned the dreaded two words...

"My wife—and I am sure you are aware that I am married—considers it a personal insult to allow me any sort of influence over her decisions, and will disagree with me on principle solely to provoke me." He gave a slight smile.

Then he told me his secret, and it's the reason that I can't tell anybody—not even you. He's getting a divorce, but he doesn't want it to be public knowledge. He's got a little girl called Alexa whom he obviously adores, but the soon-to-be ex has agreed to joint custody. He's already moved out. His mother died recently so he's been able to return to the family home.

I didn't know whether to appear sympathetic for the loss of his mother or regretful for the failure of his marriage. I did know, however, that I should try to hide the rush of excitement I was feeling. But his next words made it impossible for me to disguise my feelings.

"I'm telling you this, Laura, because although we have only just met I feel very drawn to you. I was dazzled by you at the awards dinner, and you look absolutely beautiful today. I love your hair like that."

I just looked into his eyes (dark blue, as I predicted) and I felt as if bubbles were racing through my veins. I didn't speak. Obviously I'd stopped recording him as soon as we'd moved on from talk of the charity, but I think I can remember every word he said. At least, those that were about "us." I think they're etched onto my brain!

"I would like to continue to see you, Laura, if you would permit it. Our meetings would have to be private, and it would have to be just between us for the time being, until the situation is a little less sensitive. But please be assured that I will treat you with the utmost respect and consideration."

So that's why I can't send you this, Imo. Maybe you'll never get to read it—it all depends what happens next—but I can tell you that for the first time in my life, I would have been happy to take a man home after our very first date!

With love, as always,

Laura

Imogen reached the end of Laura's letter.

She'd known all the facts, of course. She knew when and how they met, and she knew that Laura had been completely besotted with Hugo. But it was all so long ago, and so much had happened since. She was glad Laura had let her read this letter first, because it put everything that happened later into perspective.

For the moment, though, she didn't want to read anymore. She just wanted to sit back; to remember and to think. About the past, about Laura, about Will—but most of all, about Hugo.

7

There was no doubt in anybody's mind that the body in the mortuary was indeed that of Hugo Fletcher, but the formalities had to be adhered to. Laura had quietly done as she had been asked, with no outward display of emotion. Having confirmed what they already knew, Tom had suggested that she come back to headquarters with him for a while before making the return trip to Oxfordshire. It seemed callous to send her away without so much as a hot drink.

Tom gently guided her into the shoebox that passed as his office, and took a seat facing her on the other side of his relatively tidy desk. There was a quiet knock on the door.

"Ah, here's the tea. It's not particularly wonderful tea, I'm afraid, but it's hot and wet. We do need to ask you some questions, but I'm sure you'd like some time to yourself, so I'll leave you in peace. DS Robinson, whom you met last night, will come and take some background from you in a while. I'll need to ask some more in-depth questions, but we'll arrange a car back to Oxfordshire for you, and we'll follow on later today, if that's okay."

Laura spoke quietly. "Could we start the questions now, please? I'd rather get it over with, if you can spare the time."

"Unfortunately, I have something else that I need to do at eight o'clock, and I'll be a couple of hours."

Tom was surprised at the directness of the gaze that Laura Fletcher gave him. Although wearing glasses today, Tom could see her eyes were no longer red from weeping, and whilst she still spoke quietly there seemed to be a new determination in her demeanour.

"Detective Chief Inspector, as you appear to have about fifteen minutes before you must leave—I presume to attend my husband's post-mortem—do you think we could spend that time going through what you already know, please? I was too shocked last night to respond, and I want to help in any way I can."

"If you're sure you don't want a few minutes alone, Lady Fletcher?"

"No, thank you. What I'd really like is for this all to be over as quickly as possible, and if you don't mind I would prefer it if you would call me Laura. I never really wanted a title, and now that Hugo's dead I'd like to rid myself of the formality of it all. Not too many years ago, *everybody* called me Laura— from the milkman to my clients. Now it's the most difficult thing in the world to get past the bloody title."

Slightly surprised by Laura's tone of voice, Tom decided to give her some time whether she believed she needed it or not. Why was she so different today? he wondered. He could only imagine it was because she wanted to get any questions out of the way to give herself space to grieve.

"Okay, Laura it is. Please call me Tom. I'll go and find DS Robinson— Becky—and we'll spend the next ten or fifteen minutes filling in some gaps. Excuse me for a moment." He left her with her cup of tea and went to have a quick word with Becky to discuss interview tactics, but also to alert her to the change in Laura's manner.

But by the time he returned to the office with Becky, Laura's veneer of determination had seeped away, and she seemed to have retreated into herself once again. She was sitting perfectly still, gazing at nothing, her mind clearly miles away. Tom moved around to the other side of the desk and took his seat, while Becky pulled up a chair to the side. Laura turned to look at Tom, and for a moment seemed surprised that there was anybody else in the room. She appeared to mentally shake herself, straighten her back, and square her shoulders, as if to do battle.

"Okay, Laura. I'm going to bring you up to date with what we know at the moment, and please feel free to interrupt. When we come to Oxfordshire we'll need to look through Sir Hugo's things, and try to see if there is anything that would point to a motive."

"That's fine—but please just refer to him as Hugo. He would hate it; titles were something of a family obsession. But he's not here to know any different, is he?"

If he thought she was difficult to read last night, today it was impossible. It was as if she'd built a wall around her grief, which she determinedly reassembled each time it started to crumble. And now she was using antagonism against her dead husband to strengthen her defences. But anger against the deceased was a natural reaction in the early stages of grief, and Tom was more than happy to drop all formalities if that made her more comfortable.

"We know that Beryl Stubbs found your husband—Hugo—at about twelve forty-five. That's an approximation, but she was too upset and shocked to phone it in until about one forty-five. The local police arrived on the scene just before two p.m. We estimate the time of death to be between eleven thirty and noon. Mrs. Stubbs probably arrived less than an hour after your husband died, and if she hadn't missed the first bus because of an argument with her husband, she would probably have interrupted the scene." Tom smiled to try to take the edge off things a little. "Beryl likes to blame her husband for just about everything, but on this occasion he may possibly have saved her life."

Laura had once more gone very pale, the hard facts of her husband's death no doubt breaking through her carefully constructed barricade.

"Do you want more tea, Laura?" he asked with concern.

"No, I'm fine, thanks. Please carry on."

"Okay. We have one eyewitness, a neighbour who saw somebody leaving the house." Tom paused. This was never an easy thing to tell a wife. "I'm sorry, but this might be a little painful for you. The person he saw was a woman. She had long red hair and was wearing a black leather skirt, carrying a large shoulder bag. Do you have any idea who this could be?"

He paused and looked at Laura. She tilted her head back and looked at the ceiling, biting her top lip as if to prevent it from trembling. And it was about to get even more difficult.

"I'm sorry to tell you that there are indications that the murder may have been sexually motivated, so finding this woman is crucial. I know this must be very difficult for you, Laura, but any suggestions you might have would be really useful."

"You know about my husband's charity work. He dealt with a lot of women, so perhaps it was one of them. It doesn't sound like anybody I know. I'm sorry. I can't help."

She hadn't been able to look Tom in the eye when she answered, choosing instead to lower her head and stare at a pile of files on his desk. Which was worse? he wondered. To know exactly who it might be and not be surprised, or to have no idea at all, perhaps not even realising that other women—or at least another woman—featured in her husband's life.

It was Laura who broke the uncomfortable silence. "Have you discovered how he died?"

"We're not certain yet, but we'll know more later this morning, and I'll certainly keep you informed."

Tom paused as he considered how best to phrase his next question. "Your guest last night—if I remember rightly she is your sister-in-law. Is that correct?"

"Ex-sister-in-law to be precise. She was married to my brother, but they've been divorced for a long time now."

Tom nodded. "You seemed very shocked and angry at her appearance."

This wasn't the time for closed questions. He wanted more than a monosyllabic answer, but he could see that Laura was considering her words with care.

"Imogen and I were the closest of friends for many years. But we argued when she and my brother were divorced. She hadn't been to Ashbury Park since that time, so she was the last person that I was expecting to walk through the door. She lives in Canada and I had no reason to expect her. It was a surprise, that's all."

Tom knew it was more than that, and he wasn't about to let it drop. But he would choose his moment, and this wasn't it. There was a lot of other ground to cover.

"Earlier you mentioned your husband's charity. Anything you can tell us about any aspect of your husband's life, in particular the charity side, would be really helpful. We've managed to track down the staff from the office in Egerton Crescent. We've spoken to Rosie Dixon and Jessica Armstrong, and one of my colleagues met a Brian Smedley, who we understand is the chief financial officer of the property company. I know he is based in the offices in East London, but I gather he came to Egerton Terrace to see Hugo a couple of times a week. We need to interview all of them in much more detail of course, but it would be really useful to hear about the charity from your perspective."

"I'm afraid that I didn't have much to do with his charity work. I tried to offer my services in the early days of our marriage, but Hugo preferred me to be at home looking after the house, so I can only give you an overview."

"It seems a pity you weren't involved more," Tom said. "I'm sure you would have been a very valuable asset."

"I thought so too—but there we are. It wasn't to be."

"An overview is fine, then," Tom said.

"Hugo's father originally started the charity many years ago, but only locally in Oxfordshire. Initially the aim was to help young girls who had to leave home as a result of family abuse and who had ended up on the streets. They saw prostitution as the only way that they could survive. The charity focused on girls who were technically old enough to leave home with their parents' consent—although most of them actually didn't have it. They investigated each case, but if the girls really couldn't return home the charity arranged for the necessary parental permission—I'm not sure what subtle threats were issued if the abusive parents were difficult about it. Then the charity would find families for the girls to live with, and jobs too—as home helps, or in cafés or hotels. It gave the girls time to get back on their feet, and the families that took them in were helped financially too. Then the girls were given a lot of assistance to make them strong enough to make their own way in the world.

"Over the last few years, though, the work of the foundation has evolved into something much bigger than it was when Hugo first told me about it. No doubt you know all about the enormous growth in Eastern European prostitution?"

Tom nodded. He'd learned some of this from the research his team had done, but it would be good to hear about it from Laura too.

As she started to speak, he noticed that the air of detachment was being replaced by genuine enthusiasm, as if she really cared about the fate of these girls.

"When I met Hugo I was deeply impressed by the work of his charity— helping girls that appeared to have nowhere to turn. But in comparison, those girls were lucky. They spoke the language, and they were in their own country. The girls the charity helps now are often brought to England either against their will, or under the misapprehension that they're coming to work as waitresses or chambermaids. In some cases, they think they've won a modelling contract—and they are full of hope and excitement. Then, of course, it becomes obvious that life as they knew it has ended. They are smuggled in and sold into prostitution. The price of a girl can be as much as eight thousand pounds, making a significant profit for the smugglers. But they can earn up to eight hundred pounds per day for the gangs that buy them. They may have to have sex with twelve, fifteen, twenty men. Each and every day. It's practically impossible for them to escape. In theory they can buy themselves out—but there's no hope of them raising the money. Most if not all of their earnings are taken from them. They're usually here illegally, so how can they get home even if they could get the money together? If they manage to get away from wherever they're held and turn themselves in to the police, they're concerned about protection, and many of them don't want to be sent home to the lives they thought they'd escaped. They're scared of repercussions from the original smugglers, and they'd have to live with the shame of what happened to them. It's a truly terrible situation."

"So how did the charity help?" Becky asked.

"Hugo had a team of workers who would go out and find the girls. I suspect they set themselves up as punters. They would try to persuade the girls to go to the police, with the charity's help and support. But that assumed that they would be happy to be sent back to where they came from, and many of them weren't. So if that didn't work, they would offer to find the girls a safe environment and would often actually buy the girls back from the pimps, at a pretty exorbitant rate. I had a problem with this, because I thought it would just result in them just going and buying more girls. But Hugo said I didn't understand. He said I didn't need to worry about that aspect, so I really don't know. Something about supply and demand, apparently. But the rescued girls were rehoused with families—just like the original girls that the Allium Foundation helped."

"Approximately how many girls did the charity help?" Tom asked.

"Oh, not as many as they would have liked. Only about a hundred to a hundred and fifty a year. Whatever they could afford through their fund-raising, and of course Hugo did supplement the income through one of his trusts."

At that moment, a detective constable stuck his head around the door. "Sir, you're wanted for your eight-o'clock appointment."

Tom made his excuses, and thanked Laura once again for making the journey so early in the morning, promising to get to Oxfordshire as soon as possible. As he busied himself getting some papers together prior to leaving, Becky picked up the questioning. He could see that she was genuinely moved by the vision that Laura painted.

"What happens to the girls in the end?"

"What do you mean, exactly?"

Tom was rather surprised at the sharp tone that Laura used in response to what seemed to be a perfectly innocuous question.

"Well, are they just kept with the families for an agreed period, and if so, what happens to them when they leave? Do they get help with further work permits, passports, that sort of thing?"

"Oh, I see. Well, it depends on the circumstances…"

Tom didn't hear the rest of Laura's answer as he left the office, but he sensed something that sounded strangely like relief in her voice.

8

Laura slammed the front door behind her and walked wearily towards the kitchen where Imogen was having a late breakfast. The room smelled of toast and fresh coffee.

"Give me some of that, please, Imo. That was not my finest hour."

"What happened? You identified the body, I presume. Was it awful? You should have let me come with you."

Laura looked at her and let out a deep, slow breath. "You don't need to hold my hand, you know. I'm okay, and I'm in control. The body, as you put it, was just Hugo. He looked as if he was asleep, and it was nowhere near as traumatic as I thought it would be. But they asked me about the charity, and it made me very twitchy. Oh, I don't know. I'm not sure if I should be the grieving wife, a demented nutcase, or just plain old me. I suspect I seem like a bit of all three to them. I feel as if I don't know who I am anymore."

Laura plonked herself down at the scrubbed pine table in the kitchen and rested her chin on her cupped hands.

"I wouldn't worry," Imogen said. "Nobody would expect you to be normal at the moment, whatever normal is. You're supposed to be stricken with grief, and so just about anything would seem normal. I thought they were coming back with you? What's happened, did you scare them off?"

"Tom had to go to the postmortem, although he was too delicate to mention it. They're coming here soon, and then they're off to see Annabel. God knows what they'll make of Hugo's delightful ex-wife. You've never met her, have you? They have a real treat in store."

Laura gratefully picked up the cup of coffee that Imogen had put in front of her and took a deep gulp.

"They're nice, though, the police that have been assigned to this case. They seem really concerned, and the detective sergeant, who by the way is my nominated Family Liaison Officer—just what I need I'm sure—got quite emotional when I explained what Allium does."

Imogen raised her eyebrows and smiled at Laura. "You've failed to mention the good looks of the charming chief inspector. Tom, now, I note? He's a bit of a hunk, don't you think. And what was with the sexy T-shirt and oh-so-perfect jeans last night?"

"Christ, just at this moment I've got other things on my mind—as you may have noticed. Anyway, he looked completely different today, as you'll see when he turns up here in an hour or so. Smart suit—expensive, by the look of it—tie, the works. According to Becky, yesterday was supposed to be his day off, which is why he was dressed so casually. But let's be honest, even if I thought he was the sexiest man on earth, who's going to look at me these days?"

Imogen was fortunately spared the need to reply to this by a loud banging on the front door. "I'll get it," she said. "It's probably just the press again. I wish they'd leave you alone. There's a policeman at the gate, but he seems to be taken in by all sorts of stories. We should never have given him the pass code. We've had 'deliveries' from more florists than you would believe this morning. Several with carefully concealed microphones in, no doubt. I'm getting very good at being rude to them."

Propping the door open with an old brass door stop, Imogen made her way towards the front of the house, her footsteps echoing as she crossed the stone-flagged hallway. Then the peace and quiet of the house was ripped apart by the high-pitched voice of an hysterical child.

"Where's Laura? I want Laura."

Clearly Imogen had not had a chance to reply to this, because within seconds a beautiful young girl appeared in the open doorway to the kitchen and practically threw herself at Laura. She hung on, her slender body shaking with sobs.

Laura felt sick. Alexa didn't deserve this. The poor child had adored her father; had practically worshipped him, in fact. She glanced towards the doorway where a young woman of around thirty was standing. Her eyes were red and swollen, although there were no signs of tears now. They exchanged unsmiling eye contact, but not a word was spoken between them.

"Alexa, my darling. I'm so sorry. So very, very sorry. I know how much you loved him and he loved you, too, you know. He would hate to see you so upset."

Laura knew that there were no words capable of soothing Alexa, so she just held onto her tightly, stroking the white-blonde hair away from her face. At twelve years old, she was too young to be hurting so badly.

After a few minutes, Alexa's sobs had subsided slightly, but keeping a tight hold of her, Laura looked up.

"Hannah, what are you both doing here? Shouldn't Alexa be with her mother?"

"Annabel has gone to see her lawyer. She's going to be gone for most of the day, she said, and Alexa didn't want to be on her own. She's been making such a fuss, I didn't know what to do with her. Anyway, it was her idea to come here, not mine."

There had been many occasions when Laura had wanted to slap Hannah hard across the face, and this time it was so tempting. Perhaps she should just do it and put it down to her own grief.

Imogen had joined them in the kitchen, apparently having decided not to intrude until Alexa was a little calmer.

"Did I hear that right? Her mother's gone out and left her! What the hell…"

Imogen stopped as Laura gave her a warning shake of the head.

"I'll make some fresh coffee, shall I?" Imogen asked. "What about Alexa, what would you like, honey?"

Alexa turned her head slowly from where it was resting on Laura's bosom. "Who are you?" she asked with a childlike ability to get straight to the point.

It was Laura who answered. "This is Imogen, sweetheart. She used to be married to Uncle Will. Do you remember Uncle Will? You met him a couple of times when you were younger."

"Isn't he your brother? Did he go away somewhere? Was it like you, Laura, when you went away?"

"No, not like me at all. Will's an engineer and he's working in Kenya. He's been there for years now."

"So why didn't she go with him?"

"They got divorced, like Mummy and Daddy did."

Alexa turned to Imogen. "Why haven't I seen you before?"

"I've been living in Canada, Alexa. It's where I was born. I lived in England when I was a little girl, but decided to go back to my roots when I got divorced."

This wasn't strictly true, reflected Laura. Imogen had stayed in England for a couple of years after the divorce, hoping in vain to get back together with Will. Right up to the time, in fact, when Will took himself off to Kenya. By then, Laura and Imogen were no longer speaking—driven apart by the events of one single night. Despite not having spoken for nearly two years, it didn't hurt any less when Laura discovered that her one-time best friend was moving back to Canada. She had always hoped that Hugo would relent and there could be a reconciliation.

"Lexi, darling, you know you can stay here with me for as long as you like. But you look exhausted. Why don't you go upstairs for a bit and have a lie down. Hannah will make you a nice warm drink and sit with you until you go to sleep. I know it's still morning, but all that crying must have worn you out, and I bet you didn't sleep much last night, did you?"

"How could I? I just kept thinking of poor Daddy. Why would anybody want to hurt him? He was lovely, wasn't he? We had such special times together, and he loved me more than anybody in the world. He always told me that nothing could come between us."

"I know, sweetheart."

"Will you come up and see me, please, Laura? Will you tell me some stories about him?"

"Of course I will. Go on, I'll be up soon."

As Hannah and Alexa left the room, Imogen moved over towards the door and closed it firmly behind them.

"You were right about Alexa, Laura. She's an enchanting kid, and the photos you showed me don't do her justice, even after all those tears. I can see why you love her so much. Poor mite, she's going to have a bit of a tough time ahead. It's hard to believe she's twelve, though. She's such a little thing. But what's the story with Hannah? You clearly don't like her."

Laura didn't answer. She waited for Imogen to work it out, and it didn't take long.

"Ah ha! Hannah's the nanny. *That* nanny—she's the one, isn't she?"

"Yes. She's the one. She was Hugo's puppet, and couldn't see farther than the nose on her face. She still lives with Annabel, but Hugo pays her—or rather paid her." Laura paused as a thought struck her. "Now, that's interesting. I wonder what's going to happen to her, because I can't see Annabel paying Hannah out of her own pocket, and I *certainly* wouldn't. I wonder if Hugo has made any provision in his will for her."

"Do you have any idea at all what he has put in the will?" Imogen asked. "I mean, this is a family property, so I presume it goes to Alexa. I don't suppose that ever occurred to you, did it?" Imogen as usual got straight to the point.

"It may have escaped your notice, Imogen, but I've had one or two other things on my mind in the last twenty-four hours. I haven't given the will a moment's thought. Where Hugo's concerned, though, it's always wise to expect the unexpected."

Imogen appeared unfazed by Laura's slightly caustic response. "Ah, talking of expecting the unexpected, you had a phone call earlier. It was Stella. She's on her way."

"Shit! The last thing I need is my mother. She was supposed to be going off to visit Will yesterday morning. I bought her the damn ticket! What's she still doing in the country?"

"You know what she's like, Laura. She got some notion in her head about malaria, apparently. She's been taking the tablets as prescribed, but got the idea that she hadn't taken them for long enough, so wanted to delay by a week to be on the safe side. She said you'd bought her a fully flexible ticket, so she just changed the date."

"Oh God. Why, oh why did I not just buy her a fixed ticket, then she'd be gone and out of this."

Her mother had no time for pretence or artifice, and Laura could really do without her particular brand of interference at the moment. The next few days were going to be difficult enough, and she could only imagine the interrogation that would be forced upon her when her mother learned that there was apparently a woman involved in Hugo's death. Laura grabbed the pot of coffee and poured herself another cup, not caring if it was hot or cold. She sat down at the kitchen table and looked at Imogen, who was still leaning against the kitchen door.

"Didn't Will tell you any of this yesterday when you spoke to him?" Laura asked.

"He just said that he'd break the news to her himself. He probably thought you already knew she hadn't taken the flight, and you know what he's like when he talks to me—or maybe you don't. He's clipped, short, and to the point. He said he didn't have time to chat and he'd let you know when he was going to be able to get here. I keep in touch with him from time to time—just in case he has a change of heart. But it's a waste of time."

Laura felt for Imogen, and could see the sadness hovering just below the surface. "Will you still be here when he arrives, Imo? Surely you need to get back to work?"

"I've already contacted my boss. I've got my laptop, and you've got a wireless connection here. I can stay for as long as you want me to—at least until the funeral."

Oh God, the funeral, Laura thought. Something else to think about. Maybe she could give her mother that job—it might just keep her occupied.

"I've no idea when the funeral will be, though. I don't know when they'll release his body, as it's a murder enquiry. But I suppose the damage is done now—so you may as well stay."

Laura realised how ungracious that sounded, and moved on quickly.

"Look, Imo, if you don't mind I'm going to go and sit with Alexa for a little while, and then I'm going to have a bath. I need some time to think."

"Have you got any more reading for me to do?"

"Are you sure you want to? It's not obligatory, you know."

"Maybe not, but I need to understand. All of it. Is that okay?"

"Not really—but I suppose it will have to be. Actually the next letter's quite relevant, bearing in mind who we were just talking about. But Imo, whatever you read, whatever you think, please—I beg you—don't let's talk about it."

9

Dear Imo,

What can I say, apart from "My bloody, bloody mother!" Much as I love her, when I saw her at the weekend, I could cheerfully have strangled her! She thinks she's so perceptive, but sometimes she's just hurtful. And I'd brought you a letter—the first one I wrote. But because of everything she said, it just didn't seem right to give it to you. The excitement had gone. So I thought I'd write you another—and I know exactly when I'll give it to you. When you've met Hugo and you know how ridiculous my mother is being!

It's been a while since I've seen you all—you, Will, Mum and Dad—and I was really looking forward to it. Everything in my life seemed perfect, and the gorgeous warm weather—incredible for the end of March—just matched my mood. The roads were clear and I made good time, and of course I got the usual lighthearted grumbling when I rang the doorbell. You know what she's like!

"Laura, why won't you just let yourself in? This is your home. But no, I have to stop whatever I'm doing to open the door for you because of some rather bizarre principle of yours."

Of course, she wasn't really cross, and she gave me a big hug to let me know. I hugged her back and asked where Dad was. I got the predictable answer.

"God knows, and probably cares less than I do. Let's get you in and then I'll open a bottle of wine, I think. It's that sort of time, isn't it?" It wasn't, but neither of us really cared.

Despite the comments about Dad, I knew that Mum would know exactly where he was, and if he ever thought otherwise he was fooling himself. She's not had such an easy time with him, has she? I do understand that. He's not been blessed with much of a strong will, and I'm not sure he's been blessed with any conscience at all. But he's still a great dad, and I don't think Mum's prepared to give up her comfortable life just because he's a bit lacking in the backbone department. I hope not, anyway.

We sat and drank some wine, and talked about pretty much everything. I say "pretty much" because there was one thing that I was leaving out for the moment. But Mum's no idiot. Far from it.

We chatted about the awards night for a while. I think the vicarious thrill of the glamour and sophistication gave her a real buzz. Then she told me all your news (which I knew already, but didn't let on), although I could see she was watching me very carefully, and giving me one of her funny looks.

"Okay, Laura. Out with it. You're like the cat that's got the cream, and it's not just that award that's doing it. You're positively glowing. It's a man, isn't it?"

Typical! I was going to tell you all later, when you and Will arrived for supper (although I know you'd guessed there was something going on), but Mum's so perceptive! I had to respond—no choice, really—and I couldn't hide my self-satisfied smirk!

"Yes, it's a man. And this time, I think it's the real thing. I'm actually in love!"

Mum was so excited for me. She said I'd had nothing but deadbeats for years (charming!) and she couldn't wait to meet him.

Oh—oh. This was when I knew it would get a bit tricky. I tried to explain that we don't want anybody to know about us yet, so although I'd been given permission to tell my family, we weren't ready to go public. Of course, she didn't like the sound of that. Not straightforward enough for her.

So I explained.

"The thing is, Mum, he's quite famous. We've not been seeing each other for long— only a few weeks—and there are some things to be sorted out before we go public, because the press will be on us like a ton of bricks."

That perked her up again. "Famous? Wow! Who is he? Don't keep me in suspense any longer!"

I tried to keep the smug smile off my face.

"Well you'll probably have heard of him." I paused for effect. "It's Hugo Fletcher. Ring any bells?"

It was clear from her face that the name was certainly ringing bells, but plainly not the bells that I'd been hoping for.

"You don't mean Sir Hugo Fletcher, do you?"

"I most certainly do. Sir Hugo Fletcher, famous philanthropist, property tycoon, multimillionaire, thoroughly gorgeous man." *I couldn't resist the last bit, but it fell on deaf ears. She was on a roll.*

"Well, of course I've heard of him, although I don't care about his millions and neither should you. And certainly his title doesn't impress me. He got that for all his charity work, didn't he? I remember very clearly the number of television and radio programmes dedicated to his 'good works' that we all had to sit through in the months before the Honours List was announced. It was outright self-promotion, paid for by some of those millions, no doubt. If people do things for charity, it should be because they care, not because they want a title!"

See what I mean when I said my bloody, bloody mother? But things were about to get worse, and a full-scale argument ensued. I, of course, went on the defensive.

"You don't even know him, but you've judged him! He has to get publicity for the charity. It's how he raises money. It's not his profile he's promoting."

You should have seen her face, Imo! Her mouth was set in a hard line, and she had that dismissive look—as though everything I was saying was complete rubbish. You know the one, I'm sure.

"Well, it's all irrelevant anyway. Because if memory serves me right, he's married. How could you, after everything this family has been through?"

Well, what could I say? We all know that Dad was a womaniser when he was younger, but this is different. This is not some grubby little affair. Hugo loves me and he's getting a divorce! I explained all this as calmly as I could.

"So tell me, madam. Are you the cause of this divorce, then? Are you going to be named? Is he going to drop you when the time comes and move on to somebody from his own world?"

Does she have no faith in my judgement at all? I tried again.

"Look, he's divorcing Annabel because of irreconcilable differences. His mother died recently, and he wanted to move back into the family home—it's an ancestral seat, so he has to really. His mother was the daughter of an earl, or something, and inherited Ashbury Park in Oxfordshire. It's now in trust so that it can be passed down through the generations, so he has to live there. But Annabel refused. He gave her an ultimatum, but she said she wasn't budging."

"That's not a reason to divorce somebody. You work things out. I'm sorry, but the man sounds like a control freak to me. He didn't get his own way, so he divorces her!"

She made that disgusted phah sound—the one she always used to make when she was less than impressed with Dad's excuses. I'm sure you know the one I mean.

"Mum, how can you make a judgement like that on such little information? That's just one example. They haven't been sleeping together for ages—not since Alexa, their daughter, was born."

"Oh, he's got children, too. Perfect. Have I taught you nothing? He'll tell you that he's not having sex with his wife, because he knows you won't like it if he is. No doubt he hasn't told his wife that he's having sex with you either. It's what they do, child. If they're still in the same house, I'd bet you a pound to a penny that they're still in the same bed."

This was going horribly wrong, and I was near to tears.

"Mum, you really don't understand. Not only has he moved out of the house and back into his family home, but for your information—although it's none of your business—we haven't made love yet, and don't intend to until his divorce is finalised!"

That shut her up. She put her hands together as if in prayer, and lifted them to her lips.

"Laura, my love, are you telling me that Hugo, if I'm allowed to call him that, is happy with this arrangement?"

So I told her that it was his idea. Not mine. He's got his reasons. He's still not divorced, and he doesn't want my name dragging through the mud. On top of that, he thinks that if Annabel gets wind of a relationship she'll try to up the ante on her settlement, so he wants to keep me out of it. I think that shows enormous restraint, personally, but apparently I'm the only one who does.

Obviously Mum thought this all a bit odd. She gave a derisive snort, but then seemed to collect herself and asked, "Are you happy with this?"

Well, actually I'm not. I wasn't about to admit it, though. I am desperate to be with him, Imo. I am aching for us to make love. But I respect his views, and I wasn't about to show my mother the slightest chink in my armour. However, there was no stopping her.

"Have you asked yourself if this is entirely normal? You're not exactly a vestal virgin who has to be protected from the evils of premarital sex, are you?"

Sometimes, my mother even surprises me!

"Look, I know exactly when you had sex for the first time, and who with. I'm your mother. It's my job to know these things. You're not a tart, but you're no saint either, and I know that you have a healthy sexual appetite. The question is, does Hugo?"

That is something that I've never tried to hide. I find it very difficult to keep my hands off him, so of course he knows.

"No, love, you misunderstood me," she said quietly. "I meant, you have a healthy sexual appetite, but does Hugo?"

So that's why we were so subdued at supper. I couldn't tell you all this, I didn't give you the original letter, and now I just feel dejected.

Sorry, Imo—you must have thought I was in a mood. But it had nothing to do with you. Nothing at all.

Lots of love,

Laura

JUNE 1998

Dear Imogen,

How did you feel just before you got married? It's such a time of charged emotions, isn't it? I suspect every bride-to-be feels like I do.

Things are moving, but moving slowly. Hugo is divorced now. He managed to get that through really quickly, and it's been in all the papers. No doubt you've seen it. Nothing about me yet, though—which is just the way he wanted it. He says we'll make an announcement when the time is right. So we have to stay under the radar. We meet for lunch two or three times a week, on the grounds that I'm researching a documentary about his charity (which he still won't actually allow)—but apart from that, we only speak on the phone.

I hardly ever see him in private—maybe we get the odd half hour alone in his office (if he can keep Jessica out of the way). He says that until we announce that we're together, it will probably just look like a sordid little affair if I'm seen coming out of his house in the early hours of the morning.

And he still hasn't met any of you! He hasn't got any family to meet, other than Alexa—and up to now, he's consistently said it's too soon for her. She's only two, though, so I'm not sure why he thinks she would even register anything.

Anyway, back to you, Will, Mum and Dad. I've tried and tried to set up a date, but even though you've said you're happy to come to Oxfordshire, Hugo is adamant that he doesn't have the time. I thought I'd have one more attempt to try to arrange a meeting. I waited until I knew he was having a peaceful evening in Oxfordshire, then at the end of a long and loving conversation, I introduced the subject.

"Hugo, it's really important to me that you meet my family. I want them to love you like I do."

"Darling, you're worrying too much. They'll adore me! I'm sure they're thrilled that you're marrying me."

Hugo clearly has no idea about my parents, and if he expects Mum to be bowled over by his status, he's in for a surprise. But I couldn't persuade him.

"Laura, I work all day and every day. Most evenings are spent at some charity function or other, and at the weekends I have Alexa to stay. I really value any quiet time that I can squeeze in. So I'm afraid it will just have to wait. Speaking of Alexa, though, I think the time is right for you to meet her."

Well, honestly! That made me mad. But only for about two minutes. I do appreciate that Alexa is more important—she's just a child—and I really am looking forward to meeting her.

I was hoping that he would say that I should come to Oxfordshire—because I've still not seen my future home! It's all to do with this 'low-profile' business—which must end soon, surely? I've said that I would be happy to just come for an hour or something—so I can see it! But he says it's a long way to drive there and back. (Ridiculous, of course. It's only an hour or so along the M40. If he's so concerned he could always send a driver.) But then he did say that at the weekend he'd take me to my favourite restaurant in London—for lunch, of course. He's decided that we can begin to be seen together as a couple soon, and then things will be much easier, I'm sure. I wonder if that means that finally we can be a couple in all ways? Somehow, I daren't ask the question. How strange.

Hugo thinks of me all the time, though. He knows that I can't afford the type of clothes I'll need when we start to be seen in public, especially gowns for the charity functions. So nearly every day some little (or big—but always expensive) package arrives for me at work or at home. Sometimes it's flowers, sometimes it's a piece of jewellery, and sometimes it's actually clothes! Can you imagine finding a man that will go out and choose the most divine clothes for you? He says looking after me is one of his pleasures in life. He seems to know the exact size—clothes, shoes, everything. (He hasn't actually bought me underwear yet. I suspect that under the circumstances he doesn't think it appropriate.) What's most interesting about the clothes he chooses is that they are clearly so much more sophisticated than anything I would have picked. I'm beginning to think that perhaps I have looked a little cheap in the past—clothes too tight, too low cut, too revealing. Am I right? The clothes he selects for me are very subtle and elegant. He goes to some couture house where they make them to his specification! He obviously knows what he's doing—so it's best left to him, I think. I've evidently got a lot to learn.

Anyway, back to Alexa. I asked Hugo whether she'd been told that we were planning to get married.

"I want Alexa to meet you first, and then when we know that she likes you, we can tell her that we're going to be married. Annabel won't tell her, because I told her not to."

Was Hugo implying that if Alexa doesn't like me, we won't get married? Was Alexa's permission required? A child of less than three years old? And why would Annabel do anything that her ex-husband asked, or rather told, her to do?

I think I'm just getting edgy. Pre-wedding nerves and all that. Hugo is absolutely the kindest man I've ever met. He's generous, attentive, got impeccable manners. He's completely gorgeous. And he respects me. He always calls when he says he will, and he says that next month he's going to introduce me to the world as his "beautiful future wife."

Now that I'm going to meet Alexa, I thought perhaps I could twist his arm about a visit to Oxfordshire. His reply shouldn't really have been a surprise, but it was.

"I've been thinking about that, darling. I think it would be perfect if you didn't see the house at all until the wedding day. We'll be having the wedding here, of course, but it would be such a thrill for me to introduce you to the house as the new Lady Fletcher."

I had no idea that we were going to be married at the house. We had broadly set a date for September, but he'd told me to leave the arrangements up to him. I didn't know whether he meant the actual wedding ceremony to be at the house (has it got its own chapel?).

"No, of course not. There's a charming church in the village. It's absolutely beautiful. I'll speak to the vicar, of course, because as I've been married before that will be a hurdle that I need to overcome. But anything's possible, particularly if the church needs a new roof or something. I think you'll agree that the reception has to take place here at Ashbury Park, though."

Wonderful as that sounded, I'd never been—and Mum and Dad can't afford anything flash. Hugo chuckled down the phone.

"Don't be silly, darling. Ashbury Park is an extremely large manor house. It will be perfect as a wedding venue, and equally perfect as our home. But you don't have to do a thing, and your parents certainly don't have to worry. I'll get the whole thing organised as soon as we've finalised the date. All you need to do is turn up!"

I didn't know what to say. He's so considerate, but maybe I want to be involved? And I'm sure my parents want to have some input into their only daughter's wedding. How can I suggest that without hurting his feelings?

"You know, Hugo, I really appreciate you doing everything—but it would be a pleasure to be involved in the planning. It's something we could do together, isn't it?"

"Not at all. Nothing for you to worry about, darling. Just show up looking marvellous. It's all going to be my surprise! I won't hear another word about it. I want to do this for you."

I knew that the battle was lost, although I have to concede that I didn't put up much of a fight. He's so determined to make my life as easy as possible, and to give me everything. It's very sweet, and I mustn't get carried away by picking silly arguments.

Anyway, we got back to the subject of Alexa, and it was agreed that I could see her the following weekend. He would bring her to London for the day.

I wanted so much for her to like me. But I never expected to fall in love for the second time in six months.

Hugo, formal as ever (but charmingly so), introduced me to his daughter. "Alexa, I would like you to meet a good friend of mine. This is Laura."

I crouched down in front of the most beautiful little girl I have ever seen. She is absolutely exquisite. She has almost white-blonde hair that falls in soft waves just to *her shoulders, and her eyes are a mesmerising mixture of brown and green. She has the type of fragile slenderness that makes me want to pick her up very, very carefully and hug her little body with the utmost gentleness. She was looking at me a bit warily, so I thought that perhaps I should try to break the ice a little.*

"Hi, Alexa. I've bought you a little present. Do you want to open it, and see what's inside?"

I'd managed to find a pretty rag doll, dressed in palest pink gingham with a floppy hat. It's perfectly soft for a small child, and it's just the sort of doll that she can take to bed with her if she likes it.

I've never seen a child unwrap a present like she did. No tearing wildly at the paper (which is what we always did—and I still do, unless Hugo's around when I try to behave with a little more decorum). She unwrapped the present really carefully and actually folded the paper and laid it on the coffee table in front of her. She's clearly not an impetuous child. But then she looked up and smiled. It was the smile of an angel, and her little face glowed with pleasure.

"Thank you, Laura," she said, without any prompting from her father. Unbelievable!

I was smitten. It was love at first sight, and I know that I will care for this child for the rest of her life, as if she were my own.

With love,

Laura

PS—You've still not met him—so I'm hanging on to this. We'll read them all together when everything's settled down.

10

Tom popped his head round his boss's open office door. They had both attended the postmortem, although the DCS had to leave for a meeting partway through—or so he'd said. Nobody likes postmortems.

"Have you got a moment, James?"

"Come in, Tom. Excellent timing. Let's have an update on progress."

James Sinclair pushed a pile of files to one side to make space on his cluttered desk. This wasn't his only investigation, although without a doubt it had the highest profile. Tom took a seat.

"Not a lot to report yet, I'm afraid. Lady Fletcher came in and identified the body. She filled us in on Hugo's charity work, which was very interesting. By the way, she's insisting we call her Laura, and refer to her husband as Hugo. I hope you can live with that."

"It's not ideal in my opinion, as you know," Sinclair replied. "If we treat them all the same—suspects, victims, and the bereaved—we don't blur the lines. And while she may not have got her own hands dirty, we still can't rule her out completely."

"Point taken. She's very vulnerable at the moment, though, and if we'd refused to break down the formality barrier, I think she would just have shut down even further."

"Hmph. Fine. I'll leave it up to you. Do we know the cause of death yet?"

"We do. It's just been confirmed as liquid nicotine. A huge dose was injected into his groin—actually into his femoral vein. Apparently 'groin injecting,' as it's known, is quite common in drug users. There's an obvious link here, of course. Prostitution plus drug abuse? Not sure where it gets us, though."

"And I bet not many of them use liquid nicotine either," the DCS said. "How much is a lethal dose?"

"As little as sixty milligrams, and our victim was given a much higher dose. It would have worked pretty quickly, I'm told."

"How do you get hold of the stuff?"

"We don't know yet. I've Googled it on the basis that it's probably where most people would start, but I didn't turn up anything useful. I've discovered that you can dissolve it in vodka and give it to somebody to drink, but that's not what happened here. One of the lads is onto it."

Looking slightly bemused at the term *Googled*, the DCS got back onto what was, for him, safer ground. "What else have we got? Anything on the scarves?"

"No, we've probably drawn a blank there. They're from Tie Rack, and they've got branches on every high street, airport—everywhere. They're going to check the computer records, but they sell thousands of them, so it's highly unlikely we'll have any luck."

James took a deep breath and blew out slowly through puckered lips. "Okay—so please tell me we've got something on the woman that the neighbour saw?"

Tom wished he had something more positive to report. He really needed to get a result on this case. "The news is mixed. Forensics have come back on the red hair found at the scene. It is real hair, but they're pretty sure it's from a wig. Apparently hair in a wig is actually woven into a sort of cotton lace cap, which is designed specifically for the wearer—at least if it's an expensive one. There's some evidence that the hair had previously been tied, with a minute trace of the cap attached to it."

Tom paused for breath, before coming to the crunch.

"Which means that all we have to go on is that the woman seen leaving the house is of medium height and slim. Because it was a wig, we can stop looking for somebody with red hair. On the positive side, this was a real-hair wig so we can assume it was expensive and would probably have been made to measure. We can begin to trawl round all the wig makers and see what we can come up with. I don't think there are that many, to be honest."

"What about fingerprints? Did you manage to print Lady Fletcher this morning?"

"We did. Fortunately Beryl had recently cleaned everywhere very thoroughly—what she calls her 'autumn clean' as opposed to her 'spring clean'—so anything we found has to have been within the last ten days. But there's nothing exciting to report. We found Beryl's and Hugo's prints in the bedroom, together with Laura's—although strangely hers were only on the bedroom door and the wardrobe door. Her prints were also in the kitchen and the bathroom. So we need to have a chat with her about that. We did find more in the drawing room, including Laura's, plus some prints from Jessica Armstrong, his PA. But nothing else."

James Sinclair was tapping his pen on the desk in a staccato rhythm. "I know he's been dead for less than twenty-four hours, but we need to be able to show some progress. We've got no clear motive and no real suspects. No sign of anything being taken I suppose?"

"Absolutely not. There were some very saleable things in the house that I'm sure would have gone if burglary was the motive. Lots of small things in silver, not to mention a few very good paintings. We've got a couple of the lads down there at the moment with the cleaner—who seems much more cheerful today apparently—and she can't see anything missing. We'll have to check with Laura, but there's nothing obvious. We're off to talk to the charity staff in a few minutes, then heading back to Oxfordshire. I'll also see the ex-wife today."

Tom had arranged for one of his team to go and interview the bodyguard company, too. He could understand why Hugo wouldn't want them with him when he was at home, but why exactly did he need them at all? He must have thought he was in some sort of danger, but who from?

"What's your take on the bodyguards, James? I can only assume Hugo thought he should have protection because of his charity work. He must have seriously pissed off quite a lot of unsavoury people. We need to find out whether there was anybody in particular who may have had enough of a grudge to either murder him, or get somebody to do it for them. I doubt it was anything to do with his property business, though. He was quite removed from that, and they seem to be very fair and above board in everything they do."

James Sinclair rested his chin on clasped hands and stared off into space for a few moments. "Sorry to state the obvious, Tom, but we know he knew this woman—certainly well enough to invite her into his home. It looks pretty definite that sex in some form or other was on the cards, because there seems to have been no struggle to tie him up. This was no chance encounter. So he *must* have had a mistress, and if he did somebody would surely have known about it. What about family? Who was he closest to?"

Tom suppressed an exasperated groan. He'd been round and round these questions in his head. He needed to find the mistress, but nobody seemed to know anything. He was hoping and praying that somebody at the charity offices would come up with a name, because there weren't that many people to ask.

"Apart from his wife, his daughter, and his ex-wife, all his dealings seem to be with the charity or his business. He doesn't seem to have any close friends. When I spoke to Laura I alluded to the sex angle, but she didn't come up with any names. However, I have to say that she didn't seem shocked either. I certainly get the feeling she suspected something, and I'm onto that. As for family, his father died about forty years ago. His mother died in 1997, just before he met Laura, and he has a sister, Beatrice, but nobody has the remotest idea where she is."

"So how about this for a theory?" James said. "One of these Eastern European girls has been got at by her original pimp. In return for some promise or other, he gets her to offer her services to Hugo. She's a pretty girl, and he can't find it in himself to refuse. She does the deed, according to plan, and then she walks away to reap her reward. Is that a possibility?"

Tom thought for a moment. "The girls he helps are all quite young and the witness specifically said 'woman' in his statement, but we should check that again. Do you think he would take one of these girls back to his home? I'm not saying that he wouldn't give in to temptation, but would he really do it there, given his profile and reputation? We're checking out the girls, though, to see if any have suddenly come into unexpected riches or unaccountably disappeared. Ajay's on the case with that one."

"Okay then. Last question. What do you make of the sister-in-law? We were all very bemused by the greeting she got last night. Is it worth pursuing?"

Tom nodded. "Definitely. There was such venom that—like Becky—I did wonder if she might actually be the mistress. But given her hair colour I'd dismissed her until now. I've already asked Laura what it was about, and I'm not going to let it drop. I understand Imogen Kennedy is still at Ashbury Park, so I'll be questioning her as soon as I can get there."

Tom realised that Imogen's height was about right, and she'd be well worth a second look in a tight black leather skirt. The trouble was, average height was just that—average. Just about every woman they'd met in this case fitted that bill, and now that hair colour was irrelevant they were practically back to square one. But the combination of Laura's impassioned response to Imogen's arrival and her dismissal of the subject this morning gave him reason to believe that there had to be more to this, and he was going to find out what it was.

"I'd better go, James. I've got the staff gathered in the charity office, and once we've spoken to them we're heading back to Oxfordshire. I'll get back for the evening sum-up, and let's hope we've got some progress to report."

❖ ❖ ❖

Fifteen minutes later, Tom and Becky were back in her car, making their way to Egerton Crescent. At least it was a Sunday, so although the roads were quite busy, there were no traffic jams. Even though Becky felt as if they had been working for hours, it was still only late morning. No doubt they'd set off for Oxfordshire at about lunchtime, and she hoped and prayed that Tom would agree to stop and get something to eat. She'd had no time for breakfast, and was starving.

Tom looked across at her. "I was going to suggest that we split up and interview one girl each, but I've changed my mind. I think the best bet is for you to talk to both of them on your own. Make it an informal chat. Somebody else can do a formal interview and get a statement later. They might feel more like sharing gossip with you, and that's what we want. I'll talk to the finance guy, and one of the techies is meeting me there to see if we can access Hugo's computer. What do you think?"

Becky was really pleased by this suggestion. She knew that she was good with people, and women often told her things that they wouldn't talk to a man about.

"Sounds good to me, boss. Anything in particular you want me to focus on, or just general background?"

Becky was not in the least surprised to hear that she needed to probe about any possible mistresses, past or present.

"Do you want me to talk to them together, or separately?"

"What do you think would be best? You know how women work. You're all a bloody mystery to me, if I'm honest," Tom said.

Becky glanced sideways to see if he was joking, but his face was impassive. "It actually depends on their relationship. If they're good pals, they'll egg each other on to say things that they might not say alone. If they're not, they'll be more reserved in each other's company. What I'd like to do is weigh up the situation first. Maybe have a general chat about how things work in the office, who does what, and then make a decision. Is that okay?"

"Sounds good. Here we are, Becky. Let's try to aim to be out of here in an hour."

Becky didn't like Jessica Armstrong. She didn't know why, because she was perfectly pleasant. And as they walked into the offices, she was sure she could smell something rather appetising in the air.

"I know how busy you policemen are," Jessica said, "and I wasn't sure if you would have had time for breakfast. So I brought in a small selection of these rather delicious pastries. I'm happy to organise coffee for you— espresso, cappuccino, or filter. Whichever you prefer. Or tea, of course."

Becky was seriously impressed, and could understand why somebody like Jessica got to be PA to such an important man. As she munched her way through her second pastry whilst she chatted informally to the two girls, Becky voiced her thanks for Jessica's thoughtfulness. The reply seemed more like a mini-lecture.

"The art of being a good PA is in anticipating people's needs and acting before you're told to. Most people think it's about taking orders and executing them efficiently, but they're wrong. You have to second-guess what's going to happen and be prepared. That's why Sir Hugo found me irreplaceable."

Smug as Jessica was, Becky had to admit that this approach had its merits.

After the chat over coffee, she decided to talk to the two girls separately. On the face of it they seemed to get along, but it was pretty clear that Jessica saw Rosie as her inferior and a bit of an airhead. Rosie had worked for Sir Hugo for around five years, but Jessica had been with him for over twelve, so thought herself superior in every way. Funnily enough it was Rosie who had eyes red from crying, whilst Jessica seemed completely unmoved.

Wanting very much to remove the slightly arrogant look from Jessica's face, Becky was sorely tempted to interview Rosie first. But she couldn't let her personal feelings get in the way, and she needed Jessica on her side, so they made their way into a private office and sat down.

"I just want to get a bit of background, Jessica, to try to understand as much as possible about Sir Hugo, his life and his work. I'm sure that you were very close to him after all these years, and I'm hoping that you can give me some insight into the man. Perhaps you could start by telling me what you do here, and how you worked with Sir Hugo."

"I must start by saying that Sir Hugo was a truly exceptional man. He was unique in every way, and it's difficult to imagine life without him. I'm sure you think that my lack of any outward display of emotion signifies an absence of feeling, but that would be a false assumption. It's all about upbringing, Sergeant. I have been brought up not to wear my heart on my sleeve. So you won't see me cry. It's not what we do."

Bloody hell, thought Becky. She was momentarily lost for words. But she needn't have worried, because Jessica was in full flow.

"A personal assistant to somebody as important as Sir Hugo has many roles to fulfil. I liaise with Brian Smedley at the property company on Sir Hugo's behalf, but that doesn't fill my days as the majority of that work is done from head office. My main interest is in helping Sir Hugo with the day-to-day running of the charity. When we receive responses to advertisements for homes for the girls, I undertake the initial inspection. Obviously we ultimately designate somebody who is trained in social work, but I select which of the girls seems most appropriate to the family's needs, and then assign the management of the relationship to one of the qualified team. I ensure they get follow-up visits, confirm that the funding is in place, and so on. I'm also the first port of call if there are any problems with the girls or the families. So my job requires a level of expertise that can only come with years of experience."

Becky swallowed another bite of a delicious almond croissant, wondering if this really was her third pastry. "What sort of problems do you encounter?"

"Oh, some of these girls are so stupid. They get a unique second chance at life, and they just throw it away. Very occasionally we have one who steals from the family, but that's quite rare I'm pleased to say. We've had the odd instance of a girl seducing the husband of the family. That's always very difficult, because the Foundation somehow gets the blame. The wife, of course, prefers to perpetuate the myth that her husband is entirely innocent. And then some go back to the streets because they think they can earn more money. Others just leave a note and go. Who knows where? And then there are those that get picked up on the street by one of the gangs they thought they'd escaped from. It's quite hard to track them down if they're back behind locked doors. So my job's not easy. It's very challenging, actually."

Aware that Tom thought some of these girls might be pertinent to the crime, Becky thought she should pursue this angle.

"Have any of the girls gone missing recently, Jessica?"

"Oh, yes. A silly little girl who should have known better. About two weeks ago."

"And?"

"Sorry? Oh, you mean what happened to her? Ridiculous, given her history. She was living with a very nice family and working as a waitress in a local café. She met some man—he came in every day and flattered her. I'm sure you know how easily some women are seduced by a few kind words. Pathetic, really. Anyway, he had apparently asked her to go and live with him, and she said yes. She thought it was her chance for a normal life, I imagine." Jessica gave a derisive laugh. "She was too embarrassed to tell the family, because she thought they might try to stop her. I'm sure you've guessed the rest. He was a pimp. Once he'd got her, she had nowhere to go. She couldn't go back—or didn't think she could. We tracked her down through some of our street intelligence, and the owner of the café wasn't entirely blameless either. We won't be using *him* again. We've given her another chance, with another family. The first ones weren't happy to take her back. Understandable, really. As far as I'm concerned, this is her last chance, though."

"Any others before that?"

"Not recently, no. I would say it's at least two months since anybody else decided that they were better off on the streets. Some people just don't deserve our help."

Becky kept her thoughts on Jessica's sympathetic attitude to herself, and decided to move on. "How did you find working with Sir Hugo?"

"Marvellous. I couldn't fault him. He was always courteous—even when I could tell he wasn't happy, or when he was in one of his strange moods."

"Wasn't he happy, then? Did you think he was unhappy in his marriage?"

Jessica pursed her lips slightly and looked down at her hands. Becky knew without a doubt that some thinly veiled, but nevertheless derogatory remark was about to be delivered. She'd met women like this before, although generally without the superficial disguise that money and upbringing offers. But a snidey cow was a snidey cow—whether wearing posh clothes or hand-me-downs.

"I must admit that I was quite shocked when I realised that Sir Hugo was going to marry Laura—she was clearly not right for him. He needed somebody with breeding—the right background. Somebody who understood him well. Somebody with class—a kindred spirit. I didn't think that she was an appropriate choice at all.

"However, there was an air of expectation about him from the day he met her until the day he married her. Barely suppressed excitement, I would call it. His eyes literally glittered. Nobody could compete with that, could they?"

"So you think his marriage was a happy one?" Becky asked, thinking that "compete" was an interesting choice of word.

The coy look reappeared. "I couldn't possibly say. But when he returned from honeymoon, the sparkle seemed to have gone, as if something hadn't quite lived up to his expectations."

"Did you ever suspect that Sir Hugo had a mistress, Jessica? Or can you think of anybody that he might have had a relationship with?"

"Sir Hugo was a very *manly* sort of man. He had made two bad choices, in my opinion, in terms of his life partner. I think he needed somebody that would understand him, live in his world, give him all the comforts that he deserved. And I don't think that's what he has had from either of his wives. There were occasions over the years when the strange mood returned—that same mixture of elation and agitation. It was particularly noticeable in the last few weeks, but I have no idea if he was having an affair or not, although if he was I certainly wouldn't blame him."

Was this hero worship, or obsession? Becky wondered. Jessica obviously thought that Hugo should have chosen her, and so if she knew of an affair, wouldn't she say so? Wouldn't she find an opportunity to put the knife into somebody else who was unsuitable? Unless, of course, she was the one who he was having an affair with. That would make sense.

Thanking Jessica for her time, and making a note to ensure that her formal statement included information about her whereabouts at the time of the murder, Becky gave herself a minute or two to think about her next interview. Rosie seemed like a nice girl. A bit scatter-brained, perhaps, but normal. She'd obviously come from a decent background, judging by her accent; certainly better than Becky's own. But then old Hugo would undoubtedly only have employed people who spoke nicely. And at least Rosie wasn't like Jessica—with an accent so far back that she was nearly falling over.

Rosie's eyes were still red when she came through the door, but her heavy blonde fringe nearly covered them. Quite how she could see, Becky couldn't imagine. She'd obviously dressed for a Sunday, rather than an office day, in a pair of expensive-looking—and very tight—jeans, long leather boots, and a vivid green sweater. Suddenly feeling very old in one of her customary black suits and sensible flat black shoes, Becky dragged her mind back to the questioning.

"Okay, Rosie. I just want a chat with you—to try to understand what you do here, how involved you were in Sir Hugo's daily life, etcetera. Can you start by giving me a bit of a rundown on your job, do you think?"

"I'm sure you're going to think it doesn't sound like much of a job, but it does require quite a lot of managing. I book all his travel, arrange his bodyguards when he needs them, check what his charity commitments are, and keep his diaries up to date with everything. I also look after the office management—ordering stationery, answering the phone, that sort of thing. It keeps me very busy, although Jessica thinks I'm a waste of space."

"Don't you get on with Jessica?"

"She's okay. A bit posh for the likes of me, though."

"And how did you like working for Sir Hugo?"

"It was all right, really. He was a bit up himself, but it was great to tell everybody that I worked for a 'sir'—and he was surprisingly good about it when I got carried away in Harvey Nick's and didn't get back on time after my lunch. As long as I made the time up, of course. He was better than Jessica, anyway. She gets so cross if we've run out of paperclips or anything. Anybody would think it's the end of the world!"

"Tell me about his diaries, Rosie. Did he put personal stuff in, or just his appointments?"

"I have to say he was a real pain about his diaries. He wouldn't have a personal organiser. I tried to get him a Blackberry, but he wouldn't have it. He likes things he can touch—or liked, I suppose I should say. So I had his diary on my computer, and then I had to copy it all out—word for bloody word—into his desk diary, which was enormous. A huge leather thing. He had one for every year, with a great big page for each day. There were only ever a few lines on each page—just his appointments. But he kept them for years.

"Anyway, it's my job to make sure the two diaries tally, and then each day I have to produce yet another version—a typed itinerary of his movements for the day, with all the phone numbers, addresses, times and types of appointments. He would only use technology when he had absolutely no choice. Computer? 'Get thee behind me, Satan,' he would say—and he wasn't smiling when he said it! He did have a mobile phone, though, and he never went anywhere without that—but I had to programme in any useful numbers—which mainly amounted to the office, his home, and a limo service to be honest."

"His mobile phone? Where would he have kept that, Rosie? We certainly haven't found one."

"He had a leather document wallet. He kept his itinerary, meeting notes, and phone in it. He wouldn't put the phone in his pocket because it would have spoilt the cut of his suit, and we couldn't have that, could we?"

Becky was aware that Hugo's document wallet had indeed been found, although the itinerary only listed the appointments for the day before his murder. They were being checked, but didn't seem suspicious. There was definitely no phone.

"Do you know anything about Sir Hugo that would suggest that he was having an affair, Rosie?"

"Well, there's one thing that's a little odd and it could mean that. But I don't know. I could be reading too much into it."

"Go on."

"Every now and again he has an odd entry in his desk diary. It just says 'LMF.' Sometimes it's just for one day, sometimes a couple of days, sometimes just an overnight. He won't tell me what the appointments are, but he won't change them. Not for any reason at all. When I ask what LMF stands for he just smiles and says it means 'Leave me free.' But I don't believe that for a minute, because even I know it's not brilliant English. He's more likely to say, 'I'm temporarily unavailable,' or something."

"Could the F stand for Fletcher? Perhaps he goes to see somebody in the family with those initials?"

"Could be—but nobody that I've ever heard of. That means nothing, though. He wouldn't tell me, would he? I thought at first the L might stand for Laura—but I book flights for her, so I know she hasn't got a middle name."

"What about his relationship with Jessica. Was that good?"

"She worships the ground he walks on. But sadly for her, he treats her like his PA. I've never for a minute thought that he fancied her or anything."

Becky thought for a moment. If they were having a relationship, Hugo could just have been a better actor than Jessica. But this LMF sounded promising too.

"Did Jessica not know what these meetings were? She seemed to pride herself on knowing everything about Sir Hugo," Becky said, unable to resist the small dig.

"I've asked her, and she hasn't got a clue either. I always thought it might be another woman, but Jessica says it's none of our business. Perhaps if we'd *made* it our business we'd be able to help you now. Whatever his little quirks, he didn't deserve to die."

Sensing that a new bout of tears was imminent, Becky decided to wrap things up. "Okay, thanks, Rosie. If you do have any other ideas, please do let me know. However trivial you think something is, please tell us. Okay?"

Becky recounted both of the conversations to Tom as they made their way from London to Oxfordshire. For most of the journey, Tom had listened intently—when not complaining about Sunday drivers. She'd told him that she was happy to drive, but he had insisted for some reason.

"You did well," he told her. "It's interesting that the only girl that seems to have gone missing in the last couple of weeks has been found. Perhaps that rules out a theory, but not necessarily. Let's get the interview with Laura over with, and I need to speak to Imogen too, and then I can go and see the ex-wife—who by all accounts is something of a charmless individual."

"I have to tell you, I don't like Jessica. There's something about her that I just don't trust. We shouldn't ignore her in all this. She was all over Hugo like a rash, it would seem. We have to check if she was his mistress."

Tom nodded, but at that moment they swung through the gates of Ashbury Park, and made their way up the drive. They both looked at the grey, gloomy house through the even more gloomy shrubbery. The long approach to the house was bordered with tall trees that disappeared into dense woodland, under planted along the driveway with overgrown rhododendrons which might look pretty in flower, but at this time in October just added to the general dreariness and darkness of the approach. Becky shivered and saw Tom glance at her.

"You know, this house gives me the creeps. It should be really beautiful, but everything is so dark. The trees seem almost threatening, and the windows seem lifeless, as if there's nothing but emptiness behind them. It's got no soul."

Tom was right. This was definitely not a happy house, and Becky couldn't think why Laura had never done anything to make it more of a home.

The girl woke suddenly from a fitful doze. She was afraid of sleeping properly. She was afraid that something would happen to her whilst she slept—something that she couldn't control. Unsure of what had woken her, she opened her eyes in panic. Had he come? Was he here, in the room? Or had he been and gone whilst she slept?

But there was nothing. No sign that anybody had been. There was no more food, no more water, and the bed was undisturbed. She was sure that if he'd been, the bed would have been disturbed.

Then she heard a noise. It was a tapping sound, coming from the window behind her. She tried to turn her head, but realised that her neck was locked. She was desperate to turn. Perhaps somebody was trying to get in. Perhaps somebody had found her. What was wrong with her neck?

Her hands went to her throat, and then she felt it. It was the chain. During her sleep she must have twisted her body, and this was the result. The tapping stopped before she was able to turn her head. She cried out with frustration. Finally she freed herself and managed to turn towards the window. But there was nothing there.

She covered her face with her hands, fighting back the tears. Then she heard it again. Relief flooded through her and she uncovered her eyes.

But it was nothing more than a blue tit, sitting on the ledge and tapping away at the window.

Despair swept through her, and so far was she removed from reality that she failed to grasp the fact that no human hand could have touched a window so high above the ground.

11

Imogen poked her head around the bathroom door, where Laura was still lying in the bath, lost in her own thoughts. She looked at her friend and felt sad when she saw for herself how much weight Laura had lost over the years. She still had a good figure—no doubt many people would say it was an improvement—but personally she thought her previous curvaceous shape was more suited to her vibrant character. Mind you, she thought, perhaps the new body was better matched to the new personality. Would she ever get back to the old Laura?

"Hey, Laura," she said softly. "I really hate to disturb you, honey, but the police are here again. I'm happy to entertain them for a while, particularly the chief inspector, but I know they want to talk to you. How long do you think you'll be?"

Laura seemed relieved to be roused from her thoughts. "I'll be about ten minutes. Can you cope until then, Imo? Is Alexa still asleep?"

"Yes and yes. Don't look so worried, Laura. I know what I can and can't say. Horrible Hannah has gone for a walk and Alexa is fast asleep. Let's hope the poor kid stays that way until the police have gone."

With that, Imogen made her way back downstairs to where the police were waiting in the drawing room.

"Laura will be a few minutes, so can I get anybody a drink?"

"Actually, Mrs. Kennedy, we'd like to take this opportunity to ask you a few questions, if you don't mind?"

Imogen felt a slight tremor in her stomach, and wondered if everybody felt like this when interviewed by the police. She indicated that the policemen should take a seat on the sofa, and sat herself in what she hoped appeared to be a relaxed pose in a wingback chair next to the fireplace, with her feet tucked under her.

"I'll do whatever I can, Chief Inspector, although I'm not sure there's much I can help you with." Tom smiled at her, and she couldn't help thinking again what an attractive man he was. Not her sort, though; she only had one sort, and he was a stroppy, difficult, principled idiot off in the wilds of Kenya.

"We don't know much about you, Mrs. Kennedy. All we know is that you were married to Lady Fletcher's brother and you weren't given a particularly warm welcome when you arrived. Can you explain why that was, please?"

Imogen was relieved that this was such an easy question to answer with honesty. "When Laura's brother and I divorced, it was felt better that I didn't see Laura again."

Now the young woman police officer, whose name if she remembered correctly was Becky, decided to intervene.

"I was chatting a little to Lady Fletcher this morning, and she mentioned in passing that she'd known you since you were both children. Was your divorce so acrimonious that you couldn't stay in touch with your friend?"

Imogen smiled. "I suspect you're too young to have been divorced, aren't you? Well, for the record it is very difficult for anybody—family or friends—to stay in touch with both parties. Unless it's entirely amicable, people feel an obligation to take sides and it's human nature for family to side with family. Somebody is always, rightly or wrongly, perceived as the bad guy, and in this case it was me." Imogen noticed a wry smile on Tom's face, which she thought was both interesting and revealing.

"And what about your relationship with Sir Hugo, Mrs. Kennedy. Did he think it appropriate for you to break off communication with his wife?"

Imogen nearly laughed out loud. "I think he thought it was for the best, yes."

"What did you make of Sir Hugo? Did you like him?"

"I didn't really know him very well. I met him for the first time at their wedding. That was the first time that any of us met him, in fact. I probably saw him another couple of times, and then Will and I separated."

She saw that Tom Douglas was watching her very carefully. He was clearly a smart one, and she thought he would know if she lied to him.

"You didn't answer my question, Mrs. Kennedy. Did you like him?"

In an attempt to disarm him, Imogen beamed at him. "Please call me Imogen. I know Laura has asked you to dispense with the formalities. And with regard to Hugo, I wasn't desperately keen, if I'm honest."

"Can you tell me why not?"

Imogen paused to give this what she thought would be the right level of consideration. "I didn't think he was much fun. He was quite serious, and he seemed to want Laura to himself. She was very popular and full of life, and I felt that potentially he would stifle her."

"And did he?"

"Difficult for me to say, really. As I've said, it wasn't long after that before Will and I split up, so I never came here again."

"Did you really lose touch completely, Mrs. Kennedy? I find it hard to believe that you would rush to the side of somebody you hadn't seen for several years just because you heard their husband had died. We didn't even know it was murder at that point. So why *did* you come exactly?"

Imogen took a deep breath, not missing the formal mode of address that he had used. This wasn't going as well as she'd hoped. "I was at the airport when I heard. I was en route back to Canada, and I was watching the news in the British Airways Executive Lounge at Heathrow airport. It came up as breaking news. Heathrow is pretty close to here, so I raced out and grabbed a cab. Paid the driver extra to get me here as fast as possible. An impulsive decision, but I'd missed Laura so much over the years and I thought I could help her."

"You say you were en route to Canada. From where? Can you please tell me exactly where you were on Saturday morning?"

Imogen kept her tone light. "Yes. I'd been in Cannes at an exhibition. I work for an animation company in Canada and was in France promoting our services. It was an important event for us."

"I've been to Cannes, actually," Tom said. "It's quite a place. I presume the exhibition was at the Palais des Festivals. Which hotel did you stay at?"

Imogen knew he wasn't asking out of idle curiosity. "I stayed at the Majestic. A lot of people go for the Martinique, but it gets a bit noisy for me and I prefer a good night's sleep. The Majestic's an excellent hotel—not quite so overbearingly smart as the Carlton—and it's very close to the Palais. I left Cannes around midmorning on Friday, and drove to Paris. I flew into Heathrow on Saturday afternoon."

Imogen was conscious that she was probably giving far more information than was strictly necessary.

"Where were you on Friday night?" Becky asked.

"I'd hired a car in Cannes, so I meandered up through France and stayed at a little auberge just south of Paris—somewhere between Bourges and Orléans, I think."

"Do you have the name of this auberge?"

"Sorry, it was a spur-of-the-moment thing and completely unplanned."

"No receipt?" Becky asked.

"No. I'm really not sure why you want all these details, but I paid in full on arrival—in cash. I wanted to get rid of my euros. I guess I left the bill in my room."

"Won't you want to claim it on expenses?"

It didn't look as if Becky was about to give up on this one, and Imogen tried hard to disguise her irritation.

"No. It was my choice to have an extra night in France. If you must know, Will and I went to that part of France years ago so I used the opportunity to just drive around and reminisce a bit."

Imogen felt a strong sense of relief as the drawing room door opened. "Ah look, here's Laura. Did you want to ask me anything else?"

Tom smiled at her in a very pleasant way that somehow still managed to make her feel vulnerable. "No, thank you, but that was very helpful. Becky, is there anything else you want to ask?"

"Just one thing. What time did you deliver the car back to the hire company?"

"It was early. I'd gone to bed as soon as I'd arrived at the auberge—a bit tired after the long drive, I think—so I woke up at the crack of dawn. I'd already paid, so I decided to set off and it only took me a couple of hours to drive into Paris. When I got there I just put the documents and the keys through a special letterbox, you know the sort of thing. It was a budget hire company, and they didn't have a desk manned at all hours. I can give you the name of the hire company, if it would help?"

"That would be useful. Thank you."

Imogen let her breath out slowly. Hoping that would be the end of it, she turned gratefully towards Laura, who was looking so much better. She'd managed to get out of those awful middle-aged clothes and found an old pair of jeans and quite a passable dark-blue jumper. They were all slightly on the large size, but she'd obviously only had time to blitz her hair with the dryer so it was fuller round her face, and she hadn't tied it back. Some of the pallor had gone from her cheeks too, and she looked like a different person. Imogen could also see that this fact hadn't gone unnoticed by the detective chief inspector.

"I'm sorry I kept you waiting. But perhaps you can tell me why you were interrogating Imogen?" Laura sounded almost belligerent.

Tom smiled. "It's just routine, Laura. Everybody we meet who is of the right age and background and had some relationship or other with Hugo will have to be questioned."

"Imogen had no relationship at all with Hugo, as she has no doubt told you. They haven't spoken to each other or seen each other for about ten years."

Imogen thought she should calm things down a little. "It's okay, Laura. I was just telling them about the exhibition and my drive through France. I don't mind. And they know I hadn't seen Hugo. Let me go and make everybody a cup of tea while they have a chat with you."

Tom watched as the door closed behind Imogen. Interesting, he thought. She was largely telling the truth, but there were a couple of times when he detected a lie. Her eyes moved in a different direction—always a giveaway. She obviously had been in Cannes, which was easy to check, and she would also know that they could verify her story about the flight from Paris. So why slip in a couple of small and surely inconsequential lies? He was sure that the car hire company would prove a dead end too, but he wanted to unsettle her as much as possible to see what she would give away.

He looked at Laura and could just see a glimmer of the person in the photos all those years ago. For the first time, he noticed her eyes. Yesterday they had been red with crying, and when she came to identify the body she was wearing glasses that were slightly tinted and not at all attractive. Whether by accident or design they had managed to partially obscure what he could see was her best feature. They were a lovely grey colour and quite large. He suspected they were the kind of eyes that changed colour according to what she was wearing, or what mood she was in.

"Laura, I'm sorry that we have to bother you again, but we do need to get down to some formal questioning. Is that okay?"

"Of course," she replied. Tom could sense some lingering hostility, and it wasn't the atmosphere he wanted. He would have to tread carefully.

"If it's not too painful for you, can you please tell me when you last spoke to your husband?"

"Yes. I phoned him on Thursday morning to confirm that I was planning to come back on Saturday and was about to book the flight. He was at the office, and Rosie answered."

"You didn't speak to him again between then and leaving the house in Italy?"

"I did try to call him on Saturday, just to let him know what time I'd be home. I called him here, because Alexa was supposed to be coming for the weekend. But I got no answer, so I left a message."

"And that call was from your house in Italy, was it?"

Laura nodded again. Tom didn't have to tell Becky that she would need to get the phone records, although she'd had dealings with Telecom Italia before, and he was sure she wouldn't be relishing the thought of the return match.

"Will the message still be on your phone, do you know?"

"I certainly haven't deleted it. I haven't been answering the phone myself—Imogen's been filtering calls. But I don't think she would have deleted anything without asking me, so it should still be there."

"Okay," said Tom. "Perhaps we can check that later. We'll want to look at your husband's diary and his computer too, if that's okay."

Laura smiled. "Be my guest, but you'll have a problem with his computer because it's password protected. I tried to use it the other week to book a flight when my laptop was playing up, but it just asked me for the password."

Becky looked up from her notepad. "Didn't you ask your husband for the password?"

Laura's laugh was not one of amusement. "There is no way that Hugo would give me the password to his computer. He was a very private man, and he believed that we are all entitled to our own secrets."

Tom knew that he was pushing it, but somehow Laura had opened a small door, offering an insight into their relationship.

"Did you agree?"

Laura shrugged. "Each to his own, Tom. He had many good points, as I'm sure you know, so it was easy to forgive him the little things. He hardly ever used his computer anyway. I don't think he knew much more than how to turn it on."

Tom looked at her thoughtfully. He was a long way from understanding Sir Hugo and Lady Laura Fletcher's relationship. "We'll get a computer specialist out here, if that's okay. Becky, can you get onto that as soon as we're finished, please."

Turning back to Laura, Tom asked, "Did you ever use the apartment in Egerton Crescent, Laura?"

He was certain he knew the answer to this. The fact that there were no personal items belonging to a woman indicated that she didn't stay there for long periods. But then there were her fingerprints to explain.

"I haven't stayed there for years. I sometimes called in when I was in London, and perhaps I would go up to the drawing room, or to the kitchen. But I haven't stayed overnight for maybe six years."

"Wasn't it handy to stay there when you went up to London, to the theatre or to one of the charity functions?"

"I haven't been to any functions for quite some time. Hugo thought they were probably a bit tedious for me, and with his hectic schedule we didn't get much chance to go to the theatre."

But you used to go to the charity dinners, Tom thought. He'd seen the pictures. So what changed?

"When were you last there?" he asked.

"I called in last week, before I left for Italy. Hugo needed a dinner jacket, and I said I'd bring it myself. I hung it in the wardrobe in the bedroom. If you're checking fingerprints, I don't think I touched anything else in there. But I did use the bathroom. Then I went into the kitchen, made myself a cup of tea, and took it into the drawing room."

That explained all the prints they had found, particularly those in the bedroom which had seemed a bit strange as they were only in one area. There was no point in pursuing this line of questioning, so he moved on.

"What can you tell me about the bodyguards? I know that your husband employed the services of a bodyguard agency, but his use of these men seemed to be a bit sporadic. We've checked with the agency, and he definitely stood them down for the weekend."

"Hugo was expecting to be at home with Alexa this weekend. The house has good security, and he was unlikely to be going out. I've no idea why he ended up in town. To be honest, he's only been using bodyguards for a couple of years, and he tended to use them for a bit of show—to try to demonstrate that his charity put him in danger. I believe he thought it made him seem more important." Laura paused.

Tom didn't miss the slightly derisive tone. He had a vision of Laura faintly mocking Hugo in the past, and given the events of the last couple of days, now regretting it. But perhaps he was simply attributing the scathing tones of his ex-wife to Laura, who had maybe treated her husband's foibles more sympathetically.

Either way, he wasn't ready to drop the subject.

"Surely if he was effectively putting these guys out of business—the pimps, that is—they were going to feel fairly antagonistic towards him? I've always understood that he was considered to be walking a dangerous line."

Laura gave him a rueful smile. "I'm sorry, my scepticism on reflection seems ridiculous. Of course it put him in danger, and it was very brave of him. It's just that it sometimes felt as if we were living in some bad Hollywood movie. He tended to use the bodyguards when he went to well-publicised functions. Those times were perceived to be the most threatening."

At that moment, Imogen kicked the door open without ceremony, and walked in with a tray of tea, coffee, and biscuits. Tom decided that now would be a good time to break the questioning.

"Just before we pour the drinks, do you think we could listen to the phone message, please? It's just routine, but it will help us to confirm the date, time, etcetera."

"Of course. I'll show you where the phone is."

Leaving Imogen to pour tea and coffee for everybody, they walked across the austere hallway and through a door opposite the drawing room.

"This is Hugo's study. This was his private domain, and I rarely came in here. Feel free to look anywhere you like. I think the filing cabinets are locked, and I'm afraid I don't know where the keys are—but you can certainly have a look for them, or break the cabinets open if you want to. Try the computer if you like; perhaps you'll have more luck than I did." She pointed to the phone. "Help yourself."

Tom glanced at the message light, then back up at Laura. "It says four messages. Are you happy for me to listen to them all?"

Laura looked slightly surprised by this information, but not at all concerned and simply nodded. Tom pressed the play button, having first checked that the time on the machine was correct. Unless it had been tampered with, the times of the messages would be accurate.

The first message was from Laura on Saturday, exactly as she had said.

"Hugo darling, it's me. I thought you'd be at home this morning? Alexa's coming, isn't she? Could you tell her that my flight is in the afternoon, but she should still be up when I get home. I'll look forward to seeing you both this evening. I should be back about eightish. Hope everything's okay. I'm leaving for the airport soon, so don't bother to call me back. I managed to get the olives picked so we'll have lots of delicious oil to look forward to. Lots of love."

Tom noted the time was just after midday, and realised that when Laura made this call, Hugo was already dead.

"Olives?" he asked, thinking that the call may have upset Laura and wanting to lighten the mood.

"Yes, we've got about twenty olive trees. It's not many, but I find picking them quite therapeutic. I finished them on Friday afternoon. Oh God, I forgot to arrange to have them picked up this morning for pressing. They'll be ruined if I don't remember!"

Never having picked olives in his life, Tom could nevertheless see that it might be a pleasant pastime, as the sun was no doubt still shining in central Italy. But he couldn't quite see that a few litres of oil mattered much in the overall scheme of things.

There were still three messages remaining, and although he had listened to the one he was most interested in, he decided to play the others. The voice of a young girl came over the speaker.

"Daddy, I'm really upset with you. Why have you cancelled our weekend? I was really looking forward to it, and you'd promised that we could talk about getting me a new pony. *And* you said we could have some of our special time before Laura gets back. Will you phone me as soon as you get this message, please? I'm very cross, and you're going to have to do a lot to make it up to me."

Tom recognised the bargaining power of a daughter let down by her father, but looked to Laura for confirmation.

"Alexa?" he asked.

Laura nodded.

"Did you know that he'd cancelled their weekend?"

Laura shrugged. "I had no idea. As you heard, I was expecting her to be here."

As Tom pressed the button for the next message, he realised that Laura had apparently lost interest, and had turned her back to the room, looking out at the cold and dreary October weather.

"Sir Hugo? It's Peter Gregson. I apologise for calling you at home; I know I'm not supposed to. The thing is, it's Danika. You know, Danika Bojin? She's gone missing. She told me early last week that she was going to try to get hold of you. There was something that she wanted to talk to you about, but she wouldn't tell me what. She said that she should really just talk to you. And then she disappeared. She's been gone for a few days now, and we're quite worried. Can you give me a call, please? Something has obviously upset her."

Mr. Gregson left his number and hung up.

Tom felt a thrill of excitement, and turned towards Laura who still had her back to the room.

"Laura?"

Without turning round, Laura answered quietly, "That will be one of the rescue girls. I'm sorry, I really don't know anything about them. You'll have to check with the office."

Tom made a note of the number. Could this be the missing ex-prostitute they were hypothesising about this morning? The timing was perfect, and as soon as he was finished here, he would get somebody to follow this up.

He pressed the play button for the final message, but was not prepared for the explosion of sound that came from the other end.

"Hugo, you *bastard*. I've received the letter from your lawyers explaining the trick you pulled. You are such a mean *bastard*, and don't think I don't know how to get back at you. You bought my silence once, but the price has just gone up. And if you dare threaten to cut me out of your will again, I'll make sure you're dead before you get past the front gate. And don't think that I wouldn't do it, because I most certainly would. *Bastard*." The phone was slammed down.

In no doubt whatsoever that this was Hugo's ex-wife, Tom looked up at Laura. Still with her back to him, she spoke quietly.

"I'm sorry, but would you excuse me. I don't feel very well."

12

"Shit, shit, *shit!*"

Laura paced around the room, her hands on her head. Imogen just stood by the door, as if on guard.

"I should have *realised*. I should have *known*. Christ—I am so *stupid*."

"Calm down, Laura, and keep your voice down or they'll hear you. This is *not* your fault. You couldn't do anything then, and it's too late to do anything now."

"Don't be stupid, Imo. I didn't do enough, did I? I tried. God knows I tried. But it was like screaming in the wind. The sound is whipped away from you almost before it leaves your lips, and nobody hears no matter how hard you try. I just thought that now…"

"Yes, I know what you thought, but clearly you were wrong. Look, you did what you could."

"And if I don't tell them? What then? What else am I going to have to live with for the rest of my life?"

Laura sat down heavily on the edge of the bed. What a mess.

"What, exactly, do you think you *can* tell them?" Imogen persisted. "You don't *know* anything. Wasn't that what our little adventure was supposed to be about? And in view of what's happened since, I can only assume that you *still* don't know anything—so what precisely are you going to say?"

"I don't know. But my conscience tells me that I must do something."

Imogen went over to the bed and knelt down, grasping Laura's hands. "Look—Hugo's dead. Sorry, but that's a fact. He's *dead*. Nothing you say or do can possibly make any difference. And what about Alexa? I thought you wanted to protect *her*?"

"Of course I do. But I need to think. Logic says that nothing that I say or do now can make any difference. What's done is done. But emotionally I feel an obligation to people other than myself. Oh, Imo. If only you knew it all. I should have told you everything at the start. I'm so very, very sorry."

❖ ❖ ❖

After five minutes, Imogen was glad to see that Laura had calmed down. Thank God she'd been here, she thought. Otherwise the shit really would have hit the fan. She wished with all her heart that Will was here too, although in all honesty she didn't know what he would make of the situation.

A gentle knock came on Laura's bedroom door, where she had dragged Imogen after hearing the unexpected message. Imogen got up to answer it and found Becky standing outside.

"How is she?" Becky asked, clearly quite concerned.

"She's okay now. The last twenty-four hours have been quite difficult. I think it just hits her in waves from time to time."

Becky looked apologetic. "I'm really sorry, but we have to ask her some more questions, and they're quite sensitive ones."

Laura called from behind Imogen, "It's okay, Becky, I'm all right now. Let's just get it done."

Laura appeared at the bedroom door and simply nodded her head towards the top of the stairs.

"I'd like Imogen to be with me, if that's possible," she requested. "I was feeling all right, but I'm a bit wobbly now so the support would be helpful, if that's okay."

"I'm sure that will be fine. Is there anything that I can get you before we start again?"

Laura paused as if something had suddenly occurred to her. "I don't need anything, thank you Becky, but I do need to make sure that Alexa is okay. Imogen, before you join us, do you think you could track Hannah down please? She must be back from her walk by now, and I think she should persuade Alexa to have a bath or a shower after that sleep, and then perhaps she can go and watch a DVD in the sitting room. Tell her I'll be with her as soon as I can. I really need to spend some more time with her."

She turned towards Becky. "Are you likely to want to talk to Alexa? I forgot to mention that she turned up here earlier."

"I don't think so at the moment. But it would be useful to know if her dad called her back on Saturday, and if he did, whether he told her he was meeting anybody or why he cancelled the weekend. Perhaps I could go with Mrs. Kennedy, and you could go and talk to Tom in the drawing room?"

Imogen didn't really like the thought of them being separated. She had no idea what Laura might say. She needed to sort Alexa and Hannah out as quickly as possible.

❖ ❖ ❖

Tom looked up as Laura came back in, and he was pleased to see she was looking a little less pale.

"Thank you for letting us listen to all the messages, Laura. I'm sorry if the call with your husband's former wife upset you, though. She did sound more than a little angry. I'll be following it up with her as soon as we've finished here. For the record, do you think that the previous Lady Fletcher could have been involved in any way in your husband's death?"

"I really don't know the answer to that. She was certainly very demanding, and tended to use Alexa as a bargaining tool, but whether she would kill him or not, I honestly can't say."

Tom got the strong feeling that she was evading the question in some way, but he let it lie.

"When we were in the study, we found your husband's desk diary. We know that he also had one in his office. Do you know how these were updated?"

"He used to bring his desk diary home once a week from the office, and update the one here. Rosie wanted him to have an electronic solution, but he liked leather desk diaries—the bigger the better. There had to be one here so that I would know where he was. That wouldn't have worked if he'd kept everything on a Blackberry."

"We have his office diary. Do you mind if we take this one too, so that we can correlate them both?"

Laura nodded her agreement.

"One other housekeeping task—we understand he had a mobile phone, but nobody can find it. Do you have any idea where it might be?"

"He always had it with him. Perhaps he lost it." Laura shrugged.

Tom privately wondered why, if Hugo always had his mobile phone with him, Laura had chosen to call him on the landline and leave a message. But Imogen and Becky chose that moment to rejoin them. Tom was a little disappointed. He thought that Laura might be more open in a one-to-one situation, but even if he sent Becky off on some task, he felt sure that Imogen wasn't going anywhere.

"Tom, Alexa says her father didn't call her back on Saturday, so she can't help."

Tom nodded, then gave the slightest inclination of his head. This was Becky's cue to pick up the questioning.

"The next part of this conversation may be difficult for you, Laura. Tom's told you that we believe the murderer was a woman, and that his death might have been sexually motivated. What we didn't tell you is that your husband was found in a pose that suggested a sexual act was either about to take place or had already taken place. We need to know if you believe your husband was having an affair, even if you don't know who with?"

Tom had been watching Laura as Becky spoke. Although they had asked about other women before, never had it been made so clear that Hugo was actually caught with his trousers down. Or off, in his case. But Laura didn't seem to feel anything. Even if the fact of his infidelity didn't have the power to hurt her, he would have expected there to be some anger at the humiliation of it all.

"I'm sorry. I honestly don't know if Hugo was having an affair."

"I can imagine how you're feeling," Becky said. "But if you even had the slightest suspicion, it would be really helpful to us."

Laura looked as if she was gritting her teeth to prepare herself for what she had to say next.

"I'm sure you're both aware that I spent a considerable amount of time over the last few years in a care home. Hugo managed to keep it quiet from pretty much everybody until somebody grabbed a lucky photo, but on one occasion I was there for nearly two years. Perhaps during that time, Hugo found himself another woman. Who could blame him?"

Becky's face was a picture of barely suppressed indignation that Laura should find this understandable. "Can I ask you whether you noticed any change in his behaviour towards you? Most women believe that they know when their husbands are having affairs."

On the other hand, Tom thought ruefully, most men don't have the first sodding clue.

Before Laura could answer, Imogen jumped in.

"I'm sorry, but that's a really stupid question. She was mostly drugged up to the eyeballs, and could barely comprehend who she was talking to—so how she would have recognised any change in bloody Hugo, I just don't know."

Tom looked thoughtfully at Imogen. "And how, exactly, do you know she was drugged up to the eyeballs, Mrs. Kennedy, if you never saw her?"

Unexpectedly, the answer came from the doorway.

"She knows because I told her."

A tall, well-built woman in her mid-sixties stood just inside the drawing room, wearing a smart pair of black trousers and a short camel-coloured coat.

Tom watched with interest as Imogen jumped off her chair and went to give the newcomer a hug. Guessing that this was Laura's mother, he noted that contrary to his conversation with Imogen earlier, clearly not all members of the family had been forced to take sides in the matter of the divorce.

Laura merely looked up at her mother from where she sat, and gave her a watery smile. "Thanks for coming, Mum, but you really didn't need to."

Laura's mother moved to stand by her daughter's chair, gave her shoulder a gentle squeeze, and dropped a light kiss on her head. "Laura, love, of course I needed to come. I'm just glad that I hadn't already left to stay with Will. How are you coping?"

Tom intercepted a glance between Imogen and Laura's mother. Imogen just shook her head, and Laura didn't respond. He stood up and held out his hand.

"Detective Chief Inspector Tom Douglas, and my colleague is Detective Sergeant Becky Robinson. I'm leading the investigation into your son-in-law's murder. I'm sorry that we have to meet in such difficult circumstances."

Pulling off a leather glove, she grasped his hand firmly.

"I'm Stella Kennedy. I'm sorry for appearing unannounced, but Alexa saw me arrive from the window and let me in. Poor kid, she's in a bit of a state."

Laura spoke again. "We really weren't expecting you so soon, Mum. It's only about three hours since you spoke to Imo. How did you get here so quickly?"

Stella looked quite pleased with herself. "I might be collecting my pension now, but your brother's insisted on dragging me kicking and screaming into the twenty-first century by buying me a mobile phone. When I called earlier I was speaking from the train."

"Then you must be ready for a cup of tea," Imogen said. "Take the weight off your feet, and I'll go and sort it out."

Tom was beginning to wonder whether he was going to be able to get this interview back on track without being rude, when Stella saved him the trouble.

"Actually, I'm ready for something to eat too. There was no buffet on the train—something to do with it being a Sunday. If it's okay with Laura I'll go and make myself a sandwich. I've been sitting down for hours, and it's probably best if you stay here while the police finish with their questions. I'll make up a batch in case anybody else gets hungry. Do you mind if I go and help myself, Laura?"

Tom looked keenly at Laura as she responded to her mother. He could have done without this interruption, and it all seemed to be getting a bit much for Laura. And he'd lost his thread.

As Stella left the room, Tom glanced at Becky and he could see that she immediately understood him.

"I'll go and help; make myself useful," she offered.

Tom focused back on the two women in front of him. Imogen had now taken a seat beside Laura, and they seemed to be drawing strength from each other as they almost imperceptibly touched hands briefly.

"I think we've established that you weren't aware if your husband was, in fact, having an affair. I would like you to think about it, though, and let us know if you come up with any names of women he *could* have been seeing, should he have been of that frame of mind."

He paused for a moment, considering his next words and how to phrase them.

"Just briefly getting back to the diaries, Laura. We haven't had a chance to correlate them in detail yet, but when Becky was talking to Rosie this morning, she told us that Hugo had a few dates with the letters LMF pencilled in. We can't find any record of these initials in the home version of this diary. Can you shed any light on this?"

Laura spoke with what sounded like mild exasperation. "Tom, I really didn't study my husband's diary too much—only if I wanted to get hold of him. I had to check the diary to see if it was possible to interrupt him or not."

"What do you mean, 'interrupt him'?"

"If he was at an event and staying away overnight, he preferred it if I didn't contact him. Too much of a distraction, he said."

"What, not even at three in the morning, if you'd wanted to speak to him?"

Laura gave a small smile that didn't in any way signify amusement. "If I had phoned my husband at any time after midnight he would not have been amused."

"So do you have any idea at all what the initials LMF could stand for?" Tom asked again.

Laura looked him straight in the eye. "I'm sorry, but I don't have the first clue."

Tom felt certain that she was telling the truth. He was equally sure that these initials were not new to her.

Becky was having rather more luck at getting information out of Stella Kennedy in the kitchen, although interesting as it was, only time would tell if it was useful.

"Mrs. Kennedy, I know this must be a very difficult time for you, but it really helps us if we can get some decent background on a murder victim, so anything you can tell us about Hugo would be extremely valuable."

"Do call me Stella. I'm not much for standing on ceremony. To tell you the truth, though, it's really not such a difficult time for me, although I can see it is for Laura." Stella paused and wrinkled her nose in a look of slight distaste. "I may as well be up front about this because it won't take you long to work it out for yourself. I didn't like Hugo. From the moment I met him at their wedding, I didn't think he was right for her."

Stella pulled a loaf of bread towards her and started to slice it.

"Did Laura realise that you didn't like him?"

"Unfortunately I made the serious mistake of telling her what I thought, and I probably damaged my relationship with her irreparably. I could see from early on that something wasn't right, but my probing simply made her clam up. I tried again after they'd been married for a couple of years. She'd changed so much, it was breaking my heart. I thought I could use my own experiences as a way in, by talking about my marriage to her father."

Stella's head was down, focusing on the bread, but Becky could hear from her tone of voice that she was very sad about all of this.

"Laura knew about her father's infidelities," Stella continued. "It was no great secret. But she didn't realise that I'd lost all respect for him. I thought telling her about my own unhappiness would make it easier for her to tell me about hers, but that was a mistake too. Children deserve to think that their parents have been happy, I suppose. I created a barrier which I've never managed to completely break down."

Stella shook her head sadly. "He's dead now, of course, Laura's father. He died a few years after she got married. I'm glad he's not here now. Whatever else David was, he was a loving father, and seeing Laura as she has been over the past four or five years would have killed him if his heart hadn't already given out."

Keen to get Stella off the track of self-recrimination and reflection, Becky referred back to an earlier remark.

"You say you didn't meet Hugo until the day of the wedding. Wasn't that a bit unusual?"

Stella laughed without any sign of amusement. She shook her head as she started to butter the vast pile of bread that she had cut. "Oh, we tried. We offered to come to London; invited him to stay with us in Manchester; said we'd be happy to travel to Oxford, meet halfway—anything he wanted really. But we just got excuse after excuse. Laura was clearly besotted, but I thought the whole thing was a bit odd. Did you know that she hadn't even seen this place before they got married? Hugo planned the whole wedding 'as a surprise' for her. She looked gorgeous, mind you. Like a princess, as far as I was concerned. He was a lucky man—but I have a strong suspicion he thought she was the lucky one. I think he believed himself to be a bit of a catch. Arrogant, pompous man that he was."

Bloody hell, thought Becky. She really *didn't* like Hugo.

As she prepared cups, milk, sugar, and all the paraphernalia required for tea and coffee, Becky let Stella ramble on about the wedding, her thoughts about Laura's new home, and a litany of things that she disliked about Hugo. But none of it really told her anything about Laura's relationship with her husband.

"You say that she'd changed—but do you think that, in her own way, she was happy with Hugo?"

"Honestly? No. Not at all, although she just wouldn't admit it. Laura doesn't accept defeat gracefully. She never has. If there is something that she wants to succeed at, she will try and try until she gets there. When she was happy, she was so bubbly. She was still like a young girl in many ways; enthusiasm oozed out of every pore."

Stella turned to Becky as she spoke, the smile of a proud and loving mum illuminating her face. It was difficult to relate this image of Laura to the person sitting in the drawing room. Stella's smile faded as she continued.

"Even before they were married I could see that she was trying to curb her natural excesses though. I'd not met Hugo at this point, so I didn't know whether it was all down to pre-wedding nerves, or it could have been something to do with work. The moment I clapped eyes on him as he stood waiting at the altar I was sure he was responsible. But what could I do? Stand up in church when they say the bit about 'If anybody knows of any impediment...' or whatever it is, and say I didn't like the look of him?"

Stella was now slicing cheese with real aggression, as if it was some part of Hugo's anatomy that she was attacking with the sharp knife. She was in full flow, so Becky let her continue. The tea was stewed, but she would quietly throw it away and make another pot.

"I didn't think much of his speech either. Rattled on about his marvellous mother, and said Alexa was the love of his life. We all feel that about our kids, but on your wedding day...I ask you! He barely mentioned Laura. Anyway, they went off on honeymoon, and I know she was really pleased with the destination he'd chosen. When they got back, I decided to come and see how she was getting on. Let's face it, marriage isn't all about romance, and sometimes it takes a while to realise this. She'd sounded a bit down, so I thought she might just need some support, as she no longer had her work colleagues."

Stella looked up from the cheese and waved the knife in the air to punctuate her thoughts.

"That was the other thing—he'd made her give up work. It was unbecoming of such an important man for his wife to work, I expect. I was frankly quite shocked when I saw her. She'd lost weight—not a lot, but she's my daughter so I could see she was thinner. But her smile seemed forced, and she had dark circles under her eyes. I asked her what was wrong. Of course, she said there was nothing. They'd had a fantastic holiday, and now it was just back to life as normal. Then she said something that I thought was a bit strange."

Stella put the knife down and leant back against the worktop with her arms folded.

"I asked if she had any photographs. She said, 'Yes, of course. I'll get them—I think I left them in my bedroom.' Now realistically the use of the word 'my' as opposed to 'our' could just have been a slip of the tongue, but clearly it wasn't, because she became a bit flustered after she said it. I asked if I could have a tour of the house, because we'd only seen the downstairs at the wedding. Not very subtle, but I'm afraid I'm not known for my finesse. Anyway, she refused. She made some excuse about not wanting me to see it until she'd had a chance to get the decorators in, and I've never been upstairs since that day."

Becky looked puzzled. "What do you do when you come and stay, then?"

"To be honest, I've not been much. But on the rare occasions when I forced myself on them, I've been put up in the guest cottage outside. Hugo apparently thought it would be better for me to have some privacy. But I was effectively locked out of the house until Hugo decided it was time to let me in again each morning. I sensed something wasn't right, though, so I asked her outright. 'Are you happy with Hugo?' I said, 'Because I could see at the wedding that he's not an easy character.' 'What do you mean, Mum?' was her very angry retort. 'He's a wonderful man, and I'm really sorry if he doesn't meet with your approval. Perhaps you'd better not take advantage of his hospitality if that's how you feel about him.' Talk about defensive. I've never seen her like that. So I let the subject drop."

Keen as she was to explore Stella's opinion of Hugo more fully, Becky thought she should move on. "Stella, I know this is hard for you, but can you give me any background about Laura and how she came to be sent twice into a care home?"

"I'll tell you what happened, all right! Hugo had her committed—or 'sectioned' as I think it's called these days." Stella's eyes were blazing with anger. When Stella had said she didn't like Hugo much, it was undoubtedly the understatement of the century.

"The first time was for acute depression, and she stayed there for two whole years. Then Hugo claimed that she was displaying delusional behaviour or something, and was a danger to herself. He always managed to get people to back up his claims. The second time it was one of your very own chief constables, would you believe. I'm sure Hugo tried to get them to throw away the key, but that time she was out in just over a year."

Swallowing her surprise at the mention of such a senior police officer, Becky asked the obvious question. "You say he *always* managed to get people to back him up. Who was it the first time?"

"A bit less impressive than the chief constable, but equally relevant—it was that awful nanny of Alexa's. Hannah, she's called. And Laura says she was smiling smugly as they took her away. Perhaps she thought with Laura out of the way, she'd be in with a chance herself."

13

"Okay, Laura. You can relax now. The dashing DCI has gone, the sergeant's being talked to death by your mother in the kitchen, and I'm going for a walk. I desperately need some fresh air. Care to join me?"

Laura glanced up at Imogen and shook her head. "Thanks, but I'm happy to have a quiet half hour, if that's okay. Have you read all the stuff I gave you?"

Imogen gave Laura a rueful smile. "Yes, love. I have. I do want to read some more—but only when you're ready to let me. I know I said I want to understand everything and fill in the gaps, but I am aware that you're baring your soul. That must be hard."

"It is. I can't pretend that I want to do this, but I realise I owe it to you. Go for your walk, and I'll have a think about it."

Laura was relieved to have some time alone. Much as she was beginning to like Tom Douglas for the sensitive way in which he was treating her, she was glad to see the back of him. He had left Becky behind "to look after you" as he put it, but she was still ensconced in the kitchen with Stella. Laura had no idea what they were talking about, but there must have been something significant, because she had called Tom out of the drawing room for a brief conversation shortly before he left.

One of Tom's team had finally managed to track down Annabel and insisted that she either went home immediately, or she went to the police station. In either case, she had been told, DCI Douglas would be there within the hour to interview her. Annabel had chosen the former option, and Tom had kindly offered to take a still distressed Alexa back to her mother. Whilst Laura had no time at all for Annabel and even less time for her parenting skills, she knew she was far too distracted to give Alexa the love and reassurance she needed at the moment.

They had bid each other a very tearful good-bye, with lots of hugs and kisses, and Laura had promised Alexa that she'd phone her every day and make arrangements with her mother so they could meet up soon. Even though she was only Alexa's stepmother, she knew that Annabel would have no difficulty in handing the child over to her. Anything to free up time for the endless shopping, beauty treatments, and other pastimes that she constantly indulged in. If Annabel's concerns about Hugo's proposed changes to his will were justified, she may find some of her activities severely curtailed in the future.

Not that Laura cared in the slightest what he had done with his riches. She had far greater things to worry about than Hugo's will, and through careful investment she now had money of her own. Although amounting to nothing like the huge wealth that Hugo could boast, it was certainly enough to buy a decent house. She hadn't particularly hidden how her money had accumulated, but Hugo considered it so insignificant that when she mentioned it he made some scathing comment about pin money.

For now, though, she needed to sort out some practicalities. Everybody needed somewhere to sleep. Last night Imogen had ended up catnapping on the sofa, whilst Laura had spent the night in an armchair—mostly just staring into space. She decided to call Mrs. Bennett, her housekeeper, and get her to come in to make up the cottage for her mother as usual. It was always aired because Hannah used it when Alexa came to stay. Although Alexa obviously slept in the house, Hugo hadn't wanted even the loyal Hannah in the upstairs rooms.

She also knew that Imogen would not for a single moment consider sleeping in the cottage. It held the worst possible memories for her, so she could have a room in the house. And of course, Hugo wasn't here to object.

The police had already been through Hugo's room with a fine-toothed comb, apparently looking for any clues about his 'other woman,' but had turned up nothing. It clearly hadn't passed Tom Douglas by that Laura didn't share his room. She had given a rather feeble explanation about her moving out since she'd been ill.

"Hugo became used to sleeping on his own, and of course my sleep was often disturbed—so this seemed like the best arrangement." Tom had merely nodded, but his eyes had shown compassion and a glimmer of understanding that she would rather not have seen.

With a sigh, she leaned back in the chair. A few moments' peace were just what she needed.

She couldn't stop her thoughts drifting back to the days before her marriage, though, when she should have realised things were not going to be as she had expected. She'd read the next letter enough times to know that any fool could see how gullible she'd been, and Laura didn't know if she could bear to see Imogen's expression when she realised it too.

There was only one thing to do. She would have to give Imogen *all* the letters now. She didn't want to know how many she'd read—she didn't want to be trying to gauge her reaction. When shame is your own, it's hard enough to bear. When other people are witness to it, it becomes intolerable.

14

Dear Imogen,

It's ages since I've written to you. It's a bit of a joke, really, because I write you these long letters, then I never send them. I want to tell you everything. But not yet.

I've been really busy over the past few months because I've suddenly realised how much I have to learn! Once we "went public," Hugo took me shopping a few times. That was quite an experience, I can tell you, and confirmed my fears about my lack of taste. I felt that the women in the shops were smirking at me when I chose something completely inappropriate (although why it's in their shop if it's not right is quite beyond me).

Hugo was really kind, though. He let me pick colours and styles that I liked, and then talked to the women who would rush off into the depths of their stock room to come back with something similar, but perhaps a little more tasteful. Of course, this was just in the ready-to-wear shops. Going to the couture houses was something different again!

Now I have a fabulous wardrobe. So it was worth a bit of embarrassment. I'm a quick learner, and I won't make the same mistakes twice.

Going out in public with Hugo was another revelation. He knows so many really important and famous people—everybody from actors to politicians. He's even on first-name terms with the Prime Minister! Meeting these high flyers at some of the posh charity dinners is both exciting and nerve-racking. There's so much protocol involved. I had no idea what to call a minor member of the royal family when I was placed next to him at dinner. Hugo had to help me out on more than one occasion. We've developed a kind of private language. If I make some blunder—like put my napkin on my knee before the waiter had a chance to do it for me—Hugo will purse his lips and give a minute shake of the head. As soon as I see this, I watch the other women to see what they do. I actually thought he was going to turn apoplectic when I (rather discreetly, I thought) sat on my hanky. I had nowhere else to put it! I didn't have any pockets, or sleeves to push it up. And the red pepper soup was making my nose run. Funny thing is, after all these dinners that I've been to, I've never seen a single person blow their nose! How does that work? Anyway, it's all been very revealing, and I've been studying etiquette books and all sorts of things so that Hugo doesn't feel ashamed of me.

But there is one thing bothering me. Sex—or lack thereof. It was the beginning of July before we finally went public, and pretty much straight after that Hugo had to go off on some fundraising trip. So while he was away, I booked myself lots of special treatments. Whole-body exfoliations, lots of painful waxing, lovely pedicures—everything to get my body in perfect condition for him. I bought some gorgeous new underwear too. Nothing too tarty. I didn't think he'd like that based on other things he's chosen for me, but subtly sexy.

I couldn't wait for him to get back—but of course, I should have realised that he'd be a bit tired for a couple of days from the travelling. When we went out to dinner a few nights later I suggested that I went back to Egerton Crescent with him for the night. Hugo had different ideas.

"Laura, darling—there's nothing I would like more. You know how much I desire you. But we've only just announced to the press that we're together. If you're seen leaving the apartment so soon, don't you think it might make you look a little cheap?"

I hadn't thought of that, but I was still prepared to argue my case.

"Hugo, everybody has sex nowadays. Nobody would think anything about it at all!"

Then he made his pronouncement.

"There is much more to this relationship than sex, Laura. At least, I hope so. I'm very concerned that the focus on sexual activity will detract from the building of a solid relationship. We know we're compatible. We may not have actually had sex, but in our own way, we've made love."

What way was that, Hugo? Not any way that I know of.

I didn't say that, of course. I didn't want an argument. But he went on.

"We kiss—passionately. We hold each other and touch each other. It's marvellous. We are getting married in two months. I feel that we should continue the way we are at the moment. Learning about each other. Understanding each other. Building

the intensity of our desire. Just imagine how much stronger that will make us as a couple."

I don't know what to think. I wanted to ask you, but I was ashamed. Not of the fact that we don't have sex, but the fact that I don't know what's right and what's wrong. I want him so much. He made it sound so exciting, though—like one long seduction. And when we finally are together—well, it doesn't bear thinking about! He continued to try to convince me, but I was weakening.

"People never used to have sex before marriage, you know. And I've heard it said that the most successful marriages are those when both parties come together as virgins."

I hesitated to point out that this clearly wasn't the case for either of us! And I've no idea where he read that statistic. He's quite capable of making it up to suit his own purposes. But there is also something admirable about a man who clearly wants me but is prepared to restrain himself to show me some respect. Isn't there?

And now there are only two weeks to go to our wedding day, and my future husband's body is still a mystery to me! As, for that matter, is the format of the wedding. Another of Hugo's surprises. There are going to be a lot of guests—I do know that. All sorts of well-known faces, people from his charities, local dignitaries—that sort of thing. He's got no family, now that his mother's dead. I feel a bit sorry for him, really. It seems he was very close to his mother, although she was bedridden for years. He won't let me see pictures of her because he says he still can't bear to be reminded.

And I think he hated his father. I don't understand it, but perhaps he can't forgive him for killing himself. I can't remember if I told you about that? But it must have been very hard on Hugo. It's a pity his sister ran away, because everybody needs family, don't they? I don't know what I'd do without mine. Anyway, all he's got now is Alexa. And me, of course.

As he has no family, he suggested that we keep my very large and extended family to a minimum. He said it would seem odd to have lots of people on my side and none on his. I can understand that (although Mum isn't too chuffed, as I'm sure she's told you). I've invited Simon and his latest girlfriend from work, but that's it. We decided that as I couldn't invite everybody from the office, it wouldn't be right to pick and choose—so just the boss. And some of the venture capitalists. They're always useful, apparently.

Speaking of work, I'm giving up. I'm not sure how I feel about that. My job does involve me in some long hours, particularly when the filming schedule overruns—

almost inevitable, in my experience. So given Hugo's position and everything, we would never see each other if I continued in the same job. And I could never guarantee getting to the important dinners that he has to attend. I'll have plenty to do looking after the house, I expect. And I'm hoping that I can volunteer to help with the charity. We've talked about it, but Hugo thinks it's probably best for me to settle into my new life first, and then we can decide. He's always so considerate. The thing is, I don't need to work. Money isn't an issue, of course. And I want to spend as much time with Alexa as I can. I need to get to know her. And who knows, by this time next year if we're very lucky there could be another little one to look after!

I'm going to keep my shares in the company, though. Simon has hinted that it might be sold to one of the bigger outfits soon. I should make quite a packet if that's the case.

I'm getting excited and nervous and edgy. Not just about 'the big day,' but am I up to being the wife of such a prominent figure? I've learned a lot, but is it enough?

My wedding dress is gorgeous. Hugo took me to this incredible woman who makes the most glorious gowns. I told him he wasn't supposed to see it until the day, but he thought that was a load of rubbish. I think he wanted to make sure I didn't choose anything too revealing. He says that there are certain parts of my body that he thinks should be saved for his private delectation.

I can't wait.

Love and kisses,

Laura

15

Dear Imogen,

Today is the day after my wedding. And nothing is the way I expected it to be.

For a start, I didn't think I'd have time to write this before the honeymoon was over. And it's not even begun! Perhaps writing everything down will make sense of it all.

I know the morning of my wedding dawned overcast, but at least it wasn't raining, and I was more excited than I have ever been in my life; almost shaking with nerves, and desperate to see my new home. And desperate to see Hugo. I love him so much.

Do you remember when the bridal cars pulled up on the main road outside the hotel? All the staff lined up to see me leave on my dad's arm. Wasn't that lovely? I'm sorry that I couldn't ask you to be a bridesmaid, though. I did want to, but Hugo thought that adult bridesmaids—and married ones at that—were a little odd. He said you'd understand. I hope he was right.

The church was absolutely gorgeous, wasn't it? And the flowers were amazing. It had all been put together by Hugo's "team" as he called them, so it would be a complete surprise for me. I'd been so worried that he'd put lilies in the church. I hate lilies. The smell makes me feel sick. I didn't dare tell him, though, in case they'd already been chosen. But thankfully everywhere was decorated with ivory-coloured roses, and dark glossy aspidistra leaves. Hugo looked sensational, didn't he? That black tailcoat and a grey silk waistcoat—he looked like the dashing hero in a romantic film.

I was proud of my composure. Did you notice that I didn't stumble on my words? I didn't cry (although tears threatened on more than one occasion). Even my mum didn't cry, although my dad looked pretty close when he saw me in my dress.

And then it was off to Ashbury Park. I don't know what you thought when you saw the house, Imo. But I was every bit as excited about seeing my new home as I was about the wedding itself. As the car turned through the gates, I still couldn't see the house. It was almost as if it was hiding from me. I had imagined that it would be a bit like Le Manoir aux Quat'Saisons—Raymond Blanc's famous restaurant. But I was wrong, wasn't I. The narrow drive seems to have completely surrendered itself to the overgrown shrubs and trees that line its sides. It almost felt like night time as we approached. I expected the drive to end in a burst of light, but as we rounded the bend and saw the house I am horrified to say that I felt a shiver of dismay. The huge trees were swaying in the wind, their long branches scratching at the first-floor windows, and the dense shrubbery opened to the smallest of forecourts, totally overshadowed by the canopy above. I'm sure the house is a fine example of medieval architecture, with its grey stone walls and crenellated roof. But the paintwork is all black, and my eyes were drawn to the mullioned windows which seemed empty and lifeless.

This house—the very house that I am sitting in writing this—has a severity that is almost palpably hostile. Did you feel that, too?

I didn't know what to say. Hugo turned to me with a proprietary air.

"Your new home, Laura. Isn't it magnificent?"

I was speechless. Fortunately, Hugo took that as a positive, and muttered something about understanding that I would be overawed. I've never in my life thought that I would have a wild desire to buy a chain saw, but cutting back some of that forest surely had to be a priority. The house is truly enormous—you've seen it! It's on a scale that I never dreamt of, and the combination of its size and its grim austerity left me feeling shaken and unnerved. But ever the optimist, I smiled at my handsome husband. I like saying that, in spite of everything that's happened since.

My optimism was short lived, though. The inside of the house seemed even more disturbing than the outside. It's true that the wide hallway has a handsome sweeping staircase which rises rather majestically from the right-hand side. It should look spectacular. The stone floor is really beautiful (if a bit grubby looking) as is the huge sage-green Aubusson rug that practically covers the whole area. But the entire place feels so dark and neglected. Like something out of a horror film, really. Those drab walls—all a rather dirty beige colour—and the oppressive ancestral portraits! But worst of all were the stags' heads and glass cases containing stuffed animals. And that revolting-looking stoat! Did you see that?

I just stood still and gazed around. Hugo was watching me, an unfathomable expression on his face. I glanced at him nervously. I somehow knew that, against all odds, he was expecting me to go into raptures. And then I did something unforgivable. I think it must have been the tension of the day. I laughed.

I recovered quickly, but then promptly made things worse.

"I'm sorry, Hugo. Obviously it's an incredible building, and there's huge potential. I'm sure your mum loved it like this—and we can have such fun making it into a home that's more us, can't we? It's going to be brilliant."

Oh God! I was just digging deeper and deeper. I could feel him stiffen.

"We'll talk about your views regarding my home later, Laura," he said, rather coldly. "For now, we need to meet our guests. I hope the rest of the house and the arrangements I've made prove rather more acceptable to you than the grand hall clearly does."

I felt chastised. Hugo had never spoken to me in that tone of voice before. But then decided I was being ridiculous. He has such impeccable taste, he couldn't possibly think that the hall was looking its best.

"Darling, I'm sure everything that you've organised will be absolutely perfect. And I can't wait to explore the house and make plans. It'll be great fun, you'll see." I thought if I repeated the "fun" bit, it would generate some enthusiasm. It didn't.

Then I noticed my parents in the doorway. They'd still not been properly introduced to Hugo, so I turned to them and tried desperately to make up some of the lost ground.

"Mum, Dad, come in. We're just talking about this fabulous house. Isn't it going to be a great family home? I'm just so lucky!"

I could see from my mum's face that her thoughts were pretty much the same as mine. I carried on relentlessly, ignoring the look of shock on her face.

"We need to find some time for you to chat with Hugo and get to know him properly. Perhaps between dinner and the dancing later? What do you think, Hugo?"

Hugo wasn't about to show his best side to my parents, and he came across as a bit pompous, I'm sorry to say. Not an auspicious start to their relationship.

"Certainly I'd be happy to spend some time with your parents, Laura. After the wedding breakfast, as you suggest. There will be no dancing, though. It's less than a year since my mother died in this house, and a dance would be inappropriate under the circumstances."

I was a bit disappointed by this because I love dancing, and was sure I'd mentioned it when we'd talked about the wedding plans. But I suppose it did make sense. Clearly a year of mourning is considered mandatory.

Anyway, breakfast was absolutely exquisite, and the Long Gallery looked so beautiful with all the flowers that I completely forgot about the hideousness of the hallway. All I could think was that Hugo had done this for me.

The day ended all too quickly, with everybody politely taking their leave at the end of dinner. I had hoped that you would stay on a bit, but I think Hugo made it pretty clear that this wasn't what was expected. You and Will were the last to leave, and when you disappeared to find your bag, Will gave me one of his wonderful bear hugs.

He hasn't had much time to get to know Hugo, so he made a suggestion.

"We'll get together soon, shall we? Perhaps when you get back from honeymoon?"

"I'm sure we'll work something out. We'll let you know."

I know Hugo's response sounded a bit dismissive—like the end of a job interview— but I'm sure he didn't mean it to seem like that. Anyway, that's when you crept up behind me and whispered that you think he's gorgeous (I'm so pleased that you do)—then telling me to "get down and dirty."

I couldn't stop myself from giggling. I'm glad I finally managed to pluck up the courage to tell you about our vow of chastity yesterday morning. A strange thing to divulge just as you were tweaking my veil into place, I know, and I think I painted it in a more positive light than it felt to me—but still, I was glad I'd told you.

As you both left, I grabbed Hugo's arm, and told him how happy I was, and how he'd made everything so amazing. But he turned cold on me.

"I wasn't particularly impressed with the whispering with Imogen. It's impolite. I'm not sure she's a good influence on you, Laura. And I thought your display of affection with your brother was a little excessive."

Before I was able to respond, I heard a quiet cough behind us. It was Alexa's nanny, Hannah. I can't warm to her. She looks sly—like a female Uriah Heep. And she looks at Hugo as if he's God Almighty.

"I'll go to my room now, Sir Hugo. Alexa's bathed and ready for bed. She's in the kitchen."

Much as I love Alexa, I wasn't expecting this. I thought Hannah had taken her home ages ago. Hugo explained, and he did have the grace to apologise for not mentioning it. Apparently Annabel—his ex-wife (and already getting up my nose)— said Alexa couldn't come to the wedding if it was just for the day. She wasn't organising her life around Hugo, etc., etc., so Alexa had to stay the night. Our honeymoon had to be delayed by a day. But that didn't matter. I thought it was probably a good thing, because if we'd left at the end of the reception, I'd have had to get changed, then we'd have to travel—and we'd probably be a bit tired for our first night. That's what I thought anyway.

"Not to worry," I said. "She'll soon be asleep. I'm dying to see our room. Shall we take her up and then I'll get out of this dress while you put her to bed?" I was trying to be provocative. It didn't seem to have a lot of impact, though.

Hugo looked at me. "I'll go and get Alexa, and then I'll show you upstairs. I won't be a moment."

When he came back carrying Alexa, he didn't speak to me again—probably concerned about waking his little girl—and he started to walk up the elegant staircase. I picked up the long skirt of my wedding dress and followed him, trying not to shudder as I passed some of the hideous stuffed animals.

When we reached the top of the stairs, Hugo stopped.

"Wait here a minute, Laura. I'm just going to put Alexa to bed."

He disappeared through some large double doors. I looked around as I waited. Dark and gloomy portraits covered the walls. To me, everything about this part of the house speaks of death. I did wonder what the downstairs would look like when all the wedding finery was stripped away, but I didn't have much time to think, because Hugo was back in moments.

"This way," was all he said. I reached out and grabbed his hand and held on to it tightly as he walked farther down the corridor. He gently removed his hand, but lightly held my elbow.

At the third door, he stopped.

"This is your room, Laura. I hope you like it."

I looked into the room. I could see that it had been newly decorated with lavender-sprigged wallpaper, a pale apple-green carpet, and some pretty, soft furnishings, including a cream-coloured chaise longue—something I've always wanted. Through an open door I could just glimpse what appeared to be a modern tiled bathroom. But all this was meaningless, as the impact of Hugo's words hit me. I felt a hard ball of something in my chest, as if I was going to choke.

"What do you mean, Hugo? Don't you mean our room?" although it was clear to me that this was not, and never had been, a man's room.

"I prefer it if we have separate rooms, Laura. I find the idea of sleeping throughout the night with another person rather distasteful, and certainly I don't believe that sharing a bathroom is conducive to a happy and active married relationship."

For the first time that day, my optimism failed me. The ball in my chest grew and grew. It was pressing against my ribs, up through my throat, and tears were stinging the back of my eyes. I had to respond, and for once, I let him know exactly what I thought.

"Well, for your information, Sir Hugo, I personally think that sharing a bed is a very important part of a close and intimate relationship. I will happily give you your privacy in the bathroom, but I do want us to share a bed."

"We will share a bed for part of some nights, of course. You will have noticed that this is the third door along the corridor. Between our rooms is a bedroom that we can share when appropriate."

"And who, exactly, decides when it is appropriate? What happens if I want to make love in the morning? Do I have to come and knock on your door and ask you if you will move to the 'sex room,' as that's what it appears to be?"

"Don't be childish, Laura. It's been a busy and tiring day for both of us, and I have decided that tonight is not an appropriate occasion. Anyway, we have Alexa to think of."

"And where, exactly, does Alexa sleep?"

"She won't disturb you. I will take care of her if she has a bad night after all the excitement. This of all nights, she needs to feel secure. I suggest that you get some sleep. Tomorrow we leave on our honeymoon. And then we will be alone."

And then he left. Just like that. Not even a good-night kiss.

He was clearly angry with me about something—but I've no idea what. Perhaps because I was a bit disparaging about the house? Perhaps because you and I were whispering? I really don't know. But whatever it was, I felt completely bereft. It's not a word that I would commonly use, but now I know exactly what it means.

I think I was stunned. Too stunned to do anything at all. I didn't know whether to storm down to his room and demand that he join me in my bed, or to pack up and walk out of the house. But I did nothing.

I'd waited so long, and so patiently, for this night. But actually the incredible disappointment of a failed wedding night paled into insignificance when compared to the long-term implication of Hugo's words. Not to sleep together? Not to share a bed, night after night, listening to the sounds of each other in sleep, and feeling the warmth emanating from each other's bodies. Not to be able to turn over and reach for my husband, when I can't sleep, or if I've had a bad dream, or if I've just got stomach pains and need a warm and comforting hand to soothe the ache away.

I hadn't realised that tears were streaming down my face until I saw the telltale water marks on my beautiful wedding dress. I looked in the full-length mirror and saw a sight that should never be seen. A beautiful bride looking totally and completely desolate.

Slowly, I unfastened my wedding dress and hung it carefully in the wardrobe. Ripping it to shreds might vent my frustration now, but I knew I would ultimately regret it.

I decided I would get ready for bed, and perhaps Hugo would realise how cruel he'd been and come to me later. But the luxurious oils and lotions that I'd bought with such anticipation sat unopened in my bag. I knew that their delicious perfume would just intensify the sadness. I crawled under my bedclothes, dragged my knees up as high as they would go, and rolled myself into the tightest ball, trying to hold the pain inside. And I waited.

And so I woke up this morning alone. I had slept a bit—I think exhaustion kicked in. But the ball of sadness was still lying heavily in my chest.

I knew that my next move would be crucial. I so want this marriage to work. I had to think what would be the most likely approach to succeed. My natural inclination would be to argue the toss. Tell him what I want. Make him consider my point of view.

Maybe that's a bit of a joke. Why is it that it's taken a crisis to make me see what's been staring me in the face for months? Has Hugo ever considered my point of view? Has it ever occurred to him for a single moment that he could be wrong?

Everything he does, he appears to do for me. But is that just so he can remain in control? Or is he the generous, thoughtful person he has always appeared to be, constantly trying to make my life easier? He comes with me to buy clothes—he says he knows the best places, and he is footing the bill. He always chooses meals in restaurants, because he says he knows what each particular restaurant does best. He even organised the wedding—as his special gift to me.

Now, I really don't know. What is he? Control freak (as, if I remember correctly, my mother once suggested) or kind, considerate, thoughtful man? My mind was spinning in circles, and I sat on the edge of the bed with my head in my hands. I couldn't help a despairing outburst.

"Oh, God. What a bloody awful mess."

A small sound alerted me to the fact that I was no longer alone.

"Are you all right, Laura? Who are you talking to?"

When I moved my hands, I looked straight into the lovely, concerned face of Alexa. Dressed entirely in various shades of her favourite pink, the choice of clothes—no doubt her own—made me blink a little. But nothing could detract from the beauty of this child.

"Daddy sent me to find you. He says it's time you were up. Are you all right?" she repeated.

Struggling to prevent tears spilling from my eyes, I nodded.

"Would you like a cuddle? Daddy says a cuddle always helps, and he loves my cuddles."

I held out my arms and hugged Alexa's little body, wishing with all my heart that Hugo had offered me a cuddle. Just that would have been something.

"Thank you, Alexa. I needed that," I said, gently releasing her. "Tell Daddy I'm going to have a shower, and I'll be about half an hour. Can you remember that?"

Alexa gave me a slightly scornful look, as if messages of any complexity would be easy for her. Then she leant towards me and gave me a kiss on the cheek.

"I'm glad you're here, Laura. I like you." She smiled and skipped happily from the room.

Now Alexa was adding to the confusion. I made myself to get up from the bed, and went and stood under the hottest shower I could stand. I had to rationalise this situation. Hugo and I are very, very different. We were brought up with different values, and perhaps sleeping in separate rooms is the norm for people in his world.

I mustn't continue to think that my husband has made every decision with only himself in mind. I have to recognise his generosity and thoughtfulness for what it undoubtedly is.

I've overreacted. Yes, it's true that things are not the way I had envisaged. So now I have to change that. I have to make him realise that he can't sleep without me. But he won't be bludgeoned into it. The only way with Hugo is to appear compliant. Arguing will not help. I have to find different ways of making him realise what he's missing.

So here I am now at the end of the first day of my marriage, in theory having a rest before our journey this evening. I still don't know where we're going. Another of Hugo's surprises, but he says I'll love it. And I believe him.

After that dreadful start, with me feeling like the end of the world was nigh, I'm now feeling much more positive. I met the housekeeper—a pleasant lady called Mrs. Bennett who insists on calling me "your Ladyship" in spite of me telling her to call me Laura. Hugo says I can choose for myself what staff I need, as long as they don't live in. He doesn't like that (although we're not short of a room or two, that's for certain). Anyway, I've already told him that I want to cook for him, so we don't need a chef. I'll soften him up, just give me time!

There was only one slightly tricky moment. I think I need to get used to sometimes feeling like a bit of an outsider with Hugo and Alexa. They've had each other since the day Alexa was born, so it's not surprising that it might seem as though I'm intruding—I suspect that's a normal stepparent thing. Anyway, when I eventually came downstairs this morning—all signs of tears gone, I'm pleased to say—I found them in the morning room. Alexa was giggling, and the low notes of Hugo's voice obviously meant he was saying something to make her laugh. I put on the brightest smile I could muster.

"Daddy's telling me a silly story," Alexa shouted. "Go on, Daddy, finish the story." I am constantly amazed at this child's ability to speak in clear sentences; but then Annabel does pay for her to have conversation lessons several times a week. Probably an easier option than talking to her herself, I imagine.

But Hugo refused to finish the story, and I felt I had interrupted a special moment.

"Not now, Alexa. I'm sure Laura's not interested in my silly story."

"Of course I am, Hugo. I'd love to hear it." I turned to him with a smile. He mustn't know how much he hurt me last night.

"No more stories. Alexa, finish your breakfast now, please."

For a moment, my resolve flagged, but Hugo surprised me by rising from his seat and with a smile and a slight flourish, he pulled out a chair for me at the table. Relief flooded through me. Everything is going to be fine. I love my husband, and I'm sure he loves me. We just need to get used to each other.

So we're off in a couple of hours. And I'm getting excited again. I'm just "resting" in my pretty bedroom. And it is pretty. He clearly put a huge amount of thought into it. I wanted to see the other room that he told me about—that I rather unpleasantly called the "sex room." But he didn't have the key with him, so that will have to wait. Perhaps by the end of the honeymoon, though, it will be completely unnecessary, because we'll have sorted all that nonsense out.

Much love,

Laura

16

Tom Douglas was grateful for some thinking time on his journey to visit Hugo's ex-wife. He tried to make conversation with Alexa, but the child was too devastated and Hannah was uncommunicative, so he left them in peace. He did need to talk to Hannah, given what Stella had told Becky, but not with Alexa in the car.

Becky's observations of Laura were interesting, though. "Seemed more concerned about her bloody olives than whether or not her husband was having an affair!" had been her acerbic comment. "You're being very gentle with her, but it's like getting blood out of a stone. There's something not right in all this. I don't know what it is, but there's definitely something."

Tom was sure that Becky didn't understand his modus operandi, but in this type of situation he always found it better to develop a rapport with those he was interviewing. People generally revealed far more than they meant to at this stage of an investigation when there was no apparent conflict. He'd come down a bit harder on Imogen because he could sense her unease, but he knew that her alibi would check out. She was far too clever to lie about anything that could be verified.

The charity girls were a different matter, though. Although he didn't necessarily subscribe to the theory that all policemen have a "nose"—his was definitely twitching every time these girls were mentioned. He was sincerely hoping to have some news on the missing girl, Danika Bojin, by the end of the day.

Finally Tom's driver, who had been seconded from the local force for the purpose of running him around all day, pulled up outside an attractive small Georgian manor house that was home to Annabel Fletcher, her daughter, and nanny—plus, from what he understood, a regular and ever-changing number of young and increasingly unsuitable men. Painted a pale cream with white window surrounds, the property stood in well-maintained open grounds. The drive ended in a large circle, where a small fountain provided a focal point in the centre of a grass roundabout in front of the house. It was considerably smaller but infinitely more beautiful than Ashbury Park in Tom's opinion.

He opened the door to let a subdued Alexa and Hannah out of the car. He felt deep sympathy for the child. He was still struggling with the loss of his older brother just over a year ago, and whilst Jack was single-handedly responsible for Tom's current luxurious lifestyle, he would happily live in a bedsit if it brought his brother back.

He hadn't known what to expect from the former Lady Fletcher, but it certainly wasn't the person facing him in the open doorway. He knew she must be close to fifty, and he'd expected her to be fairly well preserved, but the woman that greeted him appeared even to his untutored eye to be all that is bad about plastic surgery. She was painfully thin but with large breasts that didn't quite match the rest of her body. She was wearing skin-tight pink jeans, matching high-heeled pink sandals, and a skimpy black vest top. Tom couldn't help thinking that to be dressed in clothes like this in late October, it must be very warm inside the house.

Annabel's face was fully made up, including what appeared to be false eyelashes, and she was sporting a pair of overlarge sunglasses on top of her head. A style that had always amused Tom, he thought it even more ludicrous on an overcast autumn day in Oxfordshire—particularly indoors. She smiled in greeting, placing her head coquettishly on one side, but he realised that the smile wasn't extending to any part of her face other than her mouth. Perhaps this was just her nature, he thought, or more than likely it was Botox.

"Lady Fletcher? Detective Chief Inspector Tom Douglas. I'm sorry to disturb you today, but I do need to speak to you. I don't know how close you were to your ex-husband, but I would like to extend my sympathy to you on your loss."

"Chief Inspector, it's a pleasure to meet you. Please do come in, and rest assured that Hugo is no loss to me, nor in my opinion to the rest of the world."

Tom maintained a blank expression, but now he was strangely looking forward to interviewing Annabel Fletcher.

She led him towards the back of the house and into a room that was almost entirely glass.

"What a beautiful conservatory," Tom said, looking around him at the lush plants.

"Actually, Chief Inspector, it's an orangery. The word *conservatory* always conjures up one of those revolting white plastic things that stick on the back of small houses like oversized carbuncles, don't you think?"

"My apologies, Lady Fletcher." It was fairly apparent that the former Lady Fletcher had absolutely no class herself, but was keen to give the impression of having the right background and the appropriate mannerisms to go with it. She sat down on a wicker sofa, and he took the chair facing her.

"As you know, we are now certain that your ex-husband was murdered. We suspect that the murder was committed by a woman, but that's all we know. I'm trying to understand everything possible about Sir Hugo and his life to see if we can identify somebody who may have wanted to kill him."

"Well, I for one would have happily killed him, but I didn't. He was a pompous, self-opinionated, depraved little man, Chief Inspector."

Tom could accept an ex-wife referring to her husband as pompous and self-opinionated, but depraved seemed a little strong. She took a cigarette out of a packet from a table at her side and lit it with an elegant silver lighter.

"You say that you would have happily killed him. I'm sorry to have to ask, but it's a standard question. Could you tell me where you were on Saturday between the hours of about eleven a.m. and twelve thirty p.m., please?"

She blew a long stream of smoke upwards and attempted a smile—as far as her paralysed muscles would allow. "I knew you'd ask that. I was here, of course. And before you ask the next inevitable question, I was on my own. Hannah had taken Alexa to the club for a swim. We still haven't got our own indoor pool; Hugo was far too mean to have one installed."

"So let's be clear about this. You were here all morning, and you neither saw nor spoke to anybody?"

"Correct. But I can assure you, Chief Inspector, that I have wanted to kill Hugo many times, and if I were going to do it I would have done it long ago. I'm not sorry he's dead, but I wouldn't have dirtied my own hands on the job."

She flicked the ash off the end of her cigarette and turned a defiant face towards Tom.

In all honesty, Tom couldn't somehow bring himself to believe that Hugo would have lain naked on the bed, tied up, with this woman in the room. She so obviously hated him, it didn't seem credible that he could have contemplated having any sexual relationship with her. Still, stranger things have happened.

"Lady Fletcher, when we were at Ashbury Park, we listened to a few voice mails, including one from you. You seemed to suggest that Sir Hugo had pulled some clever stunt on you, and that he was planning on changing his will. Can you explain that to me, please?"

"Oh, Christ. If I'd know the bastard was going to get himself killed, I clearly wouldn't have left that message. Fortunately, I don't think he had time to change his will—or so my lawyer told me this morning. He said any changes, codicils, or whatever would have to be typed up, and then probably sent round to Hugo for signing and witnessing. So hopefully some clever person did us all a favour and got rid of him before he could do any more damage."

She took a deep drag of her cigarette, her sucked-in cheeks giving her an even more gaunt appearance.

"He'd already pulled a fast one on me, you see. When Hugo and I divorced, I got this house, and I asked Hugo to buy me a place in Portugal too. It was just the sort of place he hated, but I wanted a nice villa with a pool and preferred to be around other English people—of the right sort of course—so although I hate the game, I chose a villa on a very exclusive development that has two golf courses."

Tom couldn't help wishing that she would put the cigarette out or at least open a window. The fumes seemed to be drawn to him as if he were harbouring an invisible smoke magnet. But fortunately she chose that moment to stand up and walk towards the door to the kitchen, although clearly she hadn't finished.

"God knows why Laura wanted the place they've got in Italy. I've seen some photos that Alexa brought back with her, and it's in the middle of nowhere, surrounded by bloody *Italians*." She paused for breath. "Look, before we go on, can I offer you something to drink? I'm having a vodka and tonic, if I can interest you in the same?"

"No, thank you, Lady Fletcher. By all means, you get your drink. But I have a few more questions to ask you, and then I have to go back into London."

Tom watched as Annabel tottered off on her high heels into the main part of the house to fix her drink. He couldn't quite work out why Hugo had actually married her. Perhaps she was a great beauty in her time, but she clearly didn't come from the sort of family that you would expect. Laura herself wasn't from a wealthy or titled background, but you nevertheless got the impression that she had class, and that she knew how to behave. Annabel, on the other hand, was something else entirely.

It didn't take her long to mix what looked like a very long drink. Tom suspected that the ratio of vodka to tonic was not quite the norm, but that was none of his business. Anyway, it might loosen her tongue.

"Perhaps we could get back to what Sir Hugo had done to upset you?"

"Yes, of course. I was talking about the house in Portugal, wasn't I? Well, when we divorced, the agreement was that I got this house, and the one in Portugal, and a million a year until Alexa is eighteen. Hugo pays any school fees for her directly, and he pays Hannah himself. Dreadful girl, dreary as hell, but I don't get any say in the matter. When Alexa leaves home my money drops to three-quarters of a million until I die—index linked, of course, as I'm quite a young woman."

Tom knew that she was nowhere near as young as she was pretending to be, but as the house they were sitting in had to be worth at least three million and it sounded like the one in Portugal was worth a bob or two as well, she was certainly a wealthy—if middle-aged—woman.

"It may surprise you that a million doesn't go very far when there are standards to keep up, so not actually having much in the way of capital, I decided that I wanted to raise some money against the house in Portugal. Its purchase had been organised through Hugo's property company, because they had better negotiating power. What I hadn't realised is that the Portuguese property is only mine to use. Due to some very clever wording in the divorce settlement, and equally due to a particularly brainless lawyer that I apparently employed, Hugo actually agreed to 'provide a holiday home in a location of my choice up to the value of two million pounds' or words to that effect. That was ten years ago, of course, so it's worth a lot more than that now. That doesn't actually mean that I personally own the house. It was only when I tried to raise some cash that I discovered what he had done. I told you he was a bastard."

She took a large swig of her drink. Tom still couldn't see what this had to do with the will, and said so.

"Well, because that's not all of it. Obviously when I realised this problem I changed lawyers immediately, and got them to look into the whole thing. It appears that his will is written in such a way that I might not continue to get the same level of maintenance if Hugo were to die. I had understood he'd set it all up in a trust so I would be protected, but I was wrong. Like so many things I believed about that appalling man."

With unnecessary force, she stubbed out her half-smoked second cigarette in a large glass ashtray, overflowing with ash and lipstick-smeared filters.

Tom smothered a cough. He didn't understand the ins and outs of trust funds, but noted down the details so they could be checked for accuracy, although he did think it would be possible to sell this house and live very comfortably off the proceeds without ongoing maintenance. Her ladyship would undoubtedly have an entirely different view of what was "living comfortably," and he couldn't help but muse about what would happen to her face if the Botox treatments were discontinued.

"So when did your ex-husband threaten to cut you out of his will?"

"My new lawyer had been trying to sort all this out for me, but progress was slow. I'm afraid I phoned Hugo last week and resorted to a few personal threats. He hung up on me. Two days later I got a message from his lawyer via mine that in view of my lack of appreciation of his generosity, he would be reviewing the contents of his will, and considering his options in relation to the trust fund. That's when I left the message that you heard."

As Tom knew from personal experience, wills could be tricky things. However, it did appear that Annabel Fletcher—discontented as she was— would be better off with Hugo alive than with him dead. Even if he changed his will he was only in his fifties, so she should have had many years of a very generous child support payment with plenty of time to get him to change his mind—and his will—to her benefit. He consulted his notebook.

"Can you tell me, Lady Fletcher, why you said, 'You bought my silence once, but the price has just gone up,' in your message to Sir Hugo?"

For the first time, Annabel looked uncomfortable. "Oh, that was something and nothing. Just something between Hugo and me. I'd rather leave it at that, if you don't mind."

"Well, I'm sorry, but I'm not prepared to leave it at that. I need to understand what you meant."

Annabel sighed. This was evidently a story she didn't relish telling. "We met when I was working for Hugo's mother, and there were certain aspects of Hugo's personality, certain…quirks, if you like, that I discovered quite by chance. Things that Hugo would definitely not have wanted to become general knowledge. My initial price was a bit of a personal makeover; a few little bits of enhancing surgery, nothing much. But then I decided that I liked the idea of becoming Lady Fletcher, and I asked him to marry me. He really had no choice, you see."

There was a conceit about her that was grating on Tom. Why would you want to marry somebody who had no choice but to comply? And what the hell had Hugo done that had put him in such an invidious position?

"Of course, *living* with Hugo was a different thing altogether. Unbearable, actually. When we divorced, I was sure he wouldn't want Laura to know all the gruesome details that I had promised to keep to myself, so my price was this house. And before you say anything, it wasn't blackmail. I just told him what I would like to happen, and he complied. When I phoned him last week, I knew it would be a bit late to threaten him with Laura. She undoubtedly knows all his grubby little secrets by now, so I was subtly threatening him with exposure to the sleazy press—something to damage his whiter-than-white reputation, if you get my drift."

"Are you saying that he *wasn't* whiter than white?"

Annabel threw her head back and laughed, although without any signs of genuine amusement. "Good God, no! I mean, yes, I *am* saying that, but no, he *wasn't* whiter than white. Not even pale grey! He was a very strange man, Chief Inspector. He had peculiar appetites that I'd rather not go into. I blame that witch of a mother of his."

"If your ex-husband was so strange, why were you comfortable with letting your daughter spend so much time with him?"

Annabel bristled with indignation. "Alexa's his daughter, too, and he pays for her, so I've not got much choice. Anyway, Hannah always goes with her. Mind you, Hugo pays for her too, and she's like a lovesick cow, so I'm not sure whether that's a help or a hindrance."

This was said with an air of indifference that Tom found very difficult to swallow, having a daughter of his own. Still, maybe Hugo's "peculiar appetites" were pertinent, given the nature of his death.

"I'm afraid I need you to be a bit more specific about your ex-husband and his sexual proclivities, even if it's uncomfortable for you. I'm not being voyeuristic here. Given that your husband was almost certainly murdered by a woman, and the mode of this death suggests some sexual activity, I'm afraid you're going to have to tell me everything you know."

Annabel Fletcher leaned back in her chair, took a long drink from her glass, lit yet another cigarette, and responded with a grimace of distaste. "Look—I'll tell you. I suppose I haven't got much choice in the matter. But it's not a pleasant story, so are you sure you won't have that drink?"

Tom had declined the drink, but as he made his way back to the centre of London for the daily debriefing, he seriously wondered if that had been a mistake, particularly as he had a driver so Becky could keep her car in Oxfordshire. He wasn't shocked by what he had heard—he'd been a policeman for far too long and thought he had seen all the depths that humans could sink to. But he was nevertheless surprised.

He couldn't decide how much of what he had been told was exaggeration or make-believe conjured up by a thwarted wife. Perhaps it would be sensible to only share this information with the DCS for now. He also needed to ask James to investigate which chief constable had been involved in the sectioning of Laura Fletcher, and what exactly his role had been. Becky had done well to elicit that piece of information from Stella Kennedy.

He stared out at the dark, wet, autumn evening, not really seeing anything but simply mulling over the events of the day and trying to piece together a puzzle that appeared to be growing in complexity and depth almost by the hour.

The girl pushed herself up from her bed and made her way wearily to the window for her nightly vigil. Despite her fear, she needed him to come, and to come soon. If only she could open a window and perhaps attract the attention of a passerby. Not that anybody ever seemed to pass by. Still, at least it would have given her some hope. Perhaps some man would walk his dog down these lonely lanes, unafraid of what the night might be hiding.

But the windows were made of toughened glass, and were screwed shut. He'd made sure she knew that. And the steel mesh on the inside meant that she couldn't reach the glass, even if she had something to break it with.

She looked at the old, soiled mattress on the floor and the plastic table sitting next to it. She knew that neither could provide a tool for breaking out, and the other furniture in the room was way beyond her reach. As soon as he'd unlocked the door to this room and pushed her inside, she was afraid. Whatever she'd done to anger him, this was her punishment. But what frightened her most was that the room was here at all—prepared, as if waiting for her.

She stared down at the chain around her ankle and followed its path to where it was firmly screwed into a strong oak ceiling beam above. She would never be able to reach it, even if she had the means to unscrew it. And she needed to sleep carefully. She mustn't get entangled in it again.

Whilst she scoured the countryside in search of any sign of an approaching vehicle she reflected that, if she were an animal—perhaps a rabbit or a fox—she would gnaw off her own foot to free herself from her trap. But she could never do that. At least, she didn't think so.

And anyway, she was sure that he would come. When he thought she'd suffered enough.

17

Tom arrived back at the office just in time to catch the end of an evening briefing delivered by two officers from Operation Maxim, the Met's human trafficking team. He was handed a piece of paper that identified the two as Inspector Cheryl Langley and DC Clive Horner. As a double act, they made Tom smile: she was a short, chubby woman with a huge smile, and he was tall and lanky with a long, lugubrious face. Cheryl was just summing up with their views of Sir Hugo.

"He did a great job, under very difficult circumstances. Human trafficking is a significant problem, as I'm sure you all know. Once the girls get here, they find they have no means of escape. They're told that the only way is to buy themselves out—but with the gangs taking about eighty percent of their earnings, it's impossible, because they are demanding upwards of twenty thousand pounds for each girl—sometimes as much as forty thousand."

It only took a second for Tom to work out that even at the lower "purchase price" the Allium Foundation must have paid a minimum of two million pounds just to buy the girls out of their miserable lives as unwilling prostitutes. And then, of course, there were all the other costs involved in running the charity.

Cheryl nodded to her colleague, who took over; his slightly high-pitched voice was at odds with his appearance.

"Sir Hugo did much more than simply buy the girls out and find homes for them. The charity had a number of well-staffed centres and even some safe houses. Those girls who were not kept under lock and key could come voluntarily to ask for help, although fear of repercussions often made them afraid of taking the risk. There were a number of campaigns in place which aimed to discourage men from using these girls, although nobody believed they had much hope of success with that particular venture."

The talk had attracted interest from all around the office, and one of the newest recruits had a question for Clive.

"I expect I'm the only person in the office that doesn't know this—but how do they get the girls from the Eastern European countries to the UK?"

Clive's confidence was growing, and he perched himself on the edge of the table and managed a smile. "It's not a bad question. You'd think there were numerous points at which they could be stopped. But some years ago, something called the Schengen Agreement was put in place between many countries in Europe. It effectively opened the borders between member countries, without the need to show passports. With no border controls in place, they only have to be smuggled out of their home countries to get free passage throughout France, Italy, Germany, and other parts of the continent. Some are smuggled by boat into Italy, others overland. And then there's only the crossing to England to worry about. However tight we try to make our own borders, the reality is that it's impossible to search every lorry or container that enters the country. We have to rely on a mixture of intelligence and luck to find them as they arrive."

Interesting as this was, Tom had a murder to solve. "In your opinion," he asked, "do you think that these gangs would have had any interest in killing Hugo Fletcher?"

It was the inspector who answered. "Frankly, we think it's unlikely. Much has been said about the personal danger that he puts himself in, but we don't buy that. Please don't take this the wrong way, but much as we admire the work he does, I think that the risk element is just good PR. He pays the gangs well for the girls—he buys them out. They set the prices, and he agrees to them, so it's unlikely that they would see any reason to kill him. Even his campaigns to persuade your man in the street not to use the girls can be seen by some of the gangs as free advertising. It's the old 'no publicity is bad publicity' thing, as far as they're concerned."

Tom was surprised by this answer. Along with everybody else he had fallen for the hype and believed Hugo to be risking his personal safety for these girls.

He wished he had time to listen to the question-and-answer session, but he didn't. He needed to share the information gleaned from Annabel with James Sinclair. It had to have some bearing on the murder, but he was damned if he knew what it was.

Tom recounted his conversation with Hugo's ex-wife almost verbatim to a silent but attentive DCS.

"So," Tom said when he'd finished, "what do you think? We can't ignore the correlation between what she claims to have witnessed and the murder scene, but she could only have known about that if she'd been there and seen it with her own eyes, because we're keeping all the detail under wraps. She'd hardly have described it so accurately if she'd killed him, would she?"

Tom continued without waiting for a response.

"She did tell me that she wanted Hugo dead but would never have sullied her own perfectly manicured hands—or words to that effect. If I'm honest I don't fancy her for it. But of course she may not be the only one who knew about Hugo's predilections. Somebody else could have been blackmailing him too, and there's always the chance that Annabel shared her knowledge of Hugo's unusual tastes, although she swears she didn't."

James Sinclair gave a worried shake of the head. "It doesn't get us any closer to *who*, though, does it? Give it some thought, Tom, and we'll have an update tomorrow. A clear head is what you need."

"I think I'd rather we keep this between ourselves for now. I don't want people to be distracted by the scandal aspect. I'm just going to tell them the facts: she was born as Tina Stibbons, she was Hugo's mother's nurse, and she changed her first name when she got married—apparently because she didn't think Tina sounded very classy."

"Your decision, Tom," James said. He screwed his face into one of his strange grimaces. "I get the feeling we've got all the bits of the puzzle. We just don't know how they fit together."

Tom nodded, knowing that it was his job to join the pieces but for the moment not having any idea what the final picture would look like.

"Just one last thing, then I'll be off. I got the distinct impression tonight that nobody actually thinks Hugo was in any danger—even his wife was a bit scathing on the subject. So why the bodyguards? Was it really just PR, or did he know of some danger that nobody else was aware of?"

It was with relief that Tom turned the key and made his way into his welcoming apartment. Pressing a single switch, the lamps around the room came on simultaneously, and he held his finger down until the dimmer lowered the lights to about half strength—a calm and soothing atmosphere was what he was looking for. He went over to his music system and selected Natalie Merchant. Setting the music to play in all parts of the apartment, he moved from room to room, shedding his clothes in the bedroom and making his way into the bathroom for a quick shower. All that he had heard today had made him feel dirty, and his quick shower turned into a ten-minute deluge of the hottest water he could stand. Pulling on a pair of ancient but very comfortable black jogging pants and a white T-shirt, he made his way into the kitchen to rustle up something simple for dinner.

Pouring himself a glass of pinot noir, he placed a pan of water on the hob to boil, and put a drop of olive oil into a deep sauté pan. He grabbed a pack of ready-chopped pancetta from the fridge and tossed it into the hot oil, leaving it until it began to sizzle. He halved a few ripe cherry tomatoes, ripped half a dozen leaves of basil, and added some pasta to the pan of boiling water.

He wasn't entirely sure that he could stomach food, but he knew from experience that he was useless if he didn't eat. At least this was quick and simple. While he waited for the pasta to cook, he sat at the counter, clasping his glass of wine between his hands, deep in thought. Who was Hugo Fletcher? Was he the paragon of virtue that everybody had always believed? Or was he the man that Annabel had described? And if he was, how had that impacted his life with Laura? Nothing fit. It was as if they were looking at two entirely different men.

The timer pinged, and he got to his feet to add the tomatoes to the pancetta for the last couple of minutes. On automatic pilot he added a couple of turns of black pepper, then added the drained pasta to the sauté pan with a bit more oil and the ripped basil. Tipping it straight onto the plate, he quickly grated some Parmesan, topped up his wine, and sat down, no further forward in his thinking than he had been when he'd walked through the front door.

No sooner had he placed the first forkful of the delicious but simple food in his mouth than he was interrupted by the buzzing of the intercom. From where he was sitting on a tall stool at the kitchen counter, he could see the video image on the screen, and was concerned to see it was Kate. He rushed over to pick up the receiver, all thoughts of his food gone.

"Kate—what are you doing here? Is Lucy okay?"

"Yes, Lucy's fine. She's with a babysitter. Can I come up, please? I'd really like to talk to you."

With immense relief that Lucy was okay, and with considerable irritation that his ex-wife was interrupting his dinner if it was nothing to do with Lucy, he pressed the entry button, took the front door off the latch, and went to sit down to continue eating. He hadn't forgotten the way she'd spoken to him the previous day.

He glanced up at her when she found him in the kitchen, and tried to hide his surprise. Her exotic good looks had been enhanced by some carefully applied makeup, and instead of her usual casual ponytail, her long dark hair was hanging straight and shiny to just below her shoulders. Resisting an impulse to comment, he pointed to the fridge.

"White wine in the fridge, if that's still your preference. Glasses are in there." Tom pointed to a wall cupboard next to the fridge. "I hope you don't mind if I finish eating, but I've been looking forward to this all the way home."

"You always were a better cook than me. That's one of the things that I miss about you."

Tom didn't look up, but thought this was very odd. Kate had never given him any indication in the past that he had *any* redeeming features—at least not in the few years since Lucy had been born.

Kate poured herself a glass of wine and sat on the stool opposite him, on the other side of the counter. She looked around with a half smile on her face. "This is a beautiful apartment, Tom. You've done really well."

Tom could imagine that in her eyes, this was the height of luxurious city living. The apartment had everything you could possibly wish for, except a soul. He hadn't chosen a single thing—it was a job lot. The dark brown leather sofas, huge flat-screen television, and shiny white kitchen represented only the best, it was true. But it said nothing about him, apart from the books and CDs piled on the floor, because clearly the modern man was not expected to read as no bookshelves had been provided.

Still extremely suspicious about this late-evening visit, Tom responded without warmth. "We both know that my earnings as a DCI didn't pay for this. Why the surprise visit? You weren't exactly friendly the last time we spoke, were you?"

"I'm sorry. I was out of order. It's just that there's a lot going on at the moment and I was a bit distracted. I didn't mean to be such a bitch."

There was only one answer to that, Tom reflected, but kept his thoughts to himself. Kate sighed quietly and continued. "There's something I need to tell you."

Tom looked up briefly, continuing to fork the pasta into his mouth.

"I wanted you to hear it from me that Declan and I are splitting up. It hasn't worked out, and it's time to do something about it. I'm sorry if I was grumpy on the phone yesterday, but that was part of the problem."

Tom was genuinely surprised. This was the first he'd heard about things not being too good between them, but then again, he'd never asked. Lucy always seemed happy enough, which was his major concern.

"What's happened?"

Kate swallowed. She looked nervous. "I left you for lots of reasons, Tom. You know that I struggled with your working hours, and Declan was so attentive. You were always distracted, thinking about your latest murder or something."

Tom picked up his plate and started to scrape the remains of his food into the bin. He'd somehow lost his appetite. He'd heard all this before, so why was she bringing it up again?

"Oh, don't look like that. It was so hard for me. Declan works long hours too—but they're consistent, so I know what to expect. I don't mind him getting up early in the morning to be at his desk at the crack of dawn, because I have to get Lucy ready anyway. And even though he gets home late, it is at least predictable, and he always *does* get home."

Kate paused. He could see she was finding this hard, but no way was he going to help her.

"Unfortunately, his attentive nature hasn't gone unnoticed by one of his colleagues it would seem, and recently he's been having lots of team outings. I found out purely by accident that the 'team' consisted of just one other member. He says he's ended it, and it was just a fling, but I don't want to know. We're not married, and I'm not prepared to stay with him and risk it happening again in a few years. I'm just going to have to find somewhere to live, and move on."

Tom was stunned. Declan had been painted as some sort of saint, and although they'd met when dropping off or picking up Lucy, for a long time Tom hadn't wanted to know anything about him. It was all he could do not to punch him in the teeth, to be honest. But that anger had long since passed.

"I'm sorry he's hurt you, Kate. I know from bitter experience how it feels when you think your partner prefers someone else."

He knew he was being petty, but after the casual way she had thrown him aside in favour of the wonderful Declan, he was struggling to feel any sympathy.

"There was no need for that, Tom. But I am *really* sorry that I was so shallow. I should have appreciated your qualities, and shouldn't have been taken in by nothing more than attention and compliments. I know now that you are by far the better man."

Tom was not remotely moved by these words, as he was also aware that Kate had been particularly attracted to Declan's six-figure income, not to mention his equally enormous annual bonus. He wasn't sure what she was up to, but he was certain he didn't like it. One thing was worrying him more than anything else.

"Where are you planning on moving to, Kate? I only relocated down here to be near Lucy; I haven't been here five minutes and you're talking about moving. Where to?"

"Oh, stop that. You know you love the job here. It's the dream job for you, so I don't feel bad about getting you to move south, even though I might not stay here myself."

Tom didn't believe what he was hearing. Since Kate had left him, many things had happened and they had all been unpleasant. And now he was just starting to get his life back together. When she had gone, she'd taken Lucy to the other end of the country without the slightest concern for him. It wasn't always easy to get weekends off, and travelling down to London had cost him the earth at a time when he could ill afford it. Divorce is an expensive business, and he was adamant that he—not Declan—would support Lucy.

Then his brother Jack had died. So he'd lost his wife and his brother—and if he hadn't taken this job he would have pretty much lost his daughter too. She'd have grown up seeing him only for the odd weekend, and he wasn't prepared to accept that.

"Where are you thinking of going, Kate? And why are you even thinking of moving away? Lucy's got friends here now, and you seem to enjoy life."

"Quite simply it's because I can't afford to live here—at least not to the level that I have been living, and I don't want Lucy's lifestyle to change."

Oh, here we go, thought Tom. Obviously when Kate had left him, she'd thought Declan's city salary was a better option. But when Jack had died, his will left everything to Tom—and it was an extraordinary amount of money as his brother had only recently sold his thriving business. It didn't take much guessing to work out what Kate was after.

"I'll buy you a house, Kate. How does that sound? I'll buy you a reasonable house, in a reasonable area, and I will happily maintain you until you find yourself another man—which you undoubtedly will do. You know Lucy is taken care of—I've already sorted that. Will that make you stay?"

"Tom, I didn't come for that."

He resisted the temptation to laugh, but when the next Natalie Merchant song turned out to be "My Beloved Wife," usually one of his favourites, he had to smile at the irony. But the mood he'd been trying to create was broken, so he walked over and turned the music off. He froze when he felt Kate close behind him. Her arms came around his waist, her full breasts rubbing his back through the thin fabric of his T-shirt.

"Tom—look at me." Tom turned round with a feeling of apprehension. Kate moved her arms until they were round his neck. He looked down into her brown eyes—eyes that had captivated him for years. He saw pleading in them and realised that Kate was not a woman who could feel complete without a man. At the moment, he was probably the best—if not the only— option.

"I'm so very, very sorry for what I did two years ago. It was a huge mistake, and I have never regretted anything more in my life."

"Kate, you had an affair. You left me. You practically destroyed me. But now I'm okay, and I'm not going to put myself through that again."

After he had discovered Kate's affair, he had tormented himself with guilt. It took him a long time to realise that it was his wife's desire to seek excitement that had been the root cause. His steady and uncomplicated love hadn't been enough. But she had never seen it that way.

"Come on. You know it's not as simple as that. I wasn't able to resist him. I know it sounds corny, but I felt lonely and he paid me a lot of attention. You don't know what it's like, Tom. It's never happened to you."

Tom grasped her arms and pulled himself free. He walked to the other side of the room, where she could no longer touch him. He realised that after all this time, he was still angry with her.

"Do you honestly think that I never had the opportunity, or the desire, to sleep with somebody else? Do you think you're the only person it happened to? Do you think I don't know what it's like to feel that flutter of excitement when somebody comes into the room, when you know that they want you as much as you want them?"

"Oh, come off it, Tom. You're a policeman. You can't have an affair with one or your fellow officers, because it's more than your job's worth. And you never *see* anybody else."

Tom was keeping his anger and frustration in check. Kate had always believed that things happened to her and that they were outside her control. She just didn't get it that she was responsible for her own actions.

"Two points, Kate. I see lots of people in my job, as you would realise if you had ever shown the slightest interest. And—more importantly—I wouldn't resist because of my *job*. I would resist because of my *marriage*. If you think it was possible for *me* to resist out of fear of losing a job, why wasn't it possible for *you* to resist for fear of losing a husband?"

Kate was not to be deterred, and she followed him across the room. She put her hands on his shoulders. He felt himself tense. She was so bloody beautiful. His body was reacting to her, but his mind was shouting no. He didn't move, either to push her away or to respond.

"I made a mistake, Tom—that's all. I'm just human, and I don't have your strength of character. But I don't want to live in a nice house in a nice area with just Lucy and me on our own. At least in Manchester we've got some friends, but here I've got nobody. Nobody, that is, except you."

Kate reached up to kiss him. Two years ago, Tom would have given his right arm for this moment. He put his hands on her waist and held her away from him. Neither of them spoke, and neither knew what was going to happen next. He couldn't let her kiss him, but when he looked at the plump pinkness of her soft lips it would have been so easy to give in.

Kate broke the silence. "Why can't we be a family again? You, me, and Lucy? She would love it, you know, and so would I. I'm so ashamed of my behaviour, and I promise you on Lucy's life that I would never do anything like that again. What do you say? We were happy once, we could try again. For Lucy's sake?"

That, of course, was playing the trump card. The thought of living with Lucy every day and seeing her every evening was enormously tempting. But Kate had unintentionally broken the spell. Common sense had prevailed, and he knew exactly what her game was. He realised that her beauty wasn't worth it; it was skin deep and nothing more. She wasn't a bad person, but she was shallow. It had never occurred to him before, but Kate didn't make proactive decisions. She just reacted to each set of events. He lifted his hands from her waist and removed her arms from his shoulders.

"I would love to see Lucy every day. But you and I...we're past the point of no return. Let me find you somewhere to live for now, so that you can leave Declan, and we'll see how it goes from there."

"Is that a definite no, or a maybe to getting back together?"

Tom held on to her hands—partly because he wanted to ensure that she didn't touch him again, and partly because he knew he was hurting her.

"Let's just say that we need to let the dust settle, and then we can talk about the right solution."

Tom knew that a definite no would be the signal for Kate be on the first train to Manchester. He needed to give her some hope, although he didn't think he could go back to her even for Lucy, knowing full well that his money was his greatest appeal. But for now, he needed to maintain the status quo.

Kate appeared to think she had made some progress. She smiled at him and squeezed his hands.

"Why don't I try to find somewhere close by? I could start looking tomorrow. Then you could see Lucy all the time, and if we're just renting it would be easy to make a more permanent move when you're ready. What do you think?"

"Have a look, let me know what the damage is, but don't commit yourself. I'll probably have to sign the rental agreement anyway, so promise me you'll just look until you've spoken to me. If you need to leave Declan urgently, then book yourselves into a hotel. I'll pay the bill."

Kate smiled at him, and he could read a hint of triumph in her eyes. He didn't have the heart to squash her dreams yet.

"I knew we could work something out. I'll phone you tomorrow when I've found somewhere."

Kissing him gently on his unshaven cheek, she smiled and made her way almost triumphantly out of the front door.

Now Tom had two things to think about: the case and his ex-wife. He somehow didn't think that the good night's sleep that he had promised himself would be forthcoming.

18

They had been a subdued group at dinner, each locked in their own private thoughts. Stella had tried to lighten the atmosphere a little, but her attempts at neutral conversation had fallen largely on deaf ears. Imogen had finally been able to escape to her room after a hurried conversation with Laura whilst Stella was in the kitchen making coffee.

"Listen, Laura, if you don't want me to read any more letters, I won't. I know that I pushed for this, because you said I didn't understand anything. But I was seriously out of order. I can stop if you like."

Laura gave her a hint of a sad smile. "I hated the idea of you reading them to start with, but now I think I really need you to carry on. I just want one person to understand, and I can't think of anybody better than you. In a way it will be an enormous relief to me. I wrote the letters because I wanted to tell you everything—but I couldn't. I nearly did once—do you remember? But we lost the moment. When I was writing, you were always in my mind. It was as if you were in the room and I was able to tell you everything. But the reality was that I was too ashamed of my stupidity and weakness. Just get rid of them as soon as you've read them, though. I never want to see or think about them again."

"If you're sure? In that case, I think I'll skip the coffee and just go up to my room. Just tell me any time if you want me to stop."

And so here she was, the shrinking pile of letters by her side, the shredder from Hugo's office standing by to dispose of them as soon as she'd read them.

Taking a quick gulp of the whisky that she had chosen as a preferable nightcap to coffee, she decisively pulled the top few sheets towards her.

❖ ❖ ❖

SEPTEMBER 1998

My dear Imogen,

Today is the day that I've decided you are never going to read these letters. So why write them? You may well ask. But you see, Imo, it soothes me, if that's not too ridiculous a word to use. I feel as if I'm talking to you—and I can kind of anticipate how you would respond. But I don't have to suffer the shame of telling you all of this to your face. Does that make sense? And I am ashamed. Although I don't really know why I should be the one feeling humiliated. Can you explain to me why people constantly feel ashamed of the actions of people close to them? Anyway, I'm rambling.

I'm in Sorrento. I'm sitting looking out over the Bay of Naples, and it's stunning. This is a sight I've wanted to see for years. But I didn't expect to be gazing over this glorious vista and feeling the way I do. Not even this view can take away the pain.

Hugo isn't with me. He stayed at the hotel making some calls. I desperately needed some time alone. Time to think. I was going to take a hire car, but Hugo insisted I had a driver. I wasn't happy about it because I'm perfectly capable of driving myself. But as we sped around all the steep bends with the road clinging precariously to the cliff face, and encountered Italian drivers overtaking on totally blind corners, I realised that Hugo was right.

As, it would appear, he always is.

The big problem is, I don't know if I'm being ridiculous. I've gone over and over everything in my head, and I can't help wondering if my romantic dreams were unrealistic. But this is what happened, and I'd love to know what you think. But I don't suppose I'll ask.

The day after the wedding, we left for honeymoon. Despite my resolution to see things from Hugo's perspective, I still felt that ache inside that I get when I'm masking unhappiness. I think I hid it well—I knew that if I'd said anything it would develop into a row, and I didn't want that. I believe I can fix this, you see.

I started to feel a bit better when we got to the airport. A chauffeured car had arrived to take us to Heathrow and I still didn't know where we were going. Hugo had helped me pick my clothes for the honeymoon and wherever we were heading it was clearly expected to be a little warmer than England, and quite glamorous if my new outfits were anything to go by. I wasn't disappointed.

On arrival at Heathrow, we were quickly whisked through to first-class departures, and Hugo leaned across and whispered one word in my ear: "Venice." This was more like my Hugo. He smiled and kissed me gently on the cheek. Whatever had ailed him the day before, he was now back to being the romantic man of my dreams, and he knows that Venice is my favourite place in the world. I've only been once before— bizarrely to a conference rather than on holiday, do you remember? But I'd found the time to ride on a vaporetto down the Grand Canal and sip a Bellini in a rather disappointing Harry's Bar. I'd always wanted to come back—preferably with a man that I loved so that I could take a gondola ride with him. Cheesy, I know—but so romantic. And now Hugo was taking me there.

And that wasn't the only exciting thing. When I asked him where we were staying, he gave the perfect answer.

"The Cipriani—where else?" Hugo actually had a twinkle in his eye. "Not my personal favourite, but I thought you would like it."

I was thrilled. Obviously I'd got things out of proportion, and now everything would be fine.

"How long are we staying?"

"Just five days." Hugo smiled. "And then we'll fly to Naples, and on to Positano for another five days."

I couldn't believe it. The Amalfi coast! He really had thought of everything.

As we were travelling first class, the flight attendant smiled at me and gave me a glass of chilled champagne as soon as we'd boarded. I could definitely get used to this life, although of course there's more to life that the luxuries that extreme wealth provides.

I really thought that everything was going to be perfect when we checked into the hotel, because when Hugo was asked if he wanted to make reservations for dinner, he gave the answer I was hoping to hear.

"Thank you, but I think we would like to eat in our suite. Perhaps I could consult the chef about the menu. In the meantime I'd be grateful if you could have a bottle of Cristal sent to the room straightaway."

I was a bit less pleased when we reached the suite and found that there were two bedrooms, and I was clearly expected to sleep in one whilst Hugo would take the other. But I'd already decided that I need to work at this, and tantrums would achieve nothing. What's odd to me is apparently not odd to Hugo.

"Darling, why don't you go and take a bath and then get dressed for dinner," Hugo asked.

I wrapped my arms round his waist and whispered in his ear.

"Dressed, my love? Are you sure that's what you want?"

Hugo gently removed my arms and smiled at me—that lovely smile that reaches his eyes.

"I'm quite sure. I would much rather see you opposite me in this glorious setting in one of your beautiful dresses than in a negligee. Humour me, please?"

That sounded fine to me, so I thought I'd take some time to get ready. I wanted to get this just right. So I ran myself a deep bath and lay back in thick bubbles. I was so looking forward to the rest of the evening—and, of course, the night ahead.

I dressed carefully in a silk shift dress in a pretty teal colour. It was a perfect foil for my red hair, which I know Hugo loves. Although the front of the dress was quite modest, the back had a deep V which reached to my waist, and the dress flowed beautifully—not too clingy, but not too loose. I knew that this was one of Hugo's favourites.

The meal that he had selected was superb. A delicious piece of ginger-marinated salmon was followed by a soft and delicate aubergine gnocchi in a salsa di pecorino, and then to complete the menu the most tender fillet of beef that I have ever tasted was served with an antiboise sauce. I couldn't even think about dessert, but Hugo fed me a mouthful of his spiced pear sorbet, and I really did think that I was in heaven. I looked across the table at my elegant and sophisticated man. He looked so handsome: smart yet casual in a classically cut pair of black trousers and pale caramel-coloured linen jacket over a white shirt, open at the neck. I couldn't help noticing a few dark hairs just below his collar line, and I ached to reach across and undo his shirt farther, and kiss the point at the base of his neck. I'm telling it like it was. This is how I felt.

I decided not to drink much, so I just had a couple of smallish glasses of wine. Hugo had a grappa after dinner, but I wanted a clear head. We went and stood outside on our private terrace, and looked out over the lagoon. Pure heaven.

I sensed that it wouldn't be right for me to touch Hugo. He likes to be in charge, so I resisted. As we gazed out across the water, he put his arm around my shoulders. I leant very slightly towards him to acknowledge his action, but not to put too much pressure on him. Then he said what I was waiting to hear.

"I am aware that we didn't make the best of starts yesterday evening, Laura, and I'm sorry if I took you by surprise with the bedroom arrangement. I'm confident you'll soon appreciate how sensible it is, but I do understand that in your world it

isn't the norm. I should have dealt with it more sympathetically. But now, my darling, this is our real wedding night. Shall we go to your room?"

I ignored the bit about our different backgrounds, because he's right, really. I actually felt quite nervous. Yesterday I had all the confidence in the world, but it took a bit of a knock, and this time I felt that I had to be very careful not to mess things up again. I wanted to tell him how much I love him, and how important he is to me. But I didn't want to break the fragile moment of closeness. I decided that he would probably prefer praise to emotion.

"Hugo, can I just say how much I appreciate this superb holiday. You've planned it so carefully, and all I want is to make you blissfully happy."

I know, Imo—it sounds a bit stilted, but it was the right thing to say. Hugo looked pleased.

We walked arm in arm through the French windows into my bedroom—a truly magnificent room decorated in silvers and golds.

My heart was beating so quickly—I don't know whether it was passion or fear of rejection! I turned to Hugo and wrapped my arms around his waist, raising my face to be kissed. I looked into his eyes, and could see real hunger there. He kissed me. Gently at first, and then with increasing passion. I put my hands between us to start unbuttoning his shirt, but he gently removed them. I told myself to slow down. Then he pulled my head onto his shoulder, and starting stroking my hair, lifting the long tresses to cover them with kisses. I was desperate to move things forward, but I made myself hang back.

Then he pushed me away—just gently—and placed his hands on my shoulders.

"Darling. You are exquisite and I want you so much. But I really want to enjoy this, and we mustn't rush. Please, go over there and let me look at you."

He walked away from me and sat down on the chair, staring at me. I didn't like this. I wanted to be held.

"I don't know what you want, Hugo. Do you just want me to stand here?"

"For a moment, yes. Your beautiful red hair is caught in the lamplight. I want to look at you in all your perfection, and remember this night."

I felt a bit stupid, but it was good to know that he thought I was beautiful—well, my hair at least. I wanted to be in his arms, though. I felt so isolated on the other side of the room.

He leaned back in the chair, and gave me that wonderful smile again.

"I'd like you to start to remove your clothes."

I frowned. I had to ask him what he meant, although it was clear enough.

"It's a simple request, Laura. Please keep your shoes on, but I'd like you to remove your clothes, whilst I watch and admire you."

I realised that he wanted me to strip for him. Oh, no! Please, not this. This was going to be the first time that he would see me naked, and I didn't want it to be like this. In the future, if it amuses him, I can't imagine I'd have an issue with it. But surely this was a night for tenderness and passion? Surely it should be about discovering each other's bodies with fingers, hands, and lips? I didn't want to give a solo performance. I tried to explain this in a non-confrontational way.

"I'm not asking you to behave like a whore," he replied. "I want to see you remove each item of clothing, piece by piece. Please continue until you are totally naked. Do you find it strange that I want to admire your body?"

What could I say? He made it sound like a compliment—but it seemed so unnatural to me; so cold and clinical. I tried again.

"Must I do this, Hugo? I just want to be touching you and holding you. Please, darling." I tried not to sound as if I was whining, but I'm not sure how successful I was.

"Think of yourself as my present. I would like to see you unwrapped very slowly. I've never considered you to be a prude, Laura. Don't make an issue of such a simple request."

He makes everything sound so reasonable. He makes everything seem as if it's me that's difficult. Perhaps he's right. Is it me? I haven't got any problem with nudity at all, in the right context. But it was clear that this was going to be entirely for his pleasure, because it certainly wasn't going to do anything for me.

Then I got a grip. I decided I was blowing everything out of proportion. So what if he wants me to strip? It's not exactly a capital offence. I had a strong word with myself and just got on with it, following his orders to the letter. Thank God I wasn't wearing tights, was all I could think. And that nearly made me laugh. Not for long, though.

One of the most awful things was that the mood was wrong. If we were familiar with each other's bodies, I could imagine doing a jokey strip, dancing to some sleazy music with Hugo lying on the bed laughing but with his eyes revealing sheer lust. Or maybe in the future I might order him to stand still and not touch me—just watch— as if I were trying to seduce him. But it didn't feel like either of these, and perhaps that's my fault. That's what I can't figure out. I could have made so much more of it. All I did was stand still and try to look sexy.

I started by unzipping the dress. Fortunately it had a very simple zip, and it just slid off my body. I don't know how I'd have made it look good if I'd had to pull it over my head. I held it just for a moment over my breasts, and then let it slide to the floor. All the time feeling vaguely absurd.

Hugo's eyes held mine, and then they slid down my body. I could practically feel them.

I was about to move on to the next bit—although there wasn't much left, to be honest, when Hugo just held up his hand. I knew this meant I had to stop.

"Is it usual for you not to wear a bra, Laura?"

"I thought you might appreciate it tonight, as we're on our own."

"I do have some preferences for underwear, but we can discuss those another time. Please carry on."

Swallowing the retort that sprang to my lips, I carried on. Any excitement that I had felt after dinner was dissipating rapidly in the face of Hugo's cold and almost analytical stare. Apart from the shoes, I only had a pair of very brief knickers left to remove, so I bent over and pulled them down slowly.

Now I can stop pretending that this was all okay, if slightly weird. I've tried to describe accurately how I felt at the time, pushing to the back of my mind the impact of what happened next.

When I'd removed my knickers, I raised my eyes to Hugo's and tried to look as alluring as possible. But the look in Hugo's eyes was not desire. His stare was cold and flat, and he stood up and walked over to the window behind me and gazed out over the lagoon. His next words, spoken without him turning round, were gutting.

"Laura, I'm deeply disappointed in you. Get dressed."

I had no idea what I'd done. Although I was shaking with a vast range of suppressed emotions, I tried to keep my tone level as I asked him to explain. He whipped round to face me.

"You're a fraud, woman. Nothing but a cheap fraud. I wouldn't have thought you capable of this level of deception."

His face showed pure contempt, and I felt exposed and vulnerable, standing naked in nothing but a ridiculous pair of high-heeled sandals. I wrapped my arms around my chest, as if to defend myself from a physical attack.

The only thing I could think was that he was disappointed with my body. I know it's not perfect, and maybe slightly more well-covered than is fashionable, but it's not bad! And yet he looked absolutely disgusted. My chest tightened. I didn't understand any of it. His next words struck me like a blow.

"You've tricked me, and I repeat, I am deeply disappointed in you."

He turned back to the window, as if there was nothing more to say.

I know that, looking back, it would perhaps have seemed natural for me to have been angry—but it's not like that when somebody you love makes you feel as if you've failed. You feel desolate. Well, that's how I felt. He'd never been unkind to me since the day we met, and I just wanted to go and kneel at his feet and beg him to explain to me what I'd done wrong.

But then there's pride. As the roller coaster of emotions continued on its path, pride kicked in. Why should I feel like this? Surely he knew he was hurting me? Didn't that matter? All these thoughts collided with the disappointment and distress, and the roller coaster reached its summit, racing down once more into the pit. That pit where reason turns to dust as pure emotion takes over. Practically crying now, I begged him to explain.

"Hugo, I have no idea what's the matter, but I need you to know that you are really upsetting me. What can I possibly have done wrong?"

He continued to stand with his back to me for a few moments, until finally he turned round.

"That!" he said, pointing rather bizarrely to my pubic region.

In another twist of my spiralling emotions, sarcasm and anger crept in—albeit briefly.

"What were you expecting? A penis?" I probably shouldn't have said that.

"You have red hair."

Now I was puzzled. What on earth could he mean? I looked down and suddenly realised that it was my dark, silky pubic hair that was inexplicably giving him a problem. I was completely bewildered.

"Yes, my hair's red at the moment, but I've been known to be blonde, although I'm naturally a brunette. I dye my hair—as do probably about fifty percent of all women. Even more than that, I suspect. Why is it an issue?"

"You really don't understand, do you? I married you partly because of your beautiful hair, and now I find it's not real."

This was so trivial that all the previous emotions evaporated into the atmosphere, leaving no residue other than a vague sense of puzzlement that anything so insignificant could be so important to him.

"But what does it matter? I didn't marry you for any reason other than the fact that I love you. Hugo, I know nothing about your body—but it's not important at all. Why would it be? I want to explore your body and get to know it—whatever its perfections and imperfections. It's you that I love!"

He just turned his back on me yet again, as if my words meant nothing.

The dull ache of yet another rejection was still there, but I was starting to feel exasperated because frankly he was being preposterous. But if I was going to have an argument, which seemed the most likely outcome, I was definitely not going to have one whilst I was standing there naked. I kicked off the high heels and grabbed a bathrobe that had been lying beautifully folded on the end of the bed. I started to feel considerably less vulnerable. If a row was what he wanted, he could have one.

"You know, Hugo, I think we've got a few options here. Number one, we could get divorced. The marriage hasn't been consummated, as I know to my huge disappointment. Number two, I could buy a bottle of red hair dye, but not until tomorrow when the shops open. Number three, you could always wear a blindfold. Or number four, you could stop being so fucking ridiculous. You decide."

After all my efforts to comply with Hugo's wishes, my anger strangely seemed to have something of an effect, because Hugo actually answered, albeit rather coldly.

"Whilst I don't appreciate the tone of voice, Laura, nor can I condone the use of foul language, I do realise that my reaction may have seemed a little out of proportion to you."

I bit back the obvious reply to this comment, and let him continue.

"You clearly don't appreciate the significance to me, but I will explain and hope that you will understand. I married you because I thought you were so like somebody who was very dear to me. In fact the most marvellous person I have ever known. She had beautiful red hair, and until I met you I had never encountered anybody who so resembled her. We were devoted to each other, and you seemed so like her—your strength, your body, but in particular your hair."

I hadn't expected anything else to wound me that night, but this was like a punch high in my chest. I choked out a response and asked him why he hadn't married her then, if she was so bloody marvellous.

"It wasn't possible. And now she's gone. I thought you could replace her."

I felt sick. All these months he's been with me not because of me, but because I'm like somebody else. Probably some married woman who had gone back to her husband. But I had to know.

"Hugo, do you love me? Ignoring any similarities between myself and this woman, do you want to be married to me?"

"Given that I am not prepared to suffer the ignominy of a second failed marriage, Laura, we will need to find a way of overcoming my disappointment. So yes, I do want to remain married to you."

As I'm writing this, I feel nothing but sorrow—for the fact that he didn't say that he loves me, the fact that he married me to replace this other woman, and for the fact that I had allowed myself to be persuaded that we shouldn't have sex before we married. I don't feel any remorse for the colour of my hair. I think he's being totally absurd.

At the time, though, the only emotion was relief—that my marriage wasn't over, and that we had a chance to fix whatever was wrong. It's hard to understand why I felt like that. I'd have expected indignation, anger, all sorts of negative feelings. But I just wanted to make things right for our marriage. So I took a deep breath, walked over to where he stood at the window, and wrapped my arms round his waist. Laying my head on the back of his shoulder, I whispered to him.

"I'm sorry I didn't tell you that this isn't my natural colour. If you'd ever come to my parents' house you would have known, because there are so many pictures of me. But it can't really be that big a deal. I'll keep it red as long as you like. Come to bed, darling? We'll get over this."

Hugo turned and put his hands on my shoulders. "You go to bed. I'll join you in a few moments."

It was clear that I wasn't going to get the pleasure of undressing him, but at least we weren't heading for the divorce courts already. I foolishly decided that a bit of levity was needed, and as Hugo turned to go I called to him.

"You never know, Hugo. Perhaps this other woman dyed her hair, too."

Hugo didn't break his stride, and perhaps I should have anticipated his response.

"I do know. She didn't."

Hugo closed the door behind him.

I don't really want to dwell too much on the next bit. The consummation of my marriage. But I'm going to tell you.

When he came back into my bedroom, he had a towel around his waist. He switched off the light before removing it, and slipped into bed. I whispered that I would really like the light on, because I wanted to explore his body, from the creases at the back of his knees to the hollow at the base of this throat, or something like that. I wanted him to understand how much I adored him. And, if I'm honest, I really did want to see my husband naked. I don't think that's particularly unusual!

Hugo, however, had a different view. He ignored my request about the light, and pulled me to him, kissing me on the neck, but not on the lips. To me, kissing has always been the most erotic of activities, and nothing turns me on more. But each time I tried to get my mouth near to his, he managed to manoeuvre himself away. When my hands started to stray around his body, he kept a tight hold on them. I wondered if this might be some sort of foreplay—perhaps he wanted me to resist touching him for as long as possible. So I went along with it. With Hugo, that always seems to be the best option.

Suddenly he rolled me onto my back and literally clambered on top of me—with no more than a couple of minutes of kissing me on the neck. I'm not sure if I can write the next bit. Do I really want to tell you this?

I felt his right hand slip between our bodies, and he guided himself into me. It was a struggle, because to be honest he was barely hard enough. I tried to gently suggest that we slow down. Perhaps we could just enjoy each other for a while. He ignored me, and what followed next was frankly unpleasant. Without any apparent interest in how I was feeling he just ground into me, clearly trying to stimulate himself, until with little more than a grunt he carefully extracted himself, and rolled over onto his back.

I couldn't speak. The tears were running down my cheeks and I was so glad the lights were out. I didn't want him to know how much he'd disappointed me. I bit back a sob, but I didn't have to worry about disguising the fact that I was crying for long. I felt some movement and realised that Hugo was actually getting out of the bed.

"Goodnight, Laura."

And that was it. Without another word, he left me.

The next morning, I woke up on my own—again. No early-morning lovemaking, or even wrapping arms and legs around each other to welcome the day. I remember that I felt completely hollow, as if my insides had been sucked out whilst I slept. For a moment, I couldn't understand why I felt that way. It's strange; people say that when something bad has happened they often wake up feeling fine until realisation hits them. In my experience, it's the exact opposite. You wake up feeling the pain, but it takes a while to remember what caused it.

There I was, two days into my marriage, and I'd already learned that my husband married me because I reminded him of somebody else, that we are to have separate rooms, and that our lovemaking is not—for the moment at least—the rapturous coming together of two people that I had anticipated.

There's more that's happened since then—because all of that was seven days ago. But I can't bring myself to write more. Not now, at least.

I so wish I could tell you this—really tell you. I don't know what to do, Imo. I'm confused and unhappy. But I've got to be positive. So I'm going to order a large glass of cold white wine and try to focus on constructive thoughts before I return to the hotel. And to Hugo.

Laura xxx

19

Monday morning dawned bright and crisp—just the sort of autumn day that Tom normally liked. After Kate had left the evening before, he had been sorely tempted to hit with a vengeance a very nice bottle of single malt that he had in the cupboard, but now he was glad he had resisted. The wine had been quite enough, and he started the day with a clear head. Well, at least it was clear of overindulgence in alcohol. In every other way it was clouded in confusion, with a million diverse and apparently unrelated thoughts vying for supremacy in his mind.

"Thank you, Kate!" Tom muttered to himself. Personal issues were the last thing he needed to resolve at the moment. He had to focus on the job in hand.

His first stop was headquarters, but he wanted to get back to Oxfordshire as soon as possible. Like Becky, he could feel the tension simmering under the surface, but unlike Becky he wanted to understand the root cause.

Despite the fact that it was only seven in the morning, he found quite a few of his team already in place. They were an enthusiastic bunch, so he called everybody together for a quick heads-up on any progress made within the eleven hours since he'd left for the supposed peace of his apartment. He leaned against a desk at one end of the room, and people pulled up chairs or sat on desks around him. Ajay was always keen to be the first to speak, and this morning was no exception.

"We've found some information about Tina Stibbons, sir. She's got a record. She was working as a nurse for an old gentleman near Cromer, and the chap's daughter accused her of stealing some valuable stamps. Her prints were all over the album—which she explained by the fact that she had been looking at the stamps with the old guy's permission. He couldn't remember if he'd given it or not. The daughter was adamant that she was going to see Tina jailed, but two days before the court case, all charges were dropped. The stamps never turned up, Tina left Cromer, and nothing more was said. The local force were livid, but as the old man was dying it seemed inappropriate to charge them with wasting police time. They strongly suspected some form of blackmail, but nothing could be proved. The daughter suddenly seemed desperate to sweep it all under the carpet. God knows what Tina had turned up."

Tom could see a pattern forming here, given what Tina, a.k.a. Annabel, had told him the day before.

"Good work, guys. Did you manage to turn up a picture of Tina?"

"We most certainly did, and it's not a pretty sight, I can tell you! What on earth was old Hugo thinking of?" Ajay said. As a man who had to have every hair in place at all times, and prided himself on his Asian good looks, it was a fairly typical comment.

"Looks aren't everything. She took care of his mother, and so perhaps he saw a different side of her. Where's the picture?"

"On the board behind you, boss. Top right."

Tom turned to look at the magnetic white board behind him, and even he was more than a little staggered by the picture. Tina Stibbons and Annabel Fletcher were unrecognisable as the same person. Yesterday she had told him that part of the deal was "a bit of a makeover," and she wasn't joking.

One of the young women handed him a much-needed cup of coffee and pointed to the picture next to it. "That one was taken of Lady Annabel just after their wedding. Their marriage was big news, although Hugo wanted it to be private so a lot of it was behind closed doors. But given his high profile, the paparazzi had a field day with their telephoto lenses. Have any of you ever watched those American programmes about makeovers?"

The men in the team looked blank, but a couple of the girls smiled and nodded.

"They take the plainest of girls and give them extensive plastic surgery. They really do turn ugly ducklings into swans, with nose jobs, chin jobs, eye tucks, tummy tucks, boob jobs, all sorts of veneers on their teeth, their skin practically removed and then regrown, laser hair removal where they have too much in the wrong place, hair implants where they haven't got enough, and when they've created a completely different physical specimen, there's the hair and makeup. It's remarkable—except that they all turn out looking pretty identical. Well, she looks like a product of one of these programmes, and I would estimate that the new look set her back about half a million."

"Does anybody but me think it's a bit odd that he turned an ugly duckling into a swan with his first wife, and then did a reverse trick with his second wife?" Ajay said, back on his favourite topic of how people look. Most of the team nodded, but Tom felt a strange compunction to defend Laura.

"I think you're all aware that she's been ill," he said, "and the depression or whatever it was has obviously had an impact on her. But I wouldn't write her off, if I were you. She's got a certain something."

Tom smiled through the whistles and ribald remarks that he might have expected. It was good to lighten the atmosphere, even at his own expense.

"Okay, what else have we got?"

He took a sip of his coffee as he looked around the room, and a young constable—who he remembered just in time was called Alice—raised her hand.

"We've checked the flights of both Laura Fletcher and Imogen Kennedy. They all tally. The only thing is, we don't know exactly where Kennedy was the night before. Given the timings, I thought it would be worth checking flights from all London airports to Paris, just in case she came and did it, then flew out and back again. But I found nothing."

"Good thinking, Alice. Well done. We've got no reason to suspect Imogen Kennedy, and she claims not to have seen Hugo for a good few years. However, when I asked what she thought of him, I detected a lie. She seemed vaguely noncommittal. She said he wasn't much fun, or something like that. There was something about her indifference that seemed calculated. On the other hand, Laura has changed from adversary to a staunch supporter where Imogen's concerned. Alibi or no alibi, I don't want Imogen Kennedy ruled out. Alice, can you please check out everything you can find on her, any visits to the UK in the last couple of years, in fact *all* trips, and we can see if these tie in with Hugo in any way."

Tom looked around the room. "Okay. Moving on. Do we have any news on Danika Bojin, the missing girl?"

"No, boss, we've not found any sign of her at all. We went round to see the family she was living with—the Gregsons—and they've not heard from her. They said she's a delightful girl, and ever so grateful to Sir Hugo. She's been with them two years, since she was just sixteen. They can't see any way that she could have been mixed up in this."

"Did they have anything useful to add?" Tom asked.

"They did say that quite a lot of the girls disappear. The gangs track down the girls and grab them again—having already been paid in full, of course. In an attempt to prevent this from happening, once the girls have been rehoused they're not supposed to keep in touch with each other. The theory is that by keeping them apart their trail goes cold, and it helps to integrate them into the lives of the families—who aren't supposed to know about each other either. It's all to do with safety and security, apparently. Gregson says he's not entirely sure of the logic of this, and some of the charity workers agree with him. But Sir Hugo is adamant, and he who pays the piper…

"Anyway, according to Peter Gregson, Danika broke that rule. When she first came to them a couple of years ago, she kept in touch with two girls." Ajay consulted his notes. "Mirela Tinescy and Alina Cozma. The girls agreed that they wouldn't tell each other where they were living—but they met up every month for an hour. Peter found out about it because Alina Cozma went missing within the first six months, and Danika asked for his help."

First this girl Alina went missing, and now Danika Bojin. Tom knew that Jessica had been quite dismissive of some of the girls for throwing away their chance of a new life, but these two didn't seem to fit that bill at all. He jotted the names down in his notebook, with an approximation of the spelling.

"Why was Danika concerned?"

"Alina had missed two of their meetings, and whilst they couldn't contact her, they were sure she would have let them know if she'd been moved. I think they'd watched one too many James Bond movies, because they'd set up a 'dead drop.'" Ajay grinned. "They agreed that if anything changed they would write a note and stick it to the base of a waste bin in Green Park—near where they met. There was nothing. Of course, the note could have dropped off, but Danika was really worried. She hadn't seen her friend for nearly three months so she decided to approach the charity. She went to Egerton Crescent, and her friend Mirela Tinescy went with her. They spoke to Jessica Armstrong to ask her if she knew what had happened to Alina. Jessica either couldn't or wouldn't help them. She just shouted at them for breaking the rules—said they'd be in serious trouble. Hugo wasn't there."

Ajay now had everybody's full attention. Nobody in the room moved as he continued.

"Danika decided she didn't care whether she got into trouble. All she cared about was her friend. So a couple of days later, she decided to try to find Hugo at his home in Oxfordshire. Mirela wasn't quite brave enough to go with her, so Danika went alone. After all her trouble, Hugo wasn't there. She told Lady Fletcher all about it, and according to Danika she was very sympathetic and helpful. She said she was going to follow it up. But she only heard from Laura once, a couple of weeks later. Danika was really disappointed—but of course it wasn't long after this that Laura was sent back to the care home. It would have been just before Christmas—a couple of years ago."

Tom was momentarily stunned. If Laura had met Danika, why had she said nothing yesterday when they listened to the message? She'd seemed disinterested, and she'd actually said she knew nothing about the girls. Why would she lie?

"How do we know all this, Ajay, if Danika is still missing?" Tom asked.

"She told Peter Gregson the whole story, because she felt she'd broken his trust. He's pretty sure that since then she's stuck to the rules. That is, until she went missing on Wednesday."

Tom was still bewildered by Laura's lack of response. Then a thought struck him. He had assumed that Laura had been upset by Annabel's message, but maybe he had misread her completely. Maybe it was the news that Danika was missing. Although it was two years since they'd met, he couldn't believe Laura would have failed to recognise Danika's name.

"Have we checked up on this"—Tom consulted his notes—"Alina Cozma with Jessica Armstrong? Becky says she's responsible for following up on any missing girls."

"No. We're going back to talk to her when the office opens this morning. We'll try to find out whether anything did happen to Alina, or whether she just did a runner. We need to talk to the other girl, Mirela Tinescy, as well, to see if she can throw any light on where Danika might be."

"Right. And get details of any girls that have gone missing in, say, the last twelve months. Any of them might be a suspect. See what you can get. Now, what else? Anything on the bodyguards?"

The room had been gradually filling with people, and Tom noticed that the DCS had arrived and was sitting listening at the back of the room. Alice raised her hand a bit more cautiously this time. She looked over her shoulder at the now full room of people, and Tom reflected that she looked way too timid to be a policeman. She was undoubtedly bright, which was just what he needed, but her cheeks went slightly pink as she started to speak.

"Yes, boss. I spoke to the company that normally looks after Sir Hugo yesterday. They said that this weekend he had specifically stood them down. He said he had private business to attend to, and wasn't attending any functions. They backed up what Lady Fletcher said—he tended to use them primarily when he needed to go to a public event, and there had never been a hint of any trouble so they didn't understand why he bothered."

"Did you ask them if, in their experience, Hugo had a mistress, or if other women accompanied him anywhere?"

"Yes, we asked the question. But all of their guys—and there were three different ones who were generally assigned to him—said that there had never been a hint of another woman."

Tom stuck his hands in his pockets. That was a bloody useless dead end, then.

"Okay. Anything on the wigs?" he asked, without much hope.

One of the older but most popular detective constables stood up. "Not much we could do yesterday, because everywhere was closed, but we're back on it today. There is one other thing, though, boss. I did a bit of digging to find out what was supposed to be wrong with Lady Fletcher. Although the doctors won't confirm anything, when that picture of her was published people started trying to rake up whatever dirt they could, no doubt paying for information. The story was that she had Delusional Disorder, and that ties in with what her mother told Becky. At least, that's what it was when she went in the second time. I wasn't sure what that meant, so I looked it up on Wikipedia, and for the thicko audience here, I've simplified it down to a couple of sentences." The policeman referred to a printout in his hand. He coughed theatrically.

"*Delusional disorder involves the person holding one or more non-bizarre delusions. They can be quite functional, and don't show odd or bizarre behaviour except as a direct result of their delusional belief.*"

Apart from a few jeers in response to the "thicko" comment, the much-reduced definition was met with silence.

Only Tom had a question. "What would be termed a nonbizarre delusion?"

"I believe it's when the delusion is actually plausible, even though patently untrue. A bizarre delusion would be if I believed that every person in this room actually had a blue face, or that the Martians have invaded my living room. A nonbizarre delusion would be believing that every time I walk out of a room, everybody laughs at me, or if I believe that my wife is having an affair with the milkman, even when evidence proves conclusively that said milkman is gay. The person who is delusional believes him or herself to be one hundred percent correct, and can't be reasoned with."

This description resulted in a smattering of laughter and derision, just as the detective had no doubt intended. Tom knew that for at least the next twenty-four hours until everybody got bored with it, each time this particular constable walked out of the room there would be loud but false laughter, and that jokes about milkmen would be rife. It kept the atmosphere light even though everybody was working hard, and he knew nobody was likely to forget this description.

"We heard yesterday that a chief constable was in some way involved in Laura's sectioning. DCS Sinclair has kindly agreed to look into this for us. Any feedback, sir?" said Tom, showing due deference to his boss in front of the rest of the team.

From the back of the room, the chief superintendent stood up. "Yes and no. It turns out that the chief constable in question is Theo Hodder."

Tom couldn't fail to notice the looks that passed around the room. Even when he'd worked in Manchester, he'd heard of Theo Hodder. Although he wasn't an officer in the Met, he had been the subject of several unsubstantiated rumours within the force. But nothing was ever proven against him. James Sinclair continued.

"Unfortunately, Mr. Hodder is currently on an exotic adventure holiday up the Amazon or somewhere, and is out of contact. You'd think he'd get enough excitement in his job, but apparently he's gone on some mission to find hidden cannibal tribes. We could probably have found him something similar on our patch, if only he'd asked. So it looks like we're either going to have to wait, or ask Lady Fletcher herself about it. But well done, everybody. You've got a lot of information, considering yesterday was a Sunday."

Good old James, Tom thought. Always encouraging.

Acutely aware that there was a shortage of plausible suspects, Tom nevertheless decided they should run through the options and brainstorm any other ideas.

"Right—Alice, can you act as scribe, please."

She jumped up and walked over to the whiteboard, pushing the photos and any other documents attached by small magnets to one side. She picked up a red marker pen.

"Let's list any and all suspects—and we'll start with the obvious, Laura Fletcher. As yet, I've not come up with any specific motive, other than Hugo seems to have been responsible for having her sectioned. That was some time ago now, although revenge *is* said to be a dish best served cold. There was something strange about their relationship that I've yet to get to the bottom of. Any comments?"

As usual, Ajay was the first to respond. "Yes, boss. The guy who saw the woman leaving—if this *is* the right woman—said she looked sexy. Would that apply to Laura Fletcher, do you think?"

"Becky said when we first met her that Laura looked like a woman who'd given up on life. I think that was the comment. But change the drab clothes, put on some makeup...I think it would have a significant impact on our perception of Lady Fletcher. However, given that she was irrefutably on a plane at the time—does anybody think this is worth pursuing?"

As Tom expected, nobody did.

"Next, the ex-wife Annabel, a.k.a. Tina. Good motive—she thought he was about to change his will, although I suspect that she'd be financially better off with him alive than dead. She's got no alibi, so in theory she's possible. She's positively scrawny, though, and I can't imagine her looking good in a leather skirt. Her legs must be like sticks. And don't forget that Hugo allowed this person to tie him to the bed, because there was no sign of a struggle. It also took a degree of intelligence. I don't want to rule her out, but I really don't think she would have done it herself. It would have been a contract job, and I don't know of many female contract killers."

Annabel's name was added to the list, with an arrow pointing to her photo.

"Same household," Tom continued. "Hannah Jacobs, the nanny. Described as a lovesick cow around Hugo, and according to Stella Kennedy she provided evidence the first time Laura was sectioned. But apparently she was in Oxfordshire with Alexa. Swimming. We need to check that out, make sure she didn't leave Alexa with one of the other nannies."

Tom had begun to pace, head down as he focused on everything he had learned over the past two days.

"Then we've got Imogen Kennedy. She was definitely in France, but there are a few timing gaps—absolutely no clue as to motive, though, and no indication that she had ever been to Egerton Crescent. But there's something odd going on there—and don't let's forget it.

"Jessica Armstrong, his PA—huge fan of Hugo—or so she says. The right age, right shape, had easy access to the apartment. Her fingerprints were in parts of the apartment, but that may be justified. She's given us no alibi. We can't find a motive, other than a potential obsession with the man, but she's not an easy one to read. We need to do some real digging and see what we can uncover. Becky thinks she is by far the most likely candidate for a mistress."

Alice wrote up Jessica's name.

"Eastern European prostitutes—rescue girls. At least one if not more are missing. They could have done this together. We don't know what their motive might have been, but they might have been put up to it. Operation Maxim thinks that's unlikely. Any ideas?"

Bob, one of the more experienced detectives, spoke up. "Given that he had all these dealings with prostitutes, both current and ex, and one of them is missing, could it be that the missing girl had become Hugo's mistress? With Laura locked away, he may well have turned to some of his own prostitutes. Perhaps he was trading the current one in for a newer model, or something, and the discarded one didn't like it much."

Tom nodded. "Good thinking, Bob. We need to get onto it as soon as the office is opened today. The only person likely to know is Jessica, so push her as hard as you can. Call me when you've got something. And speaking of Jessica, does anybody think that Rosie could be involved? For those who haven't met her, she's the social secretary—the one who helped us find Laura."

Bob was first to answer again. "Frankly, no. I was there on Saturday when she was told about Hugo, and from her reaction I'd say it's unlikely. We tracked her down in Harvey Nichols about three hours after the murder. According to the friend she was with, they'd been there for at least the previous two hours. You'd need some brass neck to go shopping an hour or so after you'd committed a murder."

From what he'd seen, and from what Becky had said, there was no way that Rosie would fit into that category.

Tom summed up. "Okay, our front-runners are the rescued girls or a mistress who is still unknown to us. Alice is checking Imogen Kennedy's movements for the last couple of years—let's see if we can catch her out in a lie about Hugo. Jessica is a contender, so we need to pursue that from every angle—money, boyfriends, social life, anything on her computer, etcetera. We also need to know from her if she knew anything about the visit that Danika Bojin paid to Hugo a couple of years ago, and according to Peter Gregson, again last week. Then there was the mysterious entry in his diary, which didn't tally with his home diary. What was it again?"

"LMF, boss," Ajay said. "We've still no idea what that's about. We've looked through all his names and addresses both on and off the computer to see if it relates to a person or a place, but we can't find a thing. The techies have his computer, but haven't come up with anything significant yet."

"Right. Keep looking. Ask every person we interview and pray for inspiration. Anybody got anything on the liquid nicotine?"

Bob briefly held up his hand again. "Yep. Same old story, I'm afraid. Dig far enough on the Internet and it will tell you how to make the stuff. It's pretty easy, too. There are other options, like getting it from somebody who works for one of the companies that make nicotine patches, but the most likely and safest way is to make your own."

"Thanks, Bob. Nothing's sacred these days, is it? Okay, folks—let's pick up from where we were and get together again this evening to see what else has come out of the woodwork. I'm off back to Oxfordshire in a while to see what else I can find out about Hugo's life. Call me about the missing girls, please. Meanwhile, I'll check with Lady Fletcher to see what she can tell me about the day that Danika called to see her."

And try to find out why she never mentioned that she knew her, he thought to himself.

20

Imogen woke up very early, after a fitful sleep. She'd stopped reading after poor Laura's first night with Hugo. The desire to read on had been strong, but somehow she felt it necessary to absorb what she'd read and take things slowly. Laura's dilemma was so clear to Imogen, as was her pain and disappointment.

She knew that nobody else would be up yet, so she propped herself up against the pillows and dragged the letters towards her.

STILL SEPTEMBER 1998!!

My dear friend,

This is the final day of our honeymoon. We're leaving Positano in about two hours. Hugo is reading the paper, and I have escaped to "the beach." It's not really a beach at this hotel, it's a wonderful rocky outcrop with steps into the sea. You have to take a lift down through the cliff to reach it. It's quite late in the year, of course, but the sun is shining and I thought I could at least go back with a tan. I still want to maintain the impression that I've had a wonderful honeymoon. What's so sad about it is that in many ways it has been perfect. Hugo has been charming and attentive, and he has chosen locations just to please me, but I can't get past the disappointment of our sex life.

Anyway, there's no way that Hugo will disturb me down here. He was fairly appalled that I was happy to venture down to a public area, when I could have just enjoyed the terrace of our suite, so he's certainly not going to follow me. Everything about this hotel is luxurious, though, and his snobbery means I'm safe to write to you. Sorry—that was an unnecessarily spiteful comment, but I'm afraid he is a bit of a snob.

Anyway, I'm going to go back to the first full day of my honeymoon and tell you all about it. Dreadful as I felt that morning—after the night before—I forced myself to get up and get dressed, although the ache of disappointment wouldn't entirely go away.

But this was Venice, city of love. "La Serenissima."

For me, this is the most romantic city on earth, with its majestic sights, stunning old palazzos, and the magnificent Piazza San Marco. It's a place known for love affairs and famous lovers; a city of contradictions—from bustling tourist sites to hushed, narrow cobbled streets that run alongside silent canals and disappear from view around a corner. I know you've never been, but when you get away from the crowds, you can hear the sounds of laughter, shouting and singing through open windows and closed shutters; the smells of cooking—garlic, herbs, and tomatoes—drift from the houses and mingle with the musty, earthy smell of the water. There's a sort of persistent joy about the place. Did you know that in Venice, a married woman's lover (a cicisbeo, apparently) used to accompany her with her husband's blessing to public events and even to church!

It's a place where sexual love was always celebrated. And Hugo had chosen to take me there. Surely that must mean something?

The events of that first evening had to have been an aberration. Tiredness from the wedding and all its preparations perhaps, or dejection after the argument we'd had. It could have been any one of a hundred things, and I don't know Hugo well enough to guess. What an admission! But to ask would be to imply criticism, and I know that to cast aspersions on a man's performance is a sure route to disaster.

So I've tried to remember that he was the one who organised this perfect honeymoon, and given that fact, I decided I owe it to him to make him happy. Perhaps he's never had a loving relationship—certainly he and Annabel weren't happy. And there's nothing that can't be fixed. "There's no such thing as a problem, only a solution," I always used to say at work. For the remainder of our stay in Venice, I was determined to do everything to make him feel good and give him the security of my love. I felt sure I could change him.

And so it was with a pleasant smile that I greeted Hugo when I walked out onto our private terrace where a delicious breakfast had been laid. I leaned down and gave him a gentle kiss on the top of his head.

"Good morning, darling. I hope you slept well. Have you planned what we're going to do today?"

Hugo seemed to have returned to his usual good, if rather restrained, spirits. If he was surprised to see me so apparently cheerful, he hid it well.

"I have worked out a small itinerary, yes. Of course I've been here many times over the years, and it will be my pleasure to show you the best bits. Have a look and see what you think?"

I pushed my plate of fruit to one side, pulled the guidebook with the marked pages towards me, and saw that Hugo had written in his neat hand a list of things to do on each of our days in Venice. My heart sank when I saw the sights that were on his priority list. You know I'm happy going to the odd art gallery, but I also love sitting outside cafés and watching the world go by. I wanted to relax in Piazza San Marco and listen to all the small orchestras competing with each other to attract business. I wanted us to hop on a vaporetto and find some quiet place full of locals for lunch.

But if I had learned one thing, it was that the way to success was not to find fault with anything that Hugo had planned. This was our first day and it had to be stress free. The easiest thing would be to go along with what he wanted, and then perhaps slip in a suggestion or two when he was in a mellow mood.

"This looks brilliant, darling. I think I'd better wear some flat shoes, though, because it looks like there's going to be quite a bit of walking."

Hugo put down the knife he was using to butter his toast and looked at me. "Is that a problem for you?"

"No, not at all. I'm just trying to think what I brought with me. I'll go and have a look after breakfast. You helped me choose what to pack—so I'm sure it will be fine."

The tone of our days was set, and the tone of our relationship. Every day we went from famous site to less famous art gallery. I tried a few tactics to try to get him to break from his itinerary, but I wasn't terribly successful—and of course, I had to be subtle so as not to cause an upset that I sensed could ruin our honeymoon.

On one occasion, we were just passing a vaporetto stop as a boat pulled in.

"Oh look, Hugo—can we just hop on this for half an hour, just to see where it takes us?"

"Laura, it's a bus!" he said. "Really, darling, I'm not in the habit of getting on buses, even if they do float and they are in the most beautiful city in the world. If you must take to the water, we'll hire a launch and you can have a ride round after lunch whilst I read the papers. How does that sound?"

I took a deep breath.

"Perfect. Thank you, Hugo, that's an excellent idea."

Hugo smiled fondly at me and pulled my arm through his. I felt very pleased with myself for creating this harmonious moment.

Now I know what you would think of this. I can imagine what you'd be saying to me. But Imo, I don't want to argue all the time. There must be a better way, surely?

My only other attempt at doing something that wasn't on Hugo's itinerary was when we were walking through Piazza San Marco on our way to some museum or other. It was our last day in Venice.

"You know, Hugo, I really fancy a cappuccino. Shall we sit down at one of these tables and listen to the orchestra for a while? We only need to stay for five minutes."

Hugo smiled at me and put his arm around my shoulders.

"If you would like a cup of coffee, then you shall have one. But not here. These pigeons are disgusting and spread so much disease. The Danieli is only a short walk away. Let's go there and have a coffee in a civilised environment."

Whilst relaxing in the luxury of this magnificent hotel would be a treat for anybody, I just love people-watching. And that doesn't mean watching the sort of clientele that the Danieli attracts, elegant and refined as they are. But Hugo had actually changed his itinerary for me and with good grace, so this was a small improvement and one that I decided to see as a positive step forward.

So our days passed in relative harmony. Hugo made plans, and I saw every important site in Venice. We ate some splendid meals, and we talked to each other—probably more than we had ever done. I really felt that we were getting closer.

And he was affectionate—both in his terms of endearment, and in the way he would hold my hand as I stepped on the launch that we took from our hotel to St Mark's Square, or hold my elbow to guide me down a narrow lane. If we saw a jeweller's or a shop selling exquisite silk scarves he would be happy to stop with me, and ask if I wanted to go in and choose something. And each time he held out my chair for me in a restaurant, he would stroke my hair or bend to kiss my cheek. So much was perfect.

But unfortunately the nights were a big disappointment. Hugo didn't suggest joining me in my bedroom again. On the second night, I did try. I said to Hugo in as calm a voice as possible, "Will you be joining me tonight?"

He merely smiled at me and shook his head. "Not tonight, darling. It's been a busy day and we're both tired. I'll let you know when I think the time is right." And then wrapped his fingers in my hair and gently pulled me towards him for a good-night kiss.

God, it's frustrating. I just know that if I make a fuss I won't win—and the following day will be a nightmare. I realised that the only thing I could do was to try to make the days as pleasant as possible, which apart from the museum and art gallery tour wasn't so difficult, to be honest. But I was striving for perfection so that he would want to join me at night.

I waited until the last night. I was as amusing and provocative as I could be during dinner, making Hugo laugh and touching him lightly when I was talking. He'd decided that we should have dinner in the main dining room of the hotel. He said he wanted the world to see his beautiful bride, and had picked out a pale-grey silk dress for me to wear, which he said made my hair look sensational. I was pretty sensitive about comments relating to my hair, as you can imagine—but I took a deep breath and calmed down.

As we walked back to our suite, I put my arm through his and rested my head on his shoulder. Holding my breath in case I put a foot wrong, I ventured an attempt at a compliment.

"I just want to tell you that these few days have been absolutely wonderful, Hugo. I can't imagine a more perfect place for a honeymoon, and I want to thank you for making it so special."

Hugo squeezed my arm against him. "It has been marvellous, hasn't it? I hope it's made you appreciate that I try to put your wishes first. I do generally know what's for the best, even though you may not always think so. I've granted you your dream of a few days in Positano, but then we can go home where we'll begin our real life together. Everything will be different then."

I wasn't sure what to make of this, but it was clear that my hard work over the last few days had paid dividends. I decided to risk pursuing the ultimate prize.

As we entered the suite, I gently pulled Hugo towards me and pressed myself lightly against him. Lifting my mouth to his, I kissed him with all the tenderness I could muster. Hugo began to respond. It started to get really passionate—and I had to struggle to keep myself under control. This was going to be it. I just knew it.

I tentatively slipped my hands inside his jacket and wrapped my arms round him, sliding my hands very slowly up the length of his back. I pressed my breasts against his chest—something that I knew he had struggled to resist before we were married.

"Hugo, shall we go into my bedroom?" I asked very gently.

I felt his whole body stiffen. His words, when they came, were harsh.

"I had fully expected to make that suggestion myself, Laura. But it is unbecoming in a woman to make the first move, don't you think?"

No, I don't think. Not even slightly. Do you? But what a stupid mistake to make. After all the hard work, then I go and make a schoolgirl error. I know he likes to be in charge. I apologised as quickly as possible, but I was flustered and got it all wrong. Again.

"I'm so sorry, Hugo. I didn't realise you felt like that, but in any past relationships I've had it's not been a problem. I can see that you think differently, so I'll just have to learn. Please forgive me."

I'd made things worse!

"I appreciate the sentiment, but I really do not want to hear or think about you in any of the whore-like relationships that you might have had before we met."

Even as recently as a few days ago, I would have reacted to his pomposity with irritation or anger. But now all I felt was a complete sense of failure. The fragile bond that I had worked so hard to create seemed to have been shattered.

"Darling, I wasn't a whore. Really I wasn't. I told you everything before we were married. Like most girls of my generation, I did have a few relationships. But you know that you're the first man I've ever loved, and the first man that I've wanted to marry and spend the rest of my life with."

I was horrified to hear a slight quiver in my voice, but I couldn't stop myself from apologising.

"I'm so sorry. I just hoped we would make love, and I don't really understand what I've done wrong."

Hugo's expression softened, and he grasped the top of my arms gently.

"I think you have quite a lot to learn about marriage, and about how men think. I didn't mean to imply that you are a whore, and I apologise. But there is a big difference between a casual relationship and a lifelong partnership. I need to respect you, Laura. And when you beg for sex it seems somehow demeaning. Do you understand?"

I wanted to shout no, no, no at the top of my voice. But I didn't.

Trying desperately not to cry, I took myself to bed. I hoped that Hugo would change his mind and join me, but as I half expected, he didn't make an appearance. My actions had destroyed what should have been a beautiful moment.

It was a long time before I went to sleep that night. I spent the last hours of my longed-for idyllic honeymoon in Venice deliberating over our relationship.

I was so very confused. I still am. Is it his age, do you think? Maybe it's his class. What do you think, Imo?

I need to remember that he had planned the wedding and honeymoon to be perfect for me. He was kind and attentive, and bought me so many small gifts. Am I making too much of things that are really trivial? So what if he wouldn't get on a vaporetto and I didn't get my longed-for gondola ride (vulgar, apparently). And maybe he saw my pushy attempts at getting him into bed as a form of criticism that he wasn't pleasing me. Perhaps, despite evidence to the contrary, he has his insecurities, too? Do you think that's the answer?

Perhaps I just need to try harder.

The next morning, though, there was no mention of the events of the previous night as we prepared to leave for Positano. I'd been so looking forward to this part of the trip, but I just felt tired and dispirited. All I could think about was the fact that I'd been married for nearly a week, with only one forlorn attempt at making love.

Despite this sense of lingering sadness, the trip to Positano has been the best part of the holiday, although I do feel guilty writing this. The fact is that Hugo isn't really interested in this part of Italy. He wouldn't even consider venturing to Pompeii— which he thinks is an overrated tourist trap—and I didn't dare suggest a trip up Vesuvius. But he was happy for me to take the driver and disappear whilst he amused himself with various papers and phone calls, and he was always pleased to see me when I got back. I think that he must have told the driver to let him know when we were due to arrive at the hotel, because there was always a chilled glass of wine being poured practically as I walked through the door.

But in some ways it was a relief that I didn't have to spend all day and every day trying to please him. I had some time to myself. Perhaps I'm really not cut out for marriage. Did you find it difficult to start with? I don't think so—you were glowing with happiness, as I remember.

There has, however, been a small improvement in our sex life! I'm learning. I need to make it clear to him that I am receptive, but not make any advances. I tried it last night—and he came to my room. So the improvement is that he wanted to try, but I'm sad to say that the lovemaking itself was still not good. No. I'm being polite. It was bloody awful. Yet another brief moment of almost violent penetration, which did absolutely nothing for me.

I know that I mustn't suggest for a minute that he isn't satisfying me, but strangely enough he made reference to it himself this morning.

"Laura, I am aware that you struggle to enjoy sex. But whatever inhibitions you are suffering from will, I feel certain, disappear when we return to Oxfordshire. I will do all possible to help you over any hurdles." He picked up my hand and kissed it.

Do you know, it really hadn't crossed my mind until this moment that Hugo genuinely thought that, if there was any problem at all, the problem was with me! Perhaps it is me? I nearly jumped to my own defence—an automatic response. But Hugo looked so concerned that I just nodded and said that I was sure we could rectify this over time.

So the honeymoon is over. I've learned a lot about Hugo, and a lot about myself. I never thought of myself as arrogant, but it's clear that I now see everything as Hugo's fault, when in fact he only ever tries to please me. And as for Hugo, he can't stand any criticism—either real or implied. I wonder if this stems from his childhood? These things normally do, I believe.

With love and some sadness,

Lxxxx

21

Stella sat in the kitchen, which was the only room in the house that she found even vaguely comfortable. It was barely light, but she had made her way across from the cottage and let herself in with the back door key. This was the first time she'd been allowed to come and go as she pleased, and she wanted to be here for Laura when she woke up. Both of her children had suffered in their marriages in one way or another, and she couldn't help feeling that this was because of their upbringing. She should have done a better job of hiding her own pain. And David should have had a bit more of a conscience, for that matter. What's the point of a husband if all he does is bring you grief?

Unlike the cold, cheerless rooms in the rest of the house, the kitchen was pleasant in an old-fashioned kind of way. The appliances were relatively new, but the cupboards looked like they were prewar, and had been covered with many coats of paint over the years. It felt like a kitchen that had hardly changed through the ages, and Stella couldn't help thinking whimsically of the number of meals that must have been served on the enormous scrubbed pine table, and the joys and sorrows it must have witnessed.

She hadn't slept well the previous night and wasn't really surprised when an equally exhausted-looking Imogen pushed open the door.

"Good morning, love," Stella said. "What's got you up so soon?" She pointed to the pot of tea in front of her, and pushed a white china mug across the table to Imogen. She knew that Imogen would prefer coffee, but she lacked the energy to get out of her chair to make it.

Imogen merely gave her a shrug, and with a distracted and rather watery smile she sat down with a muttered "Good morning." Although she could see that Imogen's mind was elsewhere, Stella needed to talk. Maybe Imogen understood what the hell had been going on in Laura's life for the past ten years. She'd tried hard enough to get through to her daughter, but she'd always thought that Hugo was the barrier. Well, he wasn't a barrier any more.

Laura was so stubborn and would never admit defeat. She had always been like that. Stella could remember her trying to climb a rope that Will had strung up in a tree in the back garden when she was about ten. She just couldn't do it—but she kept trying. Day after day. Falling flat on her back every five minutes, with rope burns on her hands and legs to boot. Nothing Stella could say would stop her. She had a look of grim determination, and eventually after about a week she did it. She made it to the top once and never bothered again. She'd succeeded against the odds, and that was enough.

Now Stella was hoping that Imogen could shed some light on why her pig-headed daughter had cut herself off from the world.

"I know you haven't seen her since you and Will split up, Imogen, but Laura wasn't happy with Hugo, you know. From the early days she just seemed to go down and down. She wouldn't speak to me, and with you two incommunicado, she had nobody. She was lost without you."

"I know, Stella. I was lost without her too."

Stella knew that this was true. She had wanted so much to help both her daughters—because Imogen was as good as, wasn't she? And Will was miserable too. Divorce was always difficult, but Laura was still married for goodness sake. In spite of that fact, Stella had watched her sink further and further into a sort of wretched hopelessness, and it had torn her apart. The two friends had needed each other more than ever and shouldn't have allowed an argument to come between them. Stella was fed up with being fobbed off by the pair of them. *And* Will. He was as bad.

"Isn't it about time somebody told me what really happened all those years ago? What could have been bad enough not only for you and Will to get divorced, but for Laura to stop speaking to you, too? And why would nobody tell me the truth? The story you all cooked up had 'rubbish' written all over it."

Imogen closed her eyes and bit her bottom lip—a childhood habit that always indicated she was stressed. She leaned across the table and caught hold of Stella's hand.

"Oh God, Stella—I'm so sorry. You're right—we didn't tell you the truth. Will wanted to protect you from knowing what a dreadful person I really am, and I just wanted you to continue to love me."

Stella could see that Imogen was fighting back the tears, but she resisted the temptation to go and give her a hug. That way, she might never find out the truth. She squeezed her hand gently, keeping quiet until Imogen was ready to continue.

"I think in some ways Laura felt to blame, as she seemed to be taking the blame for just about everything at that time. I would have told you the truth ages ago, but I kept hoping that Will would come round. So I *will* tell you, but I'm going to make myself a coffee first. I think I need the caffeine fix!"

Stella didn't want anything to distract Imogen, and weary as she was, finally getting to the bottom of something that had disturbed her for years was certainly worth getting up from her comfy seat for.

"You talk, Imogen. I'll make the coffee and some toast for us both."

As she picked up the kettle, she heard Imogen take a deep, trembling breath and let it out slowly. She was speaking quietly, as if the shame of all those years ago was rising up to overwhelm her.

"Do you remember that before we split up, Will had started looking for a job on an aid project? He really felt that he could make a difference, and I was happy to go wherever he went—as a volunteer. There was one particular project that he'd been keen to work on. So keen, in fact, that he'd asked Laura to have a word with Hugo, to see if he would consider making a donation to the charity in question. Will thought that if he could raise some cash it would make it easier to get on the team.

"We were still waiting to hear back from Laura when we got a surprise call from Hugo. He invited us for the weekend and said an old school friend of his was going to be in the area and he would love us to join them. We were stunned. Hugo had done nothing to encourage us to visit in the few months since they'd been married, and I'd only seen Laura briefly on a couple of occasions—both times at the house in London rather than here—and never alone."

Stella placed a mug of coffee in front of Imogen, who appeared to be miles away—no doubt reliving every second of that time.

"This invitation came completely out of the blue, and we were delighted to accept. We thought Hugo was coming round to us being a significant part of Laura's life. The day before we were due to come down here, Will got a phone call from the company in Ireland who were managing the aid project. They were looking for an engineer and asked Will if he could possibly fly over to see them for a meeting on Saturday morning? Neither of us thought it odd that it was a Saturday, because with these sorts of projects you just do whatever it takes. Will even wondered if Hugo had come up trumps and sent a donation. A joke, in retrospect.

"Obviously he had to go, but it was a bit late in the day to cancel the dinner invitation, particularly if Hugo had made the interview possible, so I decided to come here on my own. The company in Ireland made all the arrangements for Will, and said there would be tickets waiting at Heathrow for the Friday-night flight. So he dropped me off here and went on to the airport."

Imogen was grasping the hot mug in her hands, as if to find the strength to carry on. Stella put a plate of toast in the centre of the table and sat down to listen in silence, wondering where this was going.

"Hugo had ordered a very smart dinner with compulsory evening dress. His friend Sebastian was charming, but a little smarmy for my tastes. Anyway, Hugo kept plying us all with drinks and it turned into a surprisingly pleasant evening.

"After Hugo had dismissed the caterers, he got out the brandy. I said I didn't want any, and neither did Laura, but Hugo insisted that I be tempted with something. I tried to refuse, but he became quite indignant, and said that as the host, he would be deeply offended if I didn't take one of the liqueur selection he had bought specially for the occasion. I didn't believe that for one moment, but this had been the friendliest I had ever seen Hugo, so I complied, as did Laura. We were both a bit tipsy, but certainly not drunk. It was getting fairly late by then—well after midnight, because we hadn't started dinner until at least nine thirty. Hugo mixed our drinks himself, and they were large measures. Laura and I obviously both had the same idea—it was better to drink up than to displease his lordship."

Imogen pushed the coffee cup away from her and put her head in her hands. As she spoke, she didn't look at Stella. She just stared down at the table. Stella could feel panic rising in her chest. She knew this was going to be worse than she'd imagined, and now wished that she had never opened this can of worms. She could barely make out Imogen's words as she began to sob.

"That's the last thing I remember until the next morning. When I woke up, I was in bed in the cottage. And I wasn't alone. Sebastian was lying on top of the covers. He was naked…and so was I."

She lifted a distraught face and looked at Stella, who felt a piercing stab of dismay.

"God, Stella—you have to believe me, it was the worst moment of my life. What had woken me was the front door slamming, and the sound of feet running upstairs. When I turned to look towards the bedroom door, Will was just standing there with his hands by his sides. I'll never forget the look on his face, Stella. I might have expected anger, but it was a look of such despair that it broke my heart. I crawled across the bed to him. I was too weak to stand up, but he just turned and walked away."

Imogen put her head down on folded arms and sobbed softly. Stella was appalled, and her heart was nearly breaking at the thought of what this must have done to her son, who was so much in love with his wife. She recalled the overwhelming pain she had felt when the first of David's infidelities had come to light—it all came rushing back, and she felt her son's suffering as if it were her own. Why had he never told her? But she knew the answer. Shame. Her poor boy. She felt nothing but disgust for Imogen at that moment.

"Are you telling me, lady, that you got so outrageously drunk, you let this man—a stranger—into your bed? How could you, Imogen? How could you?"

"No. *No!* Stella, you have to believe me. I didn't. At first, I thought that's what must have happened, but although I could remember being a bit tipsy, I couldn't for a minute remember feeling drunk. One moment both Laura and I were just a bit giggly. Next moment, *wham!* I didn't remember a thing. When I eventually spoke to Laura, she said that she was the same, and that Hugo had put her to bed. She said he was ashamed of the pair of us."

Imogen stood up and went to grab a piece of kitchen roll to wipe her eyes and nose. The sobbing had stopped, but tears were streaming down her face. Stella was still sceptical, and was working hard to contain her anger.

"So what was Will doing there, Imogen? You obviously expected him to be away until the next day. Otherwise maybe you would have behaved a little better and not torn my son into pieces."

"Do you think that's what I wanted? Will said he took the flight to Dublin on Friday night, but when he arrived there was a message waiting for him to say the meeting had been cancelled and he was booked on the early-morning flight back. He had no luggage, so he was back here before eight. Later I asked him what reason the company had given, but he had never followed it up. Not top of his agenda, he said.

"Sebastian left immediately, and I never spoke to him again. Apparently Laura wasn't aware of his existence before that night, and she's told me that she never heard anything more about him. When she asked Hugo, he said he was too embarrassed to invite him again."

Imogen returned to her seat opposite Stella and wiped her face with the kitchen roll. A still-simmering Stella caught her gaze.

"I know what you must think," Imogen said. "But please let me finish before you judge me. After that night, Hugo told Laura that I was an appalling drunk who had broken her brother's heart. He said I'd disgraced him in front of Sebastian, although I don't see how I was in any way more culpable than his so-called friend, but he didn't want me in the house. Will, of course, would be welcome. He asked her to agree never to see me again.

"I had no idea what had happened, but I knew it wasn't right. I *love* Will. Anyway, about six months later, I was investigating whether all the hype about the Internet was relevant to our company, and I came across an article on the BBC website about something called Rohypnol. Nowadays everybody's heard of so called 'date rape drugs,' but then it was real news. It had been used in a few cases of rape in the US, but this was the first time in Britain. I became absolutely convinced that Rohypnol had been slipped into mine and Laura's drinks that night."

Stella had listened as requested, but she remained unconvinced. "Why would Hugo want to drug you and Laura? And where would he get hold of the stuff anyway?"

"Didn't I mention that Sebastian was American? It was easy to get hold of in the US because it wasn't illegal in Mexico, so I presume Sebastian brought it with him. Hugo must have agreed it with him in advance. The plan was to disgrace me, so that Laura could be banned from ever seeing me again."

"Well, I can't think why Hugo would want to do that, but we'll get to that later. How could anybody have known that Will would get back in time?"

"At first, I thought it was just the worst of bad luck. But it all seemed too well planned for me. So I phoned the company in Southern Ireland. They'd never heard of the man who had phoned Will. I phoned British Airways to try to find out who had paid for the tickets, but I got no joy there either. Hugo knew what this job opportunity meant to Will. The timing was all too perfect."

Stella was starting to believe that this could just hold a grain of truth, but it would make her dead son-in-law more evil than even she had believed. She grabbed a piece of toast from the plate and started to spread it liberally with jam. She made no attempt to eat it, though, and just pushed the plate away.

"I'm sorry, Imogen. It just seems too far-fetched. Why would he do that? And what did Laura think of this outlandish theory?"

"Laura was way too far under his spell, and she just wouldn't believe me about the Rohypnol. She told me not to call her again, and I was so upset that I didn't. I tried and tried to get Will to understand, but like you he was unconvinced. By this time, I'd realised what might have triggered this chain of events. A few days before we got the dinner invitation from Hugo, I was on the phone to Laura. She was crying; really sobbing. She said there was something that she desperately needed to talk to me about. I tried to get her to tell me what the problem was, but she said she couldn't say on the phone. I was all for going straight down to see her, but she begged me to wait until Hugo was away. He was due to go to Paris a few weeks later. Then she would tell me everything, but there were things she wanted to show me, too—so it had to be in Oxfordshire. Just as we were completing our plans, I heard Laura gasp. 'Shit! I've got to go,' she whispered. 'Oh please God, don't let him have heard!' and she hung up. The dinner party happened before we had a chance to meet, and we weren't left on our own for a minute after I arrived for that weekend."

Stella couldn't keep the doubt out of her voice. "So you think that Hugo heard you talking, and didn't like the fact that she was going to tell you something—or didn't like the fact that she had somebody close to talk to. You think that he engineered this whole elaborate event just to break up your friendship?"

"Yes Stella, I do—and it worked."

"And what does Laura think now?"

Neither of them had heard Laura enter the room, where she had been listening for the last couple of minutes.

"It's the truth, Mum. All of it. You have absolutely no idea what Hugo was capable of. This was the least of his crimes."

Becky stopped dead in her tracks in the hallway as she heard these words. Arriving just seconds before, Becky had found Mrs. Bennett on her hands and knees cleaning the front steps. Not wanting to make the poor lady get up, she had told her not to worry as she could make her way to the kitchen and see if anybody was out of bed yet.

The door from the hall to the back of the house was propped open with an old umbrella rack, and Laura had spoken from the open kitchen door, which swung closed behind her after she uttered the sentence which had so mesmerised Becky. Their voices were more muffled now, and hating to be an eavesdropper but remembering that primarily she was a police officer, Becky made her way towards the door. The voices were slightly raised, so it wasn't too difficult to make out the words. She recognised each of their voices from the previous day, and Stella was first to speak.

"I think you know, Laura, that I have never been comfortable with this marriage of yours. But you refused to tell me anything. Not a word against

Hugo in all these years. So now I want to know what the hell has been going on. What do you mean, this was the least of his crimes?"

"Let's not go into all this now, please, Mum. I know you never liked Hugo, and whilst I might play the devastated widow in front of the rest of the world, I'm not going to play that game in front of you."

Becky heard somebody start to say something.

"No, Imo, don't interrupt me. She's my mum and she needs to know that I am so very glad that Hugo is dead. We don't need to rake over the past, and I've no intention of doing it. But just let's get this over with."

The older voice of Stella came loud and clear through the door, and Becky realised that she must be facing this way.

"Is that all you've got to say? What were you going to tell Imogen that made Hugo do what he did? Did you *know* what he'd done? Why didn't you tell your brother? I don't know what to think."

"It doesn't matter what I was going to tell Imogen. It's all in the past, and I've no intention of repeating it. When Imogen phoned me and told me about the Rohypnol, I didn't want to believe her. I couldn't. What would that have told me about my husband? But I suspect he used it on me after that on several occasions. That, or other drugs. No, don't look like that. Not to rape me, but when he needed me to be compliant in other ways. It took me a long time to realise that Imogen was right. She knows how guilty I feel, but by then it was too late."

"So exactly how *does* Imogen know how you feel if you never saw or spoke to her after that day? You barely had time yesterday, and there were constant interruptions. What, precisely, am I missing here?"

There was a pause, and Becky was terrified of moving and giving herself away. Then Imogen answered the question. "I'm sorry, Stella. We've been lying to you. Laura and I have been in touch now for the last eighteen months or so, since just after Laura was packed away to that awful place for the second time. We didn't want anybody to know in case somebody slipped up and Hugo found out. We kept in touch over the Internet, which they allowed her to use in the home. They'd blocked all e-mail accounts, but somehow the whole concept of communication via social networking sites had passed them by."

Seeing that this had also passed Stella by, Imogen continued without further explanation.

"I was confident that there was actually nothing wrong with Laura, but she seemed to have given up. I wanted to give her back her fighting spirit. I wanted to restore the person that bastard had tried to destroy."

The words were spoken with such heartfelt venom that there was silence, complete and utter. Then Stella dropped her bombshell. "Imogen, I want you to answer me truthfully. Did you kill Hugo?"

After only the briefest of pauses, Imogen answered. "No, Stella. I can say with complete honesty that, much as I didn't think he deserved to live, I didn't kill him."

At that moment Becky sensed some movement behind her and glanced back into the hallway. Mrs. Bennett was walking towards her from the open front door. Thankfully the corridor that Becky was standing in was dark, but she knew she would be discovered in seconds. Starting to hum a little tune, she pushed open the door into the kitchen and feigned surprise that the room was full.

"Gosh, you're all up early. I hope you don't mind that Mrs. Bennett let me in. Did you all manage to get a reasonable night's sleep?"

Three pairs of eyes turned towards her as she bluffed her way through the first few seconds. They all looked slightly shocked, but she pretended she didn't notice. Mrs. Bennett was not far behind her.

"Good morning, Lady Fletcher, Mrs. Kennedy, and Mrs. Kennedy," Mrs. Bennett said. "Ah, Sergeant—I see you've not managed to get yourself a cup of tea yet. You sit down, and I'll see to it. Does anybody else want one whilst I make the breakfast?"

Becky saw Stella's puzzled frown. It clearly hadn't passed her by that since coming through the kitchen door, Becky had barely had time to walk to the kettle, let alone make herself a hot drink. She just hoped that she wouldn't have to explain herself.

After a cup of tea and yet more rounds of toast, as nobody could face anything else, all of it consumed in relative silence, people began to make excuses to leave the kitchen. Anything, Becky thought, rather than stay in this charged atmosphere. She felt sure that Stella hadn't finished questioning her daughter and daughter-in-law, but Imogen said she was going for a bath and Becky suspected that she'd make it as long as she possibly could. Close as they were, she didn't think Stella would follow Imogen into the bathroom.

An unhappy-looking Stella had returned to her cottage to get dressed. She had suggested that Laura join her, so they could have some time alone, but Laura had politely declined, saying that she needed a few minutes with Becky.

As the door closed behind Stella, Laura gave Becky a rueful smile. "Sorry, Becky, I don't really need any of your time. It's just that Mum is determined to extract every detail of my life from the last ten years. It isn't going to benefit the investigation in any way. All it does is satisfy her natural curiosity. I'd rather go and read the papers, if that's okay with you. I presume if you had anything to report, you'd have told me by now."

Becky watched Laura's retreating back with a puzzled expression. There was a layer of deceit and subterfuge here and she was struggling to understand Tom's "softly softly" approach with these women. He was firmly of the opinion that without hard evidence, tough questioning would just cause barriers to be erected and the truth might never be told. He liked to collect his little "nuggets" and store them until he could use them to maximum effect. But Becky wanted to be proactive, and as Tom was coming to Oxfordshire later, she decided that there was something that he might be able to bring with him.

She pulled her mobile phone from her bag and walked far enough away from the house to ensure she couldn't be heard.

"Tom, I've heard some interesting conversations this morning. There's quite a lot to report, but something occurred to me. We know that Imogen Kennedy flew in from Paris, and we've checked that she didn't also fly out from London the same day. But did anybody check the passenger lists for the Eurostar? It only takes a couple of hours or so. That might have given her time."

Becky was pleased to hear a note of respect in Tom's voice when he responded, but obviously he didn't believe that this idea had come out of thin air.

"What?" Becky said. "No, I've no specific reason to suspect her, and I've certainly not heard her admit to anything. In fact, quite the opposite. Stella asked her directly, and she flatly denied it. But I only heard the last part of the conversation, and I wondered what had been said before to make Stella believe that she might have done it. If you can get the printouts of the passenger lists, I'm more than happy to go through them all here. Let's face it, with them all doing a Greta Garbo on me, I've got nobody to talk to, so I could do with keeping myself occupied. I've got my laptop and my 3G card, so I can do a bit of additional research on times. And I want to look into Rohypnol and how easy it was to access at the end of the nineties."

She paused for a moment as Tom asked the inevitable question.

"I'll explain it all when I see you," she answered. "But you might also like to know that Imogen and Laura have secretly been in touch for eighteen months or so, and perhaps you should check up on that when you speak to Laura. She's tougher than you think, Tom."

She was weak. So very weak. And she was going out of her mind. Too much thinking time, that was the problem. She had begun to question her own understanding of reality, wondering if this was really happening to her or was it just some awful dream — a nightmare of such clarity that she felt sure she would wake up soon. Perhaps it would be one of those sudden awakenings; when the dreamer falls off a cliff and awakens to a dull thud somewhere around the heart. Perhaps the terror was building to such a crescendo that it would wake her. She hoped so.

But whether she was awake or asleep, she knew now how it must feel to be in solitary confinement. What did they call it? She'd read it somewhere. The Invisible Torture — that was it. Nobody can see the marks, but it drives people to madness.

She tried to think of strategies to keep herself sane. She saw a film once where somebody exercised every day in his prison cell. But she couldn't do that. She was too weak, and it might make her thirsty. That would be a disaster. She'd even tried to lick her tears, but wasn't sure whether they would still come if she had no water to drink.

And her mind kept wandering. She needed to focus, otherwise when he came for her — as she was sure he would do — he wouldn't want her anymore. And if he didn't want her, she didn't know what he would do with her.

So the best thing she could do was to think about good things. Remember the happy times in her life.

She searched her mind for a single day when it had felt good to be alive. There must have been one, surely? She'd had her share of dreams, though. Dreams of a life away from poverty; dreams of being a famous model; dreams of a life filled with love and laughter. And every dream she'd ever possessed had been shattered.

22

Imogen had locked herself in the bathroom and run a deep hot bath. She'd brought the letters with her, but she decided to soak for a while. She needed to brace herself, because reading them was so very painful.

Laura would be seeing the executors of the will later in the day, but to Imogen's relief she didn't seem at all concerned about the outcome. She was certain that Hugo wouldn't have been kind. He never was.

The signs had been there for Laura to see from the day she met him, but his clever manipulation and her eagerness to bend to his will had set the pattern for the future. Imogen could see that Laura blamed herself for lacking the strength and courage to recognise the web in which he was slowly ensnaring her. And it was almost unbearable to witness the depths of her shame.

She picked up the next letter and began to read.

JUNE 1999

My dear Imogen,

It's months since I wrote one of these stupid and pointless letters. Not since the last day of my honeymoon. The truth is, I've realised how ridiculous they are. But I have to pour my heart out to somebody, even if it's just a complete pretence.

My life now has changed. I don't work, and Hugo doesn't want me to help with the charity. I wanted to redecorate the house, although that's come to nothing either.

And now I no longer have you! I've lost my best friend, and I miss you desperately. You tried to call me yesterday, but I couldn't listen to your lies. They must be lies, surely? It's tearing me apart, Imo—my husband, or my best friend? Nobody should have to make that choice.

The last time I wrote to you we were about to return to England, where Hugo promised life—or at least sex—would be better. He seemed to think I needed to understand more about a man's desires in the bedroom. He seemed to think that he could find a way of giving me greater pleasure.

He was wrong. Oh God was he wrong. And I wanted to tell you. I was going to tell you!

Life isn't bad. We attend a lot of functions together, and Hugo is attentive towards me. He's still insisting that I buy new clothes for all the events, and he's still helping me perfect the way that I behave in the sort of circles that he moves in. I often get things wrong, though, particularly when I decide to go and choose an outfit for myself. Hugo doesn't ever get angry with me if I select something inappropriate. He just gives a slight frown when I appear dressed and ready to go out. Then I know he doesn't like it. When he approves he always does something wonderful. The other night I walked into the room, ready to go out, and he gave me one of his most glorious smiles and jumped up from the sofa to kiss my hand. He told me I would be the belle of the ball. Another night he disappeared and came back into the room with a box—and inside was a beautiful pair of emerald earrings. They're not mine to keep, because they're part of the family treasure and must be passed on—but it was so good of him to think of it.

But you know how self-opinionated I can be. I've decided more than once to ignore his obvious displeasure, and I've chosen to wear something he doesn't like. But it's not worth it. I can tell he disapproves, and he becomes so distant with me that I instantly regret it. He doesn't shout, and he doesn't say a single unpleasant word. He just speaks to me as little as possible, without appearing overtly rude, and it ruins my evening. It obviously ruins his too—so on the whole it's easier to just go with the flow. I'm beginning to dread these functions. I am almost guaranteed to do something wrong. I almost wish he would tell me what he's thinking. Then at least I would have an opportunity to put across my point of view. But you can't really fight silence.

We don't argue, which is surely a good thing? On a few occasions I've got a bit frustrated about something, and started to sound angry. But if I so much as raise my voice or sound irritated, Hugo just turns and walks out of the room. The first time it happened, he didn't speak to me for a couple of days. Eventually I had to ask him why. I suppose his response was predictable.

"I'm waiting for an apology, Laura. Your behaviour the other night was unacceptable. I will not be shouted at."

I responded with something like, "Oh for God's sake, Hugo. Don't be so bloody autocratic. I'm a person too, you know. I am entitled to my own opinion!"

He walked out again, packed a bag, and moved into Egerton Crescent until I couldn't bear it any longer. I phoned and apologised, of course. But I know that all marriages have their little spats, and we're still getting to know each other.

The greatest joy in my life is Alexa. I love the weekends when she comes to stay. She arrives on Friday and stays until Sunday. More during school holidays. She spends lots of time with me in the kitchen, and I give her little jobs to do. We have great fun making pizzas that she can decorate herself, or making hedgehog cakes that she can put the chocolate buttons on. We used to do that, do you remember? Of course, Alexa and I only cook when Hugo isn't at home. I don't think he would approve of Alexa eating pizza. Nor would he be happy to see her covered in chocolate!

I make every excuse that I can to get that awful nanny out of the house. I don't know how Annabel can stand having her around. I always feel as if she's watching me and reporting back. So I try to give her the day off or send her on as many errands as possible. I don't always succeed.

But I've avoided writing about the real issue. This is what I wanted to tell you about.

It all started when we'd been back home for about a week. I'd decided to make it my number-one priority to do something to lighten the ghastly atmosphere of this mausoleum of a house, so I sent off for samples of carpet, fabric swatches, and paint charts. My plan was to make up a few mood boards—lots of alternatives so that Hugo could have the choice. I'd started to work on a budget too—although eventually I realised that budget wasn't the issue. But more of that later. Anyway, I was keeping myself occupied during the day.

But the nights? We were still in separate bedrooms, and I didn't want to shatter the rather fragile peace by making any demands. Then one evening he said he had a "special surprise for me."

"Laura, as I mentioned on our honeymoon, I know that you've found sex within marriage difficult. I think you'll find tonight to be different." He smiled at me, and his eyes were glittering with suppressed excitement. "May I suggest that you go and have a shower. You'll see that I've laid a few items out on your bed for you. I would like you to put them on, and then come to me when you're ready. Will an hour be sufficient time?"

If this was Hugo's idea of making things more exciting, it certainly wasn't mine. I didn't want a timetable; I wanted spontaneity. And I didn't want sex, I wanted to make love. Voicing these opinions was obviously not an option.

I made my way rather despondently to my room. I had no idea what Hugo would want me to wear, and it was with a slight sense of relief that I found nothing more frightening than a set of underwear and a negligee.

The bra was pretty enough, in creamy-coloured silk with a slightly darker shade of fine lace stitched around the edges. But the set included a suspender belt and a pair of what can only be described as very large French knickers. Also made of fine silk, they came almost to my waist, and fell a good few inches over my thighs. Not my sort of thing, but I suppose I could see how they might turn somebody on. Dressing up, like stripping, isn't exactly a mortal sin. The thing that was depressing me was that it was all so cold and premeditated. But hey—it could have been worse—he could have wanted me to dress up in black latex, and that would have worried me.

When I was dressed, complete with pale cream stockings, I looked at myself in the mirror. I felt faintly ridiculous, and strangely very sad. I presumed he would want me to strip again, and that didn't fill me with delight—but if this is what it was going to take to get him to make love...

I slipped on the matching negligee and made my way with more than a little apprehension to the middle bedroom. I gave a rather hesitant knock on the door, not knowing quite what I was supposed to do. When I finally heard him summon me to the room, the sight that greeted me took me completely by surprise. He was lying full length on a huge four-poster bed and was totally naked, with the exception of a thin folded sheet which covered him from just below his navel to the top of his thighs. This was the first time that I'd been able to look at Hugo's body in any detail, as our previous encounters had taken place in total darkness, but tonight the room was brightly lit. I could tell that Hugo was already aroused (I feel oddly embarrassed mentioning that to you).

I walked towards the bed.

"Stop. Don't touch me. I'm not ready." Despite the bright lights, the pupils in Hugo's eyes were enormous, and his eyes seemed totally black.

He pointed to a small pile of what looked like silk scarves in several bright colours by the side of the bed.

"I want you to tie me up. My hands and legs to the bedposts. No—don't take your negligee off. I don't want to see you."

Why can't things just be normal! Okay, people do things like this. I know that. Is it just me? Maybe it is. I was too stunned by all of this to even ask why I'd had to wear these particular garments if he didn't want to see me. I know I keep saying it, but I'm not a prude. You know that. Far from it. It was clear from his next words, though, that somehow I'd been failing him.

"Tonight, Laura, I'm going to teach you how to please a man."

I didn't say anything. I just edged closer towards him and reached over for the scarves.

"Don't sit on the bed, don't touch me. I'll slip my hands and feet through the nooses that I've prepared, and then you tie me to the bed."

I still didn't speak. I couldn't. I just obeyed his instructions—like a zombie.

"Tighter, that's too slack. See—I can move. I mustn't be able to move. That's very important."

I tied them tighter. I was beginning to feel slightly nauseous.

Hugo closed his eyes, and I felt relief that I could no longer see into their black depths.

"Now, take off the negligee. Keep everything else on." He must have heard the swish as it dropped to the floor, because he immediately spoke again.

"Now, remove the sheet, and enjoy me!"

How could I possibly enjoy him? This wasn't something that we'd entered into together! It did nothing for me. This was a game devised to Hugo's rules, and I felt like a prostitute. Not a loving wife.

"What are you waiting for, Laura? I told you, remove the sheet and enjoy me! You must learn to take control. Just do it!"

I had so ached to see, touch, and feel his body next to mine. Perhaps I could still make this work, I thought. So I tentatively removed the sheet, and finally saw my husband completely naked for the first time. I couldn't believe that he could so obviously be feeling such intense excitement. What I wanted to do was kiss him and lick him all over, and then take him in my mouth to bring him to this peak of excitement. I wanted him to respond to me—but not like this.

I carefully knelt next to him on the bed and gently started to stroke his inner thigh. My mind was working overtime now, and my plan was to lean over and start to kiss him tenderly on his stomach, hand and mouth gradually getting closer and closer.

But it wasn't what Hugo wanted. Clearly.

"Stop! I didn't tell you to give me pleasure, I want you to take your pleasure from me."

It was pretty clear what he expected me to do. "Just go with it," I thought. "It might be better than you think."

It wasn't.

Slowly and carefully I moved myself until I was astride him. I thought once again that I might be able to seduce him into changing his mind, so instead of guiding him inside me, I leaned forward—the satin of the bra brushing his chest, and my pelvis rubbing against him. Hugo squirmed.

"Not like that. You have to learn that your pleasure is my pleasure."

"But Hugo, this is my pleasure—touching you, kissing you."

"Do it, Laura. Just do it!"

Maybe I should have just walked away. It's not easy to explain to you why I didn't. All I can say is that I'd been married less than three weeks, and more than anything in the world I wanted to make my marriage work. You don't just give up after such a short time, do you? By this time, I knew enough about Hugo to acknowledge to myself that things had to be played his way, or the repercussions would make life unbearable. I was going to have to change Hugo over time. I wasn't prepared for the consequences of arguing my point of view. So I did as he asked.

Thanks to the width of the legs of the knickers, I didn't even need to take them off, and I lowered myself onto him. I knew that any chance of an orgasm was completely out of the question for me, and I wasn't sure if Hugo expected one or not. But he kept his eyes resolutely closed, so faking wasn't a problem. God knows, I've had enough of the real thing in my time. The only question was how long was he expecting me to take. I decided to get it over with as quickly as possible; I could always excuse myself on the basis that I'd waited a long time for this. I won't go into the details of my performance—that's too much information—but it was pretty convincing. I didn't know what I was expected to do next.

"Bitch! Untie me, bitch!"

He couldn't possibly have known I was faking—I'd bet my life on it. I had no idea what was wrong, but I rushed around the bed, untying everything as quickly as possible—first his legs and then his hands. And then he opened his eyes. I had wanted to see desire in my husband's eyes, but this was just savage lust. He lunged for me, and I thought he was going to hit me. Perhaps that would have been better.

He grabbed my arm and flung me facedown on the bed. And then he took me in a way which I will never describe to you. All I will say is that it was brutal.

I cried. I couldn't help it. But either he didn't hear, or he didn't care. The only good thing was that he ejaculated in under a minute—which showed the extent of his excitement. And he never spoke another word. I stayed lying facedown on the bed, sobbing. But all I heard was the door as it closed behind him.

I don't know how long I stayed there. It could have been minutes, it could have been an hour. As soon as I could, I pulled myself together, grabbed the dressing gown and wrapped it tightly around me—almost for protection—and ran back to the safety of my own bedroom. I stripped off all the disgusting underwear and slashed it to pieces with a pair of scissors. And then I went and stood under the hottest shower I could bear. I stood there for a long time. But the hand marks where Hugo had squeezed my breasts from behind were still visible when I eventually dried my sore and aching body.

The next morning I decided that, come hell or high water, I had to have this out with him. I went down to breakfast, and he was reading the paper. Mrs. Bennett was buzzing around, but I asked her to leave us. When Hugo saw me, he gave me such a beam of pleasure. He stood up and held out my chair and then leant over me and gave me a kiss on the cheek.

"How are you this morning, my darling?"

"Hugo, I need to talk to you. About last night." My voice was trembling. I could hear it.

"Absolutely," he responded, still smiling. "But perhaps not at the breakfast table. We can talk later, if you like. There is, however, one thing that I have been meaning to say to you. I want to thank you for being so very good with Alexa. Life with her mother and I was difficult, but she was too young to understand. I am so delighted that as she grows up we will be able to offer her a stable home—at least for the days she's with us. She couldn't wish for a better stepmother."

And that was it. I was so thrilled that he thought I was good with Alexa, it seemed churlish to spoil the moment. So we never did have the conversation. The moment passed, and somehow that seemed to signal my acceptance of all that had happened. But now I never enter my bedroom without a deep sense of trepidation.

The fear of finding a gift from Hugo on the bed and all that it heralds fills my days with foreboding and my evenings with dread.

And I have nobody to tell. To find out what I should do. I don't have you anymore.

I won't give up on this marriage, though. I have to find a way to make things better—but I'm not ready to give up. Imagine what it would do to Alexa if it all fell apart.

The thing is, this is what I was going to ask you about. I phoned you. Not after the first few times, because I was so deeply ashamed, but after it had been carrying on in the same way for months, and things weren't getting any better. Hugo was so pleased with himself. I did try once more to raise the subject, but it appeared that he actually thought I was enjoying it! I tried to explain to him that I preferred more in the way of lovemaking, but he asked if I was criticising his performance, and of course, I couldn't say yes. I suggested that maybe I had things to learn, but could we try one or two alternative approaches. He simply folded his newspaper with a sigh and said something like, "Laura, you really do need to trust me on this. We're not teenagers, and you need to move on. You need to understand what adult sex is all about. I promise that you will appreciate this in time."

I bloody won't. But he's so plausible, which is why I wanted to talk to you. I waited until I thought Hugo was busy in his study, and then I called you from my bedroom. I know I was incoherent—it was just so difficult to talk about, even to you. I needed to see you, and I wanted to show you the underwear. For one awful moment, I thought Hugo had heard us talking. I was really very scared. But he can't have done. He wouldn't have invited you both to dinner if that had been the case, and he never mentioned it. We didn't get time to chat before dinner, but I thought the next morning we would grab an hour or so.

And then that awful thing happened with you and Sebastian. How could you do that, Imogen? And poor, poor Will. He is absolutely broken-hearted. I can't really blame Hugo for banishing you from the house. But it's a huge loss to me. And Will is completely beside himself with misery.

And now you've called to say you think Hugo drugged you. Imogen, you must be wrong! Why on earth would Hugo want to do that? He wouldn't have any reason to want to split you and Will up, would he? And he knew you were my best friend. I can't, and won't, believe that of my husband. That way lies madness.

Since that awful night I've been so lonely. The only thing left for me in all the lingering misery was planning the refurbishment of the house. I worked on the plans for ages, and then presented Hugo with about four different options. He barely glanced at them before telling me that this was his mother's house, and nothing could be changed.

But I wasn't prepared to give up. I decided that I would refurbish the house in Egerton Crescent as a surprise. My old company has now been sold—you probably don't know about that—and I've made a considerable amount on the shares. So I thought I'd spend some of it on a sort of present for Hugo. I would restyle the apartment, just to demonstrate what I could do. I waited until he was away. Everything was ordered and ready to go. Out with the heavy old furniture, in with something stylish and contemporary. The hideous green patterned carpet that ran throughout the apartment was ripped up, and a deep-pile apricot carpet replaced it. The walls were washed in a rich cream colour. It looked completely gorgeous, and I couldn't wait for Hugo to see it.

He didn't like it.

"Laura, I appreciate the thought and the sentiment. But I would have thought that over the last few months you would have come to understand that your taste is still in need of some development. Where is all the old furniture?"

I had to admit that I'd had it stored in some of the outbuildings in Oxfordshire. But the hideous carpet had been burnt.

With a sigh, Hugo instructed Jessica—who had witnessed this massive humiliation—to organise the return of all the new furniture to the shops, and to arrange for the old furniture to be brought back from Oxfordshire. The carpet could stay.

I feel so stupid, and I miss you.

Lxxxx

23

"Imo, you've been crying! I'm so sorry. I shouldn't have asked you to read them. I should have just told you everything."

Laura had gone in search of Imogen and had found her sitting on the side of her bed, wiping her eyes with a towel. She was ashamed that Imogen was having to sleep in this room, which was dark and gloomy—but it was the best spare room they had in this vast house.

"It's okay. I'm glad I've read them. Oh honey, I'm so sorry. It must have been awful for you. But you're such a strong person! I don't see how you could have allowed this to happen to you."

Laura gave a wry smile. "I don't know how to explain it. At the time, all I could think was that I wanted my marriage to work." She sat down on the dark green candlewick bedspread next to Imogen, and rested her head on her friend's shoulder. "You have to understand what it's like when you live with somebody who's controlling. They're clever. I don't know if they plan their every move, or whether it just comes naturally. In Hugo's case he never shouted, called me names, or hit me. If somebody locks you in a cellar for days without water, or gives you a regular black eye, you know without a shadow of a doubt that you are being abused. But when somebody appears to be considerate, never raises their voice, and appears to have your every interest in mind, how can that possibly be abuse?"

Imogen put her arm around Laura's shoulder and gave her a slight squeeze. "But you were so unhappy. Surely that didn't seem right?"

"I was unhappy—but it was hard to understand exactly *why*. Leaving aside his rather weird sexual preferences for the moment, there was nothing that I could put my finger on. I wish I could describe it to you—how it felt."

Laura paused and stared at a painting of the killing of a stag that hung on the wall next to the dressing table. Her mind wandered. Who on earth had thought it appropriate to put such a picture in a bedroom? It suited her current mood, though.

She dragged her mind back to Imogen's question. She had no words—just thoughts, images, and feelings. The hollow sensation she felt when she knew without him saying a word that Hugo was displeased, and the disproportionate joy she experienced when he smiled at her with some degree of affection. Actions and attitudes that would seem normal in most relationships took on a significance of monumental importance and flooded her with hope. But the master puppeteer knew just when her desperation point had been reached, and always rewarded her with nothing more than a kind word or a gentle kiss. And of course, over time these moments became rarer and therefore infinitely more precious.

"I can't describe how I felt, even to you. I realise I was stubborn to start with, but I was strong—or so I thought. I wasn't about to give in and admit that my idyllic marriage had failed in less than a year. Nobody gives in that easily. So I needed to give it time, and have patience. The trouble was that within those first few months I became weaker, and my self-belief was gradually eroded. Perhaps he *did* know better than me how people should behave. Perhaps I *was* overreacting to things that were perfectly normal, just because they weren't what I wanted. The problem was a lack of anything *tangible*. He always made it seem as if he was putting me first, but what he was actually doing was undermining my every thought. But I had nobody. I was no longer working, you and I weren't speaking, Will was away, and I couldn't bear to tell my mum. So I only saw myself through Hugo's eyes, and the person I saw was a failure."

Laura had never expressed these feelings out loud, and she felt a deep sense of shame. She could hear the branches of an overgrown tree scratching at the window, and the noise reminded her of the many nights she had lain awake, wondering what she was doing wrong. She had been conditioned by then to believe that every problem was a result of her own shortcomings.

"But what about the sex?" Imogen said. "I'm really sorry to raise it, but I've just read about your first night in that room. It sounds practically like rape to me!"

Laura lay back on the bed with her hands behind her head and fixed her gaze on the elaborate ceiling rose. She'd always found it easy to talk about sex—when it had been fun. Now it was incredibly difficult.

"I know. That was the one solid thing that I could hang the name 'abuse' on. But was it? It wasn't what I wanted, but was it wrong? So he liked to be tied up. Was that really strange, or was I being a prude? And he liked to be rough. But what I thought was brutal, he said was passion. I convinced myself that I had an idealised notion of romantic, earth-shattering sex. I did a lot of reading on the subject, and I was staggered to find how common bondage is, and how many people like to exert power and control during sex. I was ignorant enough to believe that all married couples make love and experience real intimacy and joy. When I discovered that I was far from alone in being dissatisfied with our lovemaking—if you could call it that—I made excuses. Perhaps that was the only way he had ever known, and I would have to help him to understand a more loving approach to sex. I constantly made allowances and fooled myself that I could change him. In a way, it was *because* of my strength and self-belief that I thought I could make things right. It's not a particularly unusual scenario for a woman, is it?"

"Did you never rebel—not even a little?"

"There was one occasion when we'd been married for a couple of years. Hugo was away, and I took the opportunity to go out to lunch with my old boss, Simon. Just that two-hour break gave me back a tiny fragment of my self-esteem. We were due to go to a charity event at the Dorchester on the night that Hugo returned, and I was meeting him there. I decided to show a bit of spirit—probably my last remaining morsel—by not wearing what he had chosen for me. I thought I was no longer the woman he'd fallen in love with. So I went shopping on my own, and I found the most glorious dress. It was a deep, deep blue, in the softest velvet you can imagine. It had a bodice top with no straps, hugged perfectly to my figure, and came just to the top of my hips. And I still had hips then. The skirt was the same fabric but cut straight to the floor, with a slit to the knee. I wore a plain silver band around my neck, and had my hair dyed back to its natural colour, getting rid of the red. It was just plain old brunette, but it looked stunning with the dress, and suddenly I felt like me again.

"I was due to meet Hugo there, so I made my way in a taxi and planned to arrive a couple of minutes late so that I could make an entrance. And I did. I wound my way through the tables to where Hugo was sitting with some of his high-flying charity people. All the men immediately stood up from the table, and even the women smiled at me. I knew I looked fabulous."

Laura could remember looking for admiration in Hugo's eyes, and when it wasn't there she suddenly felt anxious. She had been so sure that he would fall in love with her all over again.

"As was always the case at these events, Hugo and I weren't sitting next to each other, but he got up immediately and came round to pull my chair out. As I sat down, he lent down to whisper in my ear. Everybody at the table thought he was whispering some compliment, because they all smiled. What he actually said was, 'You look like a fucking whore.' It was the only time I ever heard Hugo swear. I had to sit through the whole of the meal, smiling and being polite, whilst inside I felt like I was dying."

Imogen was staring at Laura in dismay. "Why, oh why didn't you tell anybody?"

"Because by then I was so ashamed, so embarrassed, and I didn't know what I had done wrong. That was the night that I passed the point of escape. I sincerely believed that everything was my fault. I apologised to Hugo for my poor judgement. He forgave me, and I settled down to being a good wife and a stepmother to Alexa, although that part was no hardship at all. But I never dyed my hair red again, and I never tried to look sexy or attractive again. I cultivated the look of a woman who no longer cared. That way, perhaps he would leave me alone."

Laura got up from the bed and walked towards the window. She could no longer bear to look at the pity in Imogen's eyes.

And she omitted to tell Imogen that from that day onwards there was a new addition to the gifts on the bed, one that she found even more alarming.

24

Tom's attempts to get back to Oxfordshire were thwarted by a seemingly endless stream of issues, any of which could have provided a breakthrough.

The artist's impression of the woman seen leaving Hugo Fletcher's house had appeared in several newspapers, and they'd already had a number of calls. The one that seemed the most likely was from somebody who saw a woman matching the description walking from the direction of Egerton Crescent. She was heading into South Kensington underground station. Unfortunately from there she could have taken the Piccadilly, District, or Circle lines, and in either direction. But the timing was right, so now they were in the process of matching this with other sightings and CCTV footage to see if they could get an idea of where she was going. Of course, she could have changed tubes several times, but you never knew your luck.

A couple of members of the team were going over every detail of Hugo's charity, and Tom was anxious to get their report. They were missing something. He just knew it. In the meantime, Ajay had been tasked with tracking down the missing girl, Danika Bojin, and he had only just given Tom the good news that he'd got the address of Danika's friend, Mirela Tinescy, when this information was rendered superfluous. He remembered that Ajay had spoken to Peter Gregson, the man who had left the message on Laura's answer phone. Now it appeared that Mr. Gregson had turned up unexpectedly and was waiting in reception, asking to speak to a senior officer.

Tom asked Ajay to go and escort Gregson to an interview room and organise a drink for him. He would join them in a few minutes. He still hadn't had a chance to talk to Laura about Danika's visit, or to check whether the original missing girl, Alina Cozma, had ever turned up. For now, though, he needed to find out what Mr. Gregson had to say. Danika had to be high on the list of suspects.

He opened the door to the interview room and was surprised to see that Peter Gregson was not alone. With him was a young girl, so slight in build that she looked no more than about fourteen years old. Gregson stood up to shake Tom's hand.

"DCI Douglas. I'm sorry to barge in on you like this, but as you can see, Danika has returned home, and I think you might want to hear what she has to say."

Tom was more than a little surprised to hear that the girl with Peter Gregson was Danika Bojin, who he knew to be nearly nineteen.

"I'm glad to see you're safe, Danika," Tom said. "You had us a bit worried there."

"Perhaps it's best if I just give you a bit of background," Peter Gregson said. "When I talked to your colleagues the other day, I explained Sir Hugo's rather extreme rule that the girls couldn't stay in touch with each other. Did he pass that on to you?"

Tom nodded.

"Well, Danika broke that rule. That was how she and Mirela Tinescy realised that Alina Cozma was missing—because she hadn't turned up for their regular meetings. Sir Hugo was furious when he found out that they'd been in contact, and despite the fact that they never found out what had happened to Alina, Danika promised that she wouldn't disobey him again. And she hasn't, until now. Unfortunately, she recently discovered that *Mirela* has now gone missing, too. It's probably best if she explains."

Tom felt a pulse of adrenaline as Danika took up the story.

As promised, she and Mirela hadn't been in touch; she believed she owed her life to Sir Hugo, and so however painful it was, she knew she must abide by his rules. But now, everything had changed.

"Last Thursday, I went to the park and I hear a girl who speak Romanian to a little boy. I talk with her, and she say she is Allium girl. She lives with a nice family—but only because the last Allium girl has left to go back to be a working girl. She say—in Romanian, of course—'Thanks, Mirela, you lose, I win.' I ask her more questions, of course, and it is *my* Mirela. I know this. She tells me that Mirela goes about eight weeks ago. She leave a note. She say she has big chance to be high-class girl and make much money. It was bad of me to go and look for her without telling to Peter, but if he knows what I plan, he would stop me. When I come back today, Peter say we must come here to tell to you."

Tom looked with sympathy at this girl who was clearly worried about her friend.

"Why did you try to find her, Danika?"

"Because I do not believe that Mirela would do this thing. She was—how do you say it—sicked? Yes, sicked by her life as prostitute."

Nobody corrected her English, as the meaning was perfectly clear.

"She cried always and say that the men hurt her. She never want to do it again, she said. Only for husband or a kind man who take good care of her, and give her love. I don't believe she goes back to work in this way. So I go to try to find her. I had to try, Peter. Do you see?"

Danika turned her distraught face towards Peter, obviously very concerned that she had broken his trust again.

Tom spoke gently to the girl, who after all only had her friend's interests at heart.

"Where did you go, Danika? How did you try to find her?"

"I try first to find Sir Hugo. I cannot go to office, because the girl there is not nice to me when I go last time. I wait for him to come, but I never see him, so I try something else. I try to find out how to get job as high-class prostitute, like Mirela says. I don't think I'm ugly. The men always say they like my body, and I speak some English. Not so good, but okay."

Tom unfortunately knew that for some men her slight and childish body would hold great appeal.

"Well, they tell me no. Not *ever* can I be the high class. They say that everybody knows we are dirty, and nobody will touch us. They cannot get top money for Eastern Europeans."

"Why would they say you are dirty, Danika?"

Danika looked down and blushed. "The men were allowed to go with us without protection. They say they like it better. We don't want this, but we have no choice. But I have had all the tests. Peter has arranged this for me. I am not dirty, really I'm not."

Tom felt a deep sense of shame that men—possibly even men that he knew—would treat such a sweet young girl so abysmally. He couldn't help feeling some disappointment, too. Until he met her, she had been top of his very short list of suspects. Hugo dies, girl goes missing. It had seemed to be too much of a coincidence.

"I'm quite sure you're not dirty, Danika. But does that mean that you couldn't find any trace of Mirela?"

"No. I even try where we used to be—but I was very frightened that I was caught again. My nice clothes that Grace bought for me were good, though. Nobody knew I was prostitute before."

Tom assumed that Grace was Peter Gregson's wife. At least something good had happened in this girl's young life. But if they assumed that the woman seem leaving Hugo's London house was the murderer, there was no way that it could have been Danika. Even with lots of makeup she would never look like a woman. She had the stick thin arms of a child, and didn't look as if she would weigh much more than five-year-old Lucy.

In the end he left her to be interviewed by some of his colleagues. Danika might not fit the bill, but clearly this other girl, Mirela, might.

For now, he needed to get back to Oxfordshire. There were an increasing number of questions that he had to ask Laura. And he understood that Brian Smedley, Hugo's CFO for the property company and one of the Hugo's executors, was due at Ashbury Park. Tom was keen to know the detail of the will, and he wanted to be around to assess Laura's reaction to Hugo's last wishes.

It was around two thirty when he finally pulled his car up in the darkly shadowed forecourt of Ashbury Park and mounted the steps to the imposing front door. Becky was expecting him as he had phoned en route, and she opened the door before he had time to ring the bell.

"Did you bring me those passenger lists? I'm getting bored out of my brains here."

"'Hi, Tom, nice to see you too,'" he mocked. "Yes, I do have the lists, and given the number of passengers within the relevant period, you'll soon be even more bored. Has anything happened round here?"

"Nothing since this morning. We did all have lunch together, but Stella did most of the talking. Imogen looked as if she'd been crying, actually. Nobody will talk to me. They're either locked in their rooms, or they're hunting in pairs, if you know what I mean. Lots of meaningful glances—but nothing I can get a handle on. What about you?"

Tom filled her in with what had been going on back at headquarters, all the time thinking that it didn't actually add up to much.

"Do you think Danika had anything to do with it?" Becky asked.

"I'm sure she didn't, but Mirela Tinescy is missing—and she might. I think we're going to have to interview them all—at least the ones that Hugo's helped in the last twelve months. *And* all the charity staff, to see if they know of anybody who might have a grudge. All the girls apparently swear to love Hugo, but they've had a rough time, and it's just possible that one of them might have been tempted by a big payout. I've got a team setting up all the interviews, and we need to find out what we can about Mirela Tinescy. Ajay is onto that."

"Would old Hugo sleep with one of his prostitutes, do you think?"

"Well, lots of men do—although personally I've never seen it as one of my goals in life. Maybe Hugo thought of it as a perk of the job."

"Tom—that's disgusting and despicable. I can't believe you're that cynical."

He looked at Becky's snub nose, wrinkled in displeasure. If she knew what he did about Hugo's penchant for deviant behaviour, he reflected, she would think that sleeping with the charity's prostitutes was practically normal. The events of the previous evening with Kate had temporarily driven the conversation with Annabel from his mind, but now it came flooding back, and it had to be significant.

Becky showed Tom into the dining room, where she had set up a temporary office with permission from Laura. The room was papered with flock wallpaper in shades of mud, as far as Tom could make out, and one wall was practically covered by a huge, faded tapestry, which he imagined would possibly be quite beautiful with a bit of attention paid to it. Down the centre of the room ran the biggest dining table Tom had ever seen, which must have easily seated thirty people. There was no other furniture in the room, just a vast stone fireplace and heavy velvet curtains. Another welcoming room then.

"Bloody hell, Becky. Couldn't you have found somewhere a little bit more cheerful? And why have you chosen to sit at the far end of the table? It's a two-mile hike to the door."

"Precisely. It means that whatever's on my screen, I have ample opportunity to cover it up before they reach me. I don't trust them, Tom. I *like* them—but even if they're innocent of Hugo's murder, they're hiding something. Especially Imogen. She knows a lot more than she's letting on. I can see it in her eyes."

She was right, of course, and Tom knew it. Becky had a look of a bulldog about her today, her pretty face showing determination and eagerness. He knew what she thought—he was playing it too slowly. But they had nothing to go on, and certainly nothing concrete that implicated either Laura or Imogen. It wasn't even a case of circumstantial evidence. There was no evidence at all.

"I can't make any sense of it, to be honest," he said. "I need to get under their skin some more. It's absolutely freezing in here. Is there no heating on?"

Tom had taken his jacket off to drive, and he quickly shrugged his arms back into the sleeves. He wasn't much of a suit man, but it went with the territory and just now he needed whatever warmth it would offer.

"You'll get used to it. I thought you northerners were made of stronger stuff," Becky grinned. "Anyway, whilst I've been sitting here going out of my tiny mind, I did some research on Rohypnol. Being the youngster that I am, I assumed it had been around forever, but the first trace of it that I can find on the Internet is in 1999. It had apparently been available for a lot longer as a prescription drug, but that's when it was first identified as a date rape drug. The serial rapist, Richard Baker, was the first recorded user in this country. He was caught following a Crime Watch appeal. Anyway, it's the brand name of flunitrazepam and it's ten times more potent than Valium. Commonly known as a roofie, of course. According to the Internet—and I'd better read this bit—it's a 'highly-potent hypnotic drug with powerful sedative, anxiolytic'—whatever that is—'amnestic, and skeletal muscle relaxant properties.' Laura said that she thought he'd used it on her as well, but not for rape purposes. You've got to follow that up, Tom."

"I will, when I think she'll tell me the truth. She's very good at evading questions, and bombarding her just won't work."

Becky gave him a fierce look. He knew she was impatient, but she wanted to attack this like she attacked a queue of traffic: without restraint and not afraid to piss a few people off along the way. He was certain this was pointless with Laura. She would not be bamboozled. He had to win her trust.

"You'd better tell me exactly what you heard this morning," Tom said. "Let's try and get something solid to ask them about."

Becky grabbed her notebook from the end of the table and sat down. "I wrote it down afterwards—word for word as far as possible. You should have heard them, though—you could have cut the atmosphere with a knife." Becky leaned eagerly over her scribbled notes and recounted the bits of the conversation she'd heard. "Tom—the words alone don't do it. You had to hear Laura's tone of voice. It was so cold. It was absolutely clear to me that she hated Hugo. Almost as much as Imogen did."

All talk of drugs and hatred came abruptly to an end as the front door bell rang, heralding the arrival of Brian Smedley and a lawyer. Becky took her lists off to her makeshift desk at the far end of the table, and Tom made his way into the hall where Laura was greeting the arriving guests. He couldn't help but notice that Laura was looking better by the day. She was wearing a pair of black jeans and a scoop-necked raspberry-red jumper, and the cheerful colour stood out like a beacon against the dirty beige walls of the hall.

She turned towards him and seemed startled to see him standing there.

"Tom? I'm so sorry. I didn't realise that you'd arrived. Have you been offered a cup of tea or coffee?"

One thing that this house didn't seem to lack was an almost constant supply of hot beverages, but Tom expected that this was fairly normal in homes that had been ripped apart by tragedy. If nothing else, it gave people something to do.

"I'm sorry, Laura. I should have let you know I was here. Becky let me in and I didn't want to disturb you. Do you mind if I sit in and listen to the terms of the will? It might be useful in our investigation."

Tom looked keenly at Laura. She had left her hair loose and wavy again. He could see the beginnings of dark roots and wondered why anybody would dye their hair to be a shade of mouse. She had slightly more colour in her cheeks, too, and her personal confidence seemed to be growing. But she did seem on edge. No doubt she was wondering what surprises Hugo had in store in his will. Given everything he'd heard over the last few hours, he didn't blame her.

Apparently unaware of Tom's scrutiny, Laura led the way into the drawing room, asking Mrs. Bennett to prepare tea for everybody and offering a glass of something stronger to anybody that wanted it. Only the lawyer took up her offer, and Tom noticed that he looked like he needed it.

When they were all finally seated and their drinks had arrived, Brian coughed rather nervously. As executor he had drawn the short straw and had to deliver the news. Laura gave a halfhearted smile.

"It's okay, Brian. I knew Hugo very well, and anything that he's put in the will is unlikely to surprise me. Just give me an outline, that's all I need."

"Thank you, Laura," Brian responded. "As you know, Hugo was an immensely wealthy man, but had the foresight to put the vast majority of his wealth into various trusts. The trusts paid him round about a million a year for his living expenses, although of course a substantial proportion of that went in tax. But as Ashbury Park is owned by a trust, it pays all the expenses incurred in the maintenance and services for this house and the property in Egerton Crescent, so the remainder was really just for your general living expenses."

Tom couldn't help but wonder how they had managed to get through hundreds of thousands of pounds each year, especially as they had no bills to pay. From the look on Laura's face, she clearly had a similar view.

"And was that money spent each year, or was some of it saved?"

"Your living expenses ran to about thirty thousand pounds a month. Clothes, food, travel, maintaining the house in Italy. And of course, Sir Hugo withdrew twenty thousand each month in cash."

"*Twenty* thousand pounds a month in cash? Are you sure it was *twenty*?"

Tom glanced questioningly at Laura, but she was looking at the two men with a puzzled frown.

"What about maintenance for Alexa and Annabel?" Laura asked. "Was that part of it?"

"No. When Hugo divorced Annabel, he separated up some of the trusts so that one could support Alexa for the rest of her life, and one Annabel."

Laura still wore a baffled look, but remained silent.

"Now, getting back to the will, he has made some provision for you, although the terms are a little complex. Basically, you will be permitted to live here until Alexa is twenty-one, at which point she becomes the legal resident of Ashbury Park. If you remain here until that time, the property in Italy will become yours—it's currently in Hugo's name and is being transferred to the company until that date. At that point, you can either sell it to buy yourself a home in England, or go and live there. If you decide to move from this house before Alexa is twenty-one, you forfeit the house in Italy, and you will be forbidden any further contact with Alexa. Should that happen, Annabel must strictly adhere to Hugo's wishes in this regard. If she doesn't, she will forfeit a considerable portion of her inheritance, too. From what I know of Hugo's ex-wife, I imagine she will be rigorous in her compliance to these terms. In the meantime, you must spend at least ten months of the year in this house, and ensure that it is suitable for Alexa to move into when the time is right."

Tom was watching Laura's expression closely. He had deliberately chosen a seat to one side that allowed him to check her reactions without her noticing. But apart from her response to the monthly cash withdrawals, the stringent terms of the will seemed to neither surprise nor upset her. This was not the thoughtful will of a loving husband, and that had to be evident to everybody in the room.

"The trust will pay all bills for the house, and you will receive an additional allowance of fifty thousand pounds a year for your living expenses, rising with inflation, provided that you adhere to the terms mentioned previously. Should you vacate the house prior to the date of Alexa's twenty-first birthday, you will also lose your annual income. The terms of the trust are specific. The annual income can only be spent on food, clothes, and occasional travel. With the trustees' permission, you may also have additional ad hoc sums of money paid for specific items, for example a new car should that be necessary."

"Is there money available for any redecoration of the property, or work on the gardens?" Laura asked, as she no doubt contemplated the idea of living in this mausoleum for the next ten years.

"The trust will take care of that, and has specific instructions that any work undertaken has to be to repair and renew to the exact standards and style in place today."

Laura looked horrified at the prospect, and Tom couldn't blame her. To make this house into a twenty-first-century home, it needed some serious refurbishment.

"Is there anything that prevents me from spending my *own* money on changing how the house looks?" she leaned forward eagerly

Brian Smedley looked even more uncomfortable. "I'm not sure that you understand, Laura. The only money you have is the annual sum that the trust pays, and that can only be spent on items that Hugo has specified."

"But what if I had my own money, Brian? Money that I had before I married Hugo?"

An expression of hope was lighting her face and transforming it from the controlled mask that Tom was sure she had been cultivating since the postmortem. She looked quite lovely, he couldn't help thinking.

Brian looked at the lawyer, who hadn't actually said anything other than to request a small whisky when he arrived.

"Was Sir Hugo aware of this money, Lady Fletcher?" he asked.

"I told him when I sold my shares in the company I used to work for. But he wasn't interested in the amount because to him it was insignificant. I've never mentioned it since, and I've been investing it. With precious little else to do, I became quite interested in buying and selling shares, and so I certainly have enough money to redecorate the house, several times over actually. Would that be allowed?"

The lawyer checked his notes.

"It's a long and complex will, Lady Fletcher. I will check it in every detail, and the terms of the trust that owns the house. It certainly wasn't Sir Hugo's intention that anything be changed, I am sure of that. But he clearly had no idea, or had simply forgotten, that you had money of your own. I should also mention that any remarriage or cohabitation has exactly the same terms—you leave the house, forfeit the property in Italy, and will be forbidden any future contact with Alexa."

Hugo's innate cruelty must have been as obvious to everybody in the room as it was to Tom. He felt deep sympathy for Laura, but he saw she was smiling wryly. The lawyer hadn't finished.

"Do you think you'll comply with his wishes, Lady Fletcher?"

"I have no choice," she answered.

"I think Sir Hugo thought the house in Italy would see to that."

"Well, it's a pity he's not here, then," she said, leaning back in her chair. "Because it would have given me great delight to tell him that it's got nothing to do with the house. That's not why I'm staying. I'm staying for Alexa."

Tom was amazed at her composure, and he couldn't help thinking what a bastard this Hugo had turned out to be; not at all the public persona that the world had loved and respected. Laura's mask was now back in place as she listened to the remainder of the terms.

Having met Annabel, Tom could understand Laura's desire to protect Alexa. But to dictate that she should neither marry nor cohabit with a man for at least a further ten years, by which time she would be almost beyond childbearing age herself, was cruel in the extreme.

The lawyer was beginning to talk about other aspects of the will. He plainly wanted to gloss over some of the lesser bequests, and as Laura didn't press him, he sighed with relief and moved on to the terms that related to Annabel. But it was clear to Tom that there was something there that the lawyer was finding embarrassing. He needed to see a copy of that will. Maybe somebody else was benefiting, but if Laura had still been a suspect, she certainly wouldn't have killed him for his money.

Annabel was definitely not going to be happy either. In order to receive her very generous maintenance she had to agree that Alexa could stay with Laura at Ashbury Park for at least three months of every year, which could include weekends and school holidays, as agreed jointly between the two women. As she was a weekly boarder at an Oxfordshire school, this effectively meant that Alexa would spend practically no time at all with her mother. Tom had the uncomfortable feeling that Annabel wouldn't give a toss about that, as long as the money was there.

It was also determined that if the terms of the will were acceded to, the home in Portugal would become Annabel's when Alexa reached twenty-one.

It was the final section of the will that Tom found the most interesting, though. Hugo Fletcher had visited his solicitor on the day before he died and added a codicil. He had insisted that he remain at the solicitor's office until the codicil had been prepared and signed. It stated that Annabel would lose everything if she were responsible for any defamatory remarks about Hugo or his family that were made public in any media, either now or in the future.

Tom breathed a sigh of relief. Yesterday Annabel had confided a level of detail about Hugo that could certainly be considered defamatory. Fortunately he had only shared this with the DCS. He trusted his team, but it had such potential for attracting a hefty fee from the gutter press that Annabel's inheritance would more than likely have disappeared in a puff of smoke.

The lawyer and Brian Smedley left shortly after, and despite Tom's original intention to go with them to assess Annabel's reaction, he decided that it was something of a foregone conclusion and asked Becky to go instead. He hadn't had time to talk to Laura, and there were an increasing number of baffling conundrums that he needed to solve.

Laura had shown the two lawyers out, and by the time she returned to the drawing room Tom had convinced himself that she would be seriously rattled by everything she had heard. If she had been under any illusions about Hugo's feelings towards her, they had just been publicly dashed, and he was concerned for her. But it was also his job to delve under the surface and discover every secret that this family was hiding. The more he understood about the turbulent emotions of the people around Hugo, the greater his chance of understanding the man. And as a result, he hoped, the greater his chance of finding Hugo's killer. A sympathetic ear at this emotionally charged time might just break down a few of Laura's defences.

"Are you okay, Laura? It's probably not my place to say so, but that was very harsh."

He was surprised to see a genuine smile on her face as she took a seat facing him. She seemed almost amused, which was beyond his comprehension.

"Thanks for the concern, Tom, but it's fine. He really thought of everything, didn't he? There's no way that I can leave Alexa to the mercy of Annabel's indifference, you know. The poor child has enough to cope with.

"But he made one mistake," she added, with a wicked glint in her eye. "I'm just going to wait to check with the trustees, then I'm going to rip this place apart, and it's going to give me enormous pleasure. I've had years to think about what I would do. I know I'm using my own money for something that won't ultimately be mine, but I can't carry on living here for another ten years like this. Alexa deserves better than that, and there'll be plenty left for when I'm homeless."

She really didn't mind, Tom thought in amazement. But it wasn't just the virtual house arrest that was cruel.

"What about the not getting married, or cohabiting? That's a bit fierce, isn't it?"

Laura laughed and appeared to speak from the heart. "No, thank you. Never again. That's not a punishment as far as I'm concerned."

"But you clearly love Alexa. Didn't you want children of your own?"

Tom was sorry that he had broken the atmosphere, as Laura's face fell.

"Yes, I would have loved my own children. But it wasn't an option."

At that moment, Tom's mobile rang and he cursed. This was the closest he had been to seeing the real Laura. But when he saw that the caller was Kate, he knew he would have to take it. He excused himself, stood up, and walked towards the window with his back to Laura. He spoke for a minute or two, keeping his voice low, and then hung up.

"Sorry about that. It wasn't the best time to be interrupted, but that was one I had to take."

The mood was broken, and Tom was frustrated. Kate's timing had always been impeccable! Laura was looking at him enquiringly, clearly wondering if it was news about the case but perhaps not knowing whether protocol allowed her to ask.

"It was just a personal issue that I need to resolve. No great leaps forward in finding your husband's murderer, I'm afraid."

Laura looked curiously relieved. Perhaps it was good for her to know that she wasn't the only one with problems.

"Well, my husband's feelings for me have just been exposed for the world to see, so if there's anything I can do to help, just fire away. It might take my mind off the horrendous mess that my life seems to have become."

As Tom sat down again, it hit him with sudden force that he was lonely. He had never really considered it before. He never minded being alone, but since he'd moved to London he had nobody to share anything other than an occasional pint or a game of squash with. He worked long hours, saw Lucy as much as possible, and spent the rest of his time in his extravagant but soulless apartment. His real friends were two hundred miles away, but in the last two years he had lost a wife and his best friend of all—his brother.

Now Laura was looking at him with genuine interest, and he realised that most people he spoke to nowadays wore nothing more than expressions of polite indifference. He couldn't ignore her offer of support completely, and he found that he didn't want to.

"It was my ex-wife, Kate. We're divorced. It was a pretty bleak time for me, because when she left, she took our daughter with her. But now it would seem that all is not well in her new relationship, and she's decided she wants me back," Tom said, keeping the facts to a bare minimum and gazing at the fire as if the solution to his problems lay in the flames.

"Do you still love her?" Laura's softly voiced question betrayed an emotion that Tom couldn't place. He turned his head towards her and noted a slight narrowing of the eyes. Not sure what this meant, he answered her question.

"No. I did for a long time, but that's not why she wants us to get back together. Kate loves money—well, spending it anyway. It's ironic, really, having just sat through the reading of Hugo's will and seeing how you reacted. Kate would by now have been screaming about the injustice of it all."

"I've long since learned not to scream at Hugo's injustices. I would probably have worn out my vocal chords by now." She smiled to take the edge off her words. "So as far as Kate's concerned, you're the man with the money now, are you?"

"Yes, but not through my own efforts. A chief inspector doesn't do badly, but I was left a lot of money by my brother—in his will," he said with difficulty.

Laura seemed genuinely distressed by this news. "I'm so sorry. I don't see much of my brother but I would be devastated if anything happened to him. How did he die, if you don't mind me asking."

Tom paused. Even after all these months he still found it difficult to talk about. "He was smart, my brother, but not in any traditional way. He had no interest in going to university, and from the age of about fourteen he was always fiddling with electronics in his bedroom. I was the sensible and studious one. His first computer was a little thing called a ZX Spectrum—which I'm sure you've never heard of—but despite its limitations he could make that computer do the most amazing things. By the time he was eighteen, he was being paid to write programmes for all sorts of people, and by the age of twenty-five he had made his first million. He built up a multimillion-pound Internet security business, and sold it a few months before he died."

Tom paused and looked at Laura, to see if this was all too much. But she was leaning forward with her elbows on her knees, her chin resting on clasped hands, and she appeared to be truly interested.

"He went on an atypical spending spree, and amongst other things indulged himself in the fastest speedboat he could buy. And that was it. There was an accident, a real freak according to the boat manufacturers, and he died. His body was never recovered."

He spoke in a matter-of-fact voice, trying to disguise his emotion, but he guessed that Laura wouldn't be fooled. He gave himself a moment, and Laura kept a respectful silence.

"So now that I'm loaded, Kate wants to come back. If I don't agree, she's threatening to take Lucy back to Manchester. I only moved here to be close to them, and now I'm being held to ransom again. So there's the rub. Do I give in for Lucy's sake?" He looked at Laura. "You seem happy to make the ultimate sacrifice for a child that isn't even your own—so surely I should be able to live with Kate for the sake of my daughter?"

Tom watched Laura carefully to gauge her reaction. She paused for a moment before speaking.

"You know, I'm really the last person to give advice on relationships. But I do remember growing up as a child in a household where I loved both parents. The problem was, the parents didn't really love each other. Oh, they tried. And they certainly weren't nasty to each other, although there were a few cracking arguments. But the love just wasn't there. Will and I had a stable life, but I think that I would sum it up as a house that was devoid of joy. I think children need that joy in their lives. If they exist in a world where they are forever watching their parents tiptoeing around each other—even if they're not arguing—it gives them a false set of values. In retrospect, I would rather have been with one parent who was genuinely happy than with two who had so many axes to grind you could almost hear them being sharpened."

Tom thought that this was very perceptive. Having been brought up in a happy working-class home with two parents who worked hard but made each other laugh more often than they made each other cry, this had been the sort of relationship that he craved.

But this conversation had gone on long enough. He didn't have time to dwell on his own issues. Bloody Kate. He thought the days of her intruding in his thoughts had long gone. A fat lot of detecting he'd done in the last five minutes. He pulled himself together.

"I'm sorry—we're not here to talk about me. I apologise, Laura. I really shouldn't have let my personal problems intrude."

Laura was sorry that the moment had gone. Listening to Tom had reminded her that other people had problems, too, although perhaps not of the same magnitude. She had felt a brief pang of envy when he first started to talk about his ex-wife, imagining how it would be to be married to this slightly gruff but undoubtedly sensitive man. But now he was back to being a policeman and she needed to focus.

He said, "There are a number of things that I need to talk to you about, but after the news of the will I'm not sure if you're up to it. How do you feel?"

"I'm absolutely fine. Ask away." Laura knew that she needed to give herself a moment to stop being a sympathetic friend, and return to the role of the bereaved wife. "I'm just going to open a bottle of wine, which I think I deserve—presuming of course that his lordship has decreed that I'm still allowed to drink wine. Would you like some?"

"I shouldn't, but I don't think a small glass would hurt. It sounds like a great idea. Thanks."

Laura left Tom leafing through his notebook. The questions were inevitable, and she was sure Tom didn't understand her indifference to Hugo's will. How could she explain that she had known that he wouldn't have been kind to her without making herself seem even more feeble in Tom's eyes?

She returned to the drawing room with a bottle of wine and a couple of glasses, and poured the drinks, leaving Tom to his notebook. She handed him a glass and proposed a brief if somewhat ironic toast to Hugo. She didn't miss the fact that Tom barely took a sip, and she felt a twinge of guilt.

"Sorry," she said. "I forgot that you're on duty. That was thoughtless of me."

Tom gave her a good-natured smile. "Don't worry about it. I could hardly let you drink alone, could I?"

By silent but mutual consent they sat down again, and Laura braced herself for the questions, reminding herself that, considerate as he was, Tom Douglas was still a policeman.

"What can you tell me about Hugo's family?" he began. "We know his mother died in the year before you were married, but what do you know about them as a family?"

What a strange question. What bearing can Tom believe this has on Hugo's murder? Laura thought. She answered as simply as possible.

"Not a lot, really. This house is full of portraits of long-forgotten ancestors, but I never knew much about his parents. He was very close to his mother. That I *do* know, but he would never show me any pictures of her. She died of cancer shortly before I met him, and I think it was quite tough just before the end. She'd been bedridden for a good few years. It seems she took to her bed when Hugo's father died, and rarely got out of it from then on. Annabel was her nurse for a while, but she said there was actually nothing really wrong with her, and if she'd been born in a different class she'd have just got up and got on with it. I don't know if that's just Annabel speak. Eventually she did become genuinely ill, and I think she really suffered with the chemotherapy."

"You say his father died. Do you know what happened to him?"

Hugo had only mentioned this to her briefly before they were married, and with a note of such disgust in his voice that she should have realised then that empathy wasn't his strong suit. But she had put it down to distress at the facts—as always excusing Hugo's less-benign characteristics.

"He committed suicide. Hanged himself in the woods. Hugo blames his sister, Beatrice, because apparently she ran away when she was just fifteen, and his father was devastated. So a few months later he took himself off into the woods with a rope."

"And Beatrice? We haven't been able to find any trace of her, but do you know if she ever showed up again?"

"Hugo only talked about this once. He said he wanted the subject closed. Beatrice was never heard of from that day to this. It's so long ago now that I suspect nobody will ever find her, unless she wants to be found, of course."

Tom appeared to be reading his notes, but Laura could see that he wasn't. He was staring at the page, and she knew that he was trying to find the right words for the next question. She felt a cold trickle down her back.

"I do need to move on to some more personal aspects of your life, Laura. It may not seem relevant to you, but I'd like to understand a little more about your illnesses. I hope that won't be too painful for you."

As this was clearly not a direct question, Laura wasn't sure how to respond. But Tom hadn't finished, and his next words nearly took her breath away.

"Becky also told me that she overheard some of your conversation this morning. She didn't mean to eavesdrop, but she got the impression that you're not sorry that Hugo is dead. She also heard mention of Rohypnol. These might be sensitive areas, but we do need to discuss them."

Laura composed her face into a stony mask and told herself to calm down. Her salvation came from an unexpected source as Tom's mobile rang again.

She heard him curse under his breath, but having checked the caller ID, he apologised to Laura and answered. Laura could only hear one side of the conversation, but Tom suddenly seemed much more animated.

"Thanks, Ajay, that's really interesting. I'll talk to you later. Keep me updated." He clicked his phone shut and turned to Laura, his eyes glinting with excitement. "Sorry about that. I'd like to come back to those topics later if I may."

He smiled as if he were going to give her some good news.

"We've had a result. We found a red hair at Egerton Crescent. Human hair, but from a wig. One of the wigmakers told us that Hugo's mother used to be his client in the last years of her life, when she lost her hair as a result of the chemotherapy. He came here several times to measure her for new wigs, and he said he'd made five for her altogether."

Tom paused, but Laura knew exactly what he was going to say, and her body tensed in preparation.

"He also said that every one of them was made of human red hair."

25

Telling Tom that she had a pretty good idea where the wig box might be, Laura escaped to the attics. She needed some breathing space; time to slow her racing heart.

And she had to think. Not only about the wigs, but also how to answer his questions about her mental health—not to mention the Rohypnol. How had they been so careless? She had known her depression would come up, and she was prepared for that. But Becky had apparently heard way too much. Tom already knew that Hugo was far from perfect now that he'd heard the terms of the will. But the real Hugo could never be revealed. Not ever.

A shout came from the bottom of the stairs.

"Laura? Are you up there?"

"Yes, I'm pretending to look for something for the police."

Imogen's face appeared in the stairwell, followed by her body. Laura knew that she'd been working since lunchtime, but was glad of her support now.

"How did the meeting with the lawyers go? Rich lady, are you now?"

Laura scoffed. "Don't be silly. This is Hugo we're talking about. I'll explain it all later, but I've got other things to worry about now."

"What on earth are you hunting for up here anyway?"

"Wigs. Well, I'm not hunting. I know where they are. But I'm pretending to hunt."

"*What*? Jesus, I knew I shouldn't have left you alone. What the hell has happened? What have you said?"

Sometimes, Laura mused, Imogen treated her as if she didn't have a single brain cell. She explained quickly everything that Tom had told her about the wigs. Then she pointed at a large round box on the floor.

"Well, there's the wig box."

She stared at it but had no desire to touch it. She knew it would be like Pandora's box—the minute she opened it the evil and all the associated memories would come flooding out to engulf her—but she had no choice. Taking a shuddering breath, she bent down and removed the lid and the contents. She rummaged around, separating the wigs several times. This wasn't right. The hair was all matted together. Perhaps she was wrong. She *had* to be wrong. She pulled them apart again, holding down the panic until she was certain. She looked up at Imogen.

"Shit, Imo. There are only three."

Laura sat down on an old trunk. Her mind was blank. She had no explanation. She had no answer for the police, either. Imogen pushed her way onto the other end and put her arm round Laura's shoulders.

"What are you worried about? Look at it rationally. Don't let something this trivial throw you off balance. Absolutely *anybody* could have taken a wig from here at any time. Mrs. Bennett could have taken one to sell at a garage sale, for all you know. And also, if the old witch kept having wigs made you can only assume that some fell into disrepair or something, and were binned. Two missing wigs doesn't have to mean anything."

"No, maybe not. But will the police think that?"

She genuinely had no idea why there were only three, and that fact alone left her shaken.

They sat in silence as Laura tried to pull herself together. After a few moments, she pushed herself decisively from the trunk.

"Okay, here's what I'm going to say, and let's hope he believes me. When Alexa was a little girl we use to play at dressing up and we used a wig. She's too young to remember, of course. I'll say I've no idea what happened to it. And now I come to think about it, I seem to remember Hugo saying his mother was buried in one of her wigs. That accounts for both of them, and the other three are all here. Does that sound reasonable, do you think?" She looked at Imogen hopefully.

"Brilliant. Hopefully that will take the wind out of the chief inspector's rather delicious sails, although quite why you think you have to justify it, I really don't know." Imogen jumped up. But Laura was only too aware that making up a story for the police didn't actually remove the fundamental problem. There should have been more than three wigs, and it didn't make any sense at all.

She thought she had better tell her friend the rest of the bad news.

"Hang on, Imo. Before you go charging off downstairs, there's another problem. Tom wants me to explain my illness to him—what happened and why I was locked away for so long. What do you think I should say?"

Imogen looked up at Laura and shrugged. "You need to give him the evidence that they had. You don't need to give him the cause."

"But he's not daft, is he? He's going to want to know what happened to me that had sent me like that." Laura thought she had been prepared for this, but she hadn't been prepared for Tom Douglas, and his ability to weasel his way under her skin.

"Perhaps you should tell him the truth."

Laura raised her hands to grasp both sides of her head in frustration at what had to be the most stupid statement she had ever heard from Imogen.

"*What*? Are you completely *mad*? What do you expect me to say—well, you see, Tom, my husband had slipped me a roofie, but I was smart enough not to drink my wine that night. So I caught him playing his sickening games, spewed out my disgust and abhorrence for what he was doing—and my punishment was incarceration for two years in a home for the mentally disturbed."

"Laura, what on earth are you talking about? *Roofies*! I thought we'd been through all that."

"I realised a long time ago that he had drugged you, Imogen. But in spite of that, it took me a long time to recognise that he was doing the same to me." Laura was puzzled. "Haven't you read the letters?"

Imogen bowed her head.

"I'm sorry. I've been taking it slowly. I know you want me to read them, honey, but it feels voyeuristic, somehow."

"I know I'm asking a lot. I didn't want you to read them at first, and now I *need* you to read them. Go, Imogen. Go and read. God knows if I can't tell you everything face-to-face, I certainly can't tell Tom. Just read the next one. I'll wait for you here."

Laura sat down again and put her head in her hands. She suddenly realised that she'd forgotten to tell Imogen that the police knew about their conversation that morning, but its importance diminished as her memories caught up with her.

MARCH 2004

Dear Imogen,

I'm going to start writing to you again, even though I can't see you or speak to you. It allows me to pretend that life is normal. I stopped writing years ago, because I honestly didn't have anything to say. Every day was the same. Every evening was the same. Only Alexa brought me any joy. I love that child so much, but I don't know what I can do to help her. Her mother's no use, of course. But I'm rambling again. Perhaps I am mad. Perhaps they're right.

I'm in a mental home, you see. Oh, they wrap it up with nice words—a care home for the mentally deranged (they don't really say that, of course). Hugo sent me here. It's the only way he can be sure to cover everything up. Anything I say now will just be considered part of my illness. Bastard.

I don't know if I can write about how I came to be here. I'm going to try—but I've already been here for months, and I still can't come to terms with it. That's why I'm writing to you again. Maybe it will help.

Of course I need to start at the beginning and see how far I get before I can't stomach writing the rest. I'm sure that point will come. I'm not going to dwell on the years between my last letter and this. Suffice it to say that it was much of the same. On the surface, all was fine; underneath, it was anything but. Never an angry word—because by then I always did as I was told.

Hugo's made a mistake, though. He thinks that sending me here will make me even more obedient. But he's wrong.

I'm in here because of what I discovered, and it all began with a glass of wine. One that I didn't drink. I'd been waking up feeling heavy eyed, and not at all refreshed. I thought maybe it was too much wine, but when Hugo poured me my customary large glass, I couldn't refuse it. He would take it as a personal insult to his choice, and any chance of harmony during dinner would be shattered. He'd inevitably find some subtle way of punishing me for the perceived slight. So instead, I barely sipped it during the first course. As I stood up to take the plates into the kitchen, he noticed.

"You haven't been drinking your wine. Is there a problem? Is my choice unacceptable to you?"

"No, Hugo, it's delicious as always. In fact, I think I'll take it to the kitchen with me whilst I put the finishing touches to the fish. I'll just be a moment or two."

By this time, I always responded in this sycophantic way. Hugo loved it.

I really didn't want any more wine, so I poured it down the drain and topped up my glass with a rather revolting mixture of apple juice and water—just to get the right colour. Better than drinking the wine, though.

After dinner, I noticed Hugo was watching me rather carefully. A little too carefully. I realised that I was somehow acting out of character. Of course! By this time of night

I was usually getting very drowsy. Hugo often suggested that I went up to bed early, and I was always asleep in seconds. It was a sudden moment of clarity, because one large glass of wine really would not make that much difference. He'd been drugging me! The bastard had been slipping something in my wine! But why? It didn't make sense, because I was certainly not up for his little games when I felt like this. Mind you, those occasions were thankfully becoming rarer and rarer. He didn't appreciate my lack of enthusiasm.

So I feigned a yawn or two.

"I think I'll go to bed now, if that's okay with you."

"That's absolutely fine. I hope you sleep well." Hugo smiled, but there wasn't a trace of warmth in it.

Of course, I couldn't sleep at all. I tossed and turned for a couple of hours, and then I heard a sound. An unusual sound in that house, and it appeared to be coming from the room next door. It was the muffled but unmistakable sound of laughter. I listened carefully. Was it laughter, or was Hugo perhaps listening to the radio in there? The walls of the house were thick, but I could just make out the resonance of a man's deep voice, and the tinkle of high-pitched laughter.

I grabbed my towelling bathrobe, tied it tightly round my waist, and opened the door to the hallway. By this time, I was actually wishing that I'd drunk the wine because I was faced with one of those awful moments of indecision. I knew that I didn't want to see what was behind the door because the knowledge would have inevitable consequences, but I also knew I couldn't ignore it.

I turned the handle and gently pushed the door open.

The next moments were too terrible to put into words. I couldn't stop myself gasping in horror. Of course, Hugo heard me. He showed no sign of embarrassment at all as he turned towards me, naked and erect.

Instead he mocked me.

"Ah, Laura. As always I see you've come to spoil the fun. Or would you like to join us, my dear?"

I can't tell you what I saw, Imo. Not yet. But all the horror of the last few years paled into insignificance beside the tableau that was laid out before me. My whole body was shaking, and I was sure that I was going to be sick. I had never felt such raw emotion—and that emotion was hatred. Pure unadulterated hatred. Love is a powerful emotion, but it is nothing compared to the physical backlash from hate.

I struggled to control the urge to scream, but somehow I managed to find my voice. I had to try to keep it under control—I can't tell you why yet, but I had to.

"Hugo, I want to speak to you now, please. In my room. I may have spent the last five years giving in to you on everything, but not this, Hugo. Never this."

"Well, as you can see, Laura, I'm a little busy. I'll come and talk to you later, if you insist."

Shaking with rage and revulsion, I just stared at him. He read my mind. He knew exactly what my next move would be. He knew that with one single action, I could bring his world crashing down around him. And I would do it. But first I had to get him out of that room.

He sighed theatrically. "You are so tedious and provincial, Laura. I don't take kindly to blackmail, but I see that on this occasion I have no choice. I'll be with you within ten minutes if you could resist being predictable for that long?"

Without another word, I turned and left the room. I was trembling so violently that I thought my legs would give way beneath me. Whilst I waited for Hugo, my fury and disgust were building. For years Hugo had made me question every thought I'd had. But for once—just this once—I knew I was right. I thought about leaving—but I couldn't. Not tonight. Tonight I had a job to do. But there would be no more sleep for me, so I quickly got dressed in the first things that came to hand.

I was going to expose Hugo for exactly what he was. And he knew it.

Finally Hugo flung open the door to my room. Now dressed in a pair of black trousers and a startlingly white shirt, he had obviously decided that attack was the best form of defence. If I had expected excuses or apologies I was not going to get them. I should have guessed as much.

"What do you think you're doing, Laura, barging in where you're not wanted? I will not tolerate it."

I was livid. And I was not going to back down. I walked towards him until I was just inches away. I wanted to slap his miserable face, or slash him with a knife if one had been to hand. But all I had were my words.

"That was the most revolting, repugnant thing that I have ever seen. You are one sick bastard, Hugo Fletcher. I know you have a serious problem with sex, but to do what you were doing is just…I am lost for words."

I turned and walked away from him, angry that no words that I could find would adequately express my horror. Then I swung back round.

"No, I'm not lost for words at all. Perverted. There's a word. A good word, actually. You disgust me."

I practically spat that at him.

He advanced towards me. If his hands hadn't been in his pockets in an attempt to look casual and in control, I'd have been worried that for the first time ever, he may have hit me. But I didn't care. I'd have hit him back. I may have lost, but I'd have gone down fighting, and there would have been an outlet for my pent-up emotion.

I should have known that he would feel no remorse, though.

"What do you mean, I've got a problem with sex? It's not me, you foolish, suburban bitch. You're frigid! You don't know how to relax, and you don't know what men like. Do you know why? Because you were never given appropriate instruction. I imagine the first time you had sex was with a boy from school—probably when you were about sixteen. Yes, I can see that I'm right. You both fumbled around and it was altogether useless, but you persevered. And then you became an adult you got used to sex, but you've never really understood the art. Without me, you would have spent the rest of your life pretending you know how to make love, but you haven't got the remotest idea. It's all hugs, kisses, and random groping," he scoffed.

I laughed—right in his arrogant face. I was going to wipe that smug look off it, though.

"Do you honestly think I care what you think of my performance, Hugo? After what I've just seen? Thank God I never have to pretend again. And do you know what, Sir Hugo? Nobody else will come within a mile of you either. You are going to stay out of that room tonight, and I'm going to make a phone call—I am going to do everything in my power to ensure that you go to hell for this, Hugo—so..."

What happened next is a bit of a blur. I just remember Hugo advancing on me and grabbing my right arm in his left hand. Then he dragged something from his pocket. It was a syringe.

When I finally came round, I felt terrible. My eyes were sticky, and my body was aching. I had no idea how much time had passed, and I didn't know where I was. I didn't recognise the room. It was completely empty. No furniture, no carpet, and the floor and windows were filthy with ancient dust. I didn't have the strength to get up. I felt drained of all energy. And then I realised that I was naked. I couldn't imagine how I'd got there, and I had no idea where my clothes were.

To start with, I only had a vague memory of all that had happened, but it was enough for me to realise that I had failed. And then I cried. Great wracking sobs shook my body, because I knew that I was going to be powerless from now on. I had lost the fleeting advantage that I'd gained, and somehow I had wasted it. My concern had been for the moment, and it should have been for the future. I don't know how long I cried that first time, but it wasn't going to be the last.

What little strength I had was used up from the crying, so I crawled on hands and knees to the door and banged on it, screaming for help. It was locked, of course. I must have been in one of the unused wings of the house. I'd explored the whole of Ashbury Park once when Hugo was away, but it had completely spooked me—all those rooms standing empty, hiding God knows what stories from the past.

I knew deep down that nobody would hear me, so I crawled back to my corner. Hugo obviously knew where I was, and he would only come when he was ready. I lay on my side and curled into a ball. I couldn't stop shaking, but it was fear that was sending tremors through my body, not cold.

I don't know how long I waited—it seemed like hours. Then the door opened. I knew it would be Hugo, and I couldn't bear to look at him. All I wanted was to cover my nakedness from his gaze, then get out of there and out of his life. But not before I'd made sure that what I'd witnessed the night before would never happen again.

"Hello, Laura."

I could hear footsteps walking menacingly towards me across the bare boards, but I wouldn't look up.

"Stupid, useless Laura. I've come to give you a drink. I'm sure you're thirsty. Come on, take the glass."

I turned my head away. I didn't want anything he had to offer. He grabbed my hair and pulled my head back viciously. He snarled at me in a tone I'd never heard him use before.

"Drink it! Drink it now if you want to get out of this room alive. Nobody knows where you are, and nobody need ever know."

I believed him. How stupid I was. Of course he couldn't afford to let me walk away from him. I should have realised. I was far too dangerous. He'd have a plan. He always had a plan.

I should have guessed that it wasn't just water he was giving me, and it was only moments until I floated back to sleep. Next time I woke up, he came again and once more he forced me to drink. My body went limp, and I gradually drifted back into unconsciousness. Then one time after I'd taken the drink and I was barely awake, he pulled my arms away from my chest and straightened my legs. He pulled my legs wide apart, and just stood looking at me. I knew what he was doing, but I was too weak to move. Then he laughed. After that, each time he came he would twist my defenceless body into a different pose, as if I was his very own doll. My filthy, dirt-covered limbs were pulled into every kind of degrading position he could think of, exposing me to his depraved eyes, and occasional fingers. But that was all. Thank God. He wasn't interested in me. He just wanted to witness my humiliation—and my fear. Fear of what he might do whilst I was comatose.

In a rare moment of partial lucidity, I was horrified to realise that my bladder was full. It's probably what woke me. I crawled to the farthest corner; as far away from the door as I could get. And I crouched there, with tears running down my dirty cheeks. I couldn't bear for Hugo to be able to gloat at my shame any more than he was already doing.

After what seemed like weeks, I heard a shout. It wasn't Hugo's voice.

"Sir Hugo, I've found her!" The door was pushed open, and Hannah came running in. Much as I despise the girl, I was glad to see her. She stopped dead in her tracks, a look of disgust spread across her face, probably from the smell emanating from the damp patch in the corner. Hugo stood behind her in the doorway, a smile of triumph playing around his mouth. As Hannah turned to look at him though, his expression changed instantly to one of concern.

"Oh, my darling, we've been so worried about you. What happened? Nobody ever comes to this part of the house—you know that. We never thought to look for you here. And where are your clothes? You must have been here for nearly two days. We've searched everywhere. Hannah, call a doctor. Call Doctor Davidson—you'll find his details in my address book on the desk. Tell him to hurry."

With a last look of horror and distaste, Hannah turned and ran from the room.

Hugo turned back to me. He smiled cruelly.

"Now, just a little work to do on the door handle..." He laughed nastily and removed a very small screwdriver from his pocket. I watched through glazed eyes, not sure whether I was really seeing this or if it was part of some drug-induced dream. I drifted back into oblivion and didn't really register the doctor's arrival.

It took no time at all for him to declare that I was suffering from a chronic form of depression, and he gently helped me into a gown and organised a stretcher to take me to the waiting private ambulance. I tried to protest that I'd been locked in, but I *saw Hugo demonstrate sadly to the doctor that the door opened easily from both sides and that in fact there was no lock. Hannah looked on, nodding her agreement and trying not to look smug. I knew that somehow or other he'd disengaged the handle from the inside, but I also knew I couldn't prove it.*

So now I'm here. And I understand exactly why Hugo chose this place. Whilst I was "missing," he had obviously done some research and found a home that was failing badly and desperately in need of funds. I effectively bought its continued existence.

Of course, Hannah was a huge help in having me sectioned. I know she described in graphic detail what she'd found—how I was naked and filthy; how I could have got out if I'd wanted to; how I'd obviously used the floor as a toilet despite there being a bathroom—albeit unused for years—just outside the door. I know all this because the good doctor asked me questions that could only have been based on that knowledge.

And the other thing is the drugs. Hugo tried to ban all visitors, but banning my mother was too difficult even for him. She wasn't having any of that. So the doctor drugs me each time she visits. She believes, I'm sure, that I'm ill. And I can't tell her what I know—because the drugs make me into a zombie. It's only when I'm alone and drug free that I can think.

I don't know how long they'll keep me in here. Hugo can bribe them for as long as he likes, I expect. I have to suffer the indignity of the group sessions, the private therapy, and everything else that you might expect—but I feel safe here. Safer than at home. In fact, if it wasn't for one thing I would be happy to stay here. But the clock is ticking. I need a plan.

I know now without a doubt that you were right about the Rohypnol, Imo. And if I'd believed you then, what would have become of us all?

I can only say how very, very sorry I am.

With love always,

Laura

Tom was glad of a few minutes to gather his thoughts while Laura was searching for wigs, although she appeared to be taking her time finding them. As soon as she'd left the room he'd received a frantic phone call from Annabel, regretting everything that she had told him the other day given the harsh financial impact should any of it be made public. Tom had assured her that he would treat their conversation with as much confidentiality as was possible, but he couldn't make any promises.

After they disconnected, Tom went to sit in Becky's place at the end of the dining room table. She'd already told him that the list of passengers on the Eurostar hadn't revealed anything of interest, which was disappointing but not unexpected. The sightings of the red-haired lady hadn't progressed much, as people claimed to have seen her from West Ruislip to Lewisham. But had Becky's theory of the Eurostar been correct, she would most likely have changed tubes at Green Park to get to St. Pancras, although there were other options. There were some sightings that would have correlated with this, but similarly there were others that could have her on a train from Paddington to Plymouth, and he knew he was just clutching at straws.

Becky had left her laptop here, and it was lying open. He sat staring at her screen saver and tried to gather his thoughts. He felt that he was wasting his time here in Oxfordshire. He knew that Becky was fixated on the idea of Imogen Kennedy being a serious suspect, but until he'd found out what had happened to Mirela Tinescy—the most recent charity girl to go missing—he wouldn't rest easy. He hoped his team had made progress there. And with Jessica Armstrong—the most likely candidate to be Hugo's mistress.

But he needed the fully rounded picture of the victim's life that only Laura could give him, and there were so many gaps to fill in. The more he learned about Hugo, the less he liked him. So why had somebody like Laura stayed with him? He just didn't get it at all.

Although his mind was wandering all over the place, Tom decided he'd do a bit of research to see if he could find any more about this family. Using Becky's laptop to log onto the Internet, he typed Hugo's full name into Google. Of course, there were bound to be a huge number of results given the events of the last few days. Tom refined and further refined his searches, merely doodling as he mulled over the facts and theories, until one headline caught his interest.

He leaned forward in his seat, all thoughts of wigs, Eastern European girls, and mental illness thrust aside as he found what amounted to an unauthorised biography of Sir Hugo Fletcher. To his surprise, this included an account of Hugo's father's death. Although it was pretty much as Laura had said, there were a few anomalies. In fact, an open verdict was given because although a note was found, there were certain aspects of his death that were difficult to explain. Given today's forensic expertise, Tom was sure that a more definitive conclusion would have been drawn, but it nevertheless made interesting reading.

Seeing that the name of Lady Daphne Fletcher was underlined as a hyperlink, Tom clicked through. He remembered hearing at some point that Hugo's mother was the daughter of an earl, so had the courtesy title of Lady, whilst his father was a plain old "mister"—if a very wealthy one. Perhaps that explained why Hugo was so keen to get a title of his own. He continued to follow links until he found a site with images. Amongst these, there was one formal colour photograph of Daphne Fletcher in evening dress.

Tom clicked to enlarge the image. He stared at the screen. Not sure if his memory was playing tricks, he turned to Becky's stash of files. Extracting a photograph, he held it next to the screen.

"Good God," he whispered out loud to himself. Now he didn't know what to think—but whichever way he looked at it, he couldn't come up with any way of putting an acceptable spin on his discovery.

Stella was in the kitchen, busy making dinner for them all. She found chopping vegetables very therapeutic and was locked in her own world when Becky returned from Annabel's.

"What a delicious smell, Stella!"

Stella looked up and smiled. Becky didn't fool her with her innocent air, but she was a nice girl and just doing her job.

"Will you be joining us for dinner, Becky?"

"That's very kind of you, but I don't want to intrude, so I've brought a sandwich with me. I'm staying at a B-and-B down the road so that if there are any developments I can be back with you at any time during the night."

"You're not intruding at all. You're more than welcome."

"Thanks, but all the same I don't think it's the right thing to do. Laura's got you and Imogen for support, otherwise of course I wouldn't leave her on her own."

"What about Tom? Is he still around?"

"No. He had a phone call, and he needed to get back. I saw him for just a couple of minutes before he left. Something's come up. I'm waiting to have a quick word with Laura to explain why he's gone, and then I'll get off, too. I gather she was in the middle of answering some questions for him, but I'm sure they'll wait. She's lucky to have you looking after her and making sure she eats properly."

"Well, Laura's a really good cook herself, so I can't just serve up a plate of egg and chips. Anyway, she needs to get her stamina back. She wasn't always so thin, you know. She used to be really curvaceous. Laura Kennedy and Imogen Dubois—they were every young boy's dream at one time. They could just pick and choose. But Will was always the one for our Imogen."

Stella continued to chatter, but looking at Becky's face she could see that she was miles away and was looking distinctly preoccupied. Given that it couldn't possibly have anything to do with whatever she'd been saying, she left Becky to her thoughts and continued preparing the meal.

The girl no longer kept watch from the window. Her strength was fading fast. She'd started to ration her water days ago, but now it was nearly gone. She couldn't remember the last time she had eaten anything, and her thin body had precious few reserves to draw on.

She couldn't believe he had left her for so long. He'd said he was going to teach her a lesson, but when he left her with meagre supplies of dry biscuits and water she had thought he would stay away for two or perhaps three days. But not this long.

She was so cold. She wrapped the thin silk of the cream negligee around her skeletal form and tried to huddle under the bedcovers. She wanted to remove the stockings—the suspenders were biting painfully into her flesh. But she needed the warmth. And she was scared to go to sleep. Scared of the dreams. She knew she was becoming delirious.

It was such a dreadful feeling, and it was happening with increasing frequency. She felt awake, but she was strangely unable to respond to stimuli around her. She was sure somebody was in the room with her. She could feel his presence, but she couldn't force her eyes to open or her body to function. And then she knew with certainly that he was standing at the end of the mattress where she lay. He advanced, slowly, slowly towards her, looming over her. She tried to lift her arm to push him away, but her limbs wouldn't obey her commands. She tried to scream but couldn't make a sound. Finally she awoke, her body bathed in a cold, cold sweat, scared to look at whatever was waiting for her.

In a rare moment of lucidity she recognised the source of her fear. It was nothing more sinister than a long red wig, sitting on its stand on a distant chest of drawers.

Then the delirium returned, and she sank back into the abyss of her terror.

26

Tom was disappointed that he hadn't been able to complete his conversation with Laura. He'd still not had a chance to ask her about Danika, either; there were just too many interruptions. He'd received some interesting news, though. The family that Mirela Tinescy had been staying with had been interviewed, and they backed up Danika's story. Mirela had definitely left a note saying that she'd been offered a big opportunity when she left them. But it appeared Danika had misunderstood one important thing. Mirela's letter had never stated what type of opportunity. Tom remembered that Danika had heard all of this from Mirela's replacement, and this new Allium girl had clearly jumped to the conclusion that this opportunity could only have been related to prostitution. But what if this was something completely different? What if the big opportunity involved killing Hugo Fletcher in return for a chunk of cash?

It was a good theory, but that wasn't what had him racing him back to the office. He'd had people crawling all over Hugo's will in the last few hours, and it had revealed something unexpected and potentially exciting.

As soon as he walked in the door, there was a shout.

"Boss, you need to see this! We need to get Jessica Armstrong in here. With what Hugo's left her in his will, there is no way she was just his PA."

Tom took the piece of paper being waved in the air. He read the marked paragraph and opened his eyes wide in astonishment.

"Bloody hell—that's more than his *wife* got! No wonder Brian Smedley was looking so uncomfortable. Okay, I take your point, we do need to see her. But I'd like us to do some more checking before we drag her in. We need lots of background—bank accounts, credit cards, lifestyle, you know the score. Let's get that together, see where we're up to in the morning, and then get her in. I can't imagine she's going anywhere, or she'd have gone already. Everybody happy with that?"

Clearly everybody wasn't, as they'd been excited about possibly getting a result, but it made sense, and whilst he felt guilty about crushing their enthusiasm, they needed to do this right.

"One more thing," Tom said. "Becky phoned to say that Laura's checked the wig box. Only three can be accounted for, although Laura has come up with plausible reasons for where the other two could have gone. And of course they could have been tossed or given away. But somebody who had access to the house could also have taken one, and this could be our murderer. The fact that there were, at one time, five handmade red wigs but now there are only three is too much of a coincidence. Let's get thinking and see if we can come up with any ideas. Any questions?"

There weren't, and Tom was left to reflect on some of the day's more unlikely discoveries and where they were leading.

"She lives in bloody Lowndes Square! Have you any idea how much apartments there cost? Bleeding millions!"

This was the news that greeted Tom as he walked into the morning briefing. Clearly, this had to be about Jessica.

"Hang on, guys. She comes from a wealthy family. What else have we got?"

Tom took a sip from his strong black coffee. Despite an early night, sleep had been elusive. Every time he had started to drop off, an image of Kate's pleading face had sprung into his mind, oddly replaced as he drifted into sleep by a picture of Laura, laughing at Hugo's abject cruelty. So he needed a kick start, and he hoped the coffee would do it.

"The apartment cost nine hundred thousand. She bought it two years ago, and she's got a whopping seven hundred thousand pound mortgage. Can you imagine that!"

Ajay seemed incensed that somebody like Jessica should live in such luxury.

"Do we know what she earns?" Tom asked.

"Yep—a generous but not Lowndes Square–generous seventy thousand. For a bloody secretary!"

"Okay, let's not get ahead of ourselves. Whatever we think about her finances, it doesn't make her a murderer. We need to know how she pays her mortgage—there might be a reasonable explanation—and we need to know why Hugo left her so much money in his will. You never know, he might have just been feeling particularly generous." Ignoring the various expletives and mutterings from his team, Tom continued. "What I'm most interested in is the fact that the terms of the will effectively gag Jessica in the same way that Annabel has been gagged. One derogatory remark about Hugo, and she loses the lot. So what does she know? What is worth more than half a million pounds?"

He looked around the room, but clearly nobody had the answer.

"Okay—let's bring her in."

An immaculate and clearly expensively dressed Jessica was shown into the interview room. Her light brown hair was sleekly tied back from a rather hard and angular face with a sharp nose and thin lips. Her imperious manner rubbed Tom up the wrong way even before he started to question her, but of course, he had to be polite.

"Jessica, thank you for agreeing to answer some questions. I understand that you don't want any legal representation, but if you change your mind at any point, just let me know."

Jessica looked vaguely startled by the suggestion. "Why on earth would I need legal representation? I'm simply here to answer questions about Sir Hugo, I presume?"

Tom couldn't bring himself to offer reassurance. "No, that's not why we asked you to come in. We've been looking at your lifestyle, and we've looked at your earnings. The two just don't correlate, I'm afraid. We need to understand how you can afford to live in Lowndes Square given your current salary."

Jessica gave a theatrical sigh, clearly meant to signify her boredom. She closed her subtly made-up eyes as if this were the most ridiculous question she had ever been asked. "Really, Inspector, you must realise that my parents are very wealthy. Money is no object to them at all."

Tom really didn't care about titles, but on this occasion he wasn't prepared to overlook what he was sure was an intentional slight. "It's Chief Inspector. And of course we know about your parents, but we also have access to your bank details, and there is no evidence of any money coming from that source. The only money coming into your account is your salary, which after tax and deductions is used almost in full to pay your mortgage."

"Well," she responded with a superior smile, "that's your answer, isn't it? My salary covers my mortgage."

"Yes, but Jessica, you drive a Mercedes SLK, brand-new, and you still have to eat. And even I've noticed that your clothes are not exactly your average High Street brand. So how, precisely, do you manage all of that?"

"It's very simple. My father regularly supplements my earnings. I only have to ask." Jessica was leaning back comfortably in her chair. She picked an imaginary piece of fluff off her black-and-white-checked skirt.

"So if I went to your father and asked him the question, would he give the answer you're expecting?"

"Of course he would. Daddy has never been mean where money is concerned."

Tom was in no mood to give up. "By my calculations, just to pay your household bills, buy food, put fuel in the car—which we know by the way is being paid off in twelve fairly hefty monthly instalments—not to mention clothes, holidays, and entertainment, you would need several thousand each month. If we asked your father if he gave you, let's say, in excess of five thousand pounds per month, would he confirm that?"

For the first time, Tom could see that Jessica was uncomfortable. He used the moment to advantage.

"Did he, for example, pay for your holiday at the Saint Geran on Mauritius last year? Isn't that the most expensive hotel on the island?"

"Not necessarily. It's thought by many to have the most class, but there are several good hotels there now," Jessica answered, hiding behind her natural arrogance.

"You're not answering my question. How did you pay for that holiday?"

"Actually, I paid with my bonus."

"What bonus? Wouldn't a bonus be paid into the bank along with your salary?" Not that Tom had ever had a bonus, but this woman's haughty tone and condescending attitude were riling him.

She answered him with a complacent smirk. "Sir Hugo sometimes gave me a bonus in cash."

Tom banged the palms of his hands on the table, and leaned back with what he hoped she would see as a look of disbelief. "Are you telling me that Sir Hugo Fletcher, pillar of society, paid his staff on the black? I really don't think so, Jessica. Try again."

Jessica stubbornly refused to say more, so Tom changed direction—for the moment.

"Can you tell me whether you ever went into the apartment upstairs in Egerton Crescent, Jessica?"

Looking relieved, she returned to her normal slightly supercilious self. "Of course I did. Sir Hugo used to stay up in London quite a lot, and I always thought it would be nice for him if the drawing room were prepared for his evening—you know the sort of thing—newspaper at hand, lamps lit, all the decanters topped up, ice bucket filled. Just to make sure he was comfortable. I usually only went into the drawing room and kitchen, but sometimes I did take the laundry up to his room. I didn't put it away, though. I wasn't sure if he'd like that."

My God, thought Tom. What was that about her obsession with him being over some time ago?

Seeing her looking more relaxed, he switched back quickly to his previous line of questioning.

"Did he ever give you presents, Jessica, or was it just cash? Your 'bonuses'?"

Jessica looked puzzled. "He never gave me presents. Why would you want to know that?"

"Would you have any objection if a couple of my colleagues went with you to your apartment and had a look around? We could get a search warrant, but there's no need if you're prepared to cooperate."

Tom seriously doubted that he had grounds for a warrant, but hoped that Jessica wouldn't know that. As usual, he underestimated her.

"I suspect that would prove rather difficult for you, Chief Inspector. But I have nothing to hide. Be my guest." Jessica opened her bag and withdrew a set of keys, which she proceeded to dangle in front of Tom's face. She shook them. "Here you are—take them."

"We'd like you to accompany us, please."

"There's no need. I'll call my housekeeper and ask her to be there. The apartment is immaculate, and I expect it to remain that way. I would prefer to stay here and get to the end of this somewhat tedious questioning so that I can get back to work."

Tom asked Ajay to go and organise the search, and to bring back some refreshments. He didn't want to upset Jessica too much until the search had been conducted in case she withdrew her permission. But given the ease with which she had acceded to their request, he wasn't hopeful that they would find anything. She was hardly likely to have left a red wig or a phial of liquid nicotine lying around.

After their brief break, Tom was determined to wipe the smile off this girl's face. He took it slowly for a while, but not for long.

"Right, Jessica. You've already told us that Sir Hugo gave you money from time to time. What I want to know is how much, and how often."

"I don't actually believe that is any of your business."

Tom was reaching the end of his tether. He had dealt with some real crooks in his time, but he struggled to think of anybody whom he had found as frustrating as bloody Jessica Armstrong. He leaned forward.

"Are you refusing to answer the question?"

"Yes. As I said, it is none of your business."

"So exactly what was he paying you for, Jessica? Your body, or your silence?"

Jessica looked stunned. Her eyes filled and she swallowed hard. Tom had clearly hit a nerve.

"It was neither. How dare you!"

Tom's patience had passed the point of no return. He pushed his chair back with a loud scraping noise, stood up, and marched to the door, turning as he went out to deliver his parting shot.

"For Christ's sake, this is ridiculous. Ajay—would you please carry on with the interview, because we're getting absolutely nowhere."

In the end, they decided to let Jessica go home, with strict instructions to return the next day. Tom thought it would do her good to have a bit of thinking time. Or maybe worrying time.

The following day some of his irritation had dissipated, but he still needed some answers.

As expected, nothing of any interest had been revealed at the apartment, but that was inconclusive. She was an intelligent woman, and now that he knew her a little better he was sure she wouldn't have left a scrap of useful evidence.

It all came down to the money. Why did men give money to women? Only one reason, as far as Tom could see. She *must* have been his mistress, but does that mean that she murdered him? It would have been so easy for her— she had ready access to the flat, and her fingerprints were all over anyway. They weren't in the bedroom, although she did admit going in there with the laundry. But that didn't mean anything either. She could easily have gone in and put everything on the bed without touching a thing.

Tom was ready for her. He was not going to be beaten by sodding Jessica Armstrong.

"Okay, Jessica, let's start from the top. You are being taped, and if we find out later that you've lied to us, I will charge you with wasting police time. Do you understand me?"

Jessica looked momentarily alarmed, but nodded her head.

"You need to answer, Jessica. For the tape. I repeat—do you understand me?"

"Yes."

"Right. When did you buy your house?"

"Two years ago."

"How did you find the two hundred thousand pounds that was the difference between your mortgage and the price?"

"My father gave it to me. *Don't* look like that. It's true. Ask him if you don't believe me."

"How did he think that you were going to be able to pay the mortgage?"

"I don't mean to be rude, Chief Inspector, but do you have a rich father? Mine is very rich indeed, but actually has no interest in anything at all other than making money. I simply told him that Sir Hugo had decided I was invaluable and doubled my salary. He wasn't sufficiently interested in what I do to even query it. He just said something like 'jolly good, dear' and carried on reading the *Economist*."

Tom had a clear picture in his head of that scene, but it still didn't answer the question. "So how did *you* think you were going to be able to carry on paying the mortgage?"

"Sir Hugo had told me that he was very impressed with me. He wanted me to do some personal, highly confidential work for him. He said he would pay me a little extra each month. In cash."

"What did he mean by 'a little extra'?"

"A few thousand."

This was like pulling teeth. Surely by now she had realised that he was going to find out—however long it took?

"How many is 'a few,' Jessica?"

Jessica had the grace to look slightly sheepish. She shuffled a little in her chair. Then raised her chin defiantly. "He asked if eight would be enough."

"Eight thousand pounds! A month?"

"Yes."

Jessica's chin was still raised, but her cheeks were flushed with what Tom could only assume was embarrassment. Quite right, too, he thought.

"What did you have to do for the money, Jessica? You are going to have to tell us. Were you his mistress?"

"I've already told you that I wasn't. If he'd asked me, especially in the early days, I would have gladly said yes. And I can assure you that I most certainly would *not* have expected to be paid for it. But unfortunately he never did."

"So what did you do?"

"I'd rather not say. I'm sorry, but it was confidential." Jessica's obdurate expression was exasperating Tom.

"Jessica, Sir Hugo is dead. Whatever you did for him that was worth so much money—it may have a bearing on his death."

"It doesn't."

"How can you be so sure?"

"It just doesn't."

It was at times like these that Tom could understand why some policemen lost it. And then it hit him. There was one other good reason why a man might pay a woman a lot of money on a regular basis.

"Okay, you won't tell us what you did. Is that because of the terms of the will?"

"What do you mean?" Jessica asked with a frown.

"You know he left you some money?"

"Brian mentioned it, yes. I haven't got the details yet, but Brian says I should be more than happy."

Jessica was in danger of being smug again.

"Did Brian also tell you that there are some conditions attached?"

Tom was pleased to see that this news wiped the smile off her face.

"What conditions?"

"The money—a very generous sum—is to be given to you over a period of time, and during that period you cannot say anything about Sir Hugo that would bring his name into disrepute."

Ajay looked at Tom sharply. He obviously wondered why Tom had told Jessica this as it might prevent her giving them information. But Tom had a plan, and he thought he was beginning to understand Jessica quite well. He could feel a tingle of excitement.

"Well, those conditions will be no problem at all. Nothing Sir Hugo did could bring his name into disrepute."

Tom was leaning forward in his chair. This was it. He just knew it.

"What did you know, Jessica?" he asked in a soft voice. "What did you know about Sir Hugo that you have promised not to reveal?"

"There was *nothing*—how many times do I have to tell you?"

Jessica's face was set in stubborn lines, and Tom felt his excitement fading.

"So why won't you tell me what the money was for? Why does it have to remain a secret if it's not because of the terms of the will?"

"Because it's none of your business, and not in any way relevant to your enquiries. He didn't want anybody to know. He was quite modest about his generosity, you know."

Tom managed to keep his face impassive. "When did it start then, and was there was some specific trigger for this...generosity?"

"I'll tell you when it started. I *won't*, however, tell you what I did. I'm not a terrorist, so I believe I have the right to silence."

Tom sighed. God preserve us from knowledgeable suspects, he thought.

"Let's start there, then, shall we? Tell me when it started, and what prompted it."

Jessica was clasping a green suede handbag on her knee, and she was turning the handle over and over between her fingers. Two deep frown lines had appeared between her eyebrows, and Tom knew that he had rattled her—but whether he'd rattled her enough, he wasn't sure.

"Well, there were a few things that happened all around the same sort of time a couple of years ago. It started when two of the rescue girls turned up at the office, looking for one of their friends who had apparently gone AWOL. I turned them away, of course. I knew Sir Hugo was very strict about the girls not keeping in touch with each other, and I was very cross with them."

"Didn't you think that was rather a strange rule?"

"Not at all. He only had their interests at heart, and if he thought it was for the best then I supported that decision. Anyway, it was only a day or two later that the doorbell rang. I was the only one in the office apart from Sir Hugo. Rosie had gone out—ostensibly because we had run out of pens or something, although it took her an inordinately long time to buy them if I remember correctly. I opened the door, and this young girl pushed past me. She said she wanted to see 'Hugo'—not 'Sir Hugo.' I thought that very odd. Then I recognised her. I'd been looking at her file that very day. She looked very smartly dressed, though, and that had me fooled for a few moments. I tried to stop her but she pushed past me and straight into Sir Hugo's office. She slammed the door. Of course, I went after her, but Sir Hugo told me everything was okay and I could go."

Jessica paused and took a sip of water. Nobody spoke. Tom could see that she was reliving the moment, and although he was dying to ask her the question at the forefront of his mind, he had to let her finish talking. She wasn't looking at him; she was clutching the glass and gazing into the distance as the scenes of that day came back to her.

"I heard shouting coming from the office. *Shouting*. Sir Hugo never shouted, but he was clearly extremely angry about something. It didn't last long, though. After a few minutes, she came out smiling and left. Sir Hugo came out a couple of minutes later and had a word with me. He asked me never to mention that she had been there, and he wanted to know if I had overheard anything."

Much as he didn't want to interrupt the story, Tom had to know. "And did you?"

"Not really. Nothing significant. She seemed to be talking about a *pool*, of all things. I heard her mention it twice, but that made no sense to me. I knew that Annabel had been on at him about an indoor swimming pool for ages, but I couldn't see how the two things were related. Anyway, Sir Hugo said he was going home to Oxfordshire, and not to expect him back for a few days. He didn't want to be contacted. I thought that was the last of it, but when Rosie eventually deigned to return to the office, she said she'd seen Sir Hugo driving away and there was a girl in the car with him. He must have decided to give her a lift, even though she had been *extremely* rude. And that was it. That was when it started."

"Who was the girl?"

"I believe her name was Alina Cozma."

Tom took a sharp breath. This was the very girl that Danika Bojin had originally gone in search of. And he didn't believe in coincidences.

"What did Sir Hugo say? Did he ever explain?"

"Sir Hugo didn't need to explain anything to me, Chief Inspector."

Why could this girl not give a straight answer, Tom thought. But for once, she volunteered some information without being asked.

"I don't know if it's relevant, but it was shortly after that that Sir Hugo asked me to look into bodyguard companies for him. He didn't always have them, you know. And then just days later we had another most unexpected visitor. Lady Fletcher came to the office. It was very unusual, but he was extremely pleased with how I handled that. He said I demonstrated loyalty, commitment, and discretion."

This must have been after Danika had visited her at home, Tom realised. "What was the purpose of her visit?"

"She wanted to see the records from the charity, with a list of all the homes that the girls had been sent to in the past five years. She wanted contact numbers and so on. She also wanted to know if I had a record of any of the girls that had gone back to the streets, or gone back to wherever they came from. I'm quite good at anticipating what Sir Hugo would want, and I didn't think he would be happy for her to go through the files, so I refused."

"How did Lady Fletcher respond to this?"

"She stated categorically that this was work she was doing on behalf of her husband, and the records needed to be made available to her. I knew that he wouldn't have asked her to do this without telling me, so I refused to give her anything, and she left."

"Did you tell Sir Hugo about her visit?" He already knew the answer, but thought he should at least confirm it.

"Of course. He was very angry that she'd been, but absolutely delighted with me. It was a couple of days after that that he offered me the extra work. And the money. He said that confidentiality in a PA is of paramount importance, and he had to know that he could trust me with his darkest secrets. It was a funny thing to say, because I would have done it for nothing, but he said that his trust in me was worth eight thousand pounds a month." Jessica paused. "So I went house hunting."

Tom thought about this for some minutes.

"Jessica, I need you to think very carefully about this. You are not stupid, and it must have occurred to you that you were being paid a huge amount of money in return for your confidentiality. And now he appears to have bought your ongoing silence. Doesn't that seem strange to you?"

"You really don't understand, do you, Detective Chief Inspector? He was an amazing man, with depths you wouldn't even begin to comprehend."

Contrary to Jessica's view, Tom thought that he was beginning to understand those depths very well indeed—and they were a good deal darker than she obviously realised. But nothing could stop her eulogy.

"The thing that I have sworn to keep secret from the world is just one more example of the enormous philanthropy of this man. And I will not tell you. It was a solemn promise."

Recognising that at least for now this was a dead end, Tom moved on. "About the will, Jessica. In return for your ongoing silence, your mortgage is going to be paid off in full over a period of one year. Did you know that?"

Jessica nodded mutely. She may not have known the specific terms of the will—but she did know how much.

"That gives you a very clear motive for murder, I'd say. You haven't told us where you were at the time Sir Hugo was killed. I believe you thought it 'unnecessary to account for your movements.' Isn't that right? We don't know what you did for the money, and you won't tell us. I can therefore only assume that you were blackmailing him. That would make sense, wouldn't it? So I suggest you go home now and give that some thought. I want you back here again tomorrow morning. Ajay—make the arrangements, please."

Tom rose abruptly and left the room, leaving Jessica looking stunned and more than a little frightened.

It was apparent to Tom that Jessica really had worshipped Hugo Fletcher. That, of course, could provide a motive for murder, but he didn't think so in this case. She was adamant that she wouldn't reveal why she was getting so much money, but Tom was equally determined to find out. The trouble was that nothing much fazed her, and keeping her in an interview room for twenty-four hours wasn't going to achieve a thing.

But the news about Alina Cozma was seriously interesting. Tom tried to pull it all together in his head. Alina goes missing. Danika and Mirela go to see Jessica and she shows them the door. He could well imagine that scene! Danika goes to see Laura. Alina turns up and she and Hugo have an argument. That in itself was seriously odd, of course. Then Laura goes to find out about the girls—and gets equally short shrift from Jessica. Hugo finds out, employs bodyguards, and gives Jessica a little job to do. A little job that is worth eight thousand pounds a month—in cash. And now Mirela is missing. Tomorrow he was going to find out about these missing girls from Jessica. That had to be the priority.

He was just about to pack up and go home when Becky called him from Oxfordshire. She sounded tentative.

"Tom, there's something that I want to mention to you. I'm not sure it's relevant, but it's been eating at me for a while, and I thought that I should at least run it by you."

"Go on, Becky. It doesn't matter if it's bollocks—you know that. Every suggestion's a good one."

"Well, I was in the kitchen talking to Stella, and she happened to mention how gorgeous Laura and Imogen were at school. Then she mentioned their full names. Laura Kennedy, and Imogen Dubois. It niggled away at me for a while, until I remembered something. My photographic memory kicked in, if a little slowly. When I was looking through the names of the passengers on the Eurostar from London to Paris, there was an Imogen Dubois. I was certain I was right, and obviously anybody called Imogen had received a little more attention than the rest. I checked back, and there it was. I know it can't mean anything because the name on her passport is Imogen Kennedy. But it just seemed to be a bit of a coincidence."

"It's a *hell* of a coincidence, Becky. Well done. Have you actually seen her passport and checked the name?"

"Yep. It was the first thing I did. The name on the ticket always has to match the name on the passport, of course, and her passport is definitely in the name of Imogen Kennedy. I contacted the passport authorities just in case, but there are no British passports in the name of Imogen Dubois. I'm also getting the tickets checked, to see if we can find out when they were purchased, and whose name was on the credit card. I'm waiting for them to get back to me."

"Okay. Good thinking, Becky. Pity about the passport, but keep on it. I don't like coincidences. I'm going through a few things here, but I'll try and get back out there tomorrow."

"Well, when you do, prepare to be amazed."

"What does that mean?"

"Wait and see."

Realising that it couldn't have anything to do with the case, he was no more than mildly intrigued. And he wasn't to know that when he next visited, any sense of amazement would be the last thing on his mind.

The next morning Tom decided to try once more to unnerve Jessica by changing the line of questioning completely.

"I think the time has come for you to make the records that Lady Fletcher was so interested in available to me, don't you? The ones that relate to the charity girls; the ones you refused to show her."

To Tom's surprise, Jessica smiled. "Unfortunately, that won't be possible."

Tom leaned forwards. He had a feeling he'd been out manoeuvred. "What do you mean, Jessica?"

"Shortly after the incident with Lady Fletcher, Sir Hugo decided a clear-out was needed. He asked me to shred the details of any of the girls who had left their families. We only keep records of those whom the charity is still maintaining now."

"So how does the charity account for all its work, then?"

"We keep numbers, but not identities. I gave all the files to Rosie for shredding. I'm not being difficult, you understand. I'm simply unable to help you."

Tom was acutely disappointed. The combination of Laura's silence about Danika, the fact that Alina and Mirela were both missing, Jessica's unwillingness to give Laura information, and Hugo's insistence that the records were shredded made him even more certain this was significant.

"Jessica, I want you to think about everything we've discussed, and I want you to reconsider your vow of silence. You may think that what you know is insignificant, but I think you're wrong. And you still need to convince me that you weren't blackmailing Sir Hugo."

"Am I not right in thinking that the burden of proof rests with you, Chief Inspector?"

More than anything, Tom wanted to wipe the smug smile off this woman's face. But something had been niggling away at him for a while—and then it came to him. Laura's surprise at the twenty thousand pounds that Hugo had been withdrawing. She obviously was expecting something, just not that amount. Jessica accounted for less than half of it though—so what was the rest for, and what did Laura know about it?

"You mentioned before that Sir Hugo was a very generous man. We can see that by the way he treated you. So tell me, Jessica, does your secret have anything to do with him giving money to *other* people on a regular basis? People who *might* be blackmailing him?"

Jessica's mouth set in a firm line, signifying her refusal to speak. But Tom hadn't missed the flash of surprise in her eyes.

Putting Jessica to the back of his mind, Tom went in search of the DCS. He knocked briefly on his boss's door then popped his head round. James Sinclair was on the phone, but when he saw Tom he waved him in, said his good-byes, and hung up.

"James, can you spare me a minute, do you think?"

"Certainly. I could do with a progress report. What have we got?"

Tom pulled up a chair to the desk and sat down, crossing his legs comfortably. For him, nothing beat mulling over the detail with somebody as experienced as his boss.

Tom filled him in on their unsatisfactory interview with Jessica.

"Do you think she *was* blackmailing him?" James asked.

"If only! But no, I don't think so. She clearly thought he walked on water, and you don't normally leave your blackmailer a heap of money in your will, even if it is tied to your ongoing silence. But everything seems to come back to these rescue girls."

Tom uncrossed his legs, leaned forward in his seat, and rested his forearms on the desk.

"I'm on it, though. I'll let you know when I've got some answers."

Tom knew that James was giving him his full attention despite the fact that he appeared to be swinging idly from side to side on his swivel chair.

"The main thing I wanted to discuss relates to the conversation with Annabel that I told you about. I'd like you to look at these pictures."

Tom laid the images down on the table. James stopped swinging and brought his chair back to upright with a thump. Pulling his reading glasses from the top of his head, he looked at the photographs that Tom had placed in front of him.

"Who's this, then? Mm. Very attractive woman, isn't she?"

"Was, actually. It's Hugo's mother, Lady Daphne Fletcher."

Without saying another word, Tom laid the second picture down. James looked at the picture, then up at Tom. His tone was serious and rather sad. "When was this taken?"

"About ten years ago. Just about the time she met Hugo, and way before she was ill."

"It's uncanny. Given everything else we know, especially what Annabel told us, it's a little sickening too."

"I agree. It's important to understand that Laura has never seen a photograph of her mother-in-law. She said that Hugo had some, but he liked to keep them private. She says she didn't look for them because he'd asked her not to. She can have no idea about this."

James shook his head sadly. "The poor woman. Well, I think it confirms that the man had an Oedipus complex, don't you?"

"An interesting point," Tom said, "because as I understand it, an Oedipus complex is not just an obsession with the mother, it's also a desire to kill the father. Since we now know that the father's death may not have been suicide, that's certainly an intriguing thought."

The senior detective looked pensive. With his face resting on one hand, his features were realigned and for a moment his face looked almost symmetrical. He moved his hand to speak, and the skin relaxed into its habitual imbalance.

"Does this get us anywhere, do you think?"

"No. But I think it confirms the fact that Hugo Fletcher was far from the saint the world believes him to be. If he married Laura because she was practically identical to his mother, then the poor woman must have lived through hell."

"Is that enough reason to kill him, do you think?"

"I'd say that Laura is a very rational woman, despite the mental health problems, which I still have to get to the bottom of. I think she must have had a terrible life with Hugo. The more I find out about him, the more disgusted I become. If she was the murdering type, I think she had more than enough reason to kill him."

Tom paused and thought about the Laura he had spent time with after the will reading.

"She was clearly not there for the money, as evidenced by her reaction to the will. And anyway we've now checked her whereabouts for the twenty-four hours before the murder, just to be absolutely sure. We asked PC Massi—obviously of Italian descent—to speak to the locals. The villa's just outside a small town where everybody knows everybody else's business. She was seen on Friday picking olives and the local carabinieri chap passed her car on the way to the airport on Saturday and waved to her. As if that weren't enough, we've checked the message that was on the phone in Oxfordshire. It definitely came from the house in Italy, and it was definitely on Saturday morning. And there's no doubt it was Laura's voice."

"What about the friend, Imogen Kennedy. Did she have any motive?"

"Becky likes her for it. Mind you, she also refuses to rule Laura out. She says there's something fishy going on. We think Hugo had something to do with the breakup of Imogen's marriage, but that was a long time ago. On the other hand, we thought the two women hadn't been in touch for years, but Becky discovered that they have. The other interesting thing is that apparently Imogen's maiden name is Dubois, and Becky discovered that somebody with the name Imogen Dubois caught the Eurostar from St, Pancras to Paris early on Saturday afternoon. But we've checked her passport, and it's in the name of Imogen Kennedy. She never reverted to her maiden name."

James Sinclair leaned forward in his chair. "But some people can legitimately have two passports. People who travel to both Israel and its enemies, for example, or people who do so much globetrotting that they need an extra passport to use because one might have to be submitted for a visa application just when they need to travel. This is sounding very promising."

"Well, not so promising actually. We've checked with the UK passport office, and there are no passports in that name, so that's another blind alley."

"Dubois is a rather unusual name for somebody from Manchester, isn't it?"

Tom laughed. "That's because she's not originally from Manchester, she's…Oh, *shit*. How could I have been so stupid?"

Tom was on his feet and running out of the door, dragging his mobile from his pocket as he ran.

"Becky? Imogen Kennedy left Cannes on Friday—is that right?"

With Becky's incredible memory, he knew that she would confirm his recollections, and she did.

"But her flight didn't leave Paris until late on Saturday afternoon?"

Again, Becky confirmed this—squeaking "why, why?" down the phone. But Tom wasn't to be distracted.

"I want you to work out how long it would have taken Imogen to drive to Paris from Cannes, and then I want you to go through the Eurostar records in the other direction. We know that an Imogen Dubois took the Eurostar from London to Paris—with just about time to catch that plane. But she would have had to get to London in the first place. See if she could have travelled over the night before or first thing in the morning on the Eurostar. If not, we need to start checking flights again."

Tom was out of the door, and on his way to where his car was parked. Becky was still yelling in his ear in her excitement that something finally seemed to be happening.

"What? Sorry, I missed that. Yes, it's quite possible. I'll put money on her having a Canadian passport, too. No, I've no idea of motive, but one thing at a time. I'll see you in about an hour."

27

Imogen was pleased to see Laura looking so much better. She was dressed casually again in jeans and a jumper, but the rigidity seemed to have gone from her shoulders, and she seemed less tense. Except when the bell at the gate rang. She jumped each time, as though she were expecting even more bad news. Perhaps she thought it was the police returning. It was three days since Tom Douglas had been, and Imogen was sure this meant that he was pursuing some active line of enquiry, although Becky had been very quiet on the subject.

Maybe the improvement in Laura was partly due to her discovery that Hugo had indeed overlooked her private money, and there was nothing to stop her from making some of the changes to the house that she'd been planning for years. She'd already started a team of gardeners who had begun to cut back the trees and shrubs, and both the house and Laura were looking considerably more cheerful. Even the stuffed stoat had miraculously disappeared overnight, although taking down some of the other dead animals would need a strong man with a large screwdriver.

Alexa had spent the day with them yesterday, and Imogen had watched and marvelled at the love and affection that Laura showed the girl. Although twelve years old, in many ways Alexa seemed much younger. She had a very delicate build, and seemed to be lacking the early signs of maturity that Imogen might have expected. Laura had spent hours talking through the changes that she wanted to make, and the ideas seemed to take Alexa's mind off the death of her beloved father.

Imogen decided that she needed to return to Laura's letters. It wasn't easy. She hated seeing her friend's unhappiness and felt the weight of it sitting heavily on her shoulders. She understood why Laura had never told her everything. But so many things still remained unexplained.

❖ ❖ ❖

JUNE 2005

My dear Imo,

These are the ravings of a mad person!

That's how I feel. I've spent eighteen months as a crazy woman and that's how everybody sees me.

Each day starts in the same way. The nursing staff work so hard, and they are relentlessly cheerful. Every morning they waltz into my room—which I have to say is very smart indeed—with a cheery "Good morning! How are we this morning?"

I don't understand why people say "we" in this context. Am I missing something here?

Anyway, breakfast is served in the room—and I've got into a rut of always having the same thing. I'm not sure whether they see this as one more sign of madness. Does this mean that I feel safer not making decisions? It's not that at all. It's just that they do have very good chefs here, and nothing beats their scrambled eggs!

The home is very exclusive. It's a place to hide away insane members of extremely rich families. I suppose there's no predicting how many seriously wealthy people will be ill at any one time—which is probably why they got into such trouble. I suspect that Hugo is providing significant funds. All to keep me quiet.

Each day I have to have a private consultation to check whether I'm still mad, and share in some group therapy session or other. And then there are the classes. Occupational therapy they call it. I'm pretty good at flower arranging now, and the yoga class is excellent—although the meditation sessions don't go down too well with some of the more disturbed patients. Too much silence and introspection is a bit counterproductive, or so it would seem.

Lunch and dinner are both taken in the dining room. We're supposed to mix—with the more stable patients, that is. Some, of course, can't be let out of their rooms because of outbursts of violence. I keep my own counsel. Despite the persistent jollity of the staff, it's not a happy place. Mental illness is such a heartbreaking thing. From schizophrenia to personality disorders, every one of them is in a sad period of their lives. And for some, it's their future, too.

I do try to find time each day to chat to some of the people with one form of dementia or another—those who can't communicate at all. I read the papers each morning, and tell them stories about what's happening in the world. Only the happy stuff, though. Not the wars and murders. They've got enough of a burden to carry. I don't know if they can hear me, but that's no excuse not to talk to them. Imagine *that they actually know what's going on around them, and the only thing they can't do is communicate? How awful would it be if nobody spoke to them?*

And then, there are the visits from Hugo. The nurses think this is the highlight of my week! And of course, to them he is a committed (if I can use that word in this context) and devoted husband who never misses a visit. I'm drug free on these occasions. He wants to assess me. He wants to know if I am full of remorse. He wants to know if I am tamed.

I'm not, of course. I'm far less tamed than I was when I came in here. But he doesn't need to know that.

And he brings Alexa quite often. She's growing up, but I feel so guilty being in here when I should be out there giving her the love that she needs. He brings her to taunt me. He thinks that seeing me here will turn her against me. Or that I'll try to use her to find things out about what was happening "on the outside." I don't. I'd never do that. I would never say anything negative about her father, because I'm the one who would lose out. She deserves to believe that her daddy is wonderful, whatever the truth might be.

He came to see me yesterday, and things were a little different. He left me alone with Alexa for a long time, and I'm not sure why he did it. I think it was another test.

I gave her a big hug, but she felt a bit stiff. Not her normal cuddly self. I tried to break the ice gradually.

"It's so good to see you, Alexa. How's school?"

"School's fine, thank you for asking, Laura."

At nine years old, Alexa is still the most polite child that I have ever met, but even so this response seemed a bit extreme.

"Are you okay, poppet? Have I done something to upset you?"

Alexa looked at me, with a very solemn gaze.

"Why are you still in here, Laura? Why aren't you at home with us?"

"Because I've not been well, darling, and Daddy and the doctors need to decide when it's the right time for me to come home."

"You do want to come home, don't you?"

"Oh, Lexi. Of course I do. I can't wait to see you every single week."

"Daddy says you like it here, and that you're in here because you make up bad stories about people."

I wasn't sure what to say to this. Criticising Hugo wasn't an option.

"Well, I certainly don't mean to do or say anything to upset anybody. I've never wanted to do that, sweetheart, and if I have then I'm very sorry."

"Can we talk about something else, please? When we've been on our own for a few minutes, Daddy always asks me what we've been talking about, and whether you've told me any secrets."

"We can talk about anything you like, and I wouldn't say anything to you that's a secret from Daddy."

"Well, Daddy and I have lots and lots of secrets—but he says that's okay. He says that daddies and their little girls always have secrets."

My blood ran cold.

"You know, poppet, it's usually okay to tell your mummy or me about secrets with Daddy. He wouldn't keep any secrets from me, I'm sure."

Alexa gave a shy smile.

"He said that you're the last person I should tell, because you're not clever like me. But I love you anyway, Laura. You're always nice to me. Can we talk about something else now, please?"

The conversation moved onto safer ground, but by now I was really worried. Hugo didn't come back for another half an hour, and I could only speculate that he had been cooking something up with the doctor. Judging by his very superior smile when he came back into the room, it was something I wasn't going to like.

"Alexa, darling, the nurse is going to take you outside for a moment. I need to talk to Laura alone. Say good-bye to her now, and I'll come and find you in a few moments."

Alexa gave me a big hug that nearly made my heart break, then she skipped off with the nurse.

"Laura. You're looking a lot better, and I've spoken to the doctor. We've agreed that you probably need another spell in here, probably about six months, and during that time I need to prepare you to come back out into the world."

I knew it was inappropriate to display my newfound spirit, but I had to clarify what he meant.

"I'm not sure I entirely understand what I need to be prepared for, Hugo, although I will be glad to be out of here."

This wasn't entirely true if it meant I had to go back to my old life. But then, I wasn't planning on doing that.

"You need to listen and understand well. I have been divorced once, and I have no intention of being divorced twice. Once can be considered a mistake. Twice shows poor judgement. You will not divorce me, nor will you make any threats or divulge information about our life together that would prove embarrassing to me. You will remain as my faithful wife for as long as I wish it. What goes on under my roof remains under my roof. Do you understand, Laura?"

I had to fight hard to retain my self-control. It wouldn't do to show all my cards at once, but I couldn't just accept this. I looked out of the window and tried to appear nonchalant.

"And if I don't agree? What happens then?"

"Oh, that's quite simple." Hugo paused. "You die."

My head jerked round, and I just stared at Hugo, too shocked to speak immediately. Then I found my voice.

"I don't believe you just said that. You have just threatened to commit murder!"

He laughed. He actually laughed.

"It's not murder. It's an act of self-preservation. I am not prepared to be shamed by you. You are known to have a history of extreme depression. Your death by an overdose of the very medication that you will be given on leaving here would be easy to explain, and I promise you it would never be questioned. Your records will show a history of attempted suicide—the doctor and I have just agreed the terms— so the choice is entirely yours."

Of all the things that I had expected, it had never been this. And I knew without a doubt that he meant it.

"And what does living with you mean, exactly?"

His smile was entirely without sincerity.

"Oh, don't worry. I won't ask you to renew your rather tedious services in the bedroom. I can find many a willing substitute."

I couldn't just let this go. If he meant what I thought he meant.

"When I came in here, it was triggered by..."

But I froze when I saw the fury in Hugo's eyes.

"I know what triggered it. Your ludicrous overreaction to a perfectly normal event. Your behaviour has made my life exceptionally difficult, and that is something that I can't forget or forgive. But this is what we are going to do."

And then we discussed terms, as if we were negotiating a business deal to buy a secondhand car. I've been thinking about this for a long time. Let's face it, I've had plenty time to think! I can't leave him and ignore everything that I know. The consequences would be too devastating. My history of mental illness would make it difficult for me to be believed if I tell anybody about Hugo's predilections. But I can't walk away. I have to do something positive. Something proactive. So I told him my terms. I made a deal with the devil. My complicity in return for a number of concessions—one of which is the purchase of a home in Italy. Somewhere to escape to, to feel safe—somewhere that he would hate. We can appear on the face of it to be a normal couple, but during the week when we don't have Alexa I can get away from the oppressive atmosphere of our marriage. This was a concession he found easy to make. But it was by no means the most important one.

Laura shouted up the stairs to Imogen. She knew she shouldn't disturb her, but somebody was ringing the front doorbell. She didn't know how they'd got past the gate, but perhaps the gardeners had left it open. Whatever the reason, she wanted Imogen with her in case it was a reporter.

Becky had appeared out of her "office," but seeing that Imogen was making her way quickly down the stairs, Laura smiled and shook her head briefly at Becky and went to let the new arrival in. It took her a moment to register who was standing on the doorstep.

She stood in silence with her mouth slightly open as she looked into the suntanned face and bright blue eyes of one of the few people she was happy to see. She saw the sorrow in those eyes, but whether it was a sign of sympathy for her or for the sadness in his own life she didn't know. His attempt at levity broke the spell.

"Close your mouth, Sis. It's really not very becoming."

"Oh my God! It really is you. I know you told Imo that you'd come, but I never thought you'd make it so quickly. Oh, Will—it's so wonderful to see you."

Laura flung her arms around her brother's waist and clung onto him for dear life, loving the warmth of his familiar broad body. She felt his arms go round her, and she welcomed the feeling of safety that nothing but a hug from somebody close to you can offer. But it wasn't to last for long. From just above her head, she heard her brother speak quietly.

"Hello, Imogen."

Silence.

She was glad that her head was buried in his chest, because she didn't want to see the glances that passed between them. Neither of these two had ever found anybody else to love, and she knew without a doubt that this was down to Hugo. She didn't know what she could do to mend what he had so carelessly broken, but she knew she was going to try.

Pulling back, she suggested they went into the drawing room. She couldn't get enough of looking at Will. His blond hair had been bleached to pale gold by the sun, and his rugged features were bronzed by sun. His shoulders—always broad—made him seem like a giant of a man as he looked down from his six feet, four inches of solid rock. He looked like the safest port in any storm.

It was clear that Imogen and Will couldn't really decide how to behave. Should they hug each other, as they both clearly wanted to, or should they remain aloof? The latter option obviously appeared the safer to both of them.

Laura was aware of the tension in the room, and all three of them looked slightly uncomfortable, as if one person shouldn't really be there but it wasn't clear which one. They filled a ten-minute gap with small talk about Will's job, Imogen's life in Canada, and the improvements that Laura was making to the house. Then Will broke the spell.

"Okay, you two. Enough of the idle chatter. You'd better tell me what's been going on. I won't pretend to have liked your husband, Laura, but I can't imagine why anybody would have wanted to murder him."

"It's a long story," Laura said. "The last few days have been hell. Before we start on that, I'll go and tell Mum you're here. She's probably in the kitchen. She seems to be of the opinion that we all need to be fattened up, and that chocolate cake cures everything."

As she stood up, she glanced out of the window and was surprised to see Tom Douglas standing by a marked police car. And two uniformed policeman were getting out. Laura felt a tightness in her chest.

"What's going on? Tom's here and he's got uniforms with him. What do you think it means, Imo?" Laura cast an anxious look in Imogen's direction.

"Calm down, Laura. It's probably nothing. They no doubt missed something in their search, so they're coming to have another look. Go and let them in, or I'll go if you like."

Laura was out the door before Imogen could get to her feet. Becky was already opening the front door, and as her eyes briefly met Laura's she looked away.

Tom stood on the doorstep and looked at Laura.

"I'm sorry to intrude, Lady Fletcher. May we come in?" He glanced enquiringly at Will, who had followed her into the hall with Imogen close on his heels.

Laura was not slow to miss the formality, nor the grim expression on Tom's face. Trying to keep it light, she responded in kind.

"Of course, Chief Inspector. May I introduce my brother, Will Kennedy. He's just arrived. Can I offer you something to drink? The ubiquitous cup of tea, perhaps?"

Tom took a couple of steps into the hall, but came no farther. "No, thank you. I'm sorry, but we need to ask Mrs. Kennedy some questions." He turned to Imogen, who was still hovering in the door to the drawing room. "Mrs. Kennedy, there are two uniformed police officers here. They will accompany you back to New Scotland Yard for some questioning. Detective Chief Superintendent James Sinclair, whom you met briefly on the night of Sir Hugo's death, will conduct the first part of the interview. You'll be cautioned when you arrive. I'll join you later when I've asked Lady Fletcher a few more questions."

Imogen didn't move. Her face didn't alter.

Will had advanced farther into the hallway, initially to shake the detective's hand, but now he took up a belligerent stance.

"May I ask why you're taking my wife in for questioning, Detective Chief Inspector? And if you're cautioning her, does that mean you're *arresting* her?"

"We have new evidence, sir, and it relates to your ex-wife. I'm not at liberty to discuss it with you until I have spoken to your ex-wife."

Laura could see that Tom was determined to differentiate between wife past or present.

Will turned to Imogen, frowning in his concern.

"Imo, what's all this about? Do you want me to get you a lawyer?"

It was obvious that Will's mention of a lawyer had spurred Imogen to life. She gave an exaggerated sigh.

"Will, shut up. You don't know anything about this, so please just butt out."

Laura was distressed. Her voice was quiet, but shaking with emotion. "Imo, you don't need to go through this. You mustn't. It's not right. I'll speak to Tom. I'll sort it, okay?"

Imogen's jacket was lying on a chair at the bottom of the stairs and she grabbed it in one hand and turned quickly to face Laura.

"Laura, will you just shut the fuck up, too, please? I didn't kill Hugo. You know that, and I know that—and I bloody hope you know that, too, Will. So just leave it. It's just questioning. If they arrest and charge me, they'll be in trouble because they can't have any evidence if I didn't do it, can they? Now calm down, have a large gin, and I'll see you later. I don't need a lawyer. I'm absolutely fine."

Imogen turned to Tom, who seemed to have been listening intently to this conversation.

"I'm ready to go, Chief Inspector."

There had been an undercurrent in that exchange that Tom couldn't quite grasp. As they closed the door behind Imogen and the uniformed policemen, he turned to Laura and gave her a sympathetic smile.

"I'm sorry about that, Laura. I had to be quite formal at that point. I'm sure you understand."

Will interrupted before she had a chance to answer.

"Well, I don't. Unless you have evidence, you can't just hike her off to be interrogated. If it was just a couple of questions, why couldn't you ask them here?"

A force to be reckoned with, thought Tom, noting Will's aggressive pose with legs apart and hands stuffed into the pockets of his jeans.

"Mr. Kennedy, we have evidence that suggests your ex-wife was in London on the morning of the murder. Now, if you don't mind, I would like to talk to your sister."

"I'm staying with her," Will responded. "I'm sure she needs my support."

Tom could see that Laura was visibly shaken, although he wasn't sure which particular part of the conversation had done the damage.

"Will, Tom and I have a good relationship. I know you mean well, but please go and find Mum. She'll be delighted to see you, and somebody needs to tell her about Imogen. I'm comfortable talking to Tom alone. Please, Will?"

Clearly not happy with this outcome, he eventually complied and begrudgingly left the hall. Laura indicated that they should move to the drawing room, and Tom waited until they were seated before he spoke again.

"Thank you, Laura. I've got a number of things that I want to ask you, and some are quite sensitive."

He could see that she was uneasy, but he needed her to relax if he was going to get anything out of her.

"How've you been, by the way? I notice that you've been making a few changes—definitely for the better."

Tom hoped she thought he was referring to the alterations to the house and grounds, but he hadn't missed the improvements to Laura herself. Today she had some colour in her cheeks, and once again had chosen a bright jumper, this time a petrol blue—so much better for her than the washed-out beige she'd been wearing when they met. It was hard to believe it was the same person he'd seen for the first time only a few days ago. And she appeared to have more confidence.

But she was clearly very upset about Imogen being taken in for questioning, and despite her assurances to her brother, Tom could tell from her tone of voice that he wasn't her favourite person today.

"Never mind the gardens for the moment. Just tell me what you can possibly have found that in any way links Imogen to Hugo's murder?"

"I'm sorry, but I can't say anything else at the moment. As soon as I can, I promise that I'll explain it to you."

Tom knew this wasn't going to satisfy Laura, so decided it would be best to move on quickly.

"This is difficult, I know—but could you talk to me a little bit about your illnesses, do you think? I asked you this the other day, but events overtook us. I know it might not seem relevant to you, but I'm just trying to get a picture. Is that okay?"

Laura had lost the hard edge to her voice, but it was tight with tension. "The first time I was sectioned—horrible word, I know—I was classed as being severely depressed. Hannah—Alexa's nanny—and Hugo had found me huddled in a room in one of the disused areas of the house."

"Do you know what brought that on? Was there some specific incident?"

"From what I've learned about clinical depression, it can hit anybody at any time and for no apparent reason."

Recognising that this was not an answer, nor was it intended to be, Tom probed a little more.

"Were you locked in the room where they found you?" he asked gently.

"Apparently the door could be opened from the inside, so that would suggest not."

She was so good at not lying, but not actually answering either. He needed to get her to look it him. Since asking about Imogen, she had been fixing her gaze on anything but him. He could understand that this was a difficult subject, but he had wasted too much time already.

"Laura, we've not known each other long, but I think that we already hold a mutual respect for each other, and there's something you're not telling me. Your husband's ex-wife is currently in a state of near panic over information that she gave me. The will showed Hugo for what he was, and I can only conclude that there were sides to him that didn't quite live up to his public image. Becky also overhead you talking about Rohypnol. This all ties together somehow, and I'd really like you to explain it to me."

Finally she looked at him, and nobody could miss the pain that was reflected in her eyes. He saw her swallow hard, and knew that he had touched a raw nerve. He felt a sharp shard of guilt, but these questions did have to be asked, and he would rather ask them himself than pass them on to somebody who didn't feel any connection with Laura.

"Tom, this is difficult and painful for me. My husband is dead, and our marriage was far from the perfect dream that everybody was supposed to believe. But I don't think that anything is going to be gained by looking into its dismal depths now, do you?"

She needed time, Tom decided, and perhaps examining the dregs of her marriage wasn't going to be quite as productive in the short term as understanding some of the other pieces of the puzzle.

"I don't entirely agree, but for now we can move onto something else and come back to it later. I want to talk to you about Danika Bojin."

Tom was not surprised to see that Laura was plainly even more uneasy with the change of subject.

"You heard the voice mail the other day about Danika Bojin. I can't help but wonder why you didn't mention that you knew her. She's now turned up safely, thank goodness, but we know that she came to see you about two years ago. Do you want to tell me about it?"

The expressions that had flitted across Laura's face during this brief exchange of information had been indecipherable. Tom couldn't decide if it was relief or fear that he was witnessing. Laura's face hadn't changed, but her eyes were so very expressive.

"I'm delighted to hear that Danika is safe," she said. "I was concerned when I heard the message, but I'm so far removed from the charity that I didn't feel in a position to help. Danika came to see Hugo, but he wasn't in, thank goodness. He'd have been furious. Anyway, she told me that one of her friends was missing and I said I'd try to look into it for her."

Tom felt that she was brushing this off far too easily.

"Unfortunately, it wasn't long after that that I became ill again, so I was never able to help her. That's why I was so upset when I heard the message."

"Didn't you ask Hugo to help?"

Tom noticed that once again, Laura couldn't meet his eyes, a definite habit when she wanted to disguise her thoughts.

"Yes, of course I did. He told me he would deal with it, and to keep my nose out of his charity affairs."

"And did you keep your nose out of it?"

Laura raised her chin defiantly, and looked Tom straight in the eye.

"Of course I did."

Tom didn't believe her for one single moment.

28

Imogen couldn't help feeling nervous as she was led into the interview room. Perhaps everybody, guilty or innocent, felt this way. She knew she had to disguise this emotion, though. It always seemed to indicate guilt, as far as she could see. She had refused a lawyer for two reasons. She hoped it would make her appear confident of her innocence, and more to the point, she didn't want to have anybody else probing into her recent movements. She wished with all her heart that Will hadn't been there. She hadn't seen him for years, and then suddenly there he was. But within moments she'd had to suffer the indignity of being taken into police custody—or at least, taken away for questioning. All she wanted was to be where he was, just one more time.

Imogen had used the hour-long car journey to decide on the approach she was going to take, and despite an empty and slightly nauseous feeling in her stomach, she was determined to appear self-assured. All they had was circumstantial evidence. And she was seriously worried about Laura. Tom Douglas had managed to get under her skin, and there were things that he mustn't know.

She took her seat opposite DCS Sinclair and one of his officers and did her best to appear calm, while struggling to come to terms with the fact that she was being officially questioned in a murder investigation, and had even been cautioned. She looked at the deceptively kind face of the senior police officer but wasn't taken in for a moment by his apparent benevolence. It was so difficult to read his expression, anyway, as one half of his face seemed to frown whilst the other smiled. She decided she would focus on the frowning side to ensure that she didn't get lulled into a feeling of false security.

"Chief Superintendent, I do understand your point of view. If you say there was an Imogen Dubois on the Eurostar from Paris to London and then London to Paris, I can't dispute that. But surely you can check credit card payments, or online bookings, or whatever you do to get a ticket on Eurostar, and prove that it was a *different* Imogen Dubois?"

James Sinclair nodded sagely, as if this were a wise comment.

"Mrs. Kennedy, of course that's the first thing we would have done. But as luck would have it, the tickets were purchased with cash, from the sales point on Regent Street. It's quite unusual for people to pay in cash these days, you know. In fact, it's *extremely* unusual. So unusual that it makes me wonder why somebody would do it."

There was a slight note of sarcasm in his voice—something that Imogen had never encountered with Tom Douglas. She was going to have to take care.

"Who knows, Chief Superintendent. Perhaps they'd just had a lucky win on the horses or something. And if you believe it was me, that rather suggests that I was in London at the time the tickets were bought, doesn't it? I presume you've checked if that's the case?"

Imogen was feeling pleased with herself, but the policeman changed the subject abruptly, throwing her slightly off balance again.

"I understand that you have your laptop computer with you at the house in Oxfordshire. We would very much like to take a look at it, with your permission. Of course, we can go through the whole paperwork approach and get a warrant, but if you've got nothing to worry about, you won't mind if we take a look, will you?"

Imogen tried hard to control the hard jerk of fear. From the slight narrowing of his eyes, she suspected the policeman hadn't missed her reaction. She answered as calmly as possible. "Of course. It's not a problem. If you could ask Laura to get it, it's in my bedroom. She'll know where to look."

The chief superintendent signalled the policeman standing by the door, who immediately left the room. This time when he smiled, both sides of his face lifted. He was one smooth customer.

"I hope you don't mind, but we'll ask Sergeant Robinson to get it for us. Saves any doubts about contamination of evidence. You know the sort of thing, I'm sure. Now, what I really need to know—and remember that you have been cautioned—is when did you last see Hugo Fletcher?"

"It was December 1998. I can probably tell you the exact date and time, if pushed."

"And why was it so memorable, Mrs. Kennedy?"

"Because at the end of the visit, Laura and I argued, and I was never invited back to the house."

James Sinclair thrust his head forward and looked straight into Imogen's eyes. "Why did you argue? Did you fancy your chances with Laura's husband? Did you have a relationship with him?"

Imogen didn't even try to hide her revulsion at the very thought. "I had no relationship with him at all. I didn't find him remotely attractive, and apart from anything else, he was Laura's husband."

"Ah, but did he find *you* attractive? Was that the problem? Did he pester you, put you in a difficult position with your friend and your husband?"

"No. *No.*"

She hated the way he was questioning her, his large head looming across the table. She wanted to move her chair back—as far away from him as possible. She didn't believe that any criminal would have a chance in front of James Sinclair. Then he backed away slightly, and she felt a flutter of relief. The questions were still coming, but he wasn't in her face anymore.

"So tell me, Mrs. Kennedy. When did you last see Lady Fletcher, prior to the night of her husband's death?"

This was her moment. Imogen knew it. If she got this right, she would be fine. If she got it wrong—well, she couldn't even begin to think of the consequences. She sighed dramatically and for effect, hoping she hadn't overdone it.

"Okay, we haven't been entirely honest about this. Force of habit, I think. After the argument, I wasn't in touch with her until her second stay in hospital. We worked out a way that I could see her whenever I was in England without anybody knowing. Hugo would never have allowed it. We kept in touch when she returned home."

James Sinclair was slowly shaking his head, with raised eyebrows. "That doesn't quite answer my question, does it, Mrs. Kennedy. When did you *last* see her, prior to the night of Hugo's death?"

Imogen needed to think. What would Laura say if asked the same question? They had to be consistent. She didn't think that he'd missed her pause, but surely it was understandable that she had to think—to mentally check her diary?

"It would have been in the summer. Laura was in Italy, and Hugo never went with her, so it was completely safe as long as I didn't answer the telephone or anything stupid like that. I went to stay with her for a couple of days."

"And you've not seen her since?"

"No."

What do they say about people when they lie? Something about their eyes, looking down to the left? She couldn't remember, so she tried to look him straight in the eye without wavering.

"So why, exactly, was Lady Fletcher so appalled when you appeared on the doorstep? She looked as if she would like to murder *you*, let alone anybody else."

"Force of habit, I think. She was probably in another world, and when I appeared she no doubt expected Hugo to suddenly materialise from his study and strike her down. I don't know—it was a bit much, but she's over it now."

She forced herself to continue to look him in the eye. She could see that he didn't believe her.

"One more question, Mrs. Kennedy, and then we'll take a break. Why did Lady Fletcher say, 'You have absolutely no idea what Hugo was capable of. This was the least of his crimes,' and 'I am so very glad that Hugo is dead'?"

Imogen was stunned into silence for a few seconds. How in God's name did they know about that?

"I don't know how you can possibly be aware that she uttered those exact words, Chief Superintendent, but out of context it's a little difficult to say."

Sinclair clamped his lips together and shook his head again, making her feel like a child caught out in a silly lie.

"Cut the crap, please. You know very well what she meant, and you're going to tell me."

"Fine. First of all, I think you should ask her, because I would only be guessing. More importantly, I didn't like Hugo—so anything I say is inevitably going to be coloured. In my view he was a difficult, unpleasant, and manipulative man. Laura was *not* ill, but he made her seem so. I suspect she's glad he's dead because of the control he exercised over her life. But that can be nothing more than supposition, can it, Chief Superintendent, and therefore probably worthless."

She spoke with spirit. She didn't want to appear rattled, but how did they *know* all this? A quick knock came on the door, which opened to reveal a young Asian man in the doorway, beckoning the DCS, who excused himself and left the interview room.

Imogen breathed a sigh of relief. She thought she had done okay, but only time would tell.

In the corridor, James Sinclair was faced with a beaming detective. Whatever he'd found, he was certainly excited by it.

"What is it, Ajay?"

"We've just had another call from the bodyguard company. One of the guys who looked after Sir Hugo is on holiday. He was contacted at the start to answer some questions, but he was probably too busy enjoying himself to give much thought to it, and apparently he phoned back today with a bit more information. There was one incident that he thought we might be interested in. He was driving Hugo from Oxford into London one night a couple of years ago when he realised they were being followed. They hadn't quite reached the motorway, so he turned down a quiet road in the middle of nowhere. He said the guy following was pretty rubbish. So with Hugo's blessing he pulled a stunt. He raced ahead, shut off his lights, and did a one eighty—fancies himself a bit, I think—then when the other guy came round the corner he shone his lights straight into him, and he swerved onto the side of the road.

"The bodyguard was out of the car in a flash, and had the guy by the scruff of the neck within seconds. I didn't ask how they got him to talk, but they did. He said he'd been paid to follow Sir Hugo, night and day. They asked who was paying him."

Ajay paused, and James knew that he was waiting for him to ask.

"And did he answer?"

"He most certainly did. It was the wife. It was Laura Fletcher."

29

Tom's "informal chat" with Laura had been interrupted more than once, with a mix of good news and bad.

The first interruption was Kate. He wouldn't normally have taken a personal call, but this was too important. Tom had heeded Laura's words of wisdom, and much as he loved his daughter he really couldn't see himself living with her mother again. Last night they'd had an emotional discussion on the subject, but he had been resolute. Kate was calling to say she was going back to Manchester at the weekend "to think." He would have to wait and see what happened next.

He wished he could talk to Laura about it—but he knew he'd already overstepped the mark. And then James Sinclair had phoned, so he'd stepped out into the hall to take the call. He was now certain Laura knew far more than she was revealing, and he couldn't prevent a feeling of regret that he was going to have to ask her some difficult questions.

But it was the third call that really excited him.

Laura could tell by Tom's face when he returned to the drawing room that there had been some news, and she was beginning to feel very uncomfortable. She was struggling to remain in control, and increasingly she didn't want to lie to this man. He had shown her nothing but compassion and consideration, and she could tell he wasn't happy himself. She'd watched his face when he was talking to Kate, and the only thought that came to her mind was why does there have to be so much grief in the world?

Tom sat down in his usual position opposite her.

"Laura, do you want anybody with you while I ask you some more questions?"

"No, I'm fine. Just ask whatever you need to," she answered, hoping to get this over with as quickly as possible.

"We talked earlier about your illness, and you described what caused your first stay in hospital. But we have been led to believe that the second stay was different. Some sort of delusional disorder was reported in the papers, although of course that could be wrong. We also know that one of our own chief constables—Theo Hodder—was involved in some way, and we are trying to track him down to understand his involvement. But I'd really rather it came from you."

Laura had been dreading this. She knew that her answer had to be plausible, but since Tom had raised this when he last saw her, she had been practising. She would give him the facts, but try to keep emotions in check. Nevertheless, she could hear that her voice shook slightly.

"When I returned from my first stay in hospital, things were a little more stable between Hugo and me, although I could sense that things were subtly different. I assumed he had a mistress, and perhaps that was understandable as I'd been away for a couple of years. Then Danika came to see me about her missing friend Alina, and I got it into my head that something might be happening to the girls. I believed that Hugo could be involved. I dreamt up this whole conspiracy thing. I thought he might be enticing them away. Perhaps for sex, or maybe to just sell them on again. I don't know what I was thinking."

Laura thought that in all of this she had become the master of the understatement.

"Anyway, I'd met Mr. Hodder at one of the charity dinners, so I went to him with my theory. It must have been clear to him that I hadn't thought it through at all, and my imagination was working overtime. I realised I was making a fool of myself. He was one of the few people who knew I'd been ill before, and he obviously saw this as some sort of a relapse. So he called Hugo. I wasn't able to get the idea out of my head at all, so they diagnosed me as delusional, and he provided some supporting evidence. That's it, really."

Laura as usual was avoiding Tom's eyes, but she risked a glance. She saw concern, but she saw something else. She saw a glimmer of excitement in his eyes, and she realised that she hadn't been convincing enough.

"Look, Tom, I know it sounds completely ridiculous now. I made an idiot of myself. Mr. Hodder and his family apparently had one of the Allium girls themselves at one time. I gather it didn't work out too well, but he had nothing but praise for Hugo. I'm very embarrassed about it, so can we please forget it?"

"Did you know that Hugo asked Jessica to shred all the documents relating to the missing girls?"

Laura was startled. She hadn't known this—but somehow it all made perfect sense. Hugo was a bastard, but he was a clever bastard. Tom had clearly not missed her expression.

"You didn't know, did you? He also arranged to pay Jessica eight thousand pounds a month as 'a little bonus' for doing something for him that she's not prepared to divulge. He paid her in cash, so that explains where a big chunk of the twenty thousand a month went. And then you employed a private detective to follow Hugo. Hugo found out, and no doubt scared you off. Then you went to the chief constable. How am I doing so far?"

Too well, thought Laura. Far too well. But she said nothing and just looked levelly at him, hopefully hiding her surprise that most of the ten thousand she didn't know about was now accounted for.

"Well here's the good news. I've just had a call from one of my colleagues who is at the Allium offices. The delightful but apparently rather lazy Rosie has just admitted that the girls' details seemed too big a pile to shred, so she hid the boxes. We've got people going through them—starting with the past five years."

Tom's face was a picture. He thought this was going to provide all the answers, she could see that. She almost felt sorry for him, but he hadn't finished.

"Laura, I need you to tell me. Do you still think it was a delusion? You don't, do you? You never did. But what I don't understand is, if you thought something was happening to the girls, why didn't you say something to me when you heard that Danika was missing?"

She didn't know how many more lies she could tell this man. But he had a daughter of his own. Perhaps he would understand.

"I couldn't see the point in telling you—I thought it would do more harm than good. Hugo's *dead*, so it would be too late for any girls that have already disappeared, and he can't do it anymore, can he? It was so much better if you didn't investigate it. I had to protect Alexa. I kept quiet for her sake. She had to be my number-one priority. And they're safe now—the girls. They *must* be."

She suddenly felt racked with guilt. She had known so much, but not enough. She had been sure that the police would act all those months ago, but she had ended up back in a mental institution. She could have told them everything she suspected when she heard Danika was missing, but she assumed it was either too late, or that the girl would be safe now that Hugo was dead. She chose to keep quiet to protect Alexa. Tom was too smart to let it lie.

"Hang on, Laura. You said that in your delusions you imagined that something 'might be' happening to the girls, and Hugo 'could be' involved. But it sounds as if you knew for sure that something was happening. When Danika turned up, she told us the reason she'd been away. Another of her friends has gone missing very recently. Mirela Tinescy. And she left a note— a note that nobody believed. She's still missing, Laura. If Hugo took her, what do you think he's done with her?"

"You're assuming that I was right, aren't you—that it wasn't just a delusion? You believe that I wasn't mad, don't you?"

Tom was looking at her with such empathy that Laura wanted to cry. His eyes were filled with sorrow, and she knew that he was picturing her life with Hugo and her years in the care home. He stood up and came to sit next to her on the sofa, turning his body to face her. He reached out and clasped her cold hands between his. His voice was infinitely gentle as he spoke.

"Laura, James Sinclair asked Becky to retrieve Imogen's laptop from her bedroom. Lying next to it on the bed was a letter. From you, Laura."

He gently massaged some warmth back into her hands as he spoke, his compassionate eyes never leaving her face.

"And I know what it says."

30

Dear Imogen,

Today's been a peculiar day all round. The weather has been stormy one minute with the rain pelting down, and then there have been flashes of sunshine in between. But it wasn't nice enough to get out into the garden and finish tidying up for winter. I know we've got gardeners, but if I don't do something I really will go mad!

So all I did all day was sit gazing out of the window, wishing I'd gone back to Italy. At least there I can keep the demons at bay. Here, they confront me at every turn. Then I thought of you, my dear long-lost friend.

I've been back at Ashbury Park for a year now, but I've still got to be so very careful. I can't step out of line. I have to appear cowed and under Hugo's complete control. I'm here for one reason, and one reason only. A reason I haven't told you about. I don't think I could bear to see it written down, if you want the honest truth.

I really should have gone to Italy. I only stayed this week because I thought Hugo wanted me to help prepare for Christmas, and in particular to buy Alexa's presents. In the event, he seems irritated that I'm here.

We barely see each other now—which is fine by me. Hugo goes out regularly, and stays away often. Sometimes he seems positively exhilarated about the prospect of the night ahead, so I can only assume he's got a mistress. Poor woman.

Having asked me to be here to organise the shopping, he phoned earlier today to say he was going to be gone for a day or two. And he didn't want to be contacted. He sounds really angry about something, but at least I don't have to give yet another Oscar-winning performance this evening.

So I settled down by the fire with a glass of wine and a good book. Then the intercom at the gate rang. I was startled for a moment. Nobody ever comes here uninvited, and very few invitations are issued. I did wonder for a moment if it might be you!

When I answered, it was a voice I didn't recognise.

"Hello. I would like to see Sir Hugo Fletcher, please. My name is Danika Bojin."

"I'm sorry, but my husband isn't here. And I'm afraid he doesn't like doing business from the house. Perhaps you could go to the office?"

"I already go to the office two days ago, and nobody helps me. You are his wife? Please. Can you help me?"

I had no idea what this was about, but it was cold, wet, and dark outside, and the girl sounded very distressed. She looked extremely young in the video monitor, and I felt sorry for her, so I invited her in.

It turned out that she'd come to talk to Hugo about a friend of hers who's missing. She's disappeared, and Danika doesn't believe she would have gone without saying anything, so she suspects something has happened to her. She was clearly very worried.

I was impressed by her loyalty—coming all this way just to try to talk to Hugo. And she must have walked at least the last three miles in the pouring rain. Her English is amazing. I wasn't surprised to learn that she'd been an excellent student. How tragic that she'd been dragged into a life of prostitution. My own life is sad, but it's nothing compared to this girl's story. She was so very anxious.

"I know I'm told I must not to come to here, and I'm so sorry, but I don't know what I must do. Alina would not go away and not tell to us. She is happy where she live. Something has happened to her. I know this."

"Did you have any idea at all that she was thinking of leaving?"

Danika thought for a few moments. She looked very worried.

"I don't know. The last times we see her, she seem to be too happy. Big smile and shiny eyes. It was like that. Mirela see it too—so we ask her about it, and she say she has a secret, but she cannot tell to us. I think perhaps she has fallen in love with husband of family, so I asked it. She laughed and said I mistook her. The family is wonderful, and she never want to make them to be angry with her. She want to stay with them until she find a man to look after her in a proper way, you understand?

Perhaps she find him—but I do not think she would leave without explaining it to the family."

I really wanted to help her, but I didn't know how. All I could think of doing was giving her something to eat and drink, and then organising a car to take her home. But I did promise to do the best I could to find out what might have happened to her friend. I was so embarrassed by my lack of knowledge about the Allium Foundation.

"Did you ever meet my husband, Sir Hugo?"

"Oh, yes. We all meet him. He come to talk with us when we go to Allium. We line up and he choose some to talk to."

"Did he talk to you?"

"No. I am unhappy that he did not. But he talk for a long time to Alina, and he also talk to Mirela a bit. But not me. Perhaps I am too ugly."

"Of course you're not ugly, Danika. Do you have a photo of either of your friends?"

"No. But pictures are taken. They should be at Allium offices."

Since Danika went, I've been sitting and thinking for a long time about what I can do. And I've decided. Here is an opportunity to help somebody. To do something useful. If Jessica can't be bothered to help Danika, then I will. I won't tell Hugo, because he'll only find some reason to stop me. But I don't really see why he should mind. After all, I'm sure he doesn't want these girls to just disappear.

I'm going to leave this letter open, then I can tell you what happens with my investigation!

It's now six days since Danika came, and I decided that as Hugo is away yet again I'd go to the Allium offices and see what I can find out about Danika's friend, Alina. I can't go to the office when Hugo's there, so this is the first chance I've had.

When I arrived at Egerton Crescent, I went straight up to the apartment and I bumped into Rosie. She often leaves papers on Hugo's desk there. He studies them in the evening, with the lamps lit and a single malt on the desk next to him. I used to think it was bliss just to sit and watch him. That was a long time ago.

I asked Rosie to have a cup of coffee with me. She's a nice girl, even if she is a bit obsessed with shopping. I explained why I was there, and she told me that Danika and Mirela had been to the office just over a week ago, which I knew of course. She told me that several girls go missing every year, but they're not investigated if they leave a note. Hugo says there's no point going to the trouble as they've obviously left out of choice. Danika's friend left a note—so that was it.

I asked Rosie if she knew the date Alina disappeared. She could remember that Hugo was out that day, but that was all. As he's out several times a week, that wasn't very helpful. Then an idea came to her, and she pulled the diary towards her. She pointed to a date.

"This is it. I remember because we'd just heard she was missing when the BBC called to ask if Sir Hugo would be interviewed for Panorama—a special on people trafficking—and I couldn't get in touch with him to ask."

I asked why she couldn't contact him for something so important, and she pointed to some letters in his diary—LMF. Rosie explained that when the diary says LMF she can't call him, and no other appointments can be made for these days—under any circumstances. She assumed I would know what it meant, but I haven't a clue. The L could stand for Laura, I suppose—but I don't have a middle name, and anyway he'd be highly unlikely to see anything to do with me as a red-letter day.

Whilst we were chatting, Jessica called up the stairs. She didn't know I was there, and she certainly wouldn't have been happy that I was asking all these questions.

"Another girl's gone AWOL, Rosie. She's left a note, but I need to go and see the family. You'll need to come down and man the phones. God knows what you're doing up there, anyway!"

With that, the front door slammed. Rosie gave me an apologetic look and went downstairs. I decided to have a look at his diary for myself. I know he's in "noncontact mode" today, and sure enough, it says "LMF" again in his diary. Just as it did on that date three months ago when Alina went missing.

I don't know if it's me—but that seems like a hell of a coincidence. He's out of touch when Alina goes missing, and today when he's incommunicado another girl goes missing. If I hadn't known so much about Hugo—if he'd been an ordinary man—I would never have thought anything of it. But he's not.

I decided to look back through his diaries. It was strange. Every few months there was an LMF in ink, underlined. There was even one in for three months ahead. But looking backwards there were other entries in pencil that said LMF. So I took the current diary downstairs and asked Rosie about these. She said they appeared quite randomly, usually only a day or two in advance, and when he wrote them in pencil he was happy to move them for other appointments. Only the ones in ink were fixed and not to be changed under any circumstances. But in either case, once the day arrived, he could not be contacted.

Then bloody Jessica came back, because she'd forgotten some papers or something. She couldn't exactly ask me what I was doing there, but her face said it all. I told her I would like to see the files on all the girls that have gone missing. She refused. I said Hugo had asked me to do it, but she clearly didn't believe me.

I need to know whether there is any link between these girls running away, and Hugo disappearing for a couple of days. If he's taking these girls as a mistress—even temporarily—I want to know. I don't care—at least not from my perspective (I pity the girls, though)—but it could be very useful ammunition if that's what he's doing.

I had to give up on Jessica. I know she'll tell Hugo, so I need to think of some excuse. I'll tell him about Danika then say that Rosie explained about the notes, and feign a lack of interest. But I want to know what those initials stand for.

I need to be careful, though. If Hugo finds out, I'm dead (quite possibly literally).

I have made a stupid mistake and now I'm very scared. This isn't like researching a television programme. This is real life. My real life. And it's not just my life I need to think about. I got carried away with my own cleverness, and I don't know what's going to happen.

After my visit to the office, I decided the only sensible thing to do was to hire a private detective. I would have Hugo followed. I've always believed he has a mistress. But what if it's something more sinister? I need to know.

I thought I'd done my research into private detectives thoroughly. I thought I'd found somebody reputable. I should have known better.

Hugo returned from wherever he'd been, and of course I was quizzed about my trip to the office. Jessica wouldn't have wasted any time. I think I covered it reasonably well, although I was told in no uncertain terms that the charity is none of my business and they have procedures, of which I know nothing.

And then the worse thing happened. Hugo had hired a bodyguard for the evening. I should have realised that he wouldn't be up to anything as he had a potentially talkative minder with him—but I stupidly asked the detective to follow him anyway, and he was caught! And not only that, he told Hugo—no doubt with some persuasion—that it was me who had employed him.

Hugo's fury was something that I can't even begin to describe. And I could find no reasonable excuse. I couldn't say I was concerned that he had a mistress. He knows I would be delighted. I couldn't think of a single thing to say. I just sat there and let his torrent of verbal abuse roll over me. I have never seen him so furious—even more furious than that time when he locked me away.

And now I think he's trying to decide what to do with me. I need to act, and quickly. Not for me—I don't care anymore. But there's more than my life at stake.

I have to tell somebody. I have to make somebody understand. It's no good telling you—what could you do? And I don't have any other friends. If I told my mum or Will, I don't know what Hugo would do. He'd find some way of making them lose all credibility, possibly something really dreadful. So it needs to be a person with authority. It needs to be somebody who will protect me—and not just me, of course. Oh, I know what Hugo will say. He'll point back to my depressed state, and explain away my overactive imagination. I need to be convincing—and all without a scrap of evidence.

So I've decided. I'm going to go to the police. Affairs with prostitutes are not illegal, I'm sure, but if they're disappearing they'll have to investigate it. There's a chief constable that I've met a few times at charity dinners. Theo Hodder. I'm going to go to him.

I'll tell him everything. Then he'll have to act.

And I'll leave this letter somewhere where only you would ever find it, Imo—in case something happens to me. There's one place that Hugo would never think to look, but you would. Who would have thought all those years ago when we hollowed out that old copy of The Secret Garden to hide my diary that I'd need to use it again!

In fact, all my letters to you are hidden there—so if you're reading this, I wonder what's become of me?

I probably didn't tell you this often enough, Imo—but I really love you. And I'm so, so sorry.

Xxxx

31

A SMALL VILLAGE IN CRETE

Less than two thousand miles away on the island of Crete, a small group of middle-aged holidaymakers were having a pre-lunch drink in a small bar, perched on the side of a hill and well off the beaten track. Although late in the year, the sun was warm enough to sit outside at midday, and the surrounding countryside was still parched awaiting the winter rains.

"Bit of a find, this place. Look at that view!" one of the women said.

"I bet the food's good, too. Look, there's a couple of locals just coming in, and that's usually a good sign, so they say."

"Only three more days, and it's back to the rain for us."

"And on that jolly note—cheers, everybody!"

The two couples continued to talk companionably about the holiday and about some of the people they'd met, the wives making thinly disguised catty remarks about a particularly glamorous woman whom they'd caught their husbands chatting up in the bar.

The local couple hadn't been given a menu, and were just presented with a plate of food that looked quite delicious. They were keeping themselves very much to themselves, and talking quietly in what the English contingent could only guess was Greek. Unlike the Brits, who were talking at full volume on the basis that nobody would understand a word they were saying.

"I tell you what, though," one man said, "it's been good to get away from the news. It's so depressing. Bombing in Pakistan, banks going bust, unappealing politicians trying to capture our votes whilst stabbing each other in the back—at least here we can just relax. I know it's all a bit ostrich-like, but I do prefer not knowing all this stuff when I'm on holiday."

The man's wife put her glass down. "I must say I'd like to know what's been happening in the Hugo Fletcher murder case, though. We've missed all that. I couldn't believe it when we saw the newsflash at the airport. Who would want to kill a man like that? I bet it was something to do with a woman. He was a bit of a dish, wasn't he?"

The other woman nodded her agreement. "He's got a young daughter, too. She's only about eleven or twelve, I think. Poor kid."

Trying to get away from the subject, the more rotund of the two men tried to move to a topic that was closer to his heart. "Why don't we all agree to forget the news for now and enjoy this wonderful place. Okay? Let's order some lunch. I want what they're having." He rudely pointed to the only other occupied table.

The Greek couple said nothing. Their eyes met, and the man reached his hand across the table and tenderly stroked the arm of the woman sitting opposite him.

They got up quietly to leave, the man throwing a twenty-euro note on the table, their plates still half full of uneaten food.

32

It didn't take the police team long to plough through the files on the Allium girls—either accounted for or missing. There was a sense of urgency, as if everybody knew that something was about to happen. Tom received the all-important call whilst he was still in Oxfordshire. He wasn't relishing what he knew he had to do next.

"Laura, I don't know how you're going to react to this, so please sit down. You should have somebody with you. Shall I get your mother or brother?"

"No, thank you. I'd rather just hear it myself, whatever it is."

He took up a seat next to her again. He really wanted to hold her hands again, but he knew it wasn't appropriate. Instead, he tried his best to convey his deep sympathy through the warmth of his voice.

"I'm sorry, Laura. It's not often that being right is the worst option, but in this case I think it's true. And it would seem that you were right about Hugo. There's still some chance that it's coincidence, but it's highly unlikely. On or around every date in the last five years that Hugo has an underlined LMF in his diary, a girl has disappeared. They've each left a note, so there was no investigation."

Laura had bowed her head, as if she felt the acute shame of being associated with this man and whatever he had done. She didn't speak, so Tom continued.

"Only Rosie was really in a position to make the connection, and there were quite lengthy gaps—at least in the early years. And of course there were other girls that went missing in between these dates, which I think we can assume are unrelated. Given that the girls weren't necessarily reported missing immediately, it's understandable that she didn't realise the significance. And why would she even begin to *think* that he had anything to do with it?"

He was quiet for a moment, giving Laura the space to make sense of her own thoughts, if that were in any way possible. Finally she looked up. There was no hint of surprise at these revelations on her face, and it was clear to Tom that she had always known that something had been happening. Why else would she have reported her husband to a chief constable?

So why had Theo Hodder not acted? He posed the question to Laura.

She shrugged. "He refused to listen. He said that Hugo was a saint, and nothing I said would convince him otherwise. But I hadn't realised just how close he and Hugo were."

Tom was slightly puzzled by this remark. "What do you mean, close? I wasn't aware that they were actually *friends*. You should know that Hodder isn't a very popular man, and is actively disliked in some quarters."

"I think he owed Hugo a favour. But I don't know more than that. In ways that I can never explain to you, he probably did me a very good turn."

Mystified as he was by this comment, Tom had more to reveal. He was sure that now this was all out in the open, Laura would be willing to help.

"We think LMF has to represent a place. The underlined dates correspond to the dates they went missing, so we reckon the pencilled-in dates are probably when they met subsequently, but we don't know for sure. We're getting Brian Smedley to pull together a list of all the properties owned by the company to see if we can make a link. And we're looking for hotels with those initials too."

He was disappointed to see Laura shake her head. "He wouldn't have gone to a hotel. He'd have been spotted."

Tutting with exasperation, Tom made one last plea. "I'm sure we've got to solve this mystery to get to the bottom of his murder. If there's anything else you know, you must tell me."

"I don't *know* anything. It was always supposition on my part. I *do* know that you need to be looking for somewhere remote. Somewhere he wouldn't be recognised. Where nobody could see him coming and going."

"The thing is, if the girls went with him willingly, what do you think happened when he got tired of them, which he must have done as he seemed to take a new girl every three months or so? And would it be a motive for murder? It wouldn't be the first time that somebody has died at the hands of a woman scorned."

33

It felt to Laura as if a year had passed since Imogen had been taken to the police station, so when she saw a police car pull up in the drive and a weary Imogen emerge from the backseat, her relief was overwhelming. She rushed to open the front door.

"Imogen! Are you okay? I've been so worried. What did they ask you? What did you say?"

She gave her friend a hug and held on tight. Despite his warmth and understanding, when Tom had left to return to New Scotland Yard, taking Becky with him, he had declined to tell her when she could expect Imogen back, simply asking her to be patient.

Imogen moved away from the embrace and gave Laura a look of such concern that the panic lying just below the surface threatened to engulf her again.

"I'm fine. But the letters? What about the bloody letters? Christ, I'm so sorry. There was one on my bed! Did they see it when they came for the laptop?"

Relaxing slightly, Laura answered, "Becky found it. It was the one about Danika. I've spoken to Tom about it—I'll tell you later."

Imogen let out an audible breath. "Thank God I'd shredded the earlier ones! But what about the rest—the ones you wrote after that?"

"They were in your drawer, and they hadn't asked if they could search your room. So I shredded them. You know most of it anyway. It's all the stuff I told you in the home."

Imogen looked at Laura keenly. "I'd assumed the later ones would fill in the gaps—and there are some. When are you going to tell me the rest? It's like you've given me a jigsaw but kept back the vital piece that make sense of the picture."

"It's honestly better if you don't know everything until it's all over, one way or the other."

Laura could sense that Imogen wasn't going to settle for this, so she quickly changed the subject.

"Anyway, Imo—what about you? Was it really awful?"

"Hah! To say it's been a bit traumatic would be something of an understatement." Imogen wasn't really concentrating on the conversation, though. She was looking around her. They hadn't moved from the hall, and she seemed to be trying to look over Laura's shoulder. It came as no surprise to her when Imogen asked the inevitable question.

"Where's Will?"

Still always Imogen's first thought, and she was bound to be disappointed at Laura's answer.

"We were all getting upset and agitated, so he took Mum to buy some food. You know what she's like—a good hot meal and all our troubles are over. I'll ring him and let him know that you're back."

Laura moved towards the phone, but Imogen reached out a hand to stop her.

"Leave it, honey, if you don't mind. You know what I need? A stiff gin and tonic, and a very hot bath to remove the stench of the interrogation room. All I can say is there must have been a lot of very guilty people in there, judging by the stink of stale sweat." Imogen attempted a laugh. "It had ingrained itself into the walls. Come and talk to me, though, because I need to get it all off my chest. Unlike some people around her, I prefer to share."

Ignoring the barbed comment, Laura volunteered to get the gin whilst Imogen ran the bath. She shouted up the stairs to Imogen's retreating back.

"Use my bathroom, Imo, I've got some gorgeous Jo Malone stuff in there. Lime, basil, and mandarin. That will get rid of any lingering odours. Just help yourself."

Laura decided to give Imogen a bit of time to run the bath and submerge herself for a few minutes in peace. Throughout their teens and twenties all their troubles seemed to have been sorted with one or the other of them lying in the bath. Neither apparently wanted to break the habit, and a long soak seemed to cure most ills.

She sliced some lime to add to Imogen's drink, just the way she liked it, and some lemon for her own. Adding a quadruple measure of Bombay Sapphire and just a hint of tonic, she put the glasses on a tray. She was desperate to know what had happened, but she knew that Imogen wouldn't be pushed.

Knocking lightly on the door, she pushed it open and was pleased to find that Imogen had taken up her offer and the room smelt fragrant and inviting.

She had clearly dunked her hair under the water for fear of lingering odours there, and her face was scrubbed clean. Not at all like Imogen's usual subtly polished look. Stripped bare like this, Laura saw evidence of the earlier ordeal in her eyes. Or perhaps, she reflected, what she was witnessing was simply an indication of the agony that Imogen had endured since losing Will. Hugo had a lot to answer for, but her own conscience was far from clear. Never a day went by that she didn't regret the fact that she had chosen not to believe Imogen.

Forcing her face into a reassuring smile, Laura placed the drink within easy reach on the side of the bath, and perched herself on the bathroom stool.

Imogen broke the silence. "Thanks for giving me a bit of space. I'm sure you've been going out of your mind! But it's okay. Really it is. There's a problem because they know that an Imogen Dubois caught the train from Paris to St. Pancras, and then back again with only a few hours in between. They're convinced it was me, but they can't prove it. Even if they could, all they could prove is that I was in London. I could have had an urgent need of something from Harrods, for all they know. There is nothing to tie me to Hugo at all. The only thing they were hoping for was a confession."

Laura quietly sipped her drink, waiting for Imogen to continue.

"Of course, there can be no evidence at the apartment, and they'll never find any trace of me talking to Hugo. So what can they do? Oh, they've got CCTV footage of the person they 'want to interview,' and this person apparently looks like it could be me. But of course it's not a clear picture, and there's nothing on any of the other cameras—so I denied everything."

Imogen's act of bravado was impressive, but Laura knew her too well.

"Was it really awful, Imo? I'm so sorry that you've had to go through this. I could have prevented it—and I *would* have, without a moment's hesitation. I hope you know that?"

Imogen reached out a hand covered with suds, and patted Laura on the knee. "Don't be silly. If I'd done as I should have and got on that plane to Canada, everything would have been fine. So it's my own fault. I know that, and I'm sorry. And I didn't only put myself in danger, did I?"

Before Laura could answer, a shout came from downstairs.

"Laura? Where are you? Any news from Imogen?"

Will had returned, clearly as upset and worried as ever. They heard his feet pounding up the stairs. The door to Laura's bedroom flew open. As Laura hadn't bothered to shut the bathroom door, Will could immediately see that somebody was in the bath.

"Oh, sorry. I'll stand outside and you can shout to me—just bring me up to date with what's happening with Imo."

"It's not Laura, it's me, you chump. Don't you even recognise your own wife? You can come in—there are plenty of bubbles."

"Sorry. You looked just like Laura with your hair scraped back like that."

Will couldn't disguise his delight at seeing Imogen safely back, and Imogen's face took on a glow that had nothing to do with the warm and damp atmosphere of the bathroom. Laura was constantly amazed that Imogen still referred to herself as Will's wife, and equally that he didn't seem to mind. She thought that this was probably an appropriate time to leave them, and gave up her space on the stool for Will.

"Much as I know you two are extremely familiar with each other, if you don't mind I find it vaguely uncomfortable to sit here while my best friend lounges naked in the bath talking to my brother. No doubt it's another indication of my frigid nature, but there you go."

Laura smiled to take any possible sting out of her words, and as she left the room she wasn't surprised to hear Will's note of puzzlement.

"Frigid? What's all that about."

"You don't want to know."

Laura took herself down to the kitchen where she was certain she would find Stella concocting something to tempt them all with. Her nerves were shattered, and she wondered what the next bombshell was going to be.

She didn't have to wait long to find out.

Having barely found time to tell a relieved Stella that Imogen was back, the fragile peace was shattered by the ringing of the intercom. Laura picked up the receiver on the kitchen wall and glanced at the video screen. She was surprised to see a rather unkempt-looking middle-aged woman with slightly wild grey hair.

"Hello, can I help you?"

The face peered right up to the camera, obviously not at all familiar with this type of technology. It was fully dark outside now, and the white face against the black background looked eerie, the nose distorted to twice its normal size as it pressed against the lens.

"I am here to see Lady Fletcher."

The voice had without a doubt an upper-class edge to it, which didn't sit well with the image on the screen. Laura decided to be cautious.

"Could I ask your business, please?"

"No, you may not. I wish to speak to Lady Fletcher, and Lady Fletcher alone."

Stella, who could hear all this as a result of the booming voice coming from a mouth possibly less than in inch from the microphone, raised her eyebrows as she looked at Laura.

"Lady Fletcher isn't taking visitors at the moment, I'm afraid."

"I'm not a visitor. I'm family."

Laura gave Stella a questioning look, but Stella just shrugged. It was certainly nobody that she recognised from their side of the family. But Laura didn't want to appear rude.

"Could I give Lady Fletcher your name, please?"

"Just tell her that it is imperative that I speak to her. Tell her it's Beatrice."

Wondering if this day could become any more surreal, Laura pressed the entry bell to open the gate, then turned to her mother.

"It's Hugo's sister."

"I didn't even know he *had* a sister. She wasn't at the wedding, was she?"

"I've never met her. She ran away when she was about fifteen, and she's been missing for the last forty years!"

Laura made her way towards the front door, and opened it to greet Beatrice. She was surprised by the person she saw approaching the house. Her clothes were casual and inexpensive, bordering on the scruffy, consisting of some floppy black trousers and a long-sleeved white cotton jumper with a dark red anorak over it, and she tramped heavily up the drive in what looked like a pair of old trainers, a green duffel bag slung over her shoulder. Her intonation may have retained some of its upper-class British edge, but her clothes and general appearance were at odds with the voice.

"God, I'd forgotten how bloody cold England is. And what a dreary place this house is. How can you bear it? May I come in?"

Speechless, Laura stood back holding the door wide.

Beatrice walked into the hallway and stood looking around her. "How absolutely vile and depressing. Not a thing has changed, except that revolting stoat has gone. Ghastly place." She visibly shuddered. "I never thought I would be back here in a million years. Do you have any gin in this mausoleum?"

Laura still hadn't spoken. She wasn't quite sure what to say, but there was something about this rather odd woman that she liked. Perhaps it was the shared opinion of the house.

"Yes, of course. Please do go through to the drawing room and I'll organise something for you. Would you like something to eat?"

"It was you on that phone thing wasn't it? Don't blame you for not wanting visitors. I wouldn't either. I'd say sorry for your loss, but you seem a sensible girl, so I'll save my breath. And no, I'll not go into the drawing room—a dismal, gloomy place if I remember rightly. I'll come to the kitchen, if it's all the same to you."

"Yes, of course. But my mother's in the kitchen. I hope you don't mind."

"Came to console you, did she?" Beatrice barked out a laugh.

Laura really didn't know what to make of this at all, and was quite glad that Stella would be there to help.

The introductions made, Stella busied herself pouring the drinks, and there was silence for a few moments. How did you begin a conversation with somebody whose brother had just died, but who as far as she knew hadn't been in contact for decades? Beatrice seemed to be taking it all in: Laura's discomfort and the meticulous care that Stella was taking in preparing a simple gin and tonic. Anything rather than make uneasy conversation, it would seem. In the end, Beatrice broke the strained silence.

"I heard about Hugo this morning—well, lunchtime for us, but still morning here. I went straight to the airport and got a flight this afternoon. I thought I'd better."

Beatrice looked at the other women as if to gauge their reaction. Laura frowned at her mother, willing her to say something. But before Stella had a chance to speak, Beatrice continued.

"No doubt you want to know a bit about me, eh? Surely Hugo told you that I did a bunk all those years ago never to be seen again? It's perfectly true. I had to get out of this dreadful house and away from the horrendous parents. I suppose you want to know what happened to me, eh?"

Beatrice had perched herself precariously on a high kitchen stool, her short legs dangling and her head pivoting from side to side as she looked first at Laura and then Stella.

Laura nodded mutely. She knew she was being impolite, but she didn't have a clue what to say to her guest. She needn't have worried.

"I ran away to Newquay to start with. It was summer. Lots of people around and easy to blend in. A few months later, I moved to Rhodes— Lindos to be precise. People were camping out on the beach there in the sixties, and it was an easy life. I worked in bars and just did what I could to survive. Then I met my husband—he's Greek—and we moved to Crete. We've been there ever since. Most people think I'm Greek now, and I never explain. I avoid Brits at all costs."

Beatrice leaned against the wall behind her and crossed her arms over her very ample bosom. Her plain, round face was devoid of makeup, and her grey hair was cropped short. But despite her lack of both style and adornment, Laura found her strangely appealing. She was the sort of person who prided themselves on calling a spade a spade, and given the prevalence of dishonesty and deviousness that surrounded this house and its inhabitants, it was a breath of fresh air.

"How did you find out? About Hugo, I mean," Laura asked.

"I make it a rule never to check English newspapers, and we don't watch British television, so I don't usually have the first idea what's happening. But even Crete has a grapevine, usually passed on by odious tourists. I'd heard about Hugo's charity. Just what I expected, really, given our father's tastes and predilections."

Her mouth was pulled into an expression of distaste, as if she had a bad smell under her nose.

"But I only heard today about his death. Some loud English people were gossiping about him. They pretended to be concerned, but clearly were more interested in any possible scandal!"

Laura was horrified. Obviously she should have tried to find out if anybody knew how to contact Beatrice. Perhaps the lawyers would have known. The least she could have done would have been to find his last remaining relative.

"I'm so sorry you had to hear that way," she said. "It must have been a dreadful shock. If I'd known how to contact you I would have let you know personally, but I had no idea you were in touch with Hugo. He certainly never mentioned it."

Beatrice barked out another laugh. She wagged a stubby finger at Laura.

"You think I've come back to bid farewell to my long-lost brother? We haven't been in touch since the day I left, and frankly if he was the person that I suspect he was, I would rather raise a glass to his passing. No. I didn't come for him."

Beatrice looked keenly at Laura, and her voice softened.

"I only learned today that he has a daughter. I understand she's eleven or twelve—something like that. I was concerned about her. I need to know what's been happening, and how she's faring. If Hugo was anything like his father…"

Laura's eyes opened wide. She didn't know what Beatrice was going to say, but with her mother there she really didn't want to take the risk. Fortunately, Stella missed her look but Beatrice didn't. Nodding her understanding, she continued.

"She is, of course, my own flesh and blood—and I just need to see what I can do to help the girl."

Beatrice took a rather noisy sip of her gin and jumped down from the stool.

"Laura—I'd like to reacquaint myself with the old place if that would be possible? Is it okay if I bring my drink with me?"

Two minutes later they were walking from the kitchen into the hallway. At the bottom of the stairs, Laura paused. "Would you like to look upstairs first, or go through the downstairs rooms?"

"Don't be bloody ridiculous. I haven't the slightest interest in the house, but it was pretty clear to me that you didn't want me discussing your husband in front of your mother. Where's the girl? Is she okay?"

"She's fine. She's with her mother. She is a truly delightful girl and you must meet her while you're here. Whatever your worries are, it's all in hand."

Beatrice nodded slowly. Neither felt the need to explain more, and they fell into a brief silence.

When Beatrice spoke again, her tone was harsh. "My father and mother were complete bastards, you know. Strange would be a polite word, but as a boy Hugo was shaping up just to be like my father. Odd, really, because Hugo hated him. I never really understood that, given their similarity. I was so blinded by my own hatred of the whole bloody family that I really wasn't bothered what Hugo was going through. He was a self-obsessed boy who clearly thought that, as Mummy's favourite, he was something special. Never missed the little sod for a minute. But I don't suppose it was his fault entirely."

She turned and stared hard at Laura.

"Does this child know the difference between right and wrong?"

"Not completely, but I think we can get there. She just needs a bit of time now."

"Understood. What the hell did a girl like you marry a swine like Hugo for? You don't look the avaricious type. You're pretty enough, and you don't appear to be thick—although I accept that appearances can be deceptive."

Laura couldn't help but smile. She thought that Beatrice deserved the truth. She tried to explain how she was bowled over by a man that gave so much of his life to a charity that supported women in such an overt way. She knew she had put him on a pedestal, and had either failed to see his flaws or had tried to excuse them. Hugo had been unlike anybody she had ever met before. He was sophisticated, charming, and he lived a life that somebody like Laura had only ever dreamed of. She had often wondered how much she'd been influenced by his money and power, and hated the thought that either had played a part in her obsession with him. And she hadn't recognised for a long time that the thin line between consideration and control had been crossed.

Beatrice listened attentively, one arm resting on the balustrade. They still hadn't moved from the hall.

"I thought I loved him, Beatrice. I really did."

"But you were wrong, weren't you?" Beatrice responded, not without sympathy.

"Yes. I was wrong. But it took me a long time to work that out, and by then it was too late."

"What do you mean, too late? It's never too late. What stopped you from leaving?"

Laura was prevented from answering the question by the peal of the doorbell. It had to be the police as she knew the front gate was closed. Sure enough, when she opened the door, an anxious-looking Tom Douglas was standing there with Becky Robinson. Tom smiled at her with genuine apology, but when her eyes met his she had to admit to herself that she was oddly pleased to see him.

"I'm really sorry to disturb you so late, Laura. But I do need to talk to you again. Is it okay if we come in?" Tom stepped into the hall, and stopped when he saw Beatrice. "I'm sorry. I didn't realise that you had a guest."

"It's okay, Tom. This is Beatrice. Hugo's sister. Beatrice, this is Detective Chief Inspector Tom Douglas."

Tom looked intrigued. "How long have you been in the country, Mrs....?"

"Lekkas. And I've just arrived today, so if you're wondering if I killed him, the answer's no—although whoever did probably deserves a hearty round of applause!"

Laura had to smile at Tom's startled look. Beatrice's outspoken and forthright manner took a bit of getting used to, but she was liking her more by the minute. He recovered quickly.

"You might be able to help," Tom said. "Look, do you mind if we go and sit down. We desperately need to pick your brains." He gave Laura another contrite smile.

"Glad to be of help, if I can," Beatrice responded. "Where to, Laura? The dreadful drawing room?"

Without waiting for an answer she marched off, her shoes making that strange squelching noise peculiar to cheap trainers. Tom looked at Laura and raised his eyebrows questioningly. Laura gave him a brief grin, then turned to follow Beatrice. She had certainly lightened the atmosphere.

❖ ❖ ❖

As Tom took his seat in the drawing room, he thought about what Mrs. Lekkas has said about killing Hugo. Apparently it seemed impossible for *anybody* to have killed him. And everybody close to him, with the exception of Alexa, seemed delighted by his demise. But the arrival of Hugo's sister might be the stroke of luck they needed. He realised that he might have to handle this lady with care, though. She may be in for a shock when she found out what they were investigating as part of Hugo's murder enquiry.

"Mrs. Lekkas, I'd…"

"Stick to Beatrice. I lost all sense of formality years ago."

"Beatrice. I don't want to alarm you or upset you unnecessarily, but we have some suspicions about your brother's behaviour. We're not making sufficient progress, though. Laura, how do you feel about sharing this with Beatrice?"

It was Beatrice that answered. She may have lost all sense of formality, but she certainly had an ingrained view of her own importance.

"She won't have a problem, will you, Laura? Tom, is it? I think that's what Laura called you?" Without waiting for Tom to confirm or otherwise, she carried on. "I wouldn't be surprised at anything you tell me about my brother's behaviour. A chip off the old block, if you ask me. How he could emulate somebody he so clearly hated is beyond me. But ours not to reason why. What do you want to know, Chief Inspector?"

Tom glanced at Laura, who gave a brief nod.

"You're right, it is Tom, and before I go on, Beatrice, can I just explore that comment with you? The one about Hugo hating his father? We've looked through the information regarding your father's death and whilst the general view was suicide, there was quite a lot of evidence that suggested foul play, hence the open verdict. Do you think that Hugo could have killed him?"

"No. He didn't. He hated him, but he didn't kill him. Next question."

"Are you sure about that?" Tom persisted.

"Absolutely. If you want my cooperation I would be grateful if we could move on."

Fascinating as it might be, Tom realised the past could wait.

"Right. Not only are we investigating your brother's murder, but we are also looking into the possibility that he was using some of the prostitutes rescued by his charity for his own purposes. Several are missing, and there has to be a link. Maybe a scorned woman is at the root of his murder."

Beatrice's smile was entirely without humour.

"If I were you, I would assume the worst where Hugo is concerned. I think that he would have been using the prostitutes in any way that he saw fit—probably for as long as the charity has been going. My father ran a similar effort, although on a much smaller scale and with local girls only, but it was entirely for his amusement." Beatrice paused. Her eyes narrowed as if she were recalling events from her past and wasn't enjoying the moment.

"He used to insist on being present at the physical examination of each 'saved' girl," she continued. "It's a long time ago, and back then it was generally thought acceptable for some bizarre reason. Same, no doubt, as teachers caning small boys on their bare bottoms. Father said that he should be considered as a doctor, and nobody should worry about his presence. Actually he was just a pervert. So if Hugo's been playing, I wouldn't be surprised in the slightest. I'm just amazed he hasn't been found out."

She looked at Tom, and he could sense a trace of shame in the glance, as though the sins of the fathers were the responsibility of their offspring.

"If he took them as his mistresses," Tom said, "it looks as if he had a pretty high turnover with a new one every few months. What do you think would happen to them when he's finished with them, Beatrice?"

She thought for a moment.

"If you're asking for a bet, I'd say that he paid them off. He probably sent them as far away as possible, too—so that they couldn't bump into any of their old friends. If he was anything like his father, he would do whatever he had to in order to avoid a scandal." She shook her head. Tom thought she probably regretted being dragged into this. He looked at both the women sitting opposite him. He was so close, but the final puzzle piece was still missing.

"The problem is, we're having enormous trouble proving any of this, or tracing any of the girls. We need to know where he's been taking them. We might find some evidence there that will point us in the right direction. Can you think of any place from your childhood that he might have taken them, Beatrice? We've explored every other option."

Tom was literally sitting on the edge of his seat, impatient and desperate for any sort of clue and hoping that his sense of urgency would communicate itself to everybody in the room.

But Beatrice didn't appear to have anything of significance to contribute.

"I only knew him until he was about ten, but if he's anything like his parents I imagine that his fame and reputation were rather important to him." She looked at Laura, who nodded in agreement. "Then it wouldn't be anywhere where he could be caught." Beatrice shook her head. "Nowhere immediately springs to mind, I'm afraid."

Tom leaned back in the chair. One step forward, two steps backward was how it seemed to him. It was so bloody frustrating.

"This whole theory about the missing prostitutes being involved in his murder might be a complete red herring," he said. "But we've nothing else to go on at the moment."

He turned towards Laura.

"Becky will have told you, Laura, that we've been questioning Jessica, but we checked her phone records, and she can prove conclusively that she was on the phone at the time Hugo was killed. She was speaking—or rather listening—to her aunt, and the aunt has confirmed this. Jessica didn't tell us because apparently she didn't see why she should have to account for her movements, if you can believe her arrogance. And of course we've failed to get any further with your sister-in-law." He knew that was the wrong thing to say as soon as he'd opened his mouth.

Laura was quick to respond. "Tom, I know you don't believe this, but I am one hundred percent certain that she did not kill Hugo. You've told me that it was sex related, and they hated each other. If she offered him sex, he would have turned it down. Will is the only man for her."

Beatrice interrupted. "Excuse me, but who is your sister-in-law, and who is Will?"

"I'm sorry, Beatrice. Will is my brother. His ex-wife was my best friend for many years, and she's been here offering me support since Hugo died. Her name's Imogen."

"Thank you, Laura." Beatrice paused and her face creased into a puzzled frown. "*Imogen*. Why does that name mean something? Quiet, if you please. I need to think."

Tom and Laura exchanged another look. Becky had been silently taking notes throughout this exchange, but even she looked up at this comment and briefly glanced at Tom and then Laura with raised eyebrows. Two or three minutes passed. Tom was beginning to get restless. He didn't really have time for this. Just as he was about to open his mouth, Beatrice spoke again.

"Got it. I knew I would. When I was a child, I had a friend called Imogen. Do you know, I'd forgotten all about her, but when we were on holiday she often saved me from a fate worse than death."

Beatrice looked extremely pleased with herself, but the rest of the people in the room were entirely underwhelmed by this revelation. She glanced from one to the other.

"Don't you see—that's where he's taken them. It's where we used to go on holiday, and it's only a couple of hours from here at the most, and the ideal private spot."

Tom was certain that this was going to be important, but at this moment he felt like shaking Beatrice to get the information out of her. He knew he sounded exasperated, but he couldn't help himself.

"*Where*, Beatrice? You haven't told us *where*?"

Beatrice turned her face to Tom's and looked shamefaced. "Oh Lord, I'm so sorry! I got a bit carried away with my own cleverness. After my aunt—my mother's sister, that is—was killed in a car accident along with her husband, their property was left to my mother. We never went there when they were alive, because the husband was a farmer and was considered beneath us."

Tom thought he was in danger of losing it with Beatrice any minute now. He counted to ten slowly. But she hadn't yet reached the climax of her story and seemed determined to take her time.

"We visited the farm a few times after Mother inherited it for much overrated family holidays. Dreadful occasions. That's when I met Imogen. I knew the name was important."

Beatrice sat back with a self-satisfied air. Tom, on the other hand, was chomping at the bit.

"Beatrice, forgive me for being rude, but where the hell are we talking about? Where is this farm?"

Beatrice bit her bottom lip and nodded, as if realising that she had missed the crucial point.

"Ah, yes, I imagine that would be helpful. It's near Lytchett Minster in Dorset. I don't know what the place is actually called, we always referred to it as Lytchett Minster Farm."

There was a moment's silence. Tom's heart was racing, and with the exception of Beatrice, nobody in the room missed the significance of the name.

The spell was broken as Will and Imogen, closely followed by Stella, appeared in the open doorway—as if the charged atmosphere had permeated the whole house and drawn them like moths to a flame. Tom rudely ignored them and sat forward in his seat, imploring Beatrice to just tell him where in God's name he should be looking.

"Beatrice, I need you to tell me as much as you can about the farm. Do you have the address?" he asked.

"No. I'm not sure I ever knew it."

"Okay. Can you describe it at all, to give the locals something to go on? They might be able to pinpoint it for us. We'll give them the name Fletcher to check out, but something tells me that might be a waste of time."

"Oh Lord, Tom, it was so long ago. Let me think."

To Tom's frustration she paused again, but thankfully this time only for a couple of seconds.

"All I can remember is that it was in the middle of nowhere—at least it was then. No doubt it will be surrounded by identical red brick semidetached boxes now."

Although that wasn't particularly helpful, there was a buzz of excitement in the room that was strangely at odds with the seriousness of the occasion. Tom leapt up out of his chair.

"Right. I need to get to Dorset as quickly as possible. Becky—get on to the local force and see if we can identify the property with them. Beatrice—much as I hate to ask given the fact that you've had a long journey already today— it would be extremely useful if you could come with me. You can stay in the car when we arrive, but if there's any doubt about the location, we might need your help. Would you be prepared to do this?"

"Of course," she replied. "I'm quite a tough old bird, you know. And I'm intrigued. I've no doubt my brother was a nasty bastard given his parentage, but I'd love to be proved wrong. For his daughter's sake if nothing else."

Tom glanced at Laura, to see how Beatrice's words had affected her. It was one thing knowing that your husband was a bastard, but it was very different to hear it voiced by somebody else.

"Don't look so worried, Tom," Laura said. "I think we all know what Hugo was, and there's a sort of morbid fascination about it, isn't there? It's the same when people drive past a terrible car accident and feel compelled to look. I'm probably the only person in the room who hopes that Mirela turns up in a bar in Brighton, and there's nothing to find at the farm other than a secret haven that Hugo escaped to when life became too hectic." Laura paused. "Although I'm honestly not stupid enough to believe that."

Everybody was silent for a moment, each recognising a twinge of guilt at the frisson of excitement they were feeling. Tom turned to Laura.

"Becky will keep you up to date, and I'm sure your family will offer you all the support and comfort you need in what must be a dreadful time for you." Tom spoke the last sentence quite forcefully, as if instructing Laura's family to look after her and to desist from speculation and conjecture.

"Let's go, Beatrice," he said. "Becky, call us when you have any information."

Helping Beatrice back on with her anorak, he gave a last sympathetic glance at Laura and a curt nod to the rest of the assembled family, and made his way out to the car.

34

"Shit, Becky. That's not very helpful is it? Is that all they had to say?" Tom paused, holding his earpiece firmly against his head to cut out the sound of traffic on the busy A34.

"Buggeration. Right, leave it with me and I'll get back to you."

Tom switched off the phone and tutted. He sensed, rather than saw, that Beatrice was turned towards him with curiosity.

"I'm sorry, Beatrice. That was very rude of me."

"If you're apologising for your language, Tom, I wouldn't bother. I myself have a fairly comprehensive range of expletives at my disposal, and I don't hesitate to use them as you've probably gathered. What's the problem?"

"There's no trace of a property owned by anybody with the surname Fletcher, or Hugo's company. Nothing in your mother's maiden name, and we even tracked down your uncle's name. Absolutely nothing. The only good thing is that Lytchett Minster isn't a big place, so we'll just have to drive around until we see something you recognise."

"That might not be so easy," Beatrice said. She frowned. "We always called it Lytchett Minster Farm because that's the last village that we passed through before *getting* to the farm. It was a few miles from there, and I've no idea in which direction. I suspect there's more than one road in and out."

Both were lost in their own thoughts for a few moments. Beatrice broke the silence.

"Hugo was a famous man, and easily recognised, so if he had a property that was close to others, he would have been seen. If he had neighbours, they would have come round to say hello and invite him to some tedious drinks party. You should assume that the farm—and it certainly originally was a farm—is secluded, and to all intents and purposes people probably think that it's either unused or a holiday place. It used to be down an unmade road, more of a dirt track really. I'd ask the local plod to let you know which places are rarely used and very secluded. They're bound to know."

Tom had already started to phone Becky before Beatrice had finished—grasping her train of thought immediately.

Due entirely to Tom's flagrant disregard for speed restrictions, they reached the turnoff to Lytchett Minster in record time. He had arranged to meet the local force in a pub car park to discuss the possible properties.

"Beatrice, as soon as we reach the farm and you've identified it, one of the local women police officers will join you in my car, so you don't have to be subjected to anything unpleasant. And for safety, although there's no reason to suspect that there is any danger at all."

"Don't be ridiculous, Tom. I'm coming in with you. I'll know the house better than you, and I'll be useful. Don't worry—I won't touch anything. I'll follow at an appropriate distance, and I have nerves of steel. I think you need me."

Tom could just make out a look of grim determination on Beatrice's face. Neither of them knew what they were going to find, but Tom was hoping and praying that it would be Mirela Tinescy, safe and well. He had no time to argue with Beatrice as the car park was just ahead, with two police cars and an unmarked car waiting patiently for their arrival. They'd come out in force, so perhaps it was a quiet night in Poole.

Following swift introductions, and a few looks of bemusement at Beatrice—who had declared that she had expert knowledge and was vital to the investigation—the locals described the three properties as concisely as possible.

"The first one's set back from the road by about fifty metres. It's not been inhabited for about five years. It's in a bit of a state and there's no roof in a couple of places—but there's a new housing estate across the road, and we've had reports of lights in the house a few times in the last six months or so."

"It's not that one."

"Why not, Beatrice?" Tom wanted to hurry, but he didn't want to overlook something and waste even more time.

"Because it's unlikely to be 'in a state.' Much as I deplore the decor at Ashbury Park, Hugo will have liked his creature comforts. And fifty metres from the road doesn't sound far enough. Not enough privacy. Next."

Looking at Tom for approval, and getting a curt nod, the policeman moved on to the next property.

"If the fence is anything to go by, this next one is in a good state of repair, but it's a long way from the road. It doesn't look as if it's inhabited, but the fence goes all around it, and it's got an electric gate. You can't see the house from the road, and none of us has had any reason to go there, so we don't know if it's used at all."

"Sounds possible. Next."

The policeman quickly gave details of the last house.

"This one's quite grand. We know that it's used occasionally, because we've seen cars going in and out of the gates. It's just on the edge of the village, but down a lane. The local kids used to go in the gardens to steal the fruit from the trees, but when the owners come down they bring a dog—and it frightened the children so they don't go there anymore."

"It won't be that one. If children can get in, Hugo wouldn't like that. And he always hated dogs. Said they were dirty things that ate their own faeces. He got that from my mother. She always said…"

Tom interrupted her. He had no time to listen to tales of woe from Beatrice's childhood. "So you think it's property number two, Beatrice?"

"Yes. Well hidden, fence, electric gate. Of the three, it's the best option."

"Right. This is what I suggest. Given the number of us, I suggest that you, Sergeant, together with your female officer, lead us to house number two, and you, Detective Constable, follow behind." He turned to the remaining two policemen. "Perhaps you two could go in the other car to house number three—just check it out from the outside. If we're unlucky with number two, we'll meet you there. Everybody okay with that?"

Nobody argued. Although out of his jurisdiction, his seniority and the importance of this case left them all more than willing to follow his orders.

Ten minutes later, Tom's car was bumping down an unmade road in the middle of nowhere. There were no other houses within sight, and since leaving the main road they hadn't passed another vehicle. The leading police car finally pulled up by a sliding metal electric gate. Tom pulled up on the lane behind. The sergeant walked over to the car, and Tom wound down his window. The lane was dark, and other than the wind swishing in the tall trees, blowing the autumn leaves from their boughs, there wasn't a sound.

"We need to get the gate open, sir. You can't see the house from here, and it might be useful to get as close as we can in case we need any equipment. I'll hop over the gate and open up. I just need a few minutes."

"How does he propose doing that?" Beatrice asked. "It's electric."

"He'll have an Allen key in his kit. A lot of the older electric gates can be opened with one, just in case of a power cut. You need to be able to get out somehow."

"Hah! Not as secure as you might think, then. I bet Hugo didn't know that."

Within moments, the sergeant was pushing the gate open, having disengaged the motor that was holding it closed. Tom began slowly steering the car up the winding drive, avoiding potholes and overhanging branches. The place had an air of desertion about it. Weeds grew high on either side of the drive, and between the established trees there were a myriad of saplings, fighting for space and for light.

"Does it look familiar yet, Beatrice?"

"Not yet. I do get the sense that I've been here before, but that could just be wishful thinking." Beatrice peered eagerly through the windscreen. "Wait a minute. See that ramshackle building over there? That used to be a summerhouse. This is it."

Tom felt a rush of adrenaline. He put his foot down. Bugger the potholes.

They rounded the bend in the drive, and ahead of them they saw the house, eerily quiet and dark against the night sky. As they pulled up close to the front door, Tom looked up at the building. The three storeys seemed to rear up menacingly, and the gothic arched windows were lifeless. The only light came from a weak moon, which was momentarily revealed by the fast scudding clouds.

Tom turned to Beatrice.

"Wait in the car, please, Beatrice."

"No."

Beatrice made to open her door. Tom turned to her in frustration, and could see the stubborn set of her jaw.

"Beatrice, would you wait in the car, please?"

"I heard you the first time, and I said no." Beatrice got out of the car and slammed the door decisively. "I know the layout of the house. I won't get in the way."

Tom didn't have time for this. He realised that short of handcuffing her to the steering wheel, this was one battle he wasn't going to win. The other policemen were standing looking at the front door. One of them walked up and rang the bell. They could hear it echo ominously around the seemingly abandoned building. Nobody was expecting a response. They turned to look at Tom as he spoke. His voice was tight with tension, and he felt a creeping dread as he gave his instructions. If Mirela was here, she wasn't able to get to the door.

"Okay, guys. We have grounds to believe that a young girl has been abducted, and our evidence to date suggests that she may well be inside this house. There is no reason to wait for a warrant, as she may be in danger. Everybody happy with that?" There were nods all round.

"We need to get in. Suggestions?"

"The front door is solid hardwood, sir, five lever locks top and bottom. What about the windows?"

The detective was trying to peer through into the downstairs rooms.

"All of these at the front seem to be very thick glass, and there are metal grills of some type on the inside. We'd need equipment."

Tom could feel his blood racing. He was impatient and apprehensive. The amount of security suggested that this was not a house used for idle pleasures. It was a fortress. Tom felt a tap on his shoulder.

"Would an old coal chute be any use?"

Bless you, Beatrice, he thought. "It could well be. Where is it?"

"I used to slide down it when I was a child. When I needed to hide. It's probably filthy, but it comes into the cellar under the kitchen. There are some stairs that lead to a door into the rear hall. It might be locked, but unless it's been replaced it was pretty flimsy. The chute's just round this corner, I think."

Tom felt hope stirring. Hugo probably was only concerned about people getting out of the house, and climbing up a steep smooth coal chute would be impossible. Perhaps he hadn't bothered to secure it.

The chute was covered with wooden shutters set into the ground. They were very overgrown, indicating that they hadn't been used in years, and they creaked and groaned as he pulled them back. Tom peered into the opening, and even with the aid of the light from his torch, it wasn't possible to see how far down the chute went or how dangerous it was. And there could be anything waiting at the bottom. The chute was narrow, though, and filthy. There was no way that Tom would fit down there.

Tom heard a quiet voice behind him.

"I can get down there, sir." The woman officer was very slight, and Tom was sure the chute would be wide enough for her. The door at the other end, however, might be more difficult.

"Bruce has got a crowbar in the boot, sir, and I know how to use it."

The young sergeant was already running back to his vehicle, and the woman officer was slipping off her jacket and hat. Deciding that shoes might be vital for landing on a mountain of old coal, or whatever else lay at the bottom, she kept them on. She sat on the edge of the chute, clutched a torch and the crowbar that an out-of-breath Bruce had just delivered, and without hesitation pushed herself down the chute as if she were setting off on a helter-skelter ride.

They heard a clatter as she hit whatever was at the bottom, then silence. The policemen at the top of the chute held their breath, not daring to look at each other. Then an echoing voice came from the black depths below. Sounding a little less confident now that she was alone in the house, the police officer shouted up to them.

"I'm okay, sir. Sorry for the delay. I dropped the torch when I landed, so I needed to just grope around a bit before I moved. I've got it now. I can see the stairs. I'll see if I can find a way to let you in. I'll start in the kitchen."

Following Beatrice, who had set off with a purpose, the officers made their way towards the shadowy and silent back of the house, stepping through the weeds that were growing over the disused gravel paths.

Within moments they saw the flash of the officer's torch through the gloom of the windows, and heard a number of bolts being dragged back. A muffled voice came from inside.

"I can't find what's keeping it closed. It won't budge."

Tom shone his own torch on the door and saw that there were padlocked metal bars at the top and bottom. He immediately recognised the significance of them being on the outside. Bruce didn't need to be told what to do, and disappeared once more round the side of the house.

"Hang on in there. Bruce has just gone for some tool or other—we'll be with you in a second."

"It's all right, sir. This place is as quiet as the grave."

Tom didn't like the sound of that one bit.

Within minutes, Bruce had taken a sledgehammer to the padlocks, and the door was pushed open.

"Are you okay?"

The woman officer, who was herself no more than a girl, nodded. But this wasn't a comfortable house, and certainly not a place to be alone in the dark.

He tried a light switch, but nothing happened. He realised that Hugo must have switched the power off at the fuse box. That suggested that the house was empty, but he couldn't be sure. He no longer knew if he wanted to find Mirela here. Like Laura, he was beginning to hope for a phone call to say that Mirela was somewhere else entirely.

"Beatrice, do you know where the main fuse box is?"

"No idea."

"Right. We can waste time looking for it, or we can use torches. Everybody happy to use a torch?" With nods all round, they split into two groups. Tom and the woman officer, with Beatrice in tow, began their search of the downstairs rooms whilst Bruce and detective made their way upstairs to the first-floor bedrooms. They crept around like burglars in the night, as if frightened of the secrets that the house would reveal. Each footstep seemed to resonate, as if the house were hollow and empty.

And it was ominously quiet. A large stained-glass window high above the front door cast sinister shadows as the moon periodically darted out from behind a cloud.

The first door Tom tried opened into a dining room. Tom shone his torch into the shadowy depths of the room. The furniture was old but in good condition. There was a very thin film of dust, but not what Tom would have expected if the house was deserted. He couldn't believe that Hugo would clean for himself, so somebody else must have been doing it. Perhaps this was all that he wanted the girls for. Tom brushed that thought aside. With what he knew now, he was certain that it was nothing so simple.

For the moment, he cast no more than a cursory glance around each of the rooms he entered. There would be time for a proper search later, when they had established that they were definitely alone. Although he knew that Hugo was dead and there could be no threat from anybody in this house, he couldn't deny that the darkness and the silence sent a cold shiver up his spine.

He had just tried the last door and found it locked when Tom heard a shout from upstairs.

"DCI Douglas! Here! You need to come here. *Now!*"

Tom turned to the woman officer and pointed to Beatrice.

"Keep her down here, do you understand?"

He turned and ran up the stairs, taking the steps two at a time. The shadows cast by the moon appeared to be chasing him as he ran, the thump of his feet echoing dismally around the barren walls. He followed the sounds of the voices to a bedroom at the front of the house.

Pushing open the door, he could see the light from the officers' abandoned torches shining against blank walls, and didn't know what he was looking for. There was a dreadful smell in the room, but he couldn't see anybody. He flashed his torch and captured the policemen in the light, kneeling by the side of a mattress on the floor.

At that moment, the room burst into bright light. The woman officer's voice drifted up the stairs, shouting something about finding the fuse box. But Tom didn't register what she was saying. All he could do was look at the body lying on the mattress, revealed in the harsh glare of a bare light bulb.

35

Laura felt a deep sense of foreboding. She had no idea what they would discover, but she knew it wouldn't be good. Nobody knew Hugo the way that she did, and she felt a massive pressure in her chest, as if somebody were pressing down on it. In the end, nothing prepared her for the reality.

Becky came into the drawing room where they were all waiting in silence. Her face was grim.

"Laura, Tom just called. Could I speak to you in private, please?"

"Becky, whatever it is, you can tell everybody. Too much has happened now for there to be any secrets."

Becky swallowed, and asked if it would be okay if she sat down. Everybody just looked at her.

"Tell us, please."

"Tom is going to come and see you and give you more detail, but it appears that when they reached the farm, they found a girl. Mirela Tinescy."

Laura put her head down and gasped. It was Will who spoke, reaching for Imogen's hand as he did so as if it were the most natural thing in the world. "My God!" he said. "Is she okay?"

"She's alive. That's about as much as I can say, really. She was chained up in a bedroom, by her ankle. Her water had run out—we don't know how long ago."

The words *chained up* made Laura shiver, and she could feel her body covered with goose bumps. She had to ask.

"But there's only the one girl? They've not found any others?"

Becky shook her head. "Tom's going to organise a car to bring Beatrice back, but he needs to stay there. He won't be able to get back to you until late morning at the earliest. He asked me to tell you that he's really sorry, Laura. We both know how dreadful this must be for you."

Three stunned faces were turned towards Becky, and then back towards Laura, who lifted her head and leaned back heavily. She stared up at the ceiling, unable to return anybody's gaze.

Only Will broke the silence.

"My God, Laura. What were you married to?"

Imogen glared at her ex-husband, their moment of closeness apparently gone.

"Shut up, Will. Now's not the time, is it? Leave Laura alone. Stella, not the time for a cup of tea, I don't think. I know where the brandy is. Let's get it sorted, shall we?"

Laura stared into space and suddenly realised that tears were running down her face. Only Becky and Will remained in the room.

Becky broke the silence. "I'm sorry, Laura. It must be an awful time for you. I really don't know what to say."

Laura tried to smile through her tears. "It's okay, Becky. I'm not crying for me. I'm crying for those girls. If he treated them that badly, you see, I can't believe he would have risked letting them go. He *wouldn't* have let them go. They would have exposed him for what he was. Do you understand?"

Nobody spoke.

"And I knew. I *knew* he was taking them."

There was a shocked silence.

Will was looking at his sister in amazement. "What the fuck do you mean? You knew he was taking them? Why in God's name didn't you *do* anything?"

How could she ever explain?

"Don't you think I *tried*, Will? You have no idea. No idea at all. I even went to the *police* with my suspicions—a chief constable no less. And look where that got me. Back in a straightjacket, practically. There's a lot you don't understand, and clearly a lot that even I didn't understand."

She wanted to plead with them. She just wanted somebody—anybody—to begin to comprehend the life she had lead, and why she had only one option.

"I thought he was just paying them off—really I did. That's what he implied. I knew it wouldn't have been nice for them, knowing Hugo's proclivities, but I never thought he'd chain them up. I thought he'd use them in his weird games and send them away with more money than they had ever dreamed of. And when I returned here from the home, I had to do exactly as he said. I couldn't rock the boat. There was too much at stake."

Laura realised that she was in danger of saying too much. She tried to calm herself down before she continued with her explanation.

"Once he was dead, I thought they were all safe, don't you see? So there didn't seem any point raking through the dirt then. More than anything, I didn't want Alexa to ever know who her father really was. She has enough to deal with."

Laura turned to Becky, in the hope that the other woman would understand what she was saying, and why she had kept this to herself. Becky looked sympathetic, but Laura felt a sense of futility. She wished Tom were here. She thought that he would understand. He already knew some of it, and he believed in her. She was sure of that.

"Will," Laura said, "there's a lot of this that won't make sense to you. But the day after Hugo died, we heard that a girl was missing. A girl called Danika. When I heard that, I didn't know what to do. If I had thought that I could help, I would have told Tom. But I had no idea where he'd taken them—and I *promise* you I didn't think he would harm them. At least, not physically. Tom only told me that Mirela was missing a few hours ago, but there was *still* nothing I could do."

Laura was crying. She bit the inside of her mouth to try to control her urge to sob out everything—all the things that she had kept to herself for so long. Things that even Imogen didn't know. But she knew she mustn't. She told Will how she had reported her suspicions to Theo Hodder. She had no idea how much of this Becky knew—maybe Tom had told her, maybe he hadn't. But she didn't care.

"But it didn't work, Will," she sobbed. "I should have tried harder to make somebody believe me. I should have stopped him before now. But I couldn't. Hugo knew I was on to him, and he had all the cards, you see. It's much more complex than any of you realise."

She looked at Becky and Will, and could see nothing but bewilderment on their faces. They had no idea what she was talking about now.

"Those poor, poor girls. Hadn't they suffered enough? They'd been brought to England full of hope, only to find that they had to service God knows how many revolting men each day. Then they were rescued and all was well for a while. Life started to look good. Then a devil in disguise smiled at them, and they didn't recognise what he was. What's that Shakespeare quote? 'O villain, villain, smiling, damned villain.' That was my husband. That was Hugo."

36

As soon as the ambulance had left with a weak—but alive—Mirela, Tom arranged for a car to take Beatrice back to Oxfordshire.

"Beatrice, thank you so much for agreeing to come. The local police have arrived now, and they're taking over. But I'm going to stay here and work with them. You've been a great help, you know, and I do hope it hasn't been too traumatic for you."

She patted him on the arm in an almost maternal way, which seemed at odds with her previous manner. She must have been as shocked as anybody. After all, Hugo was her brother.

"I've lived a long time, Tom, and witnessed a lot of pain and suffering over the years. It's deeply disturbing that a member of my own family treated another human being in this deplorable fashion, but I don't think it's me you should be worried about." Beatrice looked genuinely concerned as she continued. "How do you think Laura's going to take this? Whatever she suspected, it's not going to be an easy thing to come to terms with."

Tom didn't want to contemplate how Laura would feel. She had lived with this man, had been his wife for several years, so on top of all the other emotions there was inevitably going to be a huge sense of humiliation—the shame of living with a monster, and the guilt of wondering whether any of the blame could rest with her. He tried to think of a way to lessen her pain.

"Beatrice, you may be able to help. At the moment, Laura will only have the bare facts. But you've seen what this place is like. One of the locals told me that the fence and gate have been here for at least twelve years, as far as he can remember, so whatever Hugo's been doing, he's been doing it for a long time. Since *before* he met Laura. She needs to be made to understand that whatever has happened, it is *not* her fault. I don't think anybody but you will be able to convince her of that—particularly given what you told me on the journey down here. Would you do that for me, please?"

Beatrice squeezed his arm. "You're a kind and thoughtful man, Tom Douglas. I would say that it will be my pleasure—but of course it won't. I'll talk to Laura and I'll do my best to make her understand, because I don't want the innocent to suffer any more than you do."

Trying his best to muster a smile of thanks, Tom quickly helped Beatrice into the waiting car and returned to the house.

"Good timing, Tom," DCI Sarah Charles, the senior investigating officer from the Dorset police, informed him. "We've managed to open the study door about ten minutes ago. Hugo clearly didn't want anybody getting in there, given the elaborate locks, so let's see what he's been hiding, shall we?"

A quiet voice interrupted them. Bruce, the ever-resourceful young sergeant, had been put in charge of searching the upper floors, and Tom could see that he still looked a little pale. But then he had been the one to find Mirela, and it couldn't have been easy for him. Even the most hardened and experienced of policemen never really become inured to acts of blatant cruelty.

"Ma'am, sir, I thought you should know that we've found lots of female clothing upstairs in the attic. Some of it's in cheap suitcases, some just in bin liners. But it's all just shoved in—there's no way it's been packed for a trip."

"All for one woman, would you say Bruce?" Sarah Charles asked.

"Doubt it, ma'am. Several different sizes—none big—from about a size six to about a ten, I'm reliably informed."

"Okay, thanks. You know the drill."

"Yes, ma'am."

Tom spoke for the first time. "What do you reckon, Sarah?"

She shook her head and gave a small shrug. "I don't feel good about this, if I'm honest. I've got that telltale tingle up my spine. You?"

"Yep. All the way."

Without another word, they turned and headed for the study. A couple of crime scene technicians were busy, but they waved them in.

"What've you got, guys?"

"We've just started, but there doesn't seem to be much. Just a pile of bills and a ledger. It's got dates, names, numbers and addresses, but they're all quite old. The most recent one is dated at least a couple of years ago."

Checking first that the crime scene team had finished with the ledger, Tom opened it on the desk, and he and Sarah leaned over it eagerly. It took Tom less than a minute to recognise the significance.

"Wait here, Sarah—I need to get something from my car," he said, turning quickly and leaving the room almost at a run.

He yanked open the car door and grabbed his briefcase from the back. He was sure that he recognised those names, but he needed to be certain. And there was one aspect of the list that he was finding particularly uncomfortable.

Sarah was watching him speculatively as he dumped his briefcase on the desk, opened it, and started rummaging through the papers.

"Here it is. I thought I'd brought a copy with me," he said with grim satisfaction. It was the list of the girls that had gone missing over the last five years.

The ledger went back much further than that, but he compared the dates and names in the diary with the list from the charity. The names matched, but the dates were all out by several months. And next to each of them were two figures. The first was a fairly consistent one thousand pounds, but the second varied—anything from a hundred to five hundred.

Tom slapped the table with his hand.

"Got it," he said. "The reason the dates are out is that these are the dates that he let the girls go, not the dates he brought them here. Look, the dates in the ledger are almost always a couple of weeks before the next girl went missing—so it's out with the old, and in with the new. Any idea about the numbers, Sarah?"

Sarah stared at the paper with a frown of concentration. "He's got their addresses. That must be relevant. Do you think he paid them off, Tom?"

"It's possible, but why do the entries stop a couple of years ago? We know he was still taking girls." He checked his list again. There were six other names, plus Mirela. It didn't make any sense.

He peered closely at the ledger page. The last entry had been struck out with what appeared to be considerable force. The paper was nearly scored through. He noticed that a couple of the letters were still just about legible. Shit. He compared the date to his list, knowing without a doubt what he was going to find. He was right. And after that final name, there were no more names, no more addresses, and no more sums of money.

Tom went cold. Perhaps he was reading too much into this. Perhaps Hugo had a different ledger that they hadn't found yet. But he didn't believe it.

The door opened and Bruce popped his head round.

"We found a couple of bits of ID in the clothes bags. Nothing much. One had an old letter in it, but it's written in a foreign language, so I've no idea what it says. The name on the envelope might be helpful, though. One of the other bags had a cleaner's security pass for a hospital. We've bagged them—I don't know if they're any use. There's nothing else."

Bruce passed the two bags to Sarah and turned to go back to his search. Pressing the bag against the contents, Sarah read out two names to Tom. He didn't need to check his list again. He knew both of these names would be there—but neither was in the ledger.

"Sarah—I'm going to give you a timeline of events and a series of known facts. I'm too close to this, so before I jump to the wrong conclusion, I want to hear what you think."

He pointed Sarah to a chair, and she sat, watching him. But he couldn't sit down. He paced backwards and forwards, hands thrust deeply in his pockets.

"We know that Hugo has been taking girls. We know when he has taken them, and judging by the ledger, we know when he let them go. It would seem he gave them money. But the last girl on that list—the one that he has scored out—has cropped up several times in our investigation into Hugo's murder. Her name is Alina Cozma. We know when he took her."

Tom paused for a moment and glanced at Sarah to check that she was with him. Then he continued pacing, staring at the floor as he concentrated.

"Alina Cozma went to Hugo's office. It was *months* after he had taken her. And according to one of Hugo's staff, she was smartly dressed. That suggests that she had either had her payoff, or Hugo had bought her some clothes—but my guess would be the payoff. She had an argument with Hugo, and later she was seen in his car, driving away from the office. The only word that the secretary heard was *pool*. She assumed that Alina meant 'a' pool—but what if she meant 'Poole'? Isn't that the closest big town?"

Sarah nodded, her eyes following Tom's movements. She probably thought he was raving, but he knew he was onto something. Alina must have known where he'd taken her, and his gut said that Hugo wouldn't have been at all happy with that.

Tom thought back. There was something else. Something to do with Laura's letter to Imogen that he had read—the one about Danika Bojin.

"Some of Alina's friends were looking for her. They went to the office in London. Then two days later, one of them went to his home in Oxfordshire to try to see Hugo. According to Hugo's PA it was also two days after the friends' visit to the London office that Alina Cozma turned up there, and was driven off in Hugo's car. It must have been the same day. But Hugo's wife said that he was away that night, and it was unexpected. She also said he was very angry about something, and he was away for a couple of days."

Tom walked over to the desk and grabbed his list of names and dates that girls went missing.

"The next girl disappeared only days later—so what happened to Alina? And why are there no more addresses?"

He felt sure that Sarah would have struggled with his timeline as the names and the whole story were new to her, but he had been speaking more to himself than to her. It was equally clear from the expression on her face that the implications had hit her with force. Hugo was still taking the girls, but why were their clothes still here, and why were there no more addresses?

"There's one more thing, Sarah. My sergeant has been talking to Hugo's wife, Laura. It is her view that if he treated them this badly, he would never have let them go. My guess is that everything escalated with Alina."

He could see from Sarah's face that her thoughts were mirroring his.

They needed to get a team here *now*. They needed to search the grounds, the cellars, and the outbuildings. And they needed specialist equipment, because by Tom's reckoning, they could be looking for the remains of six bodies.

37

Tom was beginning to feel a little superfluous at Lytchett Minster Farm. It was only a few hours since they had formulated their gruesome theory, but now the specialists had arrived and Sarah Charles had everything under control. It was, after all, her jurisdiction. He was relieved to have received a call from the hospital, though, to say that Mirela was responding well to treatment. She had been rehydrated and was weak but able to talk.

He knew that nobody in the Dorset force had his knowledge of the case and there were some questions he desperately needed answering, so after asking Sarah to keep him up to speed by telephone, he set off for the hospital. It hadn't taken long for the press to get wind of the basic facts of course, so he had to squeeze his way past the tightly packed cars and satellite vans that were now lining the narrow lane. They only knew that a girl had been found and that she was alive, but these guys had been to enough crime scenes and would easily recognise the significance of men in white coveralls. And if they brought in the dogs, Sarah would have to make a statement—something she was hoping to avoid for another couple of hours until they had more solid evidence.

He'd just made it to the main road when his phone rang.

"Tom Douglas," he said.

"Guess who's just called, boss?" said a rather smug Ajay. "Jessica sodding Armstrong! She's just seen the breaking news on the telly, and has finally twigged that her idol is not quite all he was cracked up to be. She's finally dished the dirt."

Tom slapped the steering wheel with satisfaction. "At last, she's developed a conscience. But the question is, does it help?"

"Well, I think it supports your theory. The day that Hugo rushed out after Alina Cozma, it appears he left his desk drawer not only unlocked, but slightly open, and Little Miss Nosey had a look, didn't she? She found a load of envelopes, and each one was addressed to one of the girls who had gone missing over the previous couple of years. She recognised the names, of course. And there was money inside. Hugo realised that she'd sussed him, and gave her some cock and bull story about singling girls out for special scholarships, but of course it had to remain completely confidential."

"Hah. A likely story! So what did he pay Jessica for then?" Tom asked

"He asked her to take over making the payments for him, and said he would give her a bonus for doing it. She realised, of course, that he was paying her to keep schtum and I don't think she ever believed him about the scholarships. She strongly suspected he'd taken these girls as mistresses and was just paying them off, but she thought it was his right since he was locked in such an unhappy marriage."

Tom was trying hard to maintain his concentration on the road, follow the directions he'd been given to the hospital, and listen to Ajay at the same time.

"Has he carried on with the payments?" Tom asked.

"There were no new names added to the list, according to Jessica. When she'd originally checked the envelopes, there was one addressed to Alina— but when he passed the envelopes over, the one for Alina was missing. She presumed Hugo must have given her cash or something, but her name was never on the list after that, although he kept paying the others. She thought he must have either settled on Alina as a permanent mistress, or decided that he was playing a dangerous game."

Tom was so glad that Ajay had spoken to Jessica. He thought he would have had a problem keeping his temper, and if he ever had to see her again he would feel a strong temptation to throttle her. Ajay hadn't finished, though.

"Jessica also said that this explained what she described as Hugo's 'suppressed excitement' and that he'd promised to continue to reward her loyalty as long as she stayed with him. She preferred to believe that this was an act of altruism, as she called it." Ajay snorted with derision, and Tom had great sympathy with his unvoiced opinion.

It was all slotting perfectly into place, although none of this brought them any closer to discovering who killed Hugo Fletcher. He had to admit that the murderer had probably saved at least one life, though—that of Mirela Tinescy.

The call ended as Tom parked his car in the hospital car park, and he made his way to Mirela's bedside. He had no idea how capable she would be of telling him everything he needed to know, given the trauma she had been subjected to.

He was pleased to see that Mirela had been given a private room, but he noticed how pale her face looked, with deep hollows for cheeks. He suspected that she had already been quite a slim girl, but days without food and water had taken their inevitable toll. The shape of her body was barely visible under the bedclothes. His own stomach was rumbling, but he would just have to ignore that. He walked into the room, and sat down quietly in the visitor's chair, waiting to see if she would acknowledge his arrival. Her eyes were closed, and he hated to disturb her.

"Mirela," he said quietly. Her eyes didn't open, but her head turned slightly towards him, so he knew that she had heard him. "My name is Tom Douglas. I'm a policeman, and I need to talk to you. I'm so sorry to have to do this, but if there is any way that you can talk to me I would be really grateful."

She opened her eyes. They had the look of a baby deer, caught in the headlights of a car. He should have brought a female officer with him. What a stupid mistake.

"Would you like me to ask a nurse to sit with us? Would that make you more comfortable?"

Mirela seemed to think about it for a moment, and then she gave a slight shake of the head. "It's okay. You have a kind face," she said, with an attempted smile.

"Do you think you can tell me what happened, Mirela—how you came to be in Sir Hugo's house on your own?" Tom didn't mention the fact that she was tied up—he would try to introduce that later.

Mirela spoke quietly, and he didn't catch every word. But it was enough. She explained how all the girls got follow-up visits from the charity, to check how they were settling in and to see if they had any problems.

"About six months ago, my visit is from Sir Hugo. I am very surprised by this, but pleased. He tells me that I am special, and he want to help me. He will look for a better life for me, but I must wait."

"Did he tell you what he meant by a better life?" Tom asked.

"No. He give me a phone, and say that each week I must send him SMS when I am on my own. If he can, he will call for a talk. We do this for weeks, but no big chances come. No better life. I have to keep this a big secret, and if I tell to anybody he say I may have to leave the Allium. So I don't tell. Then he say that we can meet. But not in private. We meet in museums."

Very smart, Hugo, thought Tom. Nobody would think it at all odd to see Sir Hugo Fletcher talking kindly to a young girl.

"Why did you go with him, Mirela?"

"We meet many times, and he tells me how he is unhappy with his wife. She is unwell, he says. I feel sorry for him. I start to care for him, because he is kind to me. He even gives me some money to send to my family in Romania. Then one day he tells me he has good idea. Perhaps while we wait for the big chance, I can be his housekeeper. But nobody must know this, because he cannot have a favourite girl. I must leave a note—he tells me the things to write. And then we go."

Tom took a glass of water from the side of the bed and held it to Mirela's lips for her, just as he would have done for Lucy. This girl was somebody's child, and if she had been sending money home, her family must be out of their minds with worry having not heard from her in weeks.

She gave him a weak smile of gratitude and continued. "He put a cover over my eyes. He tells me this house is his secret, and so nobody can know where it is. I cannot leave the house without him. He always comes at the night in his big car, but he takes me to go to the shops in a small car that lives at the farm."

Tom knew about this—he had seen it there and wondered what its purpose was. Clearly when Hugo was down here, he didn't want to be recognised. For such a small car, it had seemed rather odd that it had dark tinted windows. Now it all made sense.

"I had to wear the cover for my eyes until we get to the shop. Always a different shop. I don't have an idea of where we are, but I think the sea is near because of the birds. That is all I know. But he is nice to me, and I just clean the house for him."

Mirela stopped and closed her eyes. It was obvious to Tom that she was going to find the next part difficult, so he gave her some time. Finally she started to speak again.

"He start to touch me a bit. Not too bad—but I know what is coming. Then he kiss me. I don't mind—better one kind man than many who are not kind and some who smell. When he ask me for sex I decide it's okay. I like this man. We are happy together. This was at the beginning, you understand. But I don't like the sex he wants. He likes to be tied up. It is not very nice, but I have had worse."

God, thought Tom. How sad that a girl as young as this can grade sex on how bad it's been.

"Did he always chain you up, Mirela?" Tom asked, as gently as he could.

"No—no, he didn't. That was at the end. It was a few weeks, and I said I was not happy. I wanted to go outside—even in the garden. But he always say not. I am in the house all the time. No air to breathe. I start to shout at him, and say this is not the big chance. I don't like it here. He say nothing. He just look at me as if I am nothing. Then I say that I don't like the sex. I thought he was normal. But he is not. I tell him it is not a nice way to make sex, and I hate that wig he makes me to wear. His eyes goes very black. Like a *diavol*. I don't know this word in English."

Tom didn't need a translator to tell him what this meant.

"Then he hold my hair and drag me up the stairs. He take me into a room—one I don't see before because it is always locked. There is nothing. Just a mattress and a hook with a chain. And a bucket for—you know what for. He throw me on the mattress and I try to fight—but he is too strong."

Mirela's face had taken on a look of fear, as if she were reliving every moment. Tom held the water out to her again.

"Take your time, Mirela. I've got as long as it takes—don't worry."

"No—I want to say all now. Then I can forget. I can try. He put the chain on, and then he go out of the room. When he comes back he has some biscuits and some water. No other food. Then he says something horrible. He say, 'Do you remember your friend Alina?' I say that yes of course I do. He say, 'This room is to her memory.' These are not the right words, but he use a word I do not understand."

But Tom thought he did. "Did he say, 'This room is *dedicated* to her memory,' do you think?"

"I think so, but I do not know this word. He say that she was a very stupid whore. She ask for more money because she knows too many secrets. So he builds the room for her. Then he say that I will now go the way of the others. He say nobody care about prostitutes. We are forgotten forever. He leave the room. I think he is laughing. But I don't see him again. He stops coming."

Tom suddenly realised that Mirela probably had no idea that Hugo was dead. He couldn't decide whether it would be better or not to tell her, but given her fear he decided that telling her had to be the right decision.

"Mirela, Sir Hugo treated you very badly. There is no excuse for his behaviour at all, and I'm just glad that we managed to find you. But the reason he didn't come back, Mirela, is because he's dead. Somebody murdered him."

She turned her head towards him, and for the first time gave a real smile.

"Good," she said.

38

Cold as the dining room was, it felt like a haven to Becky. She sat on a hard dining chair, with her head resting on her folded arms on the table. The last few hours had been some of the most harrowing she had ever encountered with a family. The pain of telling somebody that their loved ones were dead was terrible enough, but this was a completely different experience for her. She knew now that the news Tom would be bringing for Laura was going to be the worst kind, and she knew there was no way she could even begin to imagine what Laura was going through.

Tom had told her about his conversations with Mirela, and brought her up to date on what the Dorset police were expecting to find at Lytchett Minster Farm. But he had asked her not to tell Laura—he wanted to do it himself. He must be a glutton for punishment to want to break this news, was all she could think. Thank God she didn't have to do it.

She had already had to prevent Stella from switching on the television for fear of what might be revealed, and she felt a dreadful guilt at her earlier suspicions of Laura. It seemed clear now that Tom had been right all along when he said that the Allium girls had to hold the key to the case. And all she had done was pester him about delving deeper with Laura. Imogen wasn't out of the frame, but if everything that Tom had told her was true, she couldn't help feeling that whoever killed Hugo had performed a service to mankind .

Her thoughts were interrupted by the ringing of her mobile, and she could see it was Tom.

"Hi," she said quietly. "Are you okay?" This day must have been one of the worst of his career, too.

Tom sounded tired and resigned on the phone. He told her he was on his way back and would be with them shortly. Could she let Laura know that he would be there soon?

"Of course. I think they want me to leave, though. What do you think I should do? They don't know what to do with me. I've been sitting with them in the kitchen, but I don't think they're comfortable with that, and Laura's told me at least five times that I can go because she's got all the support she needs. I'm just lurking in the dining room at the moment."

She listened as Tom spoke, told him to drive carefully, and hung up. He sounded exhausted, and the earlier exhilaration at the thought of finding one of the girls safe had been overshadowed by everything they were now expecting to discover.

Becky made her way to the kitchen, where they had all decided to gather. There wasn't a sound, but she knew they were all in there. She knocked softly on the door. It was Beatrice who shouted "Come in!" as if this was still her home. But nobody seemed to mind.

"I've just heard from Tom, Laura. He's on his way and should be here in about fifteen minutes. He didn't phone sooner in case he got held up. He wants to bring you up to date on everything himself. He thought you would understand."

Laura lifted a pale face towards Becky and attempted a smile. "Thanks, Becky. Why don't you get yourself back to the B and B now. We'll be okay until Tom gets here. You must be worn out, too."

Becky thought she should stay, but Tom had said that if Laura suggested it again, she should go.

"Can I get anything for anybody before I leave?" she asked.

"We're fine. Thanks for everything, though. It's good of you to have stayed this long," Laura answered.

Becky was about to respond that it was her job, but stopped herself just in time. It was so gracious of Laura to say that when her mind must be in turmoil. Laura wasn't at all the person Becky had first thought, and she wished she had some way of expressing her sympathy. But she merely nodded at everybody and left the room, closing the door quietly behind her.

She was surprised to find her own face wet with tears as she walked towards her car. Becky had never been much of a one for crying, but this was one day she would never forget.

When Tom finally arrived, Laura opened the door to him herself. They both looked at each other for a long moment. For reasons she couldn't explain, she felt deeply ashamed—as if she were personally responsible for the sordid revelations she felt sure Tom was about to make. All she could see in Tom's eyes, though, was compassion and exhaustion. Without a word, she pulled the door wider to let him through.

"I'm sorry I've been so long. The wait must have seemed interminable. It's not good news, I'm afraid. I really think it would be better for you to sit down." He held out one arm to indicate that she should lead him into the drawing room.

Laura perched herself on the edge of the sofa, her hands gripping the fabric on either side of her, then looked at Tom's weary eyes and waited. Before he had a chance to speak, Stella appeared in the doorway.

"Tom, I'm sure you're in need of some coffee, aren't you? Would you like something to eat, too?"

"A cup of coffee would be wonderful. But no food at the moment, thanks."

He sat down and faced a still silent Laura.

"I hope you don't mind, Laura. I haven't had anything to eat or drink for hours, and I just need to keep my batteries going a little longer."

Laura forced herself to respond. She could feel her body shaking, but more than anything she wanted to appear in control.

"Don't worry. You should have let her make you something to eat. Mum's a solution looking for a problem at the moment. It would have given her something to occupy herself with."

A light tap came on the door, and Will popped his head round. "Mum said that the police have arrived. Laura, I think you should have somebody with you. Is it okay if I join you?"

Laura looked at Tom, who simply nodded his head. There was a degree of wariness between these two as a result of Imogen's questioning, but Laura needed some moral support for what she feared she was about to hear.

"Please, Will. I'd be grateful. We don't need the whole family in this time, though. Perhaps if you listen to what Tom has to say, you can be the one to tell everybody later. I don't think I could bear it. Come and sit down."

Will took a seat next to Laura and he reached out to hold her hand. She was grateful for his strength as he gave her hand a small and comforting squeeze.

"Becky told you that we found Mirela at the farm. I've been to see her, and I'm sure you'll be pleased to hear that she's going to be fine."

Stella quietly entered the room and placed a mug of coffee in front of Tom. She looked expectantly at Laura, but Will shook his head at her and she took the hint and left.

Laura listened silently as Tom repeated his conversation with Mirela— how Hugo had managed to persuade her that she was special, and how he had given her money for her family while keeping her hanging on for her "big chance."

Tom took a sip of his coffee, and Laura didn't miss his thoughtful look as he watched her for a moment over the rim of his cup. She knew what he was thinking. He was wondering how much to tell her. Her body was icy cold, and she knew that Will must be able to sense the tremors through her hand.

"I know that you probably want to spare my feelings, Tom. But don't, please. It's all going to come out some time, and I'd rather hear it from you than anybody else."

Laura knew he would tell her the truth, but he would be considerate in his choice of words. She couldn't ask for any more than that, however awful that truth was.

Tom nodded and put his cup down. "Hugo's rule about not investigating the girls who left a note makes perfect sense now. It was his way of avoiding any investigation that could lead back to him. But he'd been doing this for years—did Beatrice tell you? It must have started before you even met him."

"But Becky said she was chained up, somehow. Is that true? Why, Tom? I don't understand why he would do that. It's barbaric."

The look of compassion in Tom's eyes was almost too much for Laura. He leaned forward as if he wanted to reach out and touch her.

"She was being punished. All she had was some water, dry biscuits, and a bucket that was overflowing in the corner. Poor kid."

Laura had gone pale, but it wasn't really with shock. It was more with the memory of her life with Hugo, and with abject pity for this young girl.

"Oh, God. I knew it would be bad, but…" Laura's voice cracked, but she had to continue. She needed to know it all. "Why did he have to punish her—do you know?"

"She complained about being locked in, and…" He paused as if debating what to say.

"And what?"

"And she didn't like the sex. She said she had to tie him up. And she always had to wear a long red wig."

Laura had a vivid picture in her mind of what that poor girl had suffered. And now she knew why there were only three wigs in the attic, although she realised she had been suppressing that particular suspicion since she'd found the wig box.

"Tom, I need to know this. Before you started to tell me about Mirela you talked about *girls*, plural, and said that he'd been doing this for a long time.

You're not just talking about Mirela being treated like this, are you? How many girls were there, and what happened to them?"

Tom couldn't meet her eyes, and that told her so much.

"We found a ledger that goes back for years. It's apparent that at one time he used to pay the girls. We think that he gave them a lump sum when they left, and then he was continuing to pay them for their silence each month. But he definitely paid them off, and they left."

"At *one time* he used to pay them? What do you mean? What changed? Why did he stop paying them?" Laura asked, her voice rising with each question. But deep inside she knew what he was going to say. She had known from the minute she heard about Mirela. She just needed to hear the words.

So Tom told her. He told her about Alina's name in the ledger. He told her what Hugo had said to Mirela, and what they'd surmised. And he told her about the team now in Dorset, ready to dig up the farm and the outbuildings.

Laura stood up and ran from the room.

It was several minutes before Laura returned, and in that time Stella had brought Tom a bacon sandwich. He felt bad about eating it, given Laura's intense distress. But he needed something to keep him going. It wouldn't help matters if he became light-headed. Neither man had broken the silence, each lost in his own thoughts.

Laura wasn't looking any better, but seemed slightly more composed.

"I'm really sorry," she said. "I just needed to get out of here for a few minutes. What are you doing about looking for the girls?"

"We've got special equipment that we're using to examine the grounds around the house. There are a lot of grounds, so it's going to be a long job. Of course, he may have put them in the car and taken them somewhere."

Laura took a long, quivering breath. She was deathly pale, and he was amazed at how well she was holding herself together.

"This is going to be hard for me to say, but it might save you some time. I think he would have strangled the girls, or possibly smothered them. He may have drugged them first so that they couldn't fight. He was an evil man without a doubt, but he didn't like mess. He wouldn't have done anything that resulted in blood flow of any kind." Laura shuddered and reached out for Will's hand again. "He wouldn't have taken the bodies out of the grounds. I'm sure of it. It would have been too risky. And if you're looking for a grave, I think you're wasting your time."

Tom gave a slight nod of encouragement, fixing his gaze on Laura's face as she continued.

"Hugo would never, ever, dig a hole or do any manual labour at all. If he killed the girls, then he would have disposed of them somewhere on the land, and somewhere that didn't require any physical effort."

Tom was baffled, but Laura seemed so certain.

"I can understand your reasoning," he said, "but I can't see where he could have hidden them in or around the property without digging."

Tom looked at Will, still grasping Laura's hand, his mouth set in a hard line. They didn't look like siblings, but they both had a similar dogged determination in their manner.

"What can you tell me about the farm?" Will asked. "Was it a working farm? How old is it approximately?"

"Why do you want to know?" Laura looked puzzled.

"Well, if it was a working farm there may have been some underground storage that might be covered up by now, or if it's old it may have had a well."

"It's a Victorian gothic farmhouse," Tom answered. "Ugly, menacing brute of a place in the dark, actually. Probably built mid- to late nineteenth century, so a well is possible. It was a sheep farm. I gather that part of Dorset is quite famous for its sheep. The land was originally quite extensive, but it's been sold off now, apart from about ten acres that surround the house. There are no outbuildings left, only an old barn that seems to be used as a garage, and a rather decrepit summer house. We'll dig out the deeds and see what we can find."

Will was on the edge of his seat. "Do you have a map of the region, and can you pinpoint the farm?"

Tom couldn't miss the note of excitement in Will's voice. "No, but we could pull something up on Google Maps. I've got my laptop. Why? What are you thinking?"

"I'd forgotten until you just mentioned it that the farm is in Dorset. Is there a pond of any sort that you know about?"

Tom thought for a moment. He'd done a quick tour of the land with the team that had been sent to perform the search for bodies.

"Not on Hugo's land, as far as I can remember. He's erected a secure fence close to the house—about a hundred metres away. There are locked gates in the fence that lead to the rest of his land, which extends in various directions beyond this. Once you're outside the fence it's pretty open countryside with nothing more than a dry stone wall between Hugo's land and the adjoining fields. We did notice a pond close to the perimeter—just in the next field—but nothing substantial. It's not a lake or anything, so probably not deep enough for…erm, Hugo's purposes. We talked about having a look, but not until everything else has been covered. Why?"

"Ever heard of ball clay?" Will asked, nodding his head slowly as if something was making sense to him.

But it meant nothing to Tom, and he shook his head.

"It's used in the manufacture of ceramics," Will explained. "Dorset's famous for it. I did some summer work there when I was at university. There are several types of ball clay mine, some open, some with mine shafts like a coal mine—but I won't bore you with the details. The interesting thing is that lots of the old mines were abandoned, and over time they filled with water. Some have been made into nature reserves, but the smaller ones were just left flooded. It might not look like much on the surface, but it could easily be very deep."

The next few hours were tense and nerve-racking. Laura didn't know what she wanted the police to find, and she kept going over and over in her mind everything that had happened. Could she have done something more than she did? If she had just tried a bit harder to convince somebody she was right about Hugo all those months ago, how many lives would have been saved? But she had never thought he was killing them. And she'd had other priorities.

Tom had been closeted in the dining room with his computer and telephone for a long time. Will had joined him to help in the search. All signs of antipathy between the two men had vanished in the face of a shared mission.

Finally, they both returned to the drawing room and sat down next to each other.

Beatrice, Imogen, and Stella had all joined Laura to offer her some support, and she was grateful, but she looked at the men and knew at once that there was news.

"It appears that Will was right," Tom said. "From the farm, it's possible to go through one of the gates in the perimeter fence—if you have a key, that is—and then there's a field that belongs to the farm bordered by nothing more than a dry stone wall. There's been no livestock on the farm for some time, so the wall has broken down in places and never been repaired. The pond is just the other side of one of the gaps. But the local lads say it looks as if this part of the wall was taken down on purpose. Apparently it looks different when it's just collapsed."

Will took up the story. "Tom's managed to confirm that the pond is, in fact, a small but nevertheless deep old mine shaft that's been flooded. With the aid of a wheelbarrow it wouldn't have been too taxing for bloody Hugo to have transported a young and probably undernourished girl to the edge of the pit, weighted her down, and disposed of the body."

Laura gasped and felt the colour drain from her face. The edges of her vision turned black, as if dark smoke was circling her eyes, and the sound of the voices around her became muffled.

She vaguely heard Will shout, "Quick, Imo. Get her head between her knees. She's going to pass out."

She felt a hand pushing down heavily on the back of her head and she leaned forward. Somebody was rubbing her back, and she took a few gulps of air. She kept her head down for a few minutes, and she could hear people making encouraging sounds. Gradually the dizziness passed, and both sound and vision returned to normal. She slowly lifted her head.

"I'm okay. I'm so sorry. This is a pathetic way to behave." She leaned right back with her head against the sofa. She turned to her mother, who looked shocked. She would know better than anybody that Laura never fainted. She might be sick through tension, but she didn't faint.

"Do you think I could have a whisky, Mum? It's just next to you on the tray."

Stella jumped up. "I think we'd all better have something," she said, making her way to the drinks cupboard. "What happens now, Tom?"

"It's too late now to do anything today, I'm afraid. It will be dark before we can set it up. We're going to get some men down there tomorrow. Either Becky or I will keep you informed."

Laura knew what they were going to find, but she wasn't about to voice that certainty. Yet more waiting. She just wanted this to be over.

Tom's gaze rested on Laura's face for a few seconds. She could practically feel its warmth, and was so grateful to him for coming in person to tell her all this. He must be dead on his feet, she thought.

As if reading her mind, he pushed himself wearily up from the sofa.

"I'm really sorry that this has been so traumatic for you," he said. "But I'm afraid I'm going to have to take my leave now. I need to report back to James Sinclair and try to catch up on some sleep. And I'm sure you could do without me around the place."

Laura tried to muster a smile for him, and made to get up to see him out.

"No, don't get up. I've been here often enough, I can let myself out."
With a final sympathetic glance, he left the room.

As Laura had guessed, Tom was truly shattered. Not just with tiredness, but with the horror of everything that had been revealed. He didn't know where this left them with the murder investigation, but for the moment it was important to discover everything possible about Hugo's activities at Lytchett Minster Farm. The red wig was an obvious link—but not the one in Mirela's room. That had been there for months, if not years. He was deep in thought as he headed across the hall. Much as he hated this house and the monster that it had sheltered, he was sorry to leave for Laura's sake. He pulled open the front door, then stopped dead and swore to himself.

"Shit, the laptop."

Closing the front door with rather more force than he intended, he made his way quietly to the dining room to collect the forgotten computer.

39

Hearing the slam of the front door, Imogen rushed to put her arms around Laura. Will was busy pouring them all stiff drinks—not the first they had had that evening. Stella moved to the other side of Laura and held her hand, rubbing it gently.

Laura felt sorry for Beatrice. She was getting all this support from her family, but after all, Hugo was Beatrice's brother as well. She was just about to voice these thoughts when Will suddenly banged the bottle he was holding down onto the table.

"Right. Laura, Imogen, I want to talk to you both. Mum, Beatrice, I would like you to leave the room, please."

"Will!" Imogen said. "You can't talk to your mother like that! And Beatrice is a guest!"

"Imogen, much as I love you—and yes, I always have—this is not your call. There's something not right about all this, and I want to know *exactly* what it is. Beatrice, do you mind? Mum, I think it's better for all concerned if you don't hear this."

Laura felt like a spectator. Everybody had something to say, it would seem. But Will only really needed to know what Laura had to say. She felt a sense of inevitability and was just waiting for the scene to play out. She knew her part, and she knew she was going to have to play it. Her mother, however, was clearly not following the script and was going to need some persuading.

She watched through detached eyes as the scene unfolded.

"William, I may be your mother, but I am not made of glass. I won't shatter if I hear something I don't like. Nothing can shock me as much as the news I've heard today, so I'm staying."

Beatrice stood up. "Come along, Stella. Let's leave them to it. I don't suppose for a moment we'll ever know what's been going on, but I for one have heard enough. Hugo was absolutely the psychotic prick that I always thought he would be."

If anybody was at all surprised at Beatrice's choice of phrase, nobody showed it.

Laura knew that it was time for her to speak. "Actually, I'd like Imogen to leave, too, please. Sorry, Imo, this isn't your decision. It's mine. Please go with Mum and Beatrice."

Stella and Beatrice left the room, but Imogen turned at the door and Laura could see the panic in her eyes.

"Imo, he has to know. I'm sorry."

"I know, I know. Shit. Will, I don't know what to say, but I want you to know that I love you. There's never been anybody else. Please don't hate me any more than you already do."

With a sigh, she left the room. Neither Will nor Laura noticed that the door hadn't closed properly.

"I want some answers, Laura." Will's face looked as if it had been carved of granite. Every line was etched deeper, and he seemed to have aged ten years since he'd walked through the front door just a few very long hours ago. He was speaking with what appeared to be barely controlled anger.

"We all now know that Hugo was a thoroughly immoral and corrupt individual," he said. "But I guess you knew that already. Is that why Imogen killed him for you? It had to be her. The police know it, but they can't prove it. God help us all. I know she's your friend and she loves you, but don't you think that was a bit much to ask? Jesus, Laura!"

Laura felt cold and strangely unemotional. So much had happened—so much that had hurt so many people. And now this almost felt like the easy bit. How many conversations had taken place in this room in the last few days? How many lives had been ripped apart? And now Will deserved the truth.

"Will, shut up. It wasn't Imogen. She didn't kill him."

"Well if it wasn't Imogen, who was it—because I think you know."

Laura took a deep breath and looked Will straight in the eye. "You're right, I do know."

"Well?"

"It was me, Will. I killed Hugo."

The room was silent. Laura couldn't even hear the sound of their breathing, and realised that she, at least, was holding her breath. She had uttered the words, and the spell was broken, the detachment gone. Admitting what she'd done was one thing, but to explain it she was going to have to relive every moment, and that would be far harder.

Will was staring at her with a look of utter bewilderment. She couldn't meet his eyes.

"It's a long story. In a way, it will be a relief to tell you. But just listen, or I won't be able to carry on. Don't interrupt. Please, Will." She held her body rigid, feeling that at the first moment of weakness she would crumble.

Will continued to stare at his sister and gave an almost imperceptible nod. Laura stood up from the sofa, clutching her large glass of whisky, and went to stand in front of the fire, drawing some warmth from the flames. She began to talk, keeping her voice steady and her emotions in check.

"It was all so meticulously planned. Every single detail. The countdown started on the afternoon of the Thursday before Hugo's death. I was at the house in Italy, of course, and I can remember checking my bags for at least the twelfth time, ticking off every item yet again from my list. Checking and rechecking. There was so much at stake, you see. I left another list on the kitchen table there, together with a small tape recorder, my passport, flight confirmation, Mercedes car keys, and Stansted car park ticket. On the floor next to the table, I left a suitcase and a carry-on case. I left them there for Imogen."

She saw Will jolt at mention of Imogen, but true to his word he didn't interrupt.

"Finally, everything was ready. I made it from the house to the car, and then I just sat there in the driving seat for ages. At first I couldn't even get the key in the ignition, my hands were shaking so much." She clutched her drink tighter as the memory of that moment hit her.

"Imogen was incredible; a real rock and an enormous source of strength. I knew I was making her an unwitting accessory, but I never thought it would be an issue for her because she'd be back in Canada before Hugo's body was found. There was no way that she would be connected to it all. Her name would just never have come up, because in theory I hadn't seen her for years. She was out of my life. She made such a huge mistake coming here, and I was livid when she arrived. She still didn't understand, you see.

"She started to visit me when Hugo had me locked up for the second time—whenever she could get over to England. We set it all up. She pretended to be visiting a sad old chap in the home who couldn't speak, and then she'd sneak in to see me. Hugo would *never* have allowed her near me."

Laura took a drink from her glass and placed it on the mantelpiece, but with nothing to hold she felt more vulnerable somehow, so she picked up the glass again and held it between her two hands.

"She knew I was supposed to be suffering from delusional disorder, and she knew what the so-called delusions were. You see, I was fairly certain Hugo was taking the girls, and I told her that the only way that I was going to be able to escape this marriage was by proving to the whole world what a depraved individual he was. I told her that I had a plan. I had to get the evidence and leak it to the press. But it was essential that any revelations couldn't be tied back to me—because I knew what the consequences would be. So I had to be able to provide irrefutable evidence that I was in Italy at the time that the news broke. That's why I had to ask for Imogen's help. At the time, all she thought I was going to do was follow Hugo and get some photographs. She had no idea what I really planned."

Imogen had been in Cannes—she had told the police the truth about that. Laura remembered very little of her drive—only that she had made it from Le Marche to Cannes in record time—just over seven hours, and no borders now, of course. That helped. She'd pulled into the car park at the Palm Beach end of La Croisette, knowing that Imogen would be waiting.

"When I arrived in Cannes Imogen had organised everything. Her suitcases were in the hire car, together with passport, flight tickets, cash— everything we'd agreed in advance.

"She could tell I was nervous, because she stroked my hair and told me I was doing the right thing. If she'd known though, I don't think she'd have helped me. She knew she was going to be breaking the law, travelling under a false passport—but she thought the risk was worth it if I could expose Hugo for what he was—or at least what I *thought* he was then."

Will stood up, and Laura realised that they had both already finished their whisky. Without taking his eyes off her face, he took Laura's glass. She thought he was going to speak, but he resisted. As he turned his back to refill the glasses, Laura felt relieved not to have his eyes burning into hers, and so she continued.

"Imogen gave me the key card to her room at the Majestic. She'd already filled in and signed the fast checkout form and left it in her room, and she was going to phone the hotel at eleven the next day to let them know that she'd just left but forgotten to hand in the form. She'd thought of everything. Then she hopped into my car as if it were the easiest thing in the world to drive through the night, back to my home in Italy.

"I needed some sleep, but I couldn't stop thinking of the bargain I'd made with Hugo. The bargain that was going to make his murder possible. I'd stopped caring about what happened to me by this time. But then I wasn't doing it for me.

"I left the hotel very early in the morning to drive to Paris. I'd got far too much time to kill, but it was the only way we could do it. Most of the driving between the villa and the south of France had to be done overnight, so I wouldn't be missed. I had to be 'seen' in the grounds of the villa—even if the person seen was actually Imogen. She was going to pick a few olives at strategic times when I knew somebody would be driving past—far enough away not to be able to make out her features, of course."

Will held out her refilled glass, and Laura took it, but went to sit down opposite him on the sofa. She was quiet for a moment as she remembered her drive to Paris—stopping to fuel herself with coffee, dropping Imogen's suitcase off at the Gare du Nord, and then leaving the car at the hire company. It had closed for the night, so nobody had seen her there. And then the interminable hours of waiting, sitting in restaurants rather than the station waiting room where somebody might have remembered her, drinking endless cups of coffee. Finally, when all other options were closed to her, she had made her way back to the Gare du Nord and hidden in the toilets to keep her face away from too much public view. It had been a terrible night. But the worst was still to come.

She swirled the whisky around the glass, gazing at it as if mesmerised by its golden vortex.

"The train was booked in the name of Imogen Dubois, a name that should never have been associated with me. I used her Canadian passport to board the train. It matched the name on the ticket, you see. The photograph was at least eight years old, and could have been anybody. It wasn't a flattering photo—how many of them are? And let's face it—my passport photo was taken just after Hugo and I were married, and I don't look remotely like that person now. I also had Imogen's other passport—her UK one. That was even older and close to its expiry date. She looked very young."

Her brother's face didn't so much as flicker. She could see that he was still far from on her side.

As she endured the never-ending hours of waiting for the train, Laura had gone over and over everything in her mind. The reason why this was the only option that made any sense. The reason why she was about to do something that sickened her to her very core.

"Finally, I was able to board the train, and it was so easy. With the briefest of glances at my passport, and slightly more scrutiny to make sure it matched the name on the ticket, I was allowed through. I huddled in a corner and pretended to be asleep so that nobody would try to engage me in conversation. Getting off the train was easy too. If I'd continued to use Imogen's Canadian passport, I'd have had to fill in a landing card. But I used her UK one, and I sailed through. No paper trail.

"I knew Hugo wouldn't be at the apartment. But he was coming. We'd planned it, you see. He thought that his final deal with me—the one that got me out of the home for the second time—was about to come to fruition. I had to get there before him to prepare myself. Getting into the house was potentially hazardous, though—I might gave been recognised by a neighbour. So I nipped into the toilets at the tube station, and I put on the hideous red wig—even though its associations with previous events made me feel sick. The rest of my outfit was waiting for me at the house, but at least with the wig nobody would make a connection."

She was now getting to the difficult part. She took three deep breaths to steady herself, and continued.

"I unlocked the front door and disengaged the alarm. I went straight to the bedroom, and opened the wardrobe door. I hadn't kept many clothes there for a long time—but there were still a few long dress bags from the early days, so I'd hidden everything I needed there just a week before.

"I'd gone through this in my head so many times that I went into automatic mode. It was the only way. I had a step-by-step list so I couldn't panic or forget anything. I pulled out the clothes and placed them on the bed. The first thing I did was put on the long, soft leather gloves that I knew were a necessity, but I'd chosen well. Hugo would think they were part of the performance.

"I unpacked a white coverall and took it into the bathroom, and pushed it deep into the clothes hamper. I went to the kitchen and took a long, sharp knife from one of the drawers. I'd sharpened it myself. This went in the clothes hamper, too. I took off everything that I travelled in, and packed the lot into a plastic bag marked 'A.' There were other bags too, each one carefully marked. The last bag wasn't empty, though. It contained five silk scarves—all bright crimson in colour. I laid the scarves on the bed."

Will was now leaning forward, a look of fascination and almost wonder on his face. Laura knew that he was amazed and slightly horrified at the cold planning that had gone into this act, and she didn't want to look at him as she told him the rest. She stood up again and went to the fireplace, this time facing the fire, with her back to him.

"Then I had a steaming hot shower. I needed it. I was frantic with worry—but I still had an hour left, and I didn't know how I was going to get through it. I knew he wouldn't be early. That might indicate that he was eager. Anyway, after the shower, I wiped the tiles down with the towel, and threw it in the tumble dryer. It would come out in half an hour and go back on the shelf with all the clean towels.

"I put the gloves back on and returned to the bedroom. Then I put on the clothes I'd chosen—clothes that Hugo would believe were for his benefit. When everything was ready, I took the final two items from a shoebox at the back of the wardrobe. One syringe and one glass bottle. I went back to the bathroom and filled the syringe with the liquid. The syringe went into the hamper, and the empty bottle was returned to the bedroom and placed in one of the marked bags.

"I was ready. There was only the room to prepare. It had to look perfect. He had to have no idea that I wasn't a willing participant in his games. I took a bottle of Cristal champagne out of the wine fridge. I knew Hugo would think this was the ultimate evidence of my submission—the very champagne he'd bought on the first night of our honeymoon. I prepared an ice bucket and flutes, and arranged the furniture. Then there was just the wig.

"All I could do then was wait."

Laura turned round and faced Will.

"So now you know. I killed him. And God help me, Will, but it was the right thing to do. You have to believe me. Do you honestly believe I would have done it—put myself through that torture—if it hadn't been the only option?"

Laura risked a glance at Will. He hadn't interrupted, and still he just stared at her through narrowed eyes.

"Is there more?" he asked. "Are you going to explain the reason for this incredibly intricate plan?"

Laura didn't like Will's tone, but she couldn't entirely blame him. Perhaps she would appear more credible if she ranted and raved, but she knew that the minute she let her emotions take control, she wouldn't be able to continue.

"I'll tell you the rest—but don't judge me. Not yet, at least." Did she see a slight softening in his eyes, or was that wishful thinking? She looked away and stared at the opposite wall, unwilling to meet his gaze as she continued with her story.

"The return journey was much the same. I'd prepared the bags so that I wouldn't panic. Some of them contained different outfits, so that I could change my look at various points along the way back to Paris. The other bags were marked for disposal, so that I didn't put more than one item of incriminating evidence in the same place. The syringe went in one, the empty bottle in another, and so on. I was back in Paris by late afternoon, and took the metro to Charles de Gaulle to fly back. Imogen landed at Stansted, picked up my car and drove to Heathrow to meet me. I'd changed into my drab Laura clothes at the airport. Then I drove back here. Imogen went into the terminal, ostensibly to catch her flight to Canada. That's it."

Will continued to stare at her, almost as if he didn't know her. After several minutes of a silence that Laura didn't feel she should break, he spoke.

"As I said, your planning was ingenious, your delivery of the plan impeccable. But to risk so much, just because you hated your husband? We know *now* what he was—but you didn't know all of that before. So why didn't you just leave him? And why involve Imogen?"

Laura had known that this was going to be hard. She was trying to keep her tone level, but inside her emotions were in turmoil. After all she had learned that day, what she really wanted to do was curl up and die. But she had to get through this. Tell Will everything, and then crawl away into a very dark corner, away from the world.

"When Imogen started to visit me, I told her just enough to make her realise what Hugo was capable of. There is a fatal flaw in him somewhere. And coupled with everything Hugo did to the pair of you, it was more than enough to persuade her to help me expose him for the person he really was. But she honestly had no idea that I was going to kill him. I couldn't believe it when she turned up here. That was a very, very bad moment. I've still not admitted it to her. That would definitely make her an accessory. She knows, though—I'm certain of it."

Will's face remained expressionless. Placing his glass on a side table, he leaned back against the sofa with his hands behind his head. Laura knew him well enough to realise that he would be weighing up her every word.

She suddenly felt panic rising in her chest. She had always thought that Will would understand. She had relied on him to be the one person who would have done the same. She had to tell him how it really was.

"He had to die, Will. If he didn't die, he was going to eventually kill me anyway. He *told* me. I had to comply—or die. He'd have used some drug or other and said it was an overdose. Given the apparent state of my mental health, it wouldn't have been difficult for people to believe. The problem was, I didn't have the first idea how to commit murder.

"I thought about so many methods. Stabbing was the favourite, but I didn't think I could do that, although I would have done if it had come to it—that's what the knife was for. I wanted something that looked as if it had been done by some lover or other, but at the same time it had to be something that Hugo would go along with.

"I knew he had other women, and I was sure they were Allium girls. He wouldn't have risked an affair if there was any danger of it being made public. When he came to visit me in the home during my second stay his words to me were chilling. He said he had normal appetites and that over the years, finding 'suitable participants' had become expensive. It was costing him over ten thousand pounds a month. We know what that was now—he was paying the girls. He said he'd found an alternative solution, but anything he'd done was due to my 'dereliction of duty' and the culpability lay at my door. I went over and over that conversation, wondering what he could have meant. But it all makes sense now. It must have been after he had started to murder them, although I honestly didn't know that."

Will whistled. "Why was he telling you this?"

"Because he wanted to issue the ultimate threat. He said that he would arrange for me to be released from the home, but he needed me to resume my marital duties. He knew I hated his idea of sex—as did the girls that he took, it would seem. We had agreed after my first time in the home that I could be excused. But he'd never found anybody that enjoyed it—and with good reason. So he wanted me back in his bed—on his terms. I hated sex with him, but the more I hated it, the more he loved it. It was power, you see. He said that it wouldn't be for long, because, as I knew, a preferable option was just around the corner."

"What on earth did that mean?"

Laura walked over to Will and knelt on the floor—not quite close enough to touch him, but so that he would find it difficult to avoid looking at her. He needed to see her face now. He needed to see the passion and the hatred. He needed to understand her.

"I'll get to that. Anyway, he told me that the only person who could stop or delay the inevitable was me. He said that I had to stop playing the vestal virgin and get back into my role as his whore. I knew what the alternative was, although he never again said specifically that he would kill me. I asked him for time. The thought of having sex with him repulsed me beyond belief, but the consequences of not doing were more than I could contemplate.

"I promised to think about it. I put it off for as long as I could. Finally he gave me an ultimatum. I would do as he asked, or I—and others—would pay the price. He played right into my hands. If he hadn't issued that ultimatum I would have had to offer myself to him—and that would have been far less credible. I said I needed to go to Italy for a few days to prepare myself, but that I wasn't happy to have sex with him here at Ashbury Park. It had to be at the apartment—a place that didn't hold such awful memories for me."

Will was now leaning forward in his seat, his hands clasped tightly between his knees. He had demanded the truth, but finally he appeared to be struggling to witness his sister's agony.

"I led Hugo to believe that I might not come. I couldn't seem too eager—and it really excited him to think that I was doing this under duress. All Imogen had to do in Italy was give me an alibi, even though she thought it was for something else entirely. On the Saturday, she phoned Hugo using a tape recording that I'd made earlier. I knew there wouldn't be anybody here, so it was a safe bet that she could just play the tape into the answering machine. We obviously couldn't phone him on his mobile, in case he answered. He still had it at the time."

Will looked at her with a mixture of admiration and horror.

"When Hugo arrived, I behaved the way he wanted me to. He genuinely believed that he had triumphed," Laura paused. She fixed her eyes on Will's.

"Then I killed him."

Will didn't speak. He picked up his drink and swallowed a large mouthful, but he didn't say a word. Laura felt compelled to continue.

"I'd taken the precaution of putting on the coverall so that I wouldn't leave any trace of me, and I kept gloves on all the time. I bought the syringe in Italy—they sell them in the supermarkets there. I made the liquid nicotine myself."

Finally, Will spoke. "Weren't you worried that it might not be the right strength or something? You could hardly try it first!"

"That was another reason for the coverall. If it hadn't worked I really wouldn't have had a choice. I took the knife with me into the bedroom, and if he hadn't died quickly, I would have had to stab him. Thank God it didn't come to that. But I forgot to put the knife back in the kitchen.

"His mobile went into one of the marked plastic bags for dumping, and the SIM card in another. Plus all the other paraphernalia—coverall, clothes, wig. Some went into bins in London, some in Paris. The phone had to go because I knew he'd been taking calls—I assumed from one of the girls. I thought once he was dead they would be safe, and I didn't want all of this to come out because of the impact on Alexa. That's why the phone had to disappear. Nobody wants the world to know that their father was a monster." Laura knew that now, of course, Alexa was going to have to be told, and she felt an intense, piercing sorrow at the thought of the child's suffering.

She could see that Will was still struggling to understand, and she knew that—soon—she was going to have to add the final detail to the image she had painted of Hugo. The one thing that would make sense of it all.

"Weren't you worried that one of you would get stopped because your face didn't match your passport? You two don't look even slightly alike!"

"Oh, Will, we're women! Look, when you came into the bathroom yesterday you thought Imogen was me, didn't you? That's because I've been wearing my hair scraped back off my face for years in an effort to divert Hugo's attention by looking as plain as possible. We're the same age, and pretty close in height and weight. When you come into the country, you hardly get a glance as long as your passport tallies, particularly if it's a UK passport. We simply did things to our appearance that minimised the difference. That was the easy part, honestly.

"It got a bit tricky for Imogen on the flight when Laura Fletcher was asked to make herself known to the crew. But she just ignored it. That's why I'd been taking cheap flights with no seat numbers—I had to stick to a recognised pattern, and anonymity was everything."

"So why the hell did Imogen come here? What a bloody ridiculous thing to do!" Will said, reaching once more for the whisky bottle—as if it could dull the pain of everything he was hearing.

"I know, and I was furious with her. But she knew something was wrong. Why else would my name have been called on the flight? And when we met at Heathrow, I refused to talk. I said I was too stressed and I'd explain everything as soon as she was back in Canada. And anyway, there wasn't time. I knew the police wouldn't be far behind me, and I needed to get back here before them. Then she heard that Hugo was dead, and she didn't know what to think. All she could think of was me.

"Hugo wasn't supposed to be found so soon. I was going to report him missing—probably late Sunday or even Monday morning. I thought I would have some time to compose myself. But Beryl went back for her purse—less than an hour after I'd left! God, what a disaster *that* could have been. And when the police came here, I was completely *beside* myself—the stress, the fear—it nearly swamped me. All I could think was how easily it could all have gone wrong. And the horror of what I'd done. And now the police suspect Imogen. I'm so ashamed of the fact that I involved her. But I couldn't think of any other way."

Will was quiet. He was studying his clasped hands between his knees. After what seemed like hours, but was probably less than a minute, he looked up. "I still can't believe this was your only option. I would have helped you. But *murder*? Why didn't you ask me?"

"I couldn't. He wouldn't have let me go. I told you, he was adamant that he would have killed me first. And if I'd involved you, he would have done something else to ruin your life. Let's face it, he's already been fairly successful in that regard."

Will looked at her with a puzzled expression on his face. He still didn't get it.

"So is that why you murdered him, then? Because you thought he was going to kill you, or because he was making your life a misery? Or was it that you thought he was abducting these prostitutes? Which was it?"

"It was none of those, Will. I didn't kill him for any of those reasons."

"So *why*, for God's sake?

"I killed him for Alexa."

Will stared at his sister. And it wasn't until much later that he realised somewhere in the house a door had closed quietly.

40

Laura sat alone in the drawing room, a room that was hard to recognise as the drab and dreary place of just six months ago. Comfortable cream sofas provided a perfect contrast to the restored dark wood panelling, and the beautiful green Aubusson rug that had previously decorated the hallway had been lifted and moved into this room, showing the newly cleaned pale stone floor to maximum effect.

She was waiting for the doorbell to ring. She forced herself to take some deep breaths and lean back, trying to relax her tense limbs, unable to decide whether it was fear or excitement that was causing the strange sensation in her chest. She hadn't seen him now for such a long time, but she'd thought about him often. With no idea how she would react when he arrived, she fought to compose herself. Wearing a simple but elegant combination of charcoal trousers and a dove-grey silk shirt, she looked neither too smart nor too casual—or at least, that was the intention. Her hair was now back to its natural brunette colour, and hung loose to her shoulders.

Finally she heard the familiar chime of the bell, and she rose quickly from the sofa, trying to slow her steps as she walked across the hallway to let him in. His dark-blond hair was a little longer, and she felt sure that he, too, had dressed with care. Not the business-like suits of a working day, but a black polo shirt and the leather jacket that she was sure he had been wearing the first time she met him. The air of sadness about him seemed even more defined, though, and there was a tightness to his smile that hadn't been there before.

"Hello, Laura. How've you been?

"Tom. It's good to see you. I've been fine, thanks. What about you?"

"Missing Lucy, but dealing with it. You've done wonders with this place. I couldn't believe it was the same house when I came up the drive."

"I'm sorry. I'm keeping you talking on the doorstep. Please—come in."

As Tom stepped into the hallway from the bright sunlight, he looked at Laura again, and she could see the surprise in his kind eyes.

"Laura, you look great!" he said. "Becky said I needed to prepare myself, but you really do look wonderful."

Laura smiled her thanks, but couldn't think of a thing to say as she led the way into the drawing room. She took a seat and clasped her hands together in an attempt to hide the trembling, and hoped Tom wouldn't notice. Instead of sitting on the sofa opposite her, though, he walked over to the French windows, open to let in the spring air, and stood with his back to her, apparently looking out at the late daffodils and early tulips blooming in the garden beyond. She'd never felt uncomfortable with him before—even when he was questioning her—but this afternoon was different. Tom was the first to break the silence.

"I've come to tell you that we're reducing the team investigating Hugo's murder. We've failed to make any real progress over the last six months, as I'm sure you know. We're not closing the case, but I've asked to be transferred onto other jobs." Tom still had his back to her.

"I can understand that, Tom. I expect you want something with a little more action. This case must be getting a bit dull for you."

"Oh, it's certainly dull. It's been dull for the past six months, actually. It's difficult interviewing suspects when you know before you start that they're innocent, and sifting through evidence that you know won't reveal anything." Tom spun round to face her, appearing almost angry.

She could see from his expression that he knew the truth, and that Will had been right. Somebody *had* been listening to their conversation. But she didn't flinch from his gaze. She was almost relieved. In some way it explained his absence over the previous few months, which she'd found unaccountably hurtful.

"I'm sorry, Tom. If you knew all that, you *did* have another option, didn't you?"

"Not really. Let's cut the crap, Laura."

She had always suspected that he'd heard them talking, but couldn't understand why he hadn't arrested her. Or at least talked to her about it. But then, of course, he would have had to act. It was such a terrible mess. Every night, Laura dreamt of the day she killed Hugo, and every morning she awoke feeling sick. She hadn't known just how evil he was, but she had known enough. And she knew without a doubt that she would do it again. In an instant.

Only the sound of the early spring birdsong penetrated the silence of the room. A happy sound in a room full of tension. After a few moments, their eyes met. The atmosphere was charged.

"I need to ask you again, Tom. Why didn't you do anything about it?"

Tom sighed and ran his fingers through his hair. His anger seemed to have been replaced by frustration, and she felt deeply sorry that she had caused this man so much stress.

"That's the question that I've been asking myself for the last six months. I heard you confess, but I had no evidence. I *still* don't have any evidence. You could have completely denied the conversation, and Will would have backed you up. But I was pretty sure that if I came to you with what I'd heard, you would have told me the truth. Then I'd have *had* to act. I wasn't sure if I could deal with that, so it was better not to see you at all."

Laura didn't know what to say. He was right, of course.

"I should tell you that Imogen is still the number-one suspect, now that all the earlier Allium girls are accounted for—the ones before Alina. We've tracked down every last one of them with Jessica's somewhat belated help."

Every time those poor girls were mentioned, she felt a sharp stab of guilt. Guilt that she hadn't done more, or done something sooner. But when it came to Imogen, Laura knew that she alone was responsible for the suspicion that had fallen on her friend.

"Have you got *anything* on Imogen at all? Are you likely to charge her?"

"No, we're not. The only evidence we have is purely circumstantial. It would be impossible to prove the stunt that you two pulled, so it seems Imogen is safe."

She was relieved for Imogen's sake. Laura had always known that the moment they charged Imogen, she would be forced to confess. There were times when she felt that the burden of guilt was too great to bear, and a confession would be so liberating. But she had more than herself to think about.

Tom was still standing by the window, as if he didn't want to get too close. She wondered what he thought of her now.

"How is Imogen, anyway? And Will?" Tom asked, momentarily lightening the atmosphere slightly.

"As you might expect, they're back together. Neither of them ever loved anybody else, and they've both been devastated at being apart all these years. I don't think it will be easy, though, because they've both changed and they need to build trust again. Imo is struggling to forgive Will for not believing her, and he is struggling to get the image of her with Sebastian out of his head. They're working on it." Laura paused briefly. "But stop changing the subject."

Tom gave a half smile, as if she knew him too well. He walked over to the facing sofa and sat down. He leaned back, his gaze not quite meeting her eyes, as if he were looking at something just above the top of her head.

"I can't help feeling a sort of impotent rage, Laura, that's my problem. This is uncharted territory for me, and for six months I have betrayed every single value that I thought I had."

"So why did you? *You* should never have had to suffer."

Their eyes met, and held for a few seconds before Tom spoke again.

"I couldn't do it. I couldn't do it to *you*. I thought you were…remarkable! The way you dealt with all the horrors that were thrown at you, and the fact that you were prepared to risk everything for somebody else. You've suffered so much. I felt compelled to protect you, inappropriate as that might sound."

Laura looked at him and tears sprung to her eyes. She closed them briefly, to hide her emotion from his perceptive gaze. Tom gave her a moment, and then he carried on.

"When I overheard you talking to Will, I heard you say that Hugo had 'a better option just around the corner'—or something like that. You also said that you killed him for Alexa. I left before you'd explained. I didn't want to be discovered listening, because then I couldn't deny what I'd heard. But I think I know what you meant."

Laura was silent. She knew that he deserved to know, but the horror of saying the words out loud was even more unbearable than the thoughts that plagued her daily. Even through her closed eyes, she could feel that Tom was watching her, and he carried on speaking, his tone softening as he no doubt recognised her anguish.

"I'll tell you what I've surmised then. I saw a photo of Hugo's mother. Do you know that you are very like her? That's probably why he never wanted you to see her picture. Annabel told me something—I don't know if you want to hear this, but I think I have to tell you. She said she'd discovered Hugo having sex with his mother. Hugo was tied to the bed, and his mother was astride him. I'm sorry—those are her words, not mine." Tom paused. "Did you know about this?"

Her shame was so deep, she still couldn't bring herself to look at Tom as she answered.

"I guessed, but not for a long time. He told me I reminded him of somebody, and then there were things he wanted me to wear when we had sex. After I changed my hair colour, he even made me wear a wig. Long red hair, of course. He used to leave it on the bed for me."

She remembered the day she found the wig box in the attic. It wasn't until after she'd returned here from the care home—for the first time. By then Hugo had stopped expecting her to play his sex games. But of course she had recognised the wigs, so she'd asked Mrs. Bennett about them. When the kind lady had explained whose they were, Laura had felt a revulsion so deep that she almost wanted to take her own life. The horror of realising just whom she had been standing in for all these years had almost demolished the last of her courage. But by then she had run out of options. She was there for one purpose only, and that was Alexa.

Tom stood up and moved across the room. He sat down on the sofa next to Laura and took her hands in his. All trace of his earlier anger and frustration had gone. As he spoke, he gently massaged her hands with his thumbs.

"On the drive to Dorset, Beatrice told me that the family tradition is for a parent to break a child in over time. They begin by sharing a bed from a very early age, and always sleep naked. The touch and feel of the adult body becomes familiar and safe. Then they fondle and play touching games as the child becomes more aware. When they're considered old enough, they tie the child to the bed—and make it seem like fun. Then finally the parent begins to have sex with the child shortly after puberty." Tom paused. Laura was watching his eyes, looking for disgust. But she saw nothing but compassion. "According to Beatrice, the relationship can continue well into adulthood, as apparently it did with Hugo and his mother. What I don't understand, Laura, is if he treated you as a replacement for his mother, why did you stay with him? And why the hell did you marry the bastard in the first place?"

His words were harsh, but his tone wasn't. His disgust was reserved for Hugo, and she was so very glad of that. She forced herself to look Tom directly in the eye. He had to know she was telling him the truth, dreadful as it was.

"I think you already understand it, or at least most of it. Before we were married, Hugo was charming and courteous. I'd never met a man like him in my life. How can I explain?"

Laura paused for a moment.

"I once made a film about abuse, and somebody told me that I didn't understand the subject at all. I now know exactly what she meant. It isn't just about definable acts of terror, such as physical cruelty or demanding obedience with overt threats. It's easy to recognise the difference between right and wrong then, even though many abused people don't act on that knowledge. The quiet but inexorable breaking down of self-esteem is much more sinister—it's violation of the soul. That's what Hugo did to me."

She looked at Tom and could see that he understood.

"What happened with Alexa?" he prodded gently. "I can guess, but I'd rather hear it from you."

He deserved to know. She owed him at least that, hard as it was for her to say out loud what she had witnessed.

"One night, when by rights I should have been sleeping, I heard noises coming from the bedroom next door. A room that should have been empty. I recognised Alexa's laugh. But it was the very room that Hugo only invited me into when he wanted sex. So I *had* to go and investigate. When I went in, he had Alexa tied to the bed. He was naked, as was she, and he had an erection. Alexa was laughing—she was only about seven. She thought it was a game."

He gave her hands a reassuring squeeze.

"Go on," he said.

"I had to get him out of that room before I could tell him what I thought. I had to protect Alexa. I wanted to run, Tom, as far away as I could. But that would have meant leaving Alexa alone with him in the house. That was impossible. So I told him I thought he was perverted, sick, everything. His response was predictable. He said my failure as a sexual partner was due to a lack of effective tuition. Fundamentally, he said that every child should have their sexuality developed by their parents, and that it was a duty he was happy to perform for Alexa. He hoped they would continue to be together for many years to come."

Tom looked white. She knew how he must be feeling, having a little girl of his own. She knew without a doubt that he would have wanted to kill Hugo every bit as much as she did. She had to tell him the rest.

"I asked if he had already had sex with Alexa and he said, 'Of course not—and I won't until she reaches puberty. She's still a child now.' I went completely wild. I was going to report him, and he knew it. That's when he injected me—I don't know what with—and locked me into a disused room. They found me there, naked and filthy. That's how he had me committed.

"But I had to stop him. I knew that nobody would ever believe me, and Alexa didn't think anything was wrong. To her it was normal; just one of her secrets with Daddy. She was proud of the fact that they shared their 'special moments,' and they were nothing new so they didn't surprise or shock her. He had never penetrated her, so there was no physical proof. Alexa was still young, though, and I thought I had time. I needed to be back here where I could protect her, so I agreed to his conditions. Without me, there was nobody to keep her safe. But I told him my terms too, one of which was that he didn't lay a finger on Alexa or me again. Despite his promises, I am fairly sure he was still grooming her. But I couldn't prove it."

She removed her hands from Tom's. She didn't really think she deserved their comfort and his reassuring strength. This time, she was the one to walk over and look out of the window, unable to bear his kindness any longer.

"I thought that if I went to the chief constable to try to get him interested in the Allium girls and Hugo was found to be as guilty as I suspected, the problem would be over. I was sure Mr. Hodder would help, but Hugo took great delight in telling me that as usual my judgement was dreadful. Apparently your colleague had raped his own Allium girl, but Hugo had managed to diffuse the situation. So he owed Hugo."

Laura had been told weeks ago that Theo Hodder had taken early retirement, but that was cold comfort now. It had been his duty to help her. She couldn't help thinking about how many of those girls could have been saved if he had acted. She now realised that, for Hugo, the prostitutes had just been convenient. She wouldn't comply with his wishes, and Alexa wasn't ready. So Hugo had taken what he needed from the handiest source—just like his father had. He had considered them worthless and disposable.

"Hugo did me a favour when he had me put away for the second time, Tom. It gave me time to prepare and plan. I had to save Alexa, and I knew that there was only one way."

She fought hard to resist the urge to go to Tom for comfort, trying desperately to remain as matter of fact as possible in the telling of her story. She had always known that one day she may have to pay the ultimate price, and maybe this was it.

"How is Alexa? How is she coping with all of this?" Tom asked.

"She's doing okay, thanks. Annabel has found some rich tycoon in Portugal, so rarely comes back to this country—which means that Alexa can spend all her weekends and holidays with me. It suits everybody. I've been seeking advice on how to deal with the fact that her father had some strange ideas about closeness, and we're working on it."

Laura turned towards Tom. She still didn't know what he was going to do, but she was glad that she'd been honest.

"So now you know everything. What now?"

Tom shook his head. He looked exhausted, as if the events of the past six months had taken a heavy toll. "You know that as a policeman, I have taken an oath? But for the last six months I have known of not one, but two murderers. And I've done nothing about either of them. What does that make me?"

"*Two*? There was only me involved—please don't drag Imogen into it. I know she was an accessory, but she wasn't guilty of murder."

Tom was shaking his head. "Did you never wonder about Beatrice? I'm fairly certain from what she said to me on the way to Dorset that she was responsible for her father's death. But there's no way of proving it now. He probably deserved it, too. Pretty good policeman, aren't I?"

"You know I think you're an excellent policeman. I'm so sorry to have put you in this position. I wouldn't have done this if I wasn't prepared to take the consequences, you know."

Tom looked surprisingly near to tears, and Laura wanted nothing more than to hold him and take away the pain she had caused. But she didn't move towards him. Nobody spoke for a few moments. Finally, Tom pushed himself up from the sofa and walked towards her. He stood about three feet away and looked into her eyes.

"I know you wouldn't blame me if I arrested you. I'm not going to, although how I'll live with myself I really don't know. But if I arrest you, I'd have to arrest Imogen—she's an accessory whether you like it or not. That would destroy her life, Will's life, and probably your mother's too. And without you, what will happen to Alexa? She's been damaged enough. Only the innocent would suffer—and enough have suffered already. You did the world a favour by killing Hugo, and you've already endured ten years of torment. I can't come to terms with putting at least five people through endless misery just because one thoroughly evil man had to die."

Laura said nothing. She knew he hadn't finished. He reached out his hands to hers, and she willingly grasped them both, although neither of them moved closer.

"The thing is, Laura, if I do this I will never be able to see you again. You do understand that, don't you? I admire you for your strength, your commitment, and your integrity—which seems is a strange thing to say under the circumstances. I can't bear the thought of your suffering, and wish I had the opportunity to help you to recover from the damage that bastard did to you. But I'm a policeman. I'm walking away, Laura, but whatever my personal feelings I can never bring myself to condone murder, even if I can justify it."

Laura said nothing, but she understood. She felt that this was a man that she could have loved, had life been kinder. But the barrier between them would be too great. And she knew she would never be able to love another man—because to her, love meant honesty, and this was a story never to be told again.

Tom dropped his arms to his sides and stepped towards her. He reached out a hand, and with the back of his index finger he gently stroked her cheek.

And then he was gone.

About the Author

Rachel Abbott was born in Manchester, England. She spent most of her working life as the managing director or an interactive media company, developing software and websites for the education market. The sale of that business enabled her to fulfil one of her lifelong ambitions – to buy and restore a property in Italy.

Rachel now lives part of each year in the completed property – a small but beautiful old monastery on the outskirts of a medieval walled hill town – with her husband and two dogs, and has finally found the time to devote to her other ambition – to write fiction.

Connect with Rachel Abbott online:
Twitter: **http://www.twitter.com/_RachelAbbott**
Facebook: **http://www.facebook.com/RachelAbbott1Writer**
Website: **http://www.rachel-abbott.com**

Acknowledgements

I owe a debt of gratitude to so many people for their help in writing this book – but in particular to John Wrintmore for his information about the workings of the police. I know I didn't always listen to his excellent advice, but only in the interests of the story. And equally my thanks go to Alan Carpenter for designing the original cover for *Only the Innocent*. I have absolutely no doubt that it made a significant contribution to the book's early success.

A special thank you to those of you who so willingly read (and re-read) this novel – especially Becky, Nic, Rachel, Kathryn, Judith and Tom. Their suggestions were invaluable.

My particular gratitude goes to my agent, Lizzy Kremer, who has guided me with huge patience and tolerance, and to the rest of the team at David Higham Associates – in particular Laura and Harriet - for their constant encouragement and enthusiasm.

And finally, I will forever be indebted to my personal support team: John – for patience and tolerance beyond the call of duty; and Giulia – for the endless cups of coffee and so much more.

Look out for Rachel Abbott's latest gripping novel

The Back Road

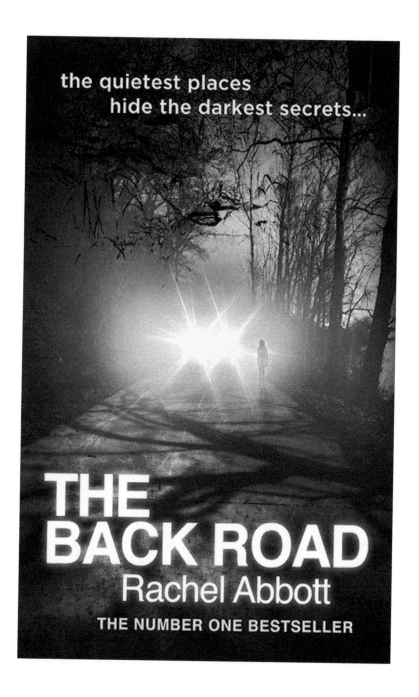

the quietest places
hide the darkest secrets...

THE
BACK ROAD
Rachel Abbott
THE NUMBER ONE BESTSELLER

Prologue

From the moment the cupboard door was slammed shut, trapping them both inside, she knew something was different. It should have seemed just like every other day, but somehow it didn't. She felt the familiar pain and discomfort—the same as always. So what was it?

The girl soundlessly inched her feet across the confined space, searching for her sister's toes with her own, both to seek and to give comfort. She had to try to make her sister feel safe. It would soon be over. But the fingers of an undefined dread were crawling up her spine.

Then her sister made a strange gurgling sound. She'd never made that sound before. It was as if something was stuck deep in her throat and she was trying to force it out. The girl silently willed her sister to stop.

Shh. Be still. Be quiet.

She rested her chin on her bony raised knees and repeated the words over and over in her head, praying that her little sister would hear her thoughts and understand. If either of them made a noise, The Mother would be angry, and it would all be so much worse. Worse than suffering in silence.

She had tried to say that they would be good. They didn't need to be put in here. But The Mother always said the same thing.

'I am The Mother. You are The Daughter. You do what I say. *Don't* argue. I've told you what happens to bad children. The Bogeyman gets them, and eats them for his dinner.' And then she laughed. The girl was scared of The Bogeyman. Perhaps he would be even worse than The Mother.

She lifted her head slightly. A narrow crack in the wooden door let in a dusty sliver of light, illuminating a slender fragment of her sister's face. It was white and shiny—a bit like a boiled egg when the shell was peeled away. She had never seen a face look like that before. Her sister lurched forward and bent over. Her hair was sticking to her forehead in damp curls, and she was making a noise in her throat. An awful noise. And there was a horrid smell too.

They had to be as silent as baby mice or they would get a beating. Luckily, at that moment the strange sounds coming from her sister wouldn't be heard. It sounded like The Grunter was here today. He made noises all the time—like a pig she'd once seen on the television. She hated the noise, but it was better than The Shouter. He always cried out, using words that sounded mean. She didn't know what they meant, but he sounded nasty when he shouted them. Then there was The Moaner. She had once tried to peep through the crack in the door because The Moaner sounded as if he was in pain, but she didn't like what she saw, so she never looked again. It didn't stop her mind from working, though, and every time she heard The Moaner, all she could see in her head was an ugly white bottom, rising and falling.

The Grunter never lasted long. Her sister was going to have to stop making that sound very soon.

The pig noises from the room outside the cupboard were much stronger and coming closer together now, and that meant The Grunter had nearly finished—he always got very loud just before the end. She didn't have much time. She needed to soothe her sister before it was too late. She hated to see her punished. The girl tried to shuffle across the confined space, but the bindings on her wrists and ankles were rubbing on the bruises and sores and she had to stifle a gasp of pain. As she got closer, her sister looked at her through eyes that had the bright shine of unshed tears, and then her little body shook with a huge force.

The girl realised with horror that her sister was being sick—but the wide brown parcel tape across her mouth was preventing the vomit from escaping. Then she watched as the little girl's eyes rolled upwards and out of sight, leaving only the glossy white showing, and she slumped over against a pile of old, dirty shoes.

Somebody had to help her sister. The girl knew she was going to be in trouble and that her punishment would hurt, but she didn't care. She threw herself sideways and rolled onto her back with her legs in the air, kicking out with her bound bare feet against the wooden cupboard door. And she kept kicking. She heard a shout of surprise and a growl of anger from the room beyond, and the door was wrenched open. A man with a huge red face and a fat blue nose leered down into the small opening of the cupboard, his trousers and a pair of dirty white underpants round his ankles.

Finally, she had met The Grunter.